One Perfect Lie

One Perfect Lie

LISA SCOTTOLINE

ST. MARTIN'S PRESS ❧ NEW YORK

ONE PERFECT LIE. Copyright © 2017 by Smart Blonde, LLC. All rights reserved. Printed in the United States of America. For information, address St. Martin's Press, 175 Fifth Avenue, New York, N.Y. 10010.

www.stmartins.com

Library of Congress Cataloging-in-Publication Data

Names: Scottoline, Lisa, author.
Title: One perfect lie / Lisa Scottoline.
Description: First edition. | New York : St. Martin's Press, 2017.
Identifiers: LCCN 2016053892| ISBN 9781250099563 (hardcover) |
    ISBN 9781250131553 (signed edition) | ISBN 9781250099587 (e-book)
Subjects: | BISAC: FICTION / Suspense. | FICTION / Thrillers. |
    GSAFD: Suspense fiction.
Classification: LCC PS3569.C725 O54 2017 | DDC 813/.54—dc23
LC record available at https://lccn.loc.gov/2016053892

Our books may be purchased in bulk for promotional, educational, or business use. Please contact your local bookseller or the Macmillan Corporate and Premium Sales Department at 1-800-221-7945, extension 5442, or by e-mail at Macmillan SpecialMarkets@macmillan.com.

First Edition: April 2017

10 9 8 7 6 5 4 3 2 1

To Shane and Liam, with love

Lying to ourselves is more deeply ingrained than lying to others.
—Fyodor Dostoyevsky

One Perfect Lie

Chapter One

Chris Brennan was applying for a teaching job at Central
Valley High School, but he was a fraud. His resume was
fake, and his identity completely phony. So far he'd fooled the
personnel director, the assistant principal, and the chairperson
of the Social Studies Department. This morning was his final
interview, with the principal, Dr. Wendy McElroy. It was make-
or-break.

Chris waited in her office, shifting in his chair, though he
wasn't nervous. He'd already passed the state and federal
criminal-background checks and filed a clear Sexual Miscon-
duct/Abuse Disclosure Form, Child Abuse Clearance Form, and
Arrest/Conviction Report & Certification Form. He knew what
he was doing. He was perfect, on paper.

He'd scoped out the school and observed the male teachers,
so he knew what to wear for the interview—a white oxford shirt,
no tie, khaki Dockers, and Bass loafers bought from the outlets
in town. He was six-foot-two, 216 pounds, and his wide-set blue
eyes, broad cheekbones, and friendly smile qualified him as
handsome in a suburban way. His hair was sandy brown, and
he'd just gotten it cut at the local Supercuts. Everyone liked a

clean-cut guy, and they tended to forget that appearances were deceiving.

His gaze took in Dr. McElroy's office. Sunlight spilled from a panel of windows behind the desk, which was shaped like an L of dark wood, its return stacked with forms, files, and binders labeled **Keystone Exams, Lit & Alg 1**. Stuffed bookshelves and black file cabinets lined the near wall, and on the far one hung framed diplomas from Penn State and West Chester University, a greaseboard calendar, and a poster that read DREAM MORE, COM-PLAIN LESS. The desk held family photographs, pump bottles of Jergen's and Purell, and unopened correspondence next to a letter opener.

Chris's gaze lingered on the letter opener, its pointed blade gleaming in the sunlight. Out of nowhere, he flashed to a memory. *No!* the man had cried, his last word. Chris had stabbed the man in the throat, then yanked out the knife. Instantly a fan of blood had sprayed onto Chris, from residual pressure in the carotid. The knife must have served as a tamponade until he'd pulled it out, breaking the seal. It had been a rookie mistake, but he was young back then.

"Sorry I'm late," said a voice at the doorway, and Chris rose as Dr. McElroy entered the office on a knee scooter, which held up one of her legs bent at the knee, with a black orthopedic boot on her right foot.

"Hello, Dr. McElroy, I'm Chris Brennan. Need a hand?" Chris rose to help her but she scooted forward, waving him off. She looked like what he'd expected: a middle-aged professional with hooded blue eyes behind wire-rimmed bifocals and with a lean face framed by clipped gray hair and dangling silver earrings. She even had on a dress with a gray-and-pink print. Chris got why women with gray hair dressed in gray things. It looked good.

"Call me Wendy. I know this looks ridiculous. I had bunion surgery, and this is the way I have to get around."

"Does it hurt?"

"Only my dignity. Please sit down." Dr. McElroy rolled the scooter toward her desk with difficulty. The basket in front of the scooter held a tote bag stuffed with a laptop, files, and a quilted floral purse.

Chris sat back down, watching her struggle. He sensed she was proving a point, that she didn't need help, when she clearly did. People were funny. He had researched Dr. McElroy on social media and her faculty webpage, which had a bio and some photos. She'd taught Algebra for twelve years at CVHS and lived in nearby Vandenberg with her husband, David, and their Pembroke Welsh corgi, Bobo. Dr. McElroy's photo on her teacher webpage was from her younger days, like a permanent Throwback Thursday. Bobo's photo was current.

"Now you know why I'm late. It takes forever to get anywhere. I was home recuperating during your other interviews, that's why we're doing this now. Apologies about the inconvenience." Dr. McElroy parked the scooter next to her chair, picked up her purse and tote bag from the basket, and set them noisily on her desk.

"That's okay, it's not a problem."

Dr. McElroy left the scooter, hopped to her chair on one foot, then flopped into the seat. "Well done, me!"

"Agree," Chris said pleasantly.

"Bear with me another moment, please." Dr. McElroy pulled a smartphone from her purse and put it on her desk, then reached inside her tote bag and slid out a manila folder. She looked up at him with a flustered smile. "So. Chris. Welcome back to Central Valley. I hear you wowed them at your interviews. You have fans here, already."

"Great, it's mutual." Chris flashed a grin. The other teachers liked him, though everything they knew about him was a lie. They didn't even know his real name, which was Curt Abbott. In a week, when it was all over and he was gone, they'd wonder how he'd duped them. There would be shock and resentment. Some would want closure, others would want blood.

"Chris, let's not be formal, let's just talk, since you've done so well at your previous interviews, and as you know, we have to get this position filled, ASAP. Mary Merriman is the teacher you'd be replacing, and of course, we all understood her need to take care of her ailing father." Dr. McElroy sighed. "She's already up in Maine, but reachable by email or phone. She would be happy to help you in any way she can."

Whatever, Chris thought but didn't say. "That's great to know. How nice of her."

"Oh, she's a peach, Mary is. Even at her darkest hour, she's thinking of her students." Dr. McElroy brightened. "If I expedite your paperwork, I can get you in class this Thursday, when the sub leaves. Can you start that soon?"

"Yes, the sooner the better," Chris said, meaning it. He had a lot to do by next Tuesday, which was only a week away, and he couldn't start until he was in place at the school. It gave new meaning to the word *deadline.*

"I must warn you, you have big shoes to fill, in Mary. She's one of our most beloved teachers."

"I'm sure, but I'm up to the task." Chris tried to sound gung ho.

"Still it won't be easy for you, with the spring semester already well under way."

"Again, I can handle it. I spoke with the others about it and I'm up to speed on her syllabus and lesson plans."

"Okay, then." Dr. McElroy opened the manila folder, which contained a printout of Chris's job application, his fake resume, and his other bogus papers. "Chris, for starters, tell me about yourself. Where are you from?"

"Mostly the Midwest, Indiana, but we moved around a lot. My dad was a sales rep for a plumbing-supply company, and his territory kept changing." Chris lied, excellently. In truth, he didn't remember his father or mother. He had grown up in the foster-care system outside of Dayton, Ohio.

Dr. McElroy glanced at the fake resume. "I see you went to Northwest College in Wyoming."

"Yes."

"Got your certification there, too?"

"Yes."

"Hmmm." Dr. McElroy paused. "Most of us went to local Pennsylvania schools. West Chester, Widener, Penn State."

"I understand." Chris had expected as much, which was why he'd picked Northwest College as his fraudulent alma mater. The odds of running into anyone here who had gone to college in Cody, Wyoming, were slim to none.

Dr. McElroy hesitated. "So, do you think you could fit in here?"

"Yes, of course. I fit in anywhere." Chris kept the irony from his tone. He'd already established his false identity with his neighbors, the local Dunkin' Donuts, Friendly's, and Wegman's, his persona as smoothly manufactured as the corporate brands with their bright logos, plastic key tags, and rewards programs.

"Where are you living?"

"I'm renting in a new development nearby. Valley Oaks, do you know it?"

"Yes, it's a nice one," Dr. McElroy answered, as he'd anticipated. Chris had picked Valley Oaks because it was close to the school, though there weren't many other decent choices. Central Valley was a small town in south-central Pennsylvania, known primarily for its outlet shopping. The factory store of every American manufacturer filled strip mall after strip mall, and the bargain-priced sprawl was bisected by the main drag, Central Valley Road. Also on Central Valley Road was Central Valley Dry Cleaners, Central Valley Lockshop, and Central Valley High School, evidence that the town had no imagination, which Chris took as a good sign. Because nobody here could ever imagine what he was up to.

Dr. McElroy lifted a graying eyebrow. "What brings you to Central Valley?"

"I wanted a change of scenery. My parents passed away five years ago, in a crash. A drunk driver hit their car head-on." Chris kept self-pity from his tone. He had taught himself that the key to evoking the sympathy was to not act sorry for yourself.

"Oh no! How horrible." Dr. McElroy's expression softened. "My condolences. I'm so sorry for your loss."

"Thank you." Chris paused for dramatic effect.

"How about the rest of your family? Any brothers or sisters?"

"No, I was an only child. The silver lining is that I'm free to go anywhere I want. I came east because there are more teaching jobs and they're better-paying. Teachers here are rolling in dough, correct?"

Dr. McElroy chuckled, as Chris knew she would. His starting salary would be $55,282. Of course it was unfair that teachers earned less than crooks, but life wasn't fair. If it were, Chris wouldn't be here, pretending to be somebody else.

"Why did you become a teacher, Chris?"

"I know it sounds corny but I love kids. You can really see the influence you have on them. My teachers shaped who I am, and I give them so much credit."

"I feel the same way." Dr. McElroy smiled briefly, then consulted the fake resume again. "You've taught Government before?"

"Yes." Chris was applying to fill the opening in AP Government, as well as the non-AP course Government & Economics and an elective, Criminal Justice, which was ironic. He had fabricated his experience teaching AP Government, familiarized himself with an AP Government textbook, and copied a syllabus from online, since the AP curriculum was nationally standardized. If they wanted to turn the public schools into chain stores, it worked for him.

"So, you enjoy teaching at the secondary level. Why?"

"The kids are so able, so communicative, and you see their personalities begin to form. Their identities, really, are shaping. They become adults." Chris heard the ring of truth in his own words, which helped his believability. He actually *was* interested in identity and the human psyche. Lately he'd been wondering who he was, when he wasn't impersonating someone.

"And why AP Government? What's interesting about AP Government to you?"

"Politics is fascinating, especially these days. It's something that kids see on TV and media, and they want to talk about it. The real issues engage them." Chris knew that *engagement* was a teacher buzzword, like *grit*. He'd picked up terms online, where there were so many teacher blogs, Facebook groups, and Twitter accounts that it seemed like the Internet was what *engaged* teachers.

"You know, Chris, I grew up in Central Valley. Ten years ago, this county was dairyland, but then the outlets came in and took over. They brought jobs, but we still have a mix of old and new, and you see that in town. There's been an Agway and a John Deere dealership for decades, but they're being squeezed out by a Starbucks."

"I see." Chris acted sad, but that worked for him too. He was relying on the fact that people here would be friendly, open-hearted, and above all, trusting.

"There's an unfortunate line between the haves and the have-nots, and it becomes obvious in junior year, which you will be teaching." Dr. McElroy paused. "The kids from the well-to-do families take the SATs and apply to college. The farm kids stay behind unless they get an athletic scholarship."

"Good to know," Chris said, trying to look interested.

"Tell me, how do you communicate with students, best?"

"Oh, one-on-one, definitely. Eye-to-eye, there's no substitute. I'm a friendly guy. I want to be accessible to them on email, social media, and such, but I believe in personal contact and mutual respect. That's why I coach, too."

"Oh, my, I forgot." Dr. McElroy frowned, then sifted through his file. "You're applying to fill our vacancy for an assistant baseball coach. Varsity."

"Yes." Chris had never coached before, but he was a naturally gifted athlete. He'd been going to indoor batting cages to get back in shape. His right shoulder ached. "I feel strongly that coaching is teaching, and vice versa. In other words, I'm always teaching, whether it's in the classroom or on the ball field. The setting doesn't matter, that's only about location."

"An insightful way to put it." Dr. McElroy pursed her lips. "As assistant baseball coach, you would report to Coach Hardwick. I must tell you, he doesn't keep assistants very long. His last one, well, moved on and wasn't replaced. Coach Hardwick likes to do it all himself, his own way. And he can be a man of few words."

"I look forward to meeting him." Chris had researched Coach Hardwick, evidently a well-known jerk. "I'm sure I can work with Coach Hardwick. He's an institution in regional high-school baseball, and the Central Valley Musketeers have one of the finest programs in the state."

"That's true." Dr. McElroy nodded, brightening. "Last year, several players were recruited for Division I and II."

"Yes, I know." Chris had already scouted the team online for his own purposes. He needed to befriend a quiet, insecure boy, most likely a kid with a troubled relationship to his father. Or better yet, a dead father. It was the same profile that a pedophile would use, but Chris was no pervert. His intent was to manipulate the boy, who was only the means to an end.

"So where do you see yourself in five years?"

"Oh, here, in Central Valley," Chris lied.

"Why here, though? Why us?" Dr. McElroy tilted her head, and Chris sensed he had to deliver on his answer.

"I love it here, and the rolling hills of Pennsylvania are a real thing. It's straight-up beautiful. I love the quiet setting and the small-town vibe." Chris leaned over, as if he were about to open his heart, when he wasn't even sure he had one. "But the truth is, I'm hoping to settle down here and raise a family. Central Valley just feels like *home.*"

"Well, that sounds wonderful! I must say, you lived up to all of my expectations." Dr. McElroy smiled warmly and closed the file. "Congratulations, Chris, you've got the job! Let me be the first to welcome you to Central Valley High School."

"Terrific!" Chris extended his hand over the desk, flashing his most sincere grin.

It was time to set his plan in motion, commencing with step one.

Step One

Chapter Two

C hris pulled into the Central Valley U-Haul dealership and parked his Jeep, a 2010 black Patriot. He slipped on a ball cap, got out of the car, and looked around. There were no other customers, which was why he'd come midmorning on a drizzly Wednesday. He didn't want any witnesses.

The U-Haul office was an orange-and-brown corrugated cube with a glass storefront, and two security cameras on its roofline aimed at the front door and the parking lot, mounted high enough that Chris's face would be hidden by the brim of his ball cap.

The dealership was smaller than the Ryder and Penske dealerships, but it had a storage facility out back, and the units were temperature- and humidity-controlled, making them the perfect place to store ammonium nitrate fertilizer, which was the main component of homemade IEDs, or improvised explosive devices, like an ANFO bomb.

Chris crossed to the lineup of gleaming white-and-orange pickups, cargo vans, and box trucks in several different lengths. The ten-foot box truck would be large enough to hold the fifty bags of fertilizer and the other equipment. If a ten-footer wasn't available, the fifteen-footer would do, though it was slower and its large size could attract attention.

Chris spotted only one ten-footer parked in the lot. According to the website, it was available next week, but he wasn't leaving anything to chance.

"Hello, sir, I'm Rick." A salesclerk came over in a green polo shirt with a logo patch and khaki pants.

"Hi, I'm Mike Jacobs. Nice to meet you." Chris extended a hand, and Rick shook it with a smile.

"How can I help you today?"

"I'm interested in the ten-footer." Chris gestured to the truck. "Is this the only one you have?"

"Yes. When do you need it?"

"Hmph." Chris paused, for show. "Let me think, today is Wednesday the thirteenth. I need it for Monday of next week, the eighteenth. Is it available?"

"I have to check and get you a rate quote. You know, you can check availability and reserve online with a credit card."

"I saw that, but I didn't want to reserve it online and send my nephew over to pick it up, only to find out that it's not available."

The clerk hesitated. "Did you say your nephew's going to be picking it up?"

"Yes, he'll be the one to come in and get it. I'm only in town for the day. I'll pay for it once I'm sure of my plans."

"How old is he?"

"Seventeen, a high-school junior." Chris didn't elaborate, because he couldn't. Not yet anyway. He'd just gotten the email confirming that he'd been hired and he was on his way to the school-district office, where he'd fill out the remaining forms. He'd start classes tomorrow and he'd have to pick a boy right away.

"Oh, that's a problem. He has to be eighteen to rent one of our box trucks."

Chris blinked. "But I'd be renting it, not him."

"Sorry, but just the same. He can't pick it up for you or drive if he's under eighteen."

"Really?" Chris asked, feigning surprise. Ryder had a minimum age of eighteen and at Penske, it was twenty-one. "But he has a driver's license, and I'll send him in with cash."

"Sorry, I can't help you out. Company rules. It's on the website in the FAQs."

"Rick, can you bend the rules, just this once? I can't come all the way back to Central Valley just to pick up the truck."

"Nope, sorry." The clerk motioned to the trailers at the end of the row. "Can you use a trailer? He'd only have to be sixteen to rent a trailer."

"No, I really need the truck."

"Then I can't help you, sorry. Did you check Zeke's?"

"What's that?" Chris's ears pricked up.

"Oh, you're not from here, that's right. Everybody knows Zeke." The clerk smiled. "He's a Central Valley old-timer. He fixes farm trucks. Actually, he can fix anything. He always has a truck sitting around to sell or rent, and all the locals use him when we don't have availability. I doubt he'd be picky about renting it to a seventeen-year-old. Most of those farm kids been driving since they were thirteen."

"Good to know," Chris said, meaning it. "Where's his shop?"

"Intersection of Brookfield and Glencross, just out of town." The clerk smiled wryly. "It doesn't have a sign but you can't miss it."

Fifteen minutes later, Chris was driving down Brookfield Road, understanding what the clerk had meant by not being able to miss Zeke's. The intersection of Brookfield and Glencross was in the middle of a soybean field, and on one corner was an ancient cinder-block garage surrounded by old trucks, rusted tractors, and used farm equipment next to precarious stacks of old tires, bicycles, and random kitchen appliances.

Chris turned into the grimy asphalt lot and parked in front

of the garage. He got out of the car, keeping his ball cap on though there were no security cameras. No one else was around, and the only sound was tuneless singing coming from one of the open bays.

"Zeke?" Chris called out, entering the garage, where a grizzled octogenarian in greasy overalls was working on an old Ford pickup on the lift. A cigarette dangled from his mouth, and his glasses had been repaired with a Band-Aid over the bridge.

"Yo."

Chris smiled pleasantly. "Hi, my name's Pat Nickerson. I hear that you might have a truck to let. My nephew's going to pick it up for me because I'm only in town for today. But he's seventeen. Can you work with that?"

"He a good boy?" Zeke's eyes narrowed.

"Yes."

"Then no!" Zeke burst into laughter, which turned into hacking, though he didn't remove the cigarette from his mouth.

Chris smiled. The guy was perfect.

"What kind of truck you need?" Zeke returned to working under the vehicle.

"A box truck, a ten-footer."

"I got two box trucks, a twelve-footer and a big mama."

"The twelve-footer will do. Does it run okay?"

"Oh, you need it to *run*?" Zeke asked, deadpan, then started laughing and hacking again.

Chris smiled, playing along, though he was deadly serious. An unreliable truck would not be the ticket. "So it runs reliably."

"Yes. I'd let you take it for a spin but it's not here. My cousin's usin' it."

"When will it be back? I need my nephew to pick it up next week, on Monday morning."

"No problem. I've got that one and another coming back. This time of year, it's slow, and nobody's been in. I've always got somethin'. You're moving Monday, we'll have it here Sunday night."

"Okay, let me double-check with my nephew to make sure, and I'll get back to you." Chris didn't explain that the truck wasn't for a move. It was for transporting an ANFO bomb that would kill as many people as possible and cause mass destruction. An ANFO bomb was easy to make and safe to assemble. Combine 96 percent ammonium nitrate fertilizer and 6 percent Number 2 fuel oil, diesel fuel, or kerosene in a drum, making a slurry the consistency of wet flour. To make it even more explosive, add nitromethane, a fuel used in motorsports or hobby rockets, readily available. Wire a blasting cap to TNT or a Tovex sausage, fire it with a simple electrical circuit, and drop it in the drum.

"Okay, fella. Call or stop back. My number's in the book. How long you need the truck for?"

"Just the day or two."

"Fine. Seventy-five bucks a day, cash. You gas it up. I'll have it here Monday morning for your nephew. Nine o'clock."

"How can I be sure?"

"Because I said so." Zeke cackled, the cigarette burning close to his lips. "Okay, fella. See ya later."

"See you," Chris said, turning to go. He had so much to do. The bombing was happening on Tuesday. Only six days away.

Kaboom.

Chapter Three

I'm Mr. Brennan, welcome to AP Government," Chris said on a continuous loop, standing at the threshold to his classroom and greeting the students. They didn't walk so much as shuffle, the girls in their Uggs and the boys in plastic slides.

"*You're* Mr. Brennan? Oh, whoa!" one female student said, flushing in a way that Chris found charming. But he wasn't tempted. The girls weren't his target. The boys were.

Chris kept smiling, greeting the students while he assessed the boys, uniformly sloppy in T-shirts, sweatpants, or school logowear. Some of them met his eye with confidence, so he eliminated them from consideration. Instead he noted the boys who had weak grips, averted their eyes, or had bad acne. Nobody with acne felt good about themselves. At seventeen years old, Chris had hated his skin, his face, and himself.

"I'm Mr. Brennan, hello, how're you doing?" Chris kept saying, as they kept coming. He had combed his class rosters and identified the boys he had both in class and on the baseball team. In this class, there were three—Evan Kostis, Jordan Larkin, and Michael "Raz" Sematov. Chris kept his eyes peeled for Evan, Jordan, or Raz, but they hadn't come yet.

"Whoa!" "Awesome!" "Look!" the students said as they reached their desks, delighted to discover that a surprise snack awaited them. Chris had placed either a soft pretzel, a packet of chocolate cupcakes, or an apple at each seat.

"Mr. Brennan, why the snacks?" one of the boys called out, holding up his cupcakes.

"Why not?" Chris called back, remembering the boy's name from the roster. The kid was Andrew Samins. "I figured you guys could use a treat."

"*Free?*" Samins asked, incredulous. "Wow, thanks!"

"You're welcome." Chris smiled, making a mental note.

"Awesome, thanks!" "Wow!" "Cool!" "Thank you!" the students chorused, the hubbub intensifying as they compared treats, leading inevitably to noisy negotiation over the snacks, which had been his intent. They were guinea pigs in an experiment, they just didn't know it. Their negotiations would give him clues about the boys' personalities: who had power and who didn't, who could be manipulated and who couldn't. Of course, the fights were over the chocolate cupcakes and the soft pretzels. Nobody wanted the apples except for the girls, either that or they settled for them. Chris wanted to see what happened with Evan, Jordan, and Raz.

"But Mr. Brennan," one girl said above the chatter, "we're not supposed to eat in class. It makes crumbs, and mice come. I saw one in the music room before break."

Another girl chimed in, "Also this is a peanut-free classroom, Mr. Brennan. I'm not allergic but some people could be."

"Ladies, the snacks are peanut-free. Dig in, and I'll take the heat." Chris watched the students take their seats. He'd arranged the desks the conventional way, five rows of six desks. He hadn't assigned them specific seating because he wanted to observe the friendships that had already formed.

Chris returned his attention to the hallway and spotted Evan, Jordan, and Raz walking toward him, looking at something on

Evan's smartphone. Chris had researched them on social media and knew that Evan Kostis was the most popular, a rich kid with a doctor father, so Evan wasn't his first choice for a pawn. Evan was the handsome one, with brown eyes, a thin nose, and thick black hair that he kept flipping back. He had a winning smile, undoubtedly thanks to orthodonture, and he dressed cool in a red Patagonia vest, Musketeers hoodie, slim jeans, and Timberland boots that looked new.

Next to Evan was Mike Sematov, whose unruly black hair curled to his shoulders. Sematov had bushy eyebrows and round dark eyes, and he was hyper, trying to grab Kostis's phone. Sematov's nickname was Raz, evidently from Rasputin, his Twitter handle was @cRAZy, and his Facebook feed was usually videos of people vomiting or popping zits and abscesses. Sematov was an excellent possibility because his father had passed away in August from pancreatic cancer. It wasn't easy to find a kid with a dead father, and Chris thought Raz might be a winner, unless the boy was too cRAZy.

Chris shifted his attention to another possibility, Jordan Larkin. Jordan was six-foot-one, but his stooped manner made him look awkward, all gangly legs and arms. The boy had a longish face with fine-boned features, but his hazel eyes were set close together and his hair, a nondescript brown, was too short. He dressed inexpensively, in a blue Musketeers Baseball sweatshirt, generic gray sweatpants, and Adidas's knockoff slides. Best of all, Jordan was the son of a single mother, which was almost as good as a dead father.

Chris smiled and extended a hand as the three boys reached the classroom. "I'm Mr. Brennan, gentlemen. Welcome to AP Government. I'll be coaching you guys, too."

Evan was the first to shake Chris's hand, looking him directly in the eye. "Evan Kostis. Ahoy! Welcome on board!"

"Good to meet you, Evan." Chris was about to turn to Jordan just as Sematov thrust his hand forward.

"Mr. Brennan, yo, I'm Mike Sematov but call me Raz. You don't look like Ms. Merriman." Raz smiled goofily.

"Can't fool you!" Chris kept his smile on, making a mental note of the fact that Sematov had offered his nickname and a hand-shake. The gestures suggested that Raz wanted a connection with him, so maybe there was something Chris could build on. "Raz, go in and pick a desk. Also I put out snacks for everybody."

"Awesome!" Raz's dark eyes lit up, and he ducked inside the classroom.

"Sweet!" Evan bolted after him, leaving Jordan alone with Chris, who extended a hand to the boy.

"You must be Jordan Larkin. Great to meet you."

"Thanks." Jordan shook Chris's hand, breaking eye contact to peek inside the classroom. "Are you for real about snacks? You know, they freak if we eat in the classroom."

"What they don't know won't hurt 'em," Chris said, then added, improvising, "We're celebrating. It's my birthday."

Jordan smiled, surprised. "Oh, jeez. Happy birthday."

"Don't say anything, I don't want to make a fuss."

"Sure." Jordan looked away, and Chris felt he had scored a point, co-opting the boy. Meanwhile Evan and Raz were racing each other to the snacks, and the only empty desks left were the first seats in each row. The remaining snacks were a soft pretzel and two apples.

"I call the pretzel!" Raz bolted toward the desk with the soft pretzel.

"I saw it first!" Evan chased after him, hip-checking Raz to grab the pretzel.

"Dude, yo!" Raz said, mock-outraged.

"Loser says what?" Evan shoved the pretzel in his mouth and claimed the desk, making the class laugh.

"Okay, everybody, let's get started!" Chris closed the class-room door, and the laughter slowly began to subside. Raz slumped into the desk at the head of the row, sulking as he set down his backpack. Jordan took the last empty desk, at the head of the row closest to Chris's desk, then he accepted the apple without complaint. The transaction confirmed to Chris that Evan Kostis was the leader, Raz was a question mark, and Jordan was the follower.

"Class, as I said, my name is Mr. Brennan and I'll be replacing Ms. Merriman. I have her syllabus, and we'll try to pick up where she left off." Chris clapped his hands together to get their attention, since they hadn't settled down. "I'm new in town. I grew up in the Midwest, taught in Wyoming, and I think we're going to have a fine rest of the semester."

"Can you ride horses?" Raz called out, and Chris took it as another attempt to make a connection.

"Yes I can," Chris answered, which was true. "Anything else you want to know? I'm happy to answer a few questions."

"Are you married?" one of the girls called out.

"No, I'm not," Chris answered to hooting and giggling.

"Are you a dog person or cat person?" asked another girl, the one who worried about peanut allergies. Her name was Sarah Atkinson, Chris knew but didn't let on.

"I like all animals but I don't have any pets right now. I'm not allowed. Last question?"

"Boxers or briefs?" Raz shouted, then burst into laughter, joined by the rest of the class.

"No comment." Chris smiled, then motioned for them to settle down. "All right, let's jump right in. I'm going to assume that you read the materials Ms. Merriman posted on her webpage and I reposted them on mine. That's how I'm going to run this class, too. Government derives its power from the consent of the governed. We also have a social compact, you and I."

The students began pulling out their three-ring binders, spiral-bound notebooks, finding pens and pencils from their backpacks. They weren't allowed to use laptops in class.

"My webpage has the syllabus, the assignments, and the quiz

and test schedule. Class participation is a third of your grade." Chris walked to his desk, which contained the Teacher's Edition of their textbook *How Government Works,* the black binder of his notes for class, and a class roster with students' faces, none of whom he cared about except Evan, Jordan, and Raz. He consulted it before he asked the next question. "Mr. Samins, Andrew Samins? Let's start with the readings. What was the first social compact in this country?"

"Uh, I don't know, I'm not sure. I was sick yesterday so I didn't do the homework."

"Okay, you get a free pass, one day only." Chris smiled, like the Cool Teacher. "Anybody else?" A bunch of girls raised their hands, and Chris glanced at his roster. "Sarah Atkinson? Sarah, why don't you tell us?"

"It was the Mayflower Compact."

"Correct, and why was the Mayflower Compact a social contract?"

"Well, the people on the Mayflower decided to get together and they said that they would make an agreement on how they were going to govern themselves."

"Right." Chris noticed Evan and Jordan hunched over their notebooks to take notes. Raz was doodling a picture of a pilgrim. "In 1620, the Mayflower made its way to the Boston area with a hundred and two passengers. On November 11, 1620, forty-one of them—only the men—wrote and signed a document that created a system of self-governance, because they had to start a settlement, plant crops, and harvest them."

Chris could see that Evan and Jordan took more notes, and Raz kept doodling. He continued, "The Mayflower Compact was a first example of popular sovereignty. Does anybody know what popular sovereignty means?"

Sarah's hand shot up again, but Chris pointed to an Asian girl behind her. "Yes, hi, please tell me your name before you answer the question."

"Brittany Lee. Popular sovereignty means that the political authority is with the people, like the citizens, and they can do what they want to the government. They can start one or they can even overthrow one."

"That's right, Brittany. The notion is that individuals have rights, and that the government has power only because it comes from the people." Chris wanted to get to the exercise he had planned, with an ulterior motive. "Now, you were supposed to read the Constitution and the Bill of Rights. These two documents embody what is unique about American government, which is that the Constitution sets the structure of government and the Bill of Rights sets the limitations on government. In other words, the Bill of Rights protects the rights of the individual. Let's do an exercise that will help us think about what it was like to be setting up a government."

Chris moved to the center of the room, and Raz turned the page, hiding his doodle. "Imagine you were one of the founding fathers, the actual people who wrote the Constitution and the Bill of Rights. Which document would you write, if you had the choice? Are you the authority, the person who wants to set up the government and establish rules that everyone can live by? *Or* are you the person who wants to set forth what rights belong to the individuals, so that they can never be taken by the authority?"

Sarah's hand shot up. "Like, do you mean are we Republicans or Democrats?"

"What about the independents?" called a boy in the back. "My brother's an independent!"

Raz turned around. "Your brother's an independent geek!"

Chris shot Raz a warning look, wondering if the boy was too much of a loose cannon for him. "Everybody, stand up, right now."

There were moans, giggles, and chatter as the students rose

by their desks, some reluctantly. Evan stood up quickly, and Jordan rose, hunched, without making eye contact with Chris.

"This unit, we're going to write our own Constitution and our own Bill of Rights. We're going to set up the government we would like and then we're going to set limitations on that government. So you need to decide if you want to write our Constitution or our Bill of Rights. Regardless of whatever political party you might be, or your parents might be, I want you to think about this for yourself."

A few students smiled and started talking among themselves.

"Don't do what your friends do. Pretend you were one of the founding fathers. Would you have been one of the people to set up the government or one of the ones to limit government? I'll give you a moment to decide. Close your eyes and think for yourself."

The students closed their eyes, giggling. Evan obeyed, and Jordan bowed his head as if it were a moment of silence. Raz closed one eye, then the other, making faces.

"Okay, the people who want to write the Constitution, walk toward the wall where the door is, with your eyes closed. And the people who want to write the Bill of Rights, walk to the side where the windows are. But don't open your eyes."

The class burst into chatter, and Sarah called out, "How can we walk with our eyes closed? We can't see! We'll bump into the desks!"

"Just do it, Sarah!" Evan called back. "You're not going to die. If you bump into something, go around it."

"Don't worry, I won't let you hurt yourself." Chris watched as the students took hesitant steps, walking with their arms outstretched, jostling each other, bumping into desks and backpacks, chattering and laughing. He kept an eye on Evan, Jordan, and Raz, as they were choosing sides.

"Keep your eyes closed!" Chris called to them. "Constitution or Bill of Rights? Up to you, people!"

There was more giggling, and one of the girls almost ended up walking out the door, but after a few minutes, the students sorted themselves into their noisy sides.

"Okay, everybody open your eyes!" Chris said, having accomplished his mission.

Chapter Four

Chris entered the faculty lounge with his lunch tray, looking for an empty seat. Teachers sat eating at tables of fake-wood veneer with blue bucket chairs. Their animated chatter filled the air, which smelled like an outlet perfume and tomato soup. The lounge was windowless, ringed by oak cabinetry and builder's-grade appliances, with walls painted Musketeer blue. An old blue couch sat against one wall underneath a mirror, and the far wall held a watercooler with backup water bottles.

Chris headed for a table that still had empty chairs, and one or two teachers flashed him friendly smiles, undoubtedly having gotten the memo with the subject line, **Give CHRIS BRENNAN a Warm Central Valley Welcome!** He'd met some of them in the cafeteria, when they'd introduced themselves and told him that the double-decker grilled cheese was on the menu, evidently a cause for celebration. Chris didn't know if it was harder to fake being a teacher or being jazzed about a sandwich.

There was a table with a few empty seats, at which sat two female teachers in shirtdresses, one with short brown hair and one with long. The one with short hair motioned to him. "Come here!" she called out, smiling. "Join us!"

"We don't bite!" she added.

Chris forced a chuckle, setting down his tray. "Thanks. I'm Chris Brennan. Great to meet you."

"Great to meet you, too. I'm Sue Deion, I teach Calculus." Sue gestured to her friend. "And this is Linda McClusky. She teaches Spanish."

"Nice to meet you, too, Linda." Chris sat down, going through his mental Rolodex. He'd researched Linda McClusky because she also taught eleventh grade. She lived in Bottsburg with her husband, Hugh, a piano teacher, and ran the Central Valley Players, which was performing *Annie* in May. Chris would miss the production.

Sue asked, "So what are you teaching, Chris?"

"Government." Chris took a bite of his grilled cheese, served on a Styrofoam plate with a cup of tomato soup, canned peaches, and red Jell-O with Cool Whip.

"Oh, here comes trouble!" Linda looked up at two male teachers approaching them with a female teacher, and Chris recognized the woman from his research because she was a drop-dead-gorgeous brunette, her great body shown to advantage in a trim black dress with black suede boots. Her name was Courtney Wheeler and she taught French, coached Cheer Club, and was married to a mortgage banker named Doug.

"Abe, Rick, Courtney, come here!" Sue motioned them over.

Chris shifted his attention to one of the male teachers, who was Abe Yomes, nicknamed Mr. Y. Abe was a tall, reedy African-American who taught Language Arts in eleventh grade, which was why Chris had researched him. Abe had on a trim checked shirt, pressed khakis, and polished loafers. He was gay and lived in town with his partner, Jamie Renette, who owned Renette Realty.

"I'm Abe Yomes, the famous Mr. Y, and you must be the new kid." Abe grinned as he set his tray on the table.

"Pleased to meet you, Abe. Chris Brennan." Chris reached across the table, and Abe shook his hand, with a smile.

"Welcome to Stepford. My partner Jamie's a Realtor, in case you decide to buy." Abe's dark eyes twinkled with amusement behind his hip rimless glasses. "I see you're drinking the Kool-Aid—I mean, eating the grilled cheese. These people, they're a cult. I tell them, the grilled cheese sucks out loud. The fact that it's a double-decker only makes it twice as gummy. I speak truth to power, and by power I mean the cafeteria ladies."

"Good to know." Chris chuckled, genuinely.

"Chris, meet Rick Pannerman, our resident hippie. He was born to teach Art. Actually he was born to be Picasso, but somebody else got the job." Abe gestured to the other male teacher, who was bald and chubby, with bright blue eyes and a smile buried in his long grayish beard. He dressed in a worn flannel shirt and jeans.

"Chris, good to see ya," Rick said, extending a meaty hand. "Welcome to the Island of Misfit Toys."

"Ha!" Chris smiled, and so did Abe.

"That's what he calls our table. Now you're one of us freaks. Gooble-gobble." Abe pulled out a chair as Courtney came walking over with her tray. "Last but not least, this lovely creature is Courtney Wheeler. She's married to Doug The Lug, the world's most boring white guy, and that's saying something."

"Abe, hush." Courtney sat down, smiling.

Abe pushed her chair in with a flourish. "Courtney is my bestie, and Prince Harry is my spirit animal. Don't you think we look alike, he and I?"

Courtney answered slyly, "Well, you both breathe oxygen."

"Not true. Oxygen breathes *him*." Abe sat down, focusing again on Chris. "So welcome, Central Valley virgin. What do you teach again?"

"Government and Criminal Justice," Chris answered, finishing the first half of his sandwich.

"I teach Language Arts, playing to type. I'm sensitive, yet curiously strong, the Altoids of teachers. Where're you from?"

"Wyoming."

"Wait. Whaaaat? Wyoming?" Abe's eyes flew open behind his rimless glasses. "Are you kidding me right now?"

Courtney burst into laughter. "Oh my God!"

Rick grinned in a goofy way. "Ha! What are the chances?"

Chris didn't like the way they said it. "Why? Have you been there?"

"*Been* there?" Abe repeated, his lips still parting in delight. "I *grew* up there! It was my childhood home! We left when I was nine but my parents moved back there, they liked it so much!"

"Really?" Chris arranged his face into a delighted mask. "What a coincidence."

"I know, right?" Abe bubbled with enthusiasm. "I'm adopted, hello. My dad was a real outdoorsman. Wyoming born and bred. He was on the Game and Fish Commission—fun fact, Wyoming is one of the few states that have a Game and Fish Commission, as opposed to a Fish and Game Commission. Anyway, my dad taught me to hunt and fish. We ate fresh elk burgers for dinner! You know how many elk are up there, and mule deer, bison, grizzlies . . ."

"Don't I know it," Chris said, though he didn't.

"Whereabouts in Wyoming are you from?" Abe leaned over, ignoring his lunch.

"Well, I'm not really *from* Wyoming—"

"I thought you said you were."

Courtney blinked. "Meanwhile Abe is being rude as usual, asking a million questions and not letting you eat."

Abe recoiled. "I'm not being rude. I never met anybody else from Wyoming out here. It's amazing!" He returned his attention to Chris. "I didn't mean to be rude, I just got excited. I'm an excitable boy. You get that, right?"

"I understand, no apology's necessary."

"I didn't think so." Abe glanced at Courtney triumphantly. "See, henny? Boyfriend and I speak the same language, though he doesn't have an accent." Abe turned back to Chris. "You don't have an accent. You must've lost it."

"I guess I did—"

"Right, you lose it. I lost mine. Can you imagine looking like me and sounding like a ranch hand? We're talking *major* cognitive dissonance."

Courtney rolled her lovely eyes. "Abe, you had the double-shot again, didn't you?"

Rick turned to Chris with an apologetic look. "We got a Starbucks in town, and Abe lives there. Buckle up."

Abe ignored them, turning back to Chris. "Anyway so are you from Wyoming or not?"

"No, I'm from the Midwest but I went to Northwest College in—"

"Cody! Of course! My dad's alma mater! In the Bighorn basin!"

"You know Northwest College, too?" Chris was kicking himself. This was a problem.

Courtney interjected, "Abe loves Wyoming. He even dragged us all out there to see it. Pretty, but really? Boring."

Rick shrugged. "I didn't think it was boring. Sachi wants us to retire there. All that natural beauty."

"Hold on a sec, I got snaps!" Abe slid his iPhone from his back pocket and started touching the screen.

Chris turned to Courtney to change the subject. "So Courtney, what do you teach?" he asked, though he already knew.

"French." Courtney smiled. "I started here five years ago, after I got married."

"Look!" Abe interrupted, holding up his phone across the

table, showing a photo of a rock formation around a body of water. "This must bring back memories, doesn't it?"

Chris plastered on a startled smile of recognition. "Man, that's great!"

Abe turned the picture around. "It looks like a lake, but it's not. I had my first kiss there—with a woman *and* a man! Tell 'em what it is, Chris! Everybody went there to make out, didn't they? That's what my dad said."

"Not me, I was a good boy. I studied hard so I could grow up, become a teacher, and eat double-decker grilled cheese." Chris took a bite of his sandwich, then acted as if he'd gotten food stuck in his throat. Suddenly he pushed away from the table, fake-choking, letting his expression reflect mild alarm, between hairball and Heimlich.

Rick's blue eyes went wide. "Chris, are you *choking*?"

"Oh no, drink something!" Courtney jumped up with a water bottle and hurried to his side.

"Chris!" Abe rushed around the table and whacked Chris on the back as Rick, Sue, and Linda came rushing over.

Chris doubled over, fake-choking as heads began to turn. Each teacher's face registered concern, then fear. He kept it up while Abe, Sue, and Linda clustered around him, calling "Oh no!" "He's choking!" "Do the Heimlich maneuver!" "Call 911!"

"It's okay, I guess it went down the wrong pipe." Chris acted as if he'd swallowed his sandwich, fake-gasping. The last thing he wanted was someone to call 911, bringing the police. They could start asking questions, which could ruin everything.

"My God!" Abe frowned with regret. "So sorry, I should have let you eat!"

"Not your fault, Abe. It was the sandwich."

"Let's sue the district," Abe shot back. Rick and Courtney laughed, and the other teachers broke into relieved smiles, then went back to their tables.

Chris smiled, but he knew that the Wyoming questions wouldn't go away forever. Abe would want to reminisce and compare notes.

Which presented a problem that he needed to solve.

Chapter Five

Heather Larkin stood by the entrance to the Lafayette Room, scanning the tables in her station, four eights in the left corner. The luncheon was for the Auxiliary Committee of Blakemore Medical Center, and fifty-two well-dressed women had been served their appetizer, mixed-greens salad with goat cheese crumbles, beet shavings, and walnuts.

Everything was going smoothly, and the room looked perfect. It was storming outside, but indirect light poured from Palladian windows and the occasional clap of thunder didn't disturb the chatter and laughter. The lights were low, emanating from tasteful brass sconces on the ivory damask walls, which matched the ivory tablecloths and slipcovered chairs. White tulips filled the centerpieces on each table, and the air smelled like costly perfume and raspberry vinaigrette dressing.

Heather kept an eye on her tables, since it was a club rule that members shouldn't have to wait for service. She wondered if they knew how many eyes were on them, waiting on them so they didn't have to wait. Waiters. Waitresses. It was even in the job name.

Heather's makeup was light, and she'd pulled her straight,

brown hair back into a low ponytail. She had on her uniform, a mint-green dirndl with a drawstring bodice intended to show her cleavage to golfers on their third Long Island Iced Tea. She hated the uniform and the required shoes, which were white with a stacked heel. But she picked her battles, and her uniform wasn't one of them.

She had waitressed at the Central Valley Country Club for fifteen years and was excellent at her job. But lately she'd been wondering if she'd gotten too good at waiting. Patience was a virtue, but there were limits. She wondered if a decade of waiting on people had trained her to wait for things to happen, rather than making them happen, or to meet other people's needs instead of her own, like an expert codependent.

Still Heather was lucky to have the job, especially as a single mother. There were cost-of-living increases, pooled tips at Christmas, plus full benefits that she and her son Jordan were eligible for. Jordan was a junior in high school, hopefully heading for college on a baseball scholarship. But what was *she* heading for? She only had two years of college because she quit when she'd gotten pregnant. Still, she never thought of her son as a mistake. Marrying his father was the mistake. Divorcing him corrected the mistake.

Heather scanned the tables. The women looked so nice with their highlights freshly done, and they had on pastel pantsuits with cute cropped jackets, undoubtedly bought at the mall. Club members didn't shop at the outlets, so they didn't have to hide the Sharpie mark on an irregular or the pulled thread of a defective garment. Heather had stopped wanting to be them, but would have settled for being somebody who wore her own clothes to work. She wanted a desk and chair, so she could sit down. She wanted a job that went somewhere, with a brass nameplate with her full name, instead of a name tag, HEATHER.

"Heather," said a voice behind her, and Heather came out of her reverie, turning. It was Emily, the new Food & Beverage

Manager. Emily was still in her twenties, but her heavy makeup made her look hard and her short brown hair was stiff with product. She had on a mint-green polo shirt with khakis, the uniform upgrade for management employees.

"Yes?"

"I need you to stay until six tonight. The luncheon is going to run late because they're going to do the silent auction and raffles after the speeches."

"Sorry, I can't. Like I said, I'd like to be home for Jordan." Heather picked her battles, and this was the one she'd picked. Her regular shift was breakfast and lunch, from 6:00 A.M. to 3:00 P.M. That would get her home so she could make dinner and they could have a meal together. It had never been a problem with her old boss Mike, and Heather had assumed that a female boss would be even more understanding. But nobody could knife a woman like another woman.

"I need you to stay." Emily pursed her lips, shiny with pink lip gloss.

"Can't Suzanne?"

"I'm not asking Suzanne. I'm asking you."

"Can't you ask her? She doesn't have kids." Heather reflexively scanned the tables but nobody needed anything.

"Your *kid* is in high school." Emily's blue eyes glittered.

"So?" Heather didn't explain that in one year, Jordan would be gone, off to college. Everything felt like the last time. "You said you'd accommodate—"

"I said I'd accommodate you *if I can*."

"But you're not trying to accommodate me. You didn't ask Suzanne—"

"Heather, if you value your job, you will do what I ask, when I ask it." Emily glanced around the dining room.

"What's that mean? You fire me if I say no?"

"Yes." Emily met her eyes directly. "When I took over, I was given carte blanche to do what needed to be done. You can take the job or leave it. Your choice."

Heather felt the blood drain from her face. She had heard the rumors that new management had been hired to cut catering costs. If Emily was looking for reason to fire her, Heather couldn't give her one. "Okay, I'll stay until six," she said quickly. Suddenly she noticed one of the women lifting an empty glass to signal a refill. "I'd better go."

"Hurry," Emily snapped. "You should've seen that earlier. Don't you know who that is? That's Mindy Kostis. She's sponsoring the luncheon."

"Okay, on it." Heather recognized the name because Jordan was on the baseball team with Evan Kostis, Mindy's son.

"Whatever. Go, go, go."

Heather made a beeline for Mindy. The Kostis family was in the Winner's Circle, the top tier of contributors to the Building Fund. Heather hadn't met or served Mindy and felt suddenly relieved that her name tag didn't have her last name. Even so, she doubted that Mindy would recognize the name, since Jordan had just made varsity.

Heather reached the table, extended a hand for the empty glass, and smiled pleasantly. "May I get you a refill, Ms. Kostis?" she asked, since it was club rules to address members by name.

"Yes, please. Tanqueray and tonic." Mindy smiled back, pleasantly enough. She had curly blonde hair, round blue eyes, and a sweet smile. She was dressed in a pink-tweed suit with a patch that read Chanel, and Heather tried not to let her eyes bug out of her head. She had never seen a real Chanel jacket.

"My pleasure," Heather answered, a scripted reply, also per club rules.

"Do I know you? You look so familiar." Mindy squinted at Heather's name tag.

Heather's mouth went dry. She didn't know how Mindy knew

her. Heather didn't go to the games because she worked. She was about to answer, *My son is on the baseball team with your son,* but she stopped herself. "No, I don't believe so," she answered, her tone polite.

"Oh, okay, sorry." Mindy smiled, blinking.

"My pleasure," Heather said again, like a CVCC fembot. The other women at the table kept chattering away, paying no attention to the conversation, which, to them, was Mindy talking to The Waitress. She turned to them. "Anyone else need a refill?"

"Uh, no," said one, without looking up, and the others didn't reply.

"Thank you." Heather left, flustered. She didn't know why she hadn't told Mindy who she was. Mindy hadn't demeaned Heather at all, so why had Heather demeaned herself? She didn't consider herself less than Mindy, so why had she acted that way? Mindy was Winner's Circle, but what was Heather? Loser's Circle?

She practically fled the Lafayette Room, heading back toward the bar, and it struck her that the luncheon had just started, but Mindy was the only woman on her second cocktail.

Chapter Six

It was pouring outside, and Susan Sematov stood at her office window, her cell phone to her ear, dismayed to hear her call go to voicemail. Her older son Ryan hadn't come home last night, and she was worried. He was nineteen, an adult, but that didn't mean she didn't worry about him anymore, especially after last year. Her husband, Neil, had passed away after a brutal battle with pancreatic cancer, and Susan, Ryan, and their younger son, Raz, were still reeling. Neil had gone from diagnosis to death in only two months, and Ryan had dropped out of Boston University, where he'd just finished his freshman year.

Susan ended the call and pressed REDIAL to call Ryan again, keeping her face to the window, so it looked as if she was surveying ValleyCo One from her window. Susan was Marketing Manager of ValleyCo, the biggest developer of outlet malls in Central Valley. The ValleyCo One outlet mall also held their corporate headquarters, a three-story brick box designed to coordinate with the brick outlet stores that lay outside her window in a massive concrete square.

Susan's call to Ryan rang and rang, and she sent up a prayer, asking God to please let him pick up. Her older son had taken his father's death so hard and felt lost at home. His friends were still at BU and their other colleges, and he was spending all day sleeping on the couch, and at night, going out drinking with God-knows-who.

Susan's call went to voicemail again, and she hung up, scanning the outlet mall. At the top of the square, its north side, were the Vanity Fair outlets—Maidenform, Olga, Warner's, Best Form, and Lillyette—which everybody in the office nicknamed BoobTown. To her right on the east side was Lee, Wrangler, Reef, Nautica, and JanSport—naturally nicknamed BallTown. To her left was Pottery Barn, Crate & Barrel, Lenox, and Corningware—or HousePorn. Behind her, out of her view, was Land of Shoes; Easy Spirit, Famous Footwear, Reebok, Bass Factory Outlet, and Gold Toe Factory. Susan had been hired straight out of Penn State as an administrative assistant in the Marketing Department and had worked her way up to running the department by the time ValleyCo Five was in blueprints.

Susan glanced at the clock—1:35. She didn't want to call the police because she knew Ryan would throw a fit. She didn't know where Ryan had gone because he'd left the house while she was on a conference call with the West Coast. Presumably he had told his younger brother Raz where he was going, but one work call had led to another, and before Susan knew it, Raz had gone up to bed without telling her where Ryan had gone.

Susan thought it over. The two brothers were thick as thieves, or at least they used to be before Neil had died, but her sons were each reacting to their father's passing in different ways; Ryan, her mild child, had grown more inward, keeping his grief inside, but Raz, her wild child, had gotten more out of control. Raz had idolized his father, and they were both baseball fanatics.

Susan let her thoughts travel backwards in time, to those memories. Raz and Neil would hit balls in the backyard for hours, and Neil went to every one of Raz's games, proud to see his son pitch for the Musketeers. Neil's illness had derailed Raz emotionally, and she had gotten recommendations for therapists, but neither boy would go. She'd started therapy, and the plan was to try to convince them to come with her, but that had yet to come to fruition.

Susan scrolled to the text function, found her last text to Raz, and texted him: **Honey, please call when you can. It's important.** Students were allowed to keep their cell phones with them, only with the sound off, and they weren't permitted to look at them during class. It was a rule more honored in the breach, and Raz and rules were never on good terms.

She slipped the phone back in her blazer pocket and went to her desk, which she kept uncluttered except for her nameplate, a digital clock, a jar of pencils and pens, and family photographs of Neil and the kids. She sat down and scanned the photos, wishing that she were in at least a few of the photographs with Neil, so she could see them over time. They'd met in college, fallen in love, gotten married upon graduation, and been happily married almost every day since then. Susan couldn't have asked for more. Except now, all she asked for was more.

Her gaze found her favorite photo, the one of Neil hugging Ryan and Raz at Ryan's graduation from CVHS. They had been so happy then, and even she didn't believe that they had had such a successful marriage, given their upbringing. She wasn't perfect, nor was he, but they were imperfect in the same way, a union of two doers who loved nothing so much as checking off boxes on a Things To Do List.

Susan shooed the thoughts away, then checked her phone, but Raz hadn't texted her back. She texted him again. **Honey, please call. Worried about Ryan.** She set the phone down, trying not to *catastrophize,* as her therapist Marcia said. Marcia had taught her to cope by occupying her mind, so Susan tapped the mousepad on her laptop. The screen filled with the red ValleyCo logo, a stylized mall nestled in the V of Valley, a branding decision made before Susan's time.

She opened an email and a PDF of a BoobTown ad for her approval. The top banner read, THIS MOTHER'S DAY IS **SUNDAY, MAY 15!** CELEBRATE MOM AND YOURSELF! Underneath was a photo of a pretty mom with a little boy, a stock image aimed at their target market. Susan had been that woman, the shopper who was ValleyCo's sweet spot, the kind of mom who put the date of a sale on her calendar the first time she heard it. That was why Susan made sure that in every ad, the sale date was the largest thing on the page, and in their email blasts, the sale date connected automatically to My ValleyCo Calendar, an app that she had commissioned herself.

My ValleyCo Calendar enabled the customer to schedule the sales at any ValleyCo outlet mall and send herself alerts at one- and two-week intervals. Susan's bosses, all male, had been skeptical, wondering why any woman would agree to be harassed, but the app took off. Susan hadn't been surprised. Its success was due to the innate belief that doing everything right would lead to happiness, a credo that she had ascribed to until Neil died.

Susan approved the ad. It was good enough. She was losing her edge now that Neil had died. He'd been her biggest supporter, and only after he was gone did she realize that she had been performing for him all along.

Susan picked up her phone. It read 1:45 P.M., which meant that Raz was in seventh period, but he hadn't called or texted. She swiped to her Favorites and pressed three—Neil would be forever number one, and Ryan was number two. The phone rang but it went to voicemail.

"Damn!" Susan said aloud, glancing behind her, but her secretary wasn't looking. Everyone had been so wonderful to her after Neil had passed, but lately her office felt like a fishbowl.

Every time they looked at her, she saw herself the way they saw her: a new widow, trying desperately to keep herself and her family from coming apart at the seams, like a factory second. The Sematovs were Irregulars now.

Susan pressed REDIAL, the phone rang twice, and finally, Raz picked up. "Raz—"

"Mom, *what?*" Raz asked, his tone irritated. "Why are you calling me? I'm at school."

"This is your free period, isn't it? I'm worried about Ryan. He didn't come home last night."

"So?"

Susan sensed he was with friends. "So he doesn't do that. He's been out all night."

"Mom." Raz snorted. "Is this what you think is important? He's a big boy. He's *out.*"

"Did he tell you where he was going last night?"

"I don't know!" Raz raised his voice.

"Where did he say he was going?"

" 'I don't know' means I don't know! I don't *remember.*"

"Raz, please think," Susan said, softening her tone. "Something could've happened to him."

"He probably got laid!"

"Raz!" Susan glanced over her shoulder and caught her secretary looking at her. "I'm worried about him."

"There's nothing to worry about! He's fine. I have to go!"

"Raz, you don't know that he's fine. Think about what he told you. Did he say where he was going or who he was with—" Susan stopped when she realized Raz had gone unusually quiet on the other end of the call.

She looked at the phone, and Raz had hung up.

Chapter Seven

Chris headed to baseball practice, more tired than he'd expected. He had no idea how teachers did it, day after day. He'd had to teach the same lesson twice, saying the same exact things to two classes of AP Government and two classes of the non-AP level, since the class size at CVHS was restricted to thirty students. Plus he had to teach his elective, Criminal Justice. He'd identified two more boys in his non-AP course and one in Criminal Justice, but neither as promising as Jordan or Raz.

Chris threaded his way down a packed hallway, having changed into his coach's gear, a blue polo shirt that read ASSISTANT COACH MUSKETEERS BASEBALL, royal-blue nylon sweatpants, and sneakers. Framed group photos of past CVHS classes were mounted on the white walls, and inspirational posters hung at regular intervals: MUSKETEERS MAKE EMPATHY A HABIT. BE THE CHANGE—NOTICE, CHOOSE, ACT. VALIDATE OTHERS. He passed a window overlooking a courtyard filled with flowerbeds. It was raining out, so practice had been moved inside to the gym.

Chris was looking forward to seeing Jordan and Raz, so he could make a final decision. He had tentatively eliminated Evan because of the boy's alpha behavior with the snacks and choice of the Bill of Rights team. Raz had also chosen the Bill of Rights team, so he was now on the bubble. Jordan was the frontrunner since he had chosen the Constitution team, suggesting that he was a boy comfortable with structure and authority, perfect for Chris. He needed a boy he could use and manipulate. Tuesday was coming up fast.

Suddenly Chris noticed that two of his players had turned onto the hallway, Trevor Kiefermann and Dylan McPhee. Chris hadn't met them yet, but he had researched them, and the two boys couldn't have been more different. Trevor was a tall, blocky redhead with a freckled face and an obsession with kettlebells and weight lifting, according to his social media. Dylan was the tallest kid on the team, at six-five, but reed-thin and wiry with wispy blond hair, fine features, and heavy wire-rimmed glasses that slid down his nose. Dylan's social media consisted of photos from NASA, the Astronomy Photo of the Day, and photographs of outer space, sent by whatever astronaut was currently orbiting the earth.

Chris flashed them a smile. "Hey guys, I'm Coach Brennan, the new assistant coach."

"Hey Coach, Trevor Kiefermann, nice to meet you. I play third base." Trevor shook his hand, squeezing it firmly.

"Coach, I'm Dylan McPhee, center field." Dylan shook Chris's hand, too, but his hand was slender, though his grip equally strong.

"Good to meet you both." Chris fell into step with them down the hallway, and Trevor seemed eager to talk, the more outgoing of the two.

"They say you're a cowboy. Moved here from Montana, right?"

"Wyoming, but news travels fast here." Chris allowed his features to reflect mild surprise.

"Raz told us. Where'd you coach before?"

"I didn't. I almost played minor-league ball but I tore my ACL the week before tryouts." Chris knew his alias couldn't be found online on any minor-league roster, should they look him up. Interestingly, the Internet made lying easier and harder, both at once.

"Sucks." Trevor shook his head. "Where'd you play?"

"Class A, Midwest League. If I tell you which team, you're gonna laugh. The Fort Wayne Tincaps of Fort Wayne, Indiana."

"What a name!" Trevor chuckled.

Dylan smiled. "Is that real?"

"Yes, totally." Chris smiled back, feeling the humor break the ice, as usual. "Still, it coulda been worse. Would you believe the Cedar Rapids Kernels."

"Ha!" Trevor laughed, and so did Dylan.

"So how's the season?" Chris asked, though he already knew. The Musketeers were on a losing streak.

"Not so good." Trevor's expression clouded. "The season started April 1, and we're one and five. Coach Hardwick might replace Raz with Jordan for tomorrow's game. We play Upper Grove, and they're undefeated."

"Is Jordan the better pitcher?"

"I think so. He just made varsity and he doesn't throw as hard as Raz, but his accuracy and control is unreal. He just stays calm, no matter what."

Dylan interjected again, "Jordan's a contact pitcher. The batter might get a piece of the ball, but they won't get a base hit. The ball will be a grounder or fly out, easy to catch."

Chris mulled it over. "So they're competing for starting pitcher and they're friends? That can't be easy, can it?"

"They're buds, but hey, it happens on a team. Only one can be the ace."

Chris was settling on Jordan, but he would need to separate him from Raz to exert the maximum influence on him. The competition for starting pitcher might be the wedge, and all Chris had to do was hammer it hard.

The hallway ended at the entrance to the boys' locker room,

and the door was propped open. Trevor gestured inside. "I'll show you where the coaches' office is. Coach Natale should be there, the JV Coach."

"Lead the way, boys."

Chapter Eight

Chris followed the boys down a ramp to a lower level and they entered a large locker room with benches and blue lockers, which was emptying. Trevor and Dylan dropped him off, and Chris walked the short hallway to the coaches' office, spotting Coach Natale through the window. Chris knew from his research that Natale taught Health, his wife Felicia was a reading specialist at the high school, and their twin girls were in fifth grade at CVMS. They owned a white poodle but Chris didn't remember the dog's name. Then it came to him— Snowflake. Confirming, *no imagination*.

"I'm Chris Brennan, the new assistant," Chris said, when he reached the entrance to the office, and Victor crossed the room with an eager grin, his meaty hand extended.

"I'm Victor Natale, welcome!" Victor pumped Chris's hand with vigor. Natale was short and chubby, with an affable Italian-guy vibe. He had large brown eyes, a big nose, and thick lips, his fleshy face framed by thick black hair. "I coach the JV team with my assistant Dan Bankoske. He's already in the gym. So I hear you're from Utah?"

"Wyoming. Everybody knows everything here, am I right?"

"Bingo!" Victor laughed. "My wife told me. She's on the Instructional Support team. She heard it from Anne in the office." He spread his arms broadly. "Well, this is our palace. The empty desk is yours."

"Thanks." Chris crossed to the empty desk and set his backpack on the black desk chair. The windowless room held four black desks facing the wall, and the other three desks were cluttered with forms, three-ring notebooks, and *Inside Pitch, Coach & Athletic Director,* and *Covering All Bases* magazines. Black file cabinets lined the opposite wall next to a dorm-size refrigerator, old microwave, and a Keurig coffeemaker.

"So, Chris, what's your deal? You single or married?"

"Single."

"Girlfriend?"

"No."

"Looking to meet somebody new? My sister-in-law's about to free up. You can take her off my hands. I can't get her out of my house."

"Not yet, thanks." Chris thought Victor was likable but he didn't need a friend.

"Lemme know. Did you get the free iPad? It's from the Boosters, God bless them."

"Yes." Chris unzipped his backpack and took out his new iPad.

"You downloaded the software, right? It's like that app, MLB Dugout."

"Right." Chris had downloaded the coaching software as per Hardwick's emailed instructions, but he had also created secret player files. "Any pointers for working with Coach Hardwick?"

"Ha!" Victor's dark eyes glittered. "The kids call him Hardass behind his back. Also Hardhead, Hardwood, Hard On, and Hard Dick."

Chris chuckled, happy to be taken into confidence so quickly. "He's not exactly Santa Claus."

"Understatement of the year."

"Are you friendly with him?"

"Is anybody? That's why Kwame left. Couldn't take it another minute. Hardwick goes through assistants like Kleenexes." Victor chuckled. "You know the secret to getting along with him? Follow the Bible."

"Really? I didn't know he was a man of faith." Chris hadn't seen anything in his research about Coach Hardwick's being religious or he would've worn a crucifix.

"No, not that Bible. Hardwick's Bible. He emailed it to you. He calls it the Bible."

"Oh, *that* Bible." Chris remembered the packet of information that Coach Hardwick had emailed him. He had it with him in his backpack.

"The Bible is the Gospel According to Hardwick. If you follow the Bible, you'll get along fine with him. The Bible is his program, his rules, rain or shine, off-season to postseason. To be fair, you can't argue with results. He wins." Victor yakked away. "I follow the Bible because it's good for JV and varsity to be consistent. But I use more emotional intelligence than he does. I like to get close to my players, get to know them personally. Hardwick's not like that. He's old-school."

"I think it's okay to get close to the players. You can still retain your authority." Chris processed the information. If Hardwick didn't get close to the players, it gave him an opening with the boys.

"I agree." Victor smiled, his approval plain. "But keep it to yourself. Follow the Bible. Stay in your lane. The kids, too. They know what's expected. If the kids follow the Bible, Hardwick doesn't sweat anything. Like hair, for example. Take Raz. Mike Sematov."

"I have him in class."

"Good luck. What a wackadoodle. He pitched last season. Throws hard. A great fastball but major control problems on and off the field." Victor snorted. "If you have him in class, you know what he's like. Hair down to his shoulders like Lincecum. Wears a man bun. Hardwick doesn't care. He even told Raz that his hair had superpowers like Samson. Now the kid'll *never* cut it."

Chris smiled. "So Raz is the starting pitcher? What about Jordan Larkin? I heard Coach Hardwick might start him instead."

"Larkin? Love that kid." Victor's coarse features lit up. "He played for me on JV last season. He's a great kid. A quiet kid, shy, but great."

"Really." Chris was targeting Larkin, more and more.

"Then over the summer, he grew. That's the kind of thing that happens in high-school ball, I see it all the time. The kids grow, put on muscle. Or they sharpen their skills, improve their mechanics, go to a camp. Larkin came into his own. He's got the stuff. He's *bringin'* it. The team's losing with Raz pitching. I think Hardwick will start Jordan."

"How did Larkin improve so much?"

"God knows. He didn't go to camp, he can't afford it."

"Do you think Raz taught him?" Chris was fishing. "Or maybe he learned from his father?"

"I don't know if Raz taught him. If he did, he regrets it." Victor frowned. "FYI, neither Larkin or Raz have a dad. Raz's dad died last summer, helluva guy. Neil, came to all the games. Larkin's dad skipped out when the kid was little. He's got a mom, a waitress. He's an only child."

"Too bad." Chris had thought as much. There had been no mention of a father in Larkin's social media.

"Yeah, it's a tough break. Larkin's praying for a scholarship."

"Guess we better get going, huh?" Chris gestured at the clock, getting a plan. They left the office and went down the hallway. The air felt hotter, and the heat intensified a weirdly strong odor.

"The stench is Axe body spray. Good luck getting it out of your clothes. My wife can smell it in my hair." Victor fell in step beside him, and they continued down a long corridor to the gym entrance, double-wide with the doors propped open. "Wait'll you see how big the gym is. Batting nets, weight room, the whole nine. Again, the Boosters buy it all."

They reached the gym entrance, and they went inside. Boys were rolling nets, dragging blue mats, and lugging mesh bags full of equipment this way and that. The noise echoed throughout the gym, ricocheting off the hard surfaces. Chris scanned for Jordan, who was with Raz, talking with Coach Hardwick.

"See what I mean? Awesome." Victor gestured with a flourish.

"It's amazing." Chris couldn't have cared less, though the gym was immense, with a high-peaked ceiling of corrugated material, bright strips of fluorescent lighting, and blue-and-white championship banners hanging from the rafters. The walls were white cinder block, and the bleachers, also royal blue, had been folded against the sidewalls, revealing a glistening hardwood floor.

"Today varsity and junior varsity are practicing. I run my guys, you run yours. They're setting up the equipment." Victor pointed to the four corners of the gym.

"I see." Chris kept his eye on Coach Hardwick, who was talking to Raz more than Jordan. The discussion seemed to be heating up, with Coach Hardwick gesturing and Raz shaking his head, no. "Victor, I'd better go check in."

"Good luck." Victor flashed him a warm smile.

Chris took off, beelining for Coach Hardwick. He plastered on a smile, but Hardwick only frowned back, and the harsh lighting of the gym showed the furrows on his forehead and the lines from his bulbous nose to his weak chin. It struck Chris that Coach Hardwick resembled the Central Valley Musketeer, the angry colonist whose painted likeness scowled from the center of the gym floor.

"You're late." Hardwick glared. Up close, his glasses looked dirty, and their bifocal windows magnified his brown irises.

"Sorry, I'm Chris Brennan. Good to see you again—"

"You were talking to Victor. Don't. He talks too much, he's Italian. Stay away from him. It'll take years off your life."

Chris let it go. "I read your email and I know what we're practicing today. I'm good to go."

Hardwick's frown eased. "Call the kids over here. Holler. We don't use whistles. They're not dogs."

"Will do." Chris turned away, cupped his hands, and shouted, "Varsity, come on over!"

Heads turned, and the boys came running almost immediately. Raz jogged over ahead of Jordan and Evan.

"Come on over and take a knee, please!" Chris clapped his hands together. The boys settled down, looking up at him with eager faces, probably twenty-five of all different shapes, sizes, and races, all of them in their blue Musketeer Varsity baseball T-shirts and shorts.

Coach Hardwick put his hands on his hips. "Boys, I'm going to make this short and sweet. Today we're going to practice hard. The Musketeer standard is excellence, on the field and in the gym. Nothing less wins."

Chris kept his game face on, noticing the boys' rapt attention. They showed every emotion on their young features, and they so wanted approval. Chris would exploit that very emotion, starting today. Jordan, Evan, Dylan, and Trevor were paying attention, but Raz's shaggy head was down, and he was picking his cuticles.

"Boys, let me tell you a story before we get started. It's from the legendary Coach John Scolinos, who coached at California Polytechnic. Coach Scolinos used to say that in high-school baseball, in college baseball, in the minor leagues, and in the major leagues, home plate is seventeen inches wide."

Chris watched as the boys listened, especially Jordan. Only Raz kept picking his cuticles.

Hardwick continued, "Baseball is a game about seventeen

inches. If you don't reach those seventeen inches, the plate does not get bigger or wider to help you. It's a standard. The standard on this team is excellence. *You* reach the *standard*. The *standard* does not reach *you*."

Chris nodded, as Hardwick kept speaking.

"How do you reach that standard? How do you reach excellence? You must hold yourself accountable at all times." Coach Hardwick gestured to Chris. "Boys, meet our new assistant coach, Coach Brennan."

"Oh, hi." Chris smiled as all the heads turned to him.

Coach Hardwick continued, "Coach Brennan was late to practice today by two minutes. Coach Brennan might be thinking, two minutes doesn't matter. It's *only* two minutes. Coach Brennan might be thinking, two minutes isn't as late as five minutes. Or ten. Or *seventeen*."

Chris felt himself flush. This would not further his plans. He needed to be an authority figure to Jordan to gain his trust. He could see their smiles fade when it dawned on them that Coach Hardwick was about to make an example of him.

"Boys, if Coach Brennan is thinking any of those things, he is sorely mistaken. Coach Brennan may have been hired by the school district, but he will not stay on this team. If any of you are thinking the way Coach Brennan thinks, you will not stay on this team, either."

Chris kept his head high. Evan started to smirk, out of nervousness or derision. Trevor and Dylan frowned. Jordan averted his eyes, and Raz kept looking down.

"Boys, the standard is arriving at practice on time. The standard never changes. Why? Because the standard is excellence, and excellence is the *only* thing that wins. The way to achieve excellence is through accountability. If you do not account to yourself, then you will fail. If Coach Brennan does not account to himself, he will fail."

Chris realized he'd been thinking about this the wrong way.

After all, the boys were identifying with him, seeing him as relatable, which was exactly what he needed. So Chris played it up, lowering his gaze as if utterly ashamed of himself.

"Tomorrow we play Upper Grove. We are ready. We have been accountable. And we will win." Coach Hardwick stood taller, hitching up his pants. "Now, boys, line up at your regular practice stations. If you read the Bible, you know the drill."

The boys scrambled to their feet, then jogged off quickly.

Chris turned to Coach Hardwick. "Coach, it won't happen again."

"Damn right it won't."

Chris took it on the chin. "I saw you talking with Jordan and Raz. Anything I should know?"

"Raz wants to stay as starting pitcher."

"Over Jordan?"

"No, over Cy Young."

Chris smiled at the bad joke. "From what I hear, Jordan doesn't have the stuff to start."

"What?" Hardwick's eyes narrowed behind his glasses. "Did Victor tell you that? What does *he* know? He coaches JV for a reason. He hasn't seen Jordan throw since last season. You don't believe me, go see for yourself."

"You mean have a catch with Jordan?" Chris asked, which was exactly what he wanted.

"Yes. Let him show you what he's got. I know talent when I see it. Hmph."

"Okay, Coach. Will do." Chris jogged off after the team, smiling inwardly. He was looking forward to his catch with Jordan. Just the two of them, alone. Like father and son.

Or so Chris imagined.

Chapter Nine

C hris approached Jordan, who was standing in line for batting practice. "Got a minute?" he said, tossing the boy a glove. "Coach wants us to have a catch, so I can see what you got."

"Okay." Jordan came out of line, and a few of the boys glanced over, including Evan and Raz.

"Let's go on the other side of the curtain, for safety's sake." Chris started walking along a blue plastic drape that hung from the ceiling, sectioning off a portion of the gym. Chris had already moved the portable pitcher's mound and other equipment to the other side.

Jordan said nothing, trailing him. The gym was filled with the activity and noise of fifty boys running, drilling, and catching.

"I hear a lot of nice things about you from Coach Natale." Chris kept his tone light, to get some good vibes going. "He told me he really enjoyed coaching you."

"Oh." Jordan half-smiled, head down.

"He also said you've really improved."

Jordan didn't say anything, walking in his characteristic stooped fashion along the plastic curtain.

"It's hard to improve, I find. But you did it. You made varsity."

Jordan nodded, with a slight smile.

"You might even start tomorrow."

Jordan nodded again.

"How did you do it?"

"I don't know." Jordan shrugged.

"Somebody teach you?"

"Not really."

"You wanna know who taught me to play baseball? My mom." Chris rolled his eyes, self-deprecating, as they reached the opening in the curtain and entered the isolated part of the gym, which was empty.

"Huh." Jordan half-smiled, and Chris decided to carry the conversational ball, hoping to lay a foundation for Jordan to open up.

"My mom is awesome, *was* awesome. I was close to her. Unfortunately, my dad was a real jerk. A drunk, actually." Chris heard the ring of truth in his words, since one of his foster fathers had lived inside the bottle. "My mother tried to be the mom and a dad, both. She was tall and bowled in a league. She's the one who bought me my first glove, even helped me oil it. She took me to the park and taught me how to throw."

"Huh." Jordan met Chris's eyes for the first time. "I learned from YouTube."

"Really?" Chris couldn't remember when YouTube had started.

"Sure, I watched a lot of YouTube videos. I still do. There are professional ones like MLB Network. They have Pedro Martinez talking about Colon. I like them but I like the amateur ones, like, from college and high-school coaches. They take it slower and explain. I think that's how I got better. I worked on my mechanics. That's what recruiters look for. Good mechanics."

"It's true, you can't get to the next level without good mechanics." Chris realized that Jordan warmed up when the subject was baseball. "I like videos, but some aren't worth it. Is there one you recommend? A favorite?"

"Yeah, it's from Texas. It's mad technical but the coach explains it in a way you can understand."

"Can you send me the link? My email's on my teacher page."

"Sure."

"Thanks." Chris had just opened up a line of communication to the boy. "I also heard you picked up some new pitches."

"Yeah. I had a fastball, two-seam, and a change-up. My curve was okay. I added a three-seam, a slider, and a sinker."

"Wow, terrific." Chris imagined Jordan training himself with only videos for guidance. Overall, Chris was hearing solitude, even loneliness, which he would exploit to his advantage.

"Plus I worked on my legs. They were too skinny. I was all arms before, when I pitched."

"Legs matter."

"The power comes from the legs and hips."

"Exactly. Good for you." Chris decided to plant another seed. "Hey, listen, before we get started, I'm sorry about what happened at the beginning of practice, with me and Coach Hardwick. That was kind of, uh, embarrassing."

"I know, right?" Jordan's eyes flared. "On your birthday, even."

"Right." Chris had totally forgotten that it was his fake birthday, but Jordan hadn't, an excellent sign. "I was late because I was talking to Coach Natale, but I don't want you to think I disrespected the team."

"No, Coach, I wouldn't think that. I don't think that."

"I care about the team as much as I care about my class. Coaching and teaching, they're two sides of the same coin." Chris looked down as if he were feeling shame anew, then screwed the baseball into his glove. "Did you enjoy class today, by the way? It was fun, right?"

"Sure, yeah." Jordan smiled.

"Okay, let's have a catch. You need to warm up, and I need to blow off steam."

"Okay." Jordan smiled, warmly.

"Then we'll move into your new pitches. I heard so many good things that I wanted to see it for myself." Chris backed up, and Jordan walked in the other direction. Chris rotated his arm to loosen it up, ignoring the ache from his batting-cage workouts, then threw to Jordan. The boy threw it back effortlessly, the ball making a smooth arc that was a product of innate athletic talent and muscle memory.

Chris caught it and tossed it back harder to establish some credibility, and the ball made a solid *thump* when it reached Jordan's glove. Jordan threw it back harder, too, and as they went back and forth, Chris could discern an overall relaxation of the boy's body, his movements becoming more fluid, throwing and catching as if at play. Jordan even laughed when Chris's throws went wide or high, and each time he did, Chris made sure to say "attaboy" or "well done."

Chris realized that playing catch was a bonding thing, better than conversation, especially with a boy who was more comfortable with action than words. He thought of that old movie *Field of Dreams,* about the son who wanted to have a catch with his father. Oddly, Chris found himself wondering why so many fathers were missing, including his own. He only rarely thought about his father anymore, a man he'd never met. It was past.

Chris tossed the ball to Jordan for the last time. "You good to go?"

Jordan nodded.

Chris got the face mask, put it on, and positioned himself about the right distance, then dropped into a catcher's crouch. "Okay, don't kill me!"

Jordan stepped up onto the pitcher's mound, of white rubber. "Don't worry, if you got good insurance!"

"Ha!" Chris put down one finger, an old-school signal for a fastball.

Jordan wound up, lifting his front leg and rearing back, then pitched perfectly, releasing at the right moment and following through, back leg raised. The ball zoomed toward the strike zone.

"Nice!" Chris caught the ball, impressed. The ball speed had to be at least eighty or eighty-five miles an hour. He threw it back.

"I can do that better!" Jordan called out, catching the ball.

"That was terrific!" Chris crouched again, put down four fingers, and wiggled them, signaling for a change-up.

Jordan wound up, reared back, and pitched the ball again, following through. The ball zoomed toward the strike zone, where it changed speeds at the last instant, dipping down the way God intended.

"Very nice!" Chris tossed the ball back and then put Jordan through his three-seam fastball, a sinker, a slider, and only one curveball because there was no point adding to the wear and tear on his arm. When they were finished, Chris rose, took off the face mask, and walked forward. "That'll do!"

"Okay!" Jordan jogged off the mound, reaching him with a happy, relaxed smile.

"Okay, Coach?"

"More than okay! Awesome!" Chris clapped him on the shoulder.

"Thanks." Jordan grinned.

"Really, your hard work paid off. You're throwin' heat." Chris sensed a new closeness between them, so his mission had been accomplished—or at least part of it had. He wanted to get closer to Jordan, but he also wanted to separate Jordan from Raz. Chris couldn't get as close to Jordan as he needed to be if Jordan had a best friend, and the crack in the relationship between the boys was already there. All Chris had to do was stick a chisel in the fissure and hammer it into pieces.

Chris motioned beyond the curtain. "Now, run and go get Raz."

"Raz?" Jordan hesitated. "Why?"

"You'll see. Hurry, go. We don't have much time."

"Sure okay. Be right back." Jordan took off, tucking the glove under his arm. He ran through the opening in the curtain and arrived only a few minutes later with Raz jogging behind him, his dark eyes flashing with eagerness and his glove already on.

"Raz, hi. I need you." Chris motioned to him.

"Sure, Coach." Raz tucked a strand of hair into his man bun.

Chris turned away pointedly from Raz and faced Jordan. "Jordan, I was thinking it would be a great idea to videotape you. Between us, I have a buddy who knows a scout. I can send him the video through back channels, if you know what I mean."

"Really?" Jordan's eyes rounded with delight. "What school?"

"I can't say." Chris was improvising. Of course there was no scout, no school, and no back channel. "Just leave it to me."

"That'd be great! I appreciate that, Coach."

"Good, and keep it on the QT." Chris turned back to Raz. "Raz, you catch while I film Jordan."

Raz blinked. "Then are you gonna film me, too?"

"No, just Jordan."

Raz cleared his throat. "But Coach Brennan, I pitched last season. I'm the pitcher."

"So?" Chris faked confusion. "Raz, are you telling me you can't catch Jordan?"

"No, I can catch him, of course I can catch him, but *I'm* the pitcher. Not Jordan."

Jordan recoiled. "Raz, I pitched last season."

"On JV." Raz waved his glove at him dismissively.

"I'm on varsity now."

"Because you're a tryhard, Jordan."

"No I'm not!" Jordan shot back, pained.

"Whoa, boys," Chris broke in, acting surprised, as if he hadn't instigated the conflict. He didn't need it to go too far. He only needed to turn one boy against the other. He frowned at Raz. "Can't say I like your attitude, Raz. This is a team. We function as teammates. And don't give me attitude."

"Sorry, Coach Brennan." Raz swallowed hard. "But yo, can I pitch after Jordan? Like, can you film Jordan, then film me? And you could send the video of me to your friend and—"

"Not today. It's late." Chris motioned Raz backwards. "Get in position now. Catch."

Raz stalked away, simmering.

Chris took Jordan by the arm and walked him toward the pitcher's mound. "Jordan, I didn't know he'd react that way. I'm trying to do a nice thing for you. Where did that come from?"

"I know." Jordan walked with his head down. "He wants to stay as the starter. He just brought it up with Coach Hardwick."

"Coach Hardwick will make that decision, not Raz."

"That's what Coach says."

"I'm surprised Raz would take that to Coach Hardwick. I thought you and he were friends." Chris paused, letting the silence do its work. The implication was that Raz wasn't acting like a friend. "Well. You're not doing anything wrong. You understand that, right?"

Jordan nodded, walking.

"You worked hard and you improved. You put in the time, built up your legs, studied the videos. You earned this shot. A good friend would be happy for you."

Jordan pursed his lips as they reached the other side of the gym, where Chris motioned to the pitcher's mound.

"Okay. Put Raz out of your mind. Get up there. Give it everything you've got, you hear me?"

Jordan nodded, averting his eyes, then headed toward the

mound. He threw a practice pitch, then started pitching in earnest, but the fight with Raz had gotten to him. His pitching had none of its earlier brilliance, and one of his fastballs went wild. Chris hadn't been sure that would be the result, but even if it hadn't been, it worked for his purposes. Now Jordan would be mad at Raz for causing him to blow his big chance. Chris filmed the debacle and patted Jordan on the back afterwards, telling him they'd do it again, another time. Jordan and Raz didn't say another word to each other for the rest of practice and they left the gym separately.

It couldn't have gone worse for Jordan and Raz.

And it couldn't have gone better for Chris.

Chapter Ten

After practice, Chris sat in his Jeep, pretending he was talking on the phone. The dashboard clock read 6:15, and the sky was darkening. Lights in the parking lot cast halos on the empty spaces. He kept an eye on his rearview mirror, watching the players walk toward the student parking lot. It was too dark to see their faces, but he recognized Jordan's lurching gait and Evan at the center of the group. Raz lagged behind, alone.

Chris left the faculty lot and turned into the student lot, slowing and rolling down his window when he reached the boys, who were clustered around a brand-new BMW M 235i convertible coupe, gleaming darkly under the light. The engine thrummed like six cylinders of German precision engineering.

"What's up, guys?" Chris shouted to them, though he knew.

"Coach Brennan!" "Yo!" "Hi, Coach!"

"Coach, you like my ride?" Evan grinned, sitting next to Jordan in the passenger seat. Raz was trying to shove himself into the backseat, which was nonexistent.

"Love it! Is it really yours?"

Raz interjected, "He got it from Daddy!"

"Wow!" Chris acted surprised, though he had seen Evan's

posts about the car on Instagram. "Hey listen, I was about to email the team. I'm having a get-together at my house tomorrow night, to introduce myself to the team. Why don't you guys come over? Have some pizza?"

Evan answered, "Okay!"

"Sure, okay, yes!" the others called back.

"For your birthday?" Jordan asked from the passenger seat.

"Coach, it's your birthday?" "Whaaaa!" "Happy Birthday!"

Meanwhile, Chris palmed his smartphone, thumbed to Settings, then to WIRELESS. His screen filled with the wireless networks, including **Evan4EvaEva,** which had to be Evan's car. Chris pressed the screen to connect. Most people didn't think about cyber-security in their cars, but the software that operated most cars, especially new ones, had plenty of vulnerabilities, and any wireless signal could be hacked—even a car's braking system.

"Coach, what time you want us over?" Jordan called out.

"How about eight?" Chris kept his grin on.

"Woohoo, party!" Evan shouted, and Jordan and the other boys laughed, turning up the music again.

"Drive safe, gentlemen! See you tomorrow!" Chris waved good-bye, fed the car gas, and drove through the lot. **Evan4-EvaEva** evaporated, and he took a right turn onto Central Valley Road, passing development after development. In no time he reached the entrance of Valley Oaks, where balloons lay deflated on the fresh sod, tethered to the MODEL HOME AVAILABLE sign.

He turned into the driveway, and the development was dark, with only the newly built sections lit up. There was a segment of new homes still under construction, their wood frames wrapped in Tyvek HomeWrap, and he drove to Building 12, parked in the pocket lot behind, then entered the building and let himself into his apartment on the second floor. He walked through the living room to the kitchen, a small rectangle with white cabinets, no-name appliances, and beige counters. He opened the refrigerator, which was packed with groceries for his party, grabbed a bottle of beer, and uncapped it, returning to the living room.

Chris surveyed the apartment, a two-bedroom with a rectangular living room furnished with a rented sectional couch, a teak coffee table, and end tables with glazed pottery lamps—but otherwise, the place was designed to make a teenage boy feel like it was a cool place to hang. An entertainment center with a large-screen TV and an Xbox system occupied one side of the room. The bottom shelf held Halo, Call of Duty, and Grand Theft Auto, and Chris had bought the games used, so it looked like he played, which he didn't. He knew what real violence was like, and gaming had none of the thrill.

On the opposite wall was his locked gun case with a thick glass front, which held several hunting rifles, two long guns, an AR-15 assault weapon, and two handguns, a Beretta and a Colt .45 revolver. Chris had the appropriate licensing for each one, and they were unloaded and under lock and key. The case was intended to invite the admiring eyes of teenage boys, and he bet that most of his team had gone hunting, with brothers or dads. Chris was an excellent shot, though nobody but him would know that.

He wanted to make sure everything was set for tomorrow night, so he set down the beer bottle and crossed to the digital clock, turned it upside down, and checked the connection, which was fine. Though the clock looked normal, it was a hidden camera with audio. He double-checked the camera in the artificial plant in the corner and in the electrical outlet on the wall.

Chris scanned the ceiling fixture, which was a hidden camera, like the smoke detector. In the kitchen, there was a hidden camera on top of the refrigerator and behind the coffeepot. He couldn't be everywhere tomorrow night, but the cameras could pick up all sorts of stray information. He needed to know as much about these boys as soon as possible, for step one and beyond.

Chris picked up his backpack and went to his office, which was small with two windows, bare white walls, and a massive computer workstation with two large monitors aglow, stacked with files. He had a lot of information to absorb, so it was going to be a long night.

A teacher's work was never done.

Chapter Eleven

Heather Larkin wished she had time to make a decent dinner, but tonight it was scrambled eggs. She loved Ina Garten and wanted to be a home cook, but there was a difference between imagination and reality, beginning with her kitchen—too small to be a galley kitchen, she called it an "alley" kitchen—with refaced brown-wood cabinetry, Formica-knockoff countertops, and ancient appliances from a scratch-and-dent store. Their apartment was two bedrooms in a low-rise complex between a do-it-yourself car wash and a Friendly's. Their view was the lighted Friendly's sign, and at night, if she drew the curtains, the apartment took on a radioactive red glow.

Heather turned off the eggs, scooped them onto the plate, and brought them to Jordan, who was studying at the table. "Sorry, honey. I wanted to make chicken, but the witch kept me late again."

"No problem, Mom," Jordan said without looking up, and Heather knew he meant no disrespect. He was supposed to have read *The Great Gatsby,* but he hadn't gotten it done. His schedule was as busy as hers, with school, homework, baseball practice, and games. He grabbed the upside-down bottle of ketchup from the table, popped the top, and squeezed it onto his eggs.

"How about I make chicken tomorrow night?"

"Sure, fine." Jordan picked up a fork and plowed into the eggs, then turned the page of his book, tucking it underneath the rim to keep it open.

"Let me get your toast." Heather went back to the kitchen, plucked the pieces from the toaster, put them on a plate, and brought them back to the table with her new Kerrygold butter. She had overheard the members at the club talking about Kerrygold like it was magical, but Whole Foods was the only store that carried it. Heather didn't shop there because it was expensive, but she'd made an exception to get the Kerrygold. She didn't realize until the checkout line that she was the only customer in a uniform—with a *name tag,* for God's sake. Self-conscious, she'd zippered her coat up.

"Thanks," Jordan said through a mouthful, opening his lips to let the heat from the eggs escape his mouth.

"Want coffee, honey?"

"If it's made already."

"It is." Heather cheered up as she went back into the kitchen, feeling a wave of gratitude for her son. He kept his room clean, took their garbage to the incinerator chute, did his own laundry in the machines in the crummy basement. He'd set up her email, showed her how to G-chat, and fixed Netflix so they could use her sister's account. Jordan never gave her a moment's trouble. She didn't know how she'd gotten so lucky, in him.

"How was practice?" Heather asked from the kitchen, sliding the pot of coffee from Mr. Coffeemaker and pouring him a mug, then herself. They both drank it black, which made her feel good, for some reason. They were no-frills, a tough little half a family.

"Fine." Jordan turned the page, then tucked the paperback under his plate.

"How was school?" Heather brought the mugs back and placed Jordan's coffee in front of him.

"Fine."

"Good." Heather pulled out the chair and sat opposite him. She wasn't hungry because she had eaten at the club, scarfing down so many leftover pigs-in-blankets that she felt like one.

"Got a new assistant coach."

"Oh? What's his name?"

"Brennan. I have him for AP Government, too."

"Is he nice?"

"Yes. I got a game tomorrow. I might start." Jordan glanced up with a quick smile.

"You mean you might be the starting pitcher?" Heather asked, surprised. "Not Raz?"

"Yep." Jordan nodded, returning to his book.

"Good for you, honey!" Heather felt happy for him, though she knew he would have mixed feelings, competing with Raz. She could have asked him about it, but she'd learned not to bug him. She wished she could go to his games, to cheer for him, to be there for him, but she had to work, which was just another way she fell short.

Heather sipped her coffee, keeping him company, or maybe he was keeping her company. Either way, silence fell between them. Jordan didn't talk much, but on the plus side, he never complained. She used to worry that he *internalized* his emotions, like it said in the magazines, but he was a boy, after all, and so much like her father.

Heather laced her fingers around her mug, and her gaze traveled to the window. She hadn't closed the curtains yet, and it was already dark outside. The Friendly's sign glowed blood-red—TRY OUR HUNKA CHUNKA PB FUDGE—and the lights were on in the Sunoco gas station. Traffic was congested on Central Valley Road, and car exhaust made chalky plumes in the night air. Jordan had been spooked by exhaust when he was little.

Mommy, are those ghosts coming from inside the cars?

No, honey. They're farts.

Heather smiled to herself, wondering if she had been a better mother then or if it had just been easier. Her mother always said, *big kids, big problems,* and Heather worried constantly about college for Jordan, where he would get in, how they would pay for it. Heather lowered her gaze, watching him. She loved watching her son eat, even though she watched people eat all day, but that was different.

Suddenly a text alert sounded on Jordan's phone, which was on the table, and Heather glanced over to see a skinny banner pop onto the screen:

From Evan K: bro

Heather blinked, surprised. Evan K had to be Evan Kostis, Mindy's Kostis's son. It was funny, since she'd seen Mindy just today at the luncheon.

Do I know you? You look familiar.

Heather felt a tingle of excitement at the thought that Jordan could become friends with Evan. Jordan didn't have any close friends besides Raz, but Raz was such a wacko. A popular kid like Evan could bring Jordan out of his shell. And Evan was the captain of the baseball team and in the local newspaper, whether for National Honor Society or some other thing. Evan was Winner's Circle, like his parents. Maybe the Larkin's could get out of the Loser's Circle, or at least Jordan could.

The banner flashed a second time, but Jordan kept reading and Heather watched the phone screen go black. Her father always said, *it's not what you know, it's who you know,* and she saw proof of that every day, watching the club members exchanging business cards, taking each other's stock tips and vacation-spot recommendations, hiring each other's lawyers, doctors, babysitters, whatever.

"Jordan, you got a text." Heather rose, reaching for his plate to clear the table, but he grabbed the other side of the plate, stopping her.

"You don't have to clear, Ma. I will."

"If I clear, you can text Evan back."

"I'm not like you, Ma. I don't get excited every time I get a text. I'm not an *olds*." Jordan stood up with a crooked smile, picking up the dirty plates, silverware, and crumpled napkin, stacking them the way he learned to at the club, where he bused tables in summer.

"I just think if Evan texted you, you should text him back."

"I don't."

"Why not? Don't you want to see what he wants?"

"I know what he wants." Jordan walked into the kitchen with the plates and silverware, then opened the dishwasher only wide enough to slide the plates in the bottom rack and drop the fork and the knife in the silverware bin.

"What does he want?" Heather could see Jordan getting testy, but she had him in her clutches and wasn't about to let go.

"He wants to go to the movies Saturday night."

"That sounds like fun," Heather said, too quickly. "Are you going to go with him?"

"I can't."

"Why not?"

"I'm doing something with Raz."

"Did you already make plans with Raz?"

"I always do things with Raz on the weekend. You know that."

"But it's not like you have plans."

"I'm *not* gonna ditch Raz." Jordan frowned.

"You're not ditching him if you don't have plans."

"Mom, I have homework to do." Jordan went to the table, palmed his phone, and grabbed his paperback.

"I'm just saying. Maybe you can go out with Raz on Friday night and Evan on Saturday night." Heather followed him into the living room, knowing she had already said too much. She always said to herself, *with boys, say as few words as is humanly possible.* The hardest part about being a mother was shutting up.

"Don't want to." Jordan walked through the living room, where he'd left his backpack, and Heather dogged his heels.

"Or why not go with Evan, but see if Raz can come, too?"

"No." Jordan swung his backpack over his shoulder, its black straps flying.

"Why not? Why can't you take Raz?" Heather went after him, talking to his back.

"Evan doesn't like Raz." Jordan disappeared down the hallway.

"Wonder why," Heather said, but by then, she was talking to herself.

Chapter Twelve

M indy Kostis took a sip of her G & T, on her laptop at the kitchen island. She knew the alcohol wasn't helping her diet, but no matter what she did, she couldn't lose weight anyway. She worked out with a personal trainer and had just started yoga, but she knew it wouldn't work. Her goal weight was 125, and Mindy was pretty sure she would be 125 years old before she reached it, then she would be dead. Her epitaph would read, SHE REACHED HER GOAL WEIGHT, THEN DIED OF SHOCK.

Mindy scrolled down on the Photos page, scanning their vacation pictures. They'd spent spring break in the Cayman Islands, and she wanted to pick the best photos for a Facebook album, **The Kostis Family in the Kaymans!** The vacation was a true getaway for her, her husband Paul, and their son Evan. She'd scheduled parasailing, paddleboard, and scuba lessons, and Evan had left his phone behind, which was a miracle. Mindy had even gotten Paul's attention, a rarity of late.

She eyed a photo of Paul gazing out at the water. He was a hematology oncologist at Blakemore Medical Center, and his cases often weighed on his mind. But this was different. She knew him better than that. They'd met in the cafeteria line at Blakemore, where she was a nurse and he was a resident. They had been married twenty-two years, happy until he'd had an affair with a nurse fifteen years younger and thirty pounds skinnier. Mindy didn't know which hurt more.

Mindy glanced at the clock on her laptop, surprised to see that it was 10:16. It was strange that Paul still wasn't home. He'd said he'd be home by ten. She prayed he wasn't having another affair, but she couldn't bring herself to ask him. Last time he'd denied it, and she'd believed him. But that time, she had proof. This time, she had nothing but an underlying worry that drove her to read his texts while he was in the shower, go through his pockets before she dropped his clothes off, and try to get into his email, though it was password-protected.

"Mom?" Evan scuffed into the kitchen in his sweats and slides, holding his phone. "I need a check for our jackets tomorrow."

"Jackets?" Mindy couldn't focus, wondering where Paul was. She glanced at her phone. There were no calls or texts from him.

"Yes, for the team. You know. Tomorrow's the last day to bring in the money."

"Oh, right, of course." Mindy shifted mental gears. She herself had organized the bulk purchase. She went into the side drawer and found the checkbook they used for household expenses. She dug around for a pen, wrote the check, then tore it off and handed it to him. "Here we go."

"Thanks." Evan turned to leave, starting to text.

"Did you finish your homework?"

"Yes." Evan walked away, and Mindy felt a pang. On vacation, they'd had nice, long walks on the beach, and Evan had told her about girls he was dating, Ashley Somebody, a freshman at CVHS, and Brittany Somebody Else at Rocky Springs. Mindy was pretty sure he'd had sex already. In fact, he was probably having more sex than she was. But maybe not more than his father.

"Honey, hold on," Mindy called after Evan, on impulse.

"What?" Evan turned, texting. She couldn't see his face, and the lights were recessed spots on a dimmer, and the granite countertops, black with orange flecks, glistened darkly around him. The kitchen was state-of-the-art and top-of-the-line, but sometimes it struck her as a stage set, since they never ate at the same times.

"Did you get dinner?" Mindy hadn't gotten home in time to feed him.

"Sure."

"What'd you have?"

"A sandwich. The leftover tuna."

"How was school?"

"Okay," Evan answered without looking up, texting.

"How's Ashley and Brittany?"

"Fine."

"Is that who you're texting?"

"Mom . . ." Evan didn't have to finish the sentence. Mindy had already agreed it was rude to ask him who he was texting.

"Okay, so how's the car?"

"Awesome!" Evan looked up with a smile. "The sound system is incredible."

"Good!" Mindy felt cheered. It had been Paul's idea to get Evan the BMW for his birthday, and she'd gone along with it because she'd rather have him in something with state-of-the-art safety. The best use of their money was taking care of their only son, and their standard of living was the trade-off for Paul's long hours, after all.

"Can I go now, Mom?"

"Sure, honey. Don't spend too long on the phone. Love you."

"Love you too."

"Good night now." Mindy blew him a kiss, but Evan didn't look up, shuffling from the kitchen. She swiveled back to the laptop, where the vacation picture was still on. She found herself getting back on the Internet, going to Gmail, and logging in as Paul.

She took another stab at guessing his password.

Chapter Thirteen

Susan Sematov clutched her cell phone like a security blanket. It was 10:30 P.M., and Ryan still wasn't home, nor had he called or texted. She stood in the family room and looked out the picture window, which ghosted her reflection against the Dutch colonials, clipped hedges, and green recycling bins. Her makeup had worn off, emphasizing the bags under her eyes and the shine on her upturned nose. Her eyes were tired, and her mouth made a tight line. Her brown hair hung limply to her shoulders, and she still had on her navy suit from J. Crew Outlet and brown pumps from DFW. ValleyCo employees were required to shop its outlets, which had been Susan's idea.

The scene outside the picture window was dark and quiet. They lived on a cul-de-sac, and their neighbors were home, so if any headlights appeared, they would belong to Ryan. Susan had spent the entire day worrying about Ryan. She'd called the local hospitals, the police, and two of Ryan's high-school friends, but neither of them had heard from Ryan in months. Still she couldn't just stare out the window.

Susan went to the bottom of the stairwell, calling upstairs. "Raz, I'm going out to look for Ryan!"

There was no reply. Raz was probably G-chatting and texting while he did his homework. She worried that he was rewiring his brain circuitry, being on electronic devices all the time.

"Raz? Raz!"

No reply.

Susan considered going upstairs to talk to him, but she didn't want to have a fight. He hadn't apologized for hanging up on her today, and his angry outbursts were becoming common. She'd been walking on eggshells around him and she told her therapist that Raz was turning into a bully. She texted him, **I'm going out to see if I can find Ryan.**

Raz texted back, **wtf mom.**

Susan didn't like profanity. She texted, **See you in an hour. Let me know if he comes home in the meantime.**

Susan crossed to the console table and got her car keys out of the basket, her gaze falling momentarily on Neil's. Her first thought was, *Oh no, Neil left his keys,* then her mouth went dry. She wondered when that would stop happening, if ever. She took her keys, turning around and half expecting to see him. He wasn't there, but everything reminded her of him. The family room had a pseudocountry look made real by the greenish-blue end tables that he had painted. She loved old furniture, which Neil would refinish and paint whatever color she wanted, back when they were young and all about each other, before the kids. It made her feel like a bad mother to admit it, but she had felt more special then.

Susan's reverie was interrupted by a noise upstairs, and the next moment she turned to see Raz coming downstairs, his expression predictably cross.

"Mom, what are you doing?" Raz reached the bottom of the stairs with a thud, his tread heavy. He was a good-looking boy, even when he was angry, his thick, dark eyebrows knitted together, dramatic against his long dark hair. He had his father's big brown eyes, and his nose had a bump, also like Neil's, but it fit his face. His mouth was big, in more ways than one.

"I'm just going out to look for Ryan."

"Where? You don't even know where to look."

"I'm just going to look around at some of the places in town."

"Where?"

"Houlihan's. TGI Fridays. He could be at any of those."

"He doesn't go places like that." Raz strode toward her, and Susan edged backwards, unaccountably.

"Where does he go then? Enlighten me."

"I don't know, that sketchy bar on Stable Road."

"What's the name of it?" Susan didn't know.

"Oh God." Raz rolled his eyes. "This is so dumb, Mom. He's fine."

"What's the name of it? Where is it?"

"I told you. It's on Stable Road. You don't have to go out looking for him like he's a dog."

"I want to," Susan replied, modulating her tone. "I can't sleep anyway. I'll just take a nice drive and see if I can see him."

"He's not gonna be at Houlihan's."

"Okay, I know, you said that. Then I'll go to Stable Road and look for the bar there."

"You won't find it."

"If you remember the name, I'll find it. I'll look it up."

"It's easier just to show you." Raz stalked past, heading for the door.

"You don't have to do that. It's late." Susan didn't want him to go with her. She didn't want to fight with him in the car. She would have preferred a peaceful drive through town, alone. She was officially the worst mother in the world, avoiding her own son.

"Let's go already!" Raz stepped outside, letting the screen door bang behind him.

"Okay." Susan left the house, locking the front door and following him to her car, a white Lexus sedan. She backed out of the driveway and left the cul-de-sac, with Raz texting. They traveled north, heading into town. Silence fell between them, making her tense. She hadn't had a chance to talk to Raz since she'd been on the phone for the dinner hour. They'd had pizza delivered, again.

"How's school?" Susan asked, after a time.

"Fine," Raz answered, his head down, texting.

"How's the season going?"

"We're losing."

"Oh, sorry about that." Susan tread lightly. "How's your arm? Feeling good?"

"Fine."

"I looked at the schedule and your next home game is tomorrow, right? I was thinking that I could leave work early and come see you." Susan turned right. Large homes lined the street, their warm yellow lights on, the families within safe and sound. The Sematovs used to be one of those families.

"You mean, watch the game?"

"Yes, of course." Susan kept her tone light. Neil was the one who went to the games, not her.

"You don't have to."

"I want to." Susan couldn't see his expression. His hair fell in his face, lit from below by the bluish light of his phone, where the text bubbles were floating by.

"You have work."

"I can get out early. I'd love to come."

"No you wouldn't. If you did, you would have come before."

Susan's mouth went dry. "I'd like to go," she said anyway. "I know Dad used to go, but I'd like to go. I'd like to see you pitch."

"I might not be pitching."

"Why not?" Susan took a right turn, heading into Central Valley proper.

"I don't know. I just might not pitch. It's not, like, a given."

"Who would pitch, if not you?"

"Jordan."

"But he's JV, isn't he?" Susan knew Jordan Larkin, a great kid. Jordan and Raz were good friends. Jordan had even cried at Neil's funeral, and Susan had been touched. Raz had cried, too, but not Ryan. Ryan kept it all inside. Now both of her sons were losing their way.

"Jordan made varsity. He's gotten better."

"Oh." Susan knew it was bad news for Raz. "Well, even if you don't pitch in the beginning, you'll get in the game. You'll play even if you don't start, right?"

"Does it matter?"

"What do you mean?"

Raz didn't reply.

"It doesn't matter to me if you don't start," Susan answered anyway. "Does it matter to you?"

"Not at all. I'm stoked. I can't wait to sit on the bench with my dick in my hands."

"Raz, really?" Susan didn't like that language. "If starting pitcher is what you want, maybe you can get the position back."

"How would I do that?"

Susan was about to answer, then stopped. Neil was the answer. Neil had taught Raz to pitch. Neil would've taken Raz in the backyard, and the two of them would have drilled forever. "Okay, well, I'm sure there's a way. Maybe there's someone I can hire, like a tutor. A coach. A pitching coach."

"I don't want to work with a pitching coach. You're not gonna hire me a pitching coach. It's stupid."

"No it's not. There's nothing wrong with helping yourself. If you were nearsighted, you'd wear glasses."

"I knew you would say that. You always say that."

Susan spared him the lecture on goal-directed behavior. She wasn't certain of it herself lately. Her goals had scaled down to:

Last the entire day without blubbering like a baby. Save the kids. Keep the wheels on your life.

"Mom. I don't want a pitching coach. How many times do I have to say it? No pitching coach!"

"Okay, fine." Susan felt her temper flare, but reminded herself again to stay patient. Raz wanted only one pitching coach, his dad.

"What if I don't play? What if I don't even get in?"

"You'll get in. They need more than one pitcher a game." Susan was pretty sure that was true. "In any event, I'm going to the game."

"Whatever," Raz answered, leaving Susan to her thoughts. She had to face the fact that the kids had been closer to Neil than her. She didn't know if she could ever bridge that gap. Worse, she couldn't shake the sensation that they thought the wrong parent had died. She even agreed.

Suddenly her phone rang. They both looked over, and the screen read **Ryan calling.**

"Thank God." Susan grabbed the phone and swiped to answer. "Ryan, are you okay? Where are you?"

"I'm at the police station in Rocky Springs. Can you come?"

Chapter Fourteen

The morning sun shone through the classroom windows, and Chris stood as the students went to their seats, dug in their backpacks, and opened spiral notebooks. Evan slipped his phone away, but Jordan was already writing in his notebook. Raz was late, and Chris hoped he showed up. He had to make the final choice between Jordan and Raz today. There was too much to do before Tuesday. He wanted to pull the trigger after class, and he had one more trick up his sleeve.

"Good morning, everyone!" Chris began. "We're going to start with an exercise about the Bill of Rights."

Suddenly Raz hurried into the classroom and sat down heavily in his seat, dropping his backpack loudly on the floor. "Sorry I'm late," he mumbled, but Chris kept his attention on the class.

"Okay, gang, your homework was to write an essay about which Amendment is the most important. But our forefathers didn't write the Bill of Rights by submitting a paper. They hammered it out together. So that's what we're going to do today, have a real debate." Chris returned his attention to Raz, slumped in his chair. "Raz, which Amendment did you decide was the most important?"

"Um, the Second?"

"Okay, come on up here." Chris gestured to the front of the classroom, and Raz rose uncertainly. Chris looked back at the class. "Now, let's get an adversary." Chris turned to Jordan, apparently spontaneously. "Jordan, which Amendment did you think was the most important?"

"The Fourth."

"Then come on up."

"Okay." Jordan rose and lumbered to the front of the room, barely glancing over at Raz.

Chris stood between the two boys like a boxing referee. "Raz and Jordan, you will each state your case. If anybody has a question, they can ask and you have to answer, then keep going. The class will decide who wins, and that will be the end of the first round. We'll keep going until we see which Amendment is left."

Raz raked back his hair, and up close, he looked unusually pale, even drawn. "Well, uh, I said the Second Amendment was the most important because everybody should have a right to protect themselves, like, against whatever. Like bad guys. You're not safe if you can't protect yourself and that should be your right as a citizen—"

"Raz, what's the Second Amendment?" one of the boys shouted. "It's called a *definition*. We learned it in middle school."

The class laughed, and Raz looked shaken. "The Second Amendment is the right to bear arms. It says that a citizen has a right to bear arms and the government can't take that away from them."

Sarah raised her hand. "My dad says the militia is allowed to have the arms, not the people. It says it right there, 'a militia,' doesn't it?"

"My mom says that's from lobbying—" shouted another boy, but Chris shot him a warning glance, not wanting a gun-control debate. He knew more about guns than these kids ever would, and that wasn't the point of the exercise.

"Raz," Chris interjected, "what do you think is the reason the Second Amendment is the most important?"

"Well, um, see," Raz fumbled. "Because you gotta *live*. You can talk about the pursuit of happiness, or free speech, but none of it makes any difference if you're *dead*. Once you're dead, you're *dead* and *gone* . . . and it doesn't matter what your rights were or whatever happiness you were pursuing because, let's face it, you're . . . like, dead."

The class burst into laughter.

Sarah's hand rose. "Raz, is your argument that if you're dead, you don't have any rights? Is that really the best argument you can come up with? That dead people don't have rights?"

"It's not that." Raz licked his dry lips, his dark eyes filming. "You have to be able to protect yourself! You have to be able to live! Do you want to die? Do you really want to *die*?"

"What?" Sarah and the class laughed, but Chris waved them into silence, realizing that Raz was probably talking about his late father.

"Okay Raz, time's up. Thank you." Chris gestured to Jordan. "Jordan, state your case."

Jordan faced the class, surprisingly poised. "I wrote that the Fourth Amendment was the most important. It says that citizens should be safe in their houses, and that the government is not allowed to have unreasonable searches and seizures."

"Good *definition*!" the boy in the back said pointedly, and the class chuckled.

Jordan paused. "Most of the Amendments are about making sure you're able to do something, like the right to speak freely or to practice whatever religion you want, but the Fourth Amendment says you don't have to do *anything*."

"It's the chillest Amendment!" another boy called out, and everybody laughed.

Jordan smiled shyly. "In a way, it is. It says you have the right to be free and happy in your own home. The right *to be left alone.*

Justice Brandeis of the Supreme Court said that, and that's what makes the Fourth Amendment the most important. Thank you."

The class erupted into applause, which Chris silenced by motioning to them. "Okay, class, now that you have heard both arguments, it's time to vote. Clap if you think Raz is the winner of the debate."

Only two students clapped, and the others giggled. Raz sagged, embarrassed.

Chris gestured to Jordan. "Now clap if you think Jordan won the debate."

Everybody else clapped, and Jordan stood taller. Raz looked away.

Chris made his decision. He was going with Jordan. The boy had risen to the occasion, overcoming his natural reserve to defend himself and his position, performing under pressure and thinking on his feet. The classroom exercise paled in comparison to what lay ahead, and Chris couldn't rely on a boy who might fall apart when things got tough.

And lethal.

Chapter Fifteen

Chris chewed his sandwich, eating at his desk. He'd brought lunch from home to avoid the other teachers. He didn't need an instant replay of yesterday and he could choke credibly only so many times. He had his laptop open as if he were working in his classroom, but he sat scanning his files on Jordan, confirming the correctness of his choice.

"Chris, you're working through lunch?" someone called out, and Chris looked up to see Abe, Rick, and Courtney standing in the threshold, holding trays of cafeteria food. Abe looked stylish, Rick looked organic, and Courtney looked tempting, but they were the last thing Chris needed right now.

"Guys, I have to look over a lesson plan." Chris hit a key so that the local newspaper, the *Central Valley Patch,* would come on the screen.

"Listen to you—'lesson plan'! I like when you talk dirty." Abe pulled up three desks around Chris's desk. "I came to talk about Cody with my new best friend!"

"Ha!" Chris hid his dismay. He had gone online last night and learned as much as possible about Cody, Northwest College, and the Bighorn basin, but he didn't know how long he could keep this up.

Rick hesitated. "We don't mean to bother you, Chris."

Courtney shot Abe a sideways glance. "Abe, I told you this was a bad idea. Chris has to work."

"Oh, sit down, everybody." Abe set down the tray with sodas, a slice of pizza on a styrofoam plate, and a garden salad. "Chris, don't be such a goody-goody. We're the mean girls of Central Valley. On Wednesdays we wear pink."

"We're not the mean girls, they are." Courtney sat down. "They hate us because they ain't us."

Rick smiled in his goofy way, as he took a seat. "We won't stay long, Chris. We didn't want you to feel left out."

Courtney's phone started ringing in her purse, and she slipped it out and looked at the screen. "I swear, Doug has radar for when I get a minute to breathe."

Abe smiled. "Courtney, he knows your schedule. B Lunch is 11:15 to 11:45."

"Excuse me." Courtney rose with the phone, answering the call on the way out of the classroom.

" 'Hi Courtney, this is Lug,' " Abe said, mimicking a caveman voice. "He's one *big* beefsteak patty, but she loves the guy, what can I say? And she's loyal. She's stuck with me through thick and thin. I was so sick a few years ago, and she was there, every step of the way."

"What was the matter, Abe?" Chris asked, to keep him talking about anything but Wyoming.

Rick fell suddenly silent, eating his pizza, which turned the beard hairs around his mouth reddish.

"I had anorexia. I was manorexic!" Abe fluttered his eyes behind his hip glasses. "My whole life, off and on, I just couldn't beat it. For me it was about depression, anyway, blah blah, that's my tale of woe." He leaned forward. "So Chris, we're sons of Wyoming! Tell me you had your first kiss at the reservoir, too."

"I swear, I didn't." Chris had determined that the body of water in Abe's photo was a reservoir. "I had my first kiss at fourteen in the hayloft at my granny's farm."

"Well, quite the junior achiever! Where was the farm?"

"Little town on the west side of the state, Evanston."

"You ever get up to Jackson? Can you believe the changes in Jackson?"

"Tell me about it," Chris said offhand. *No, really, tell me about it.*

"The place is so chichi now! The celebrities, ski-in developments, and the shopping. It even has its own *Hermès*! Courtney taught me how to pronounce it so I sound cool."

"And you do," Chris said, tense. Sooner or later, Abe would figure him out, and he couldn't deny it was a problem.

"I took Jamie there on vacation and he said the only way he'd go back to Wyoming is if we went to Jackson. But I told him, Jackson is *not* Wyoming."

"Damn straight."

Rick finished his pizza. "Sachi and I were just talking about that trip last night. She loved it."

"Right?" Abe flashed Rick a happy smile, then returned his attention to Chris. "Where did your dad go to high school, Chris?"

Chris had an answer, as of last night. "Sheridan."

"Whoa, small."

"Right. I didn't get that far out."

"Nobody does, except cattle." Chris had hoped as much, which was why he'd picked it online. He was trying to contain the damage.

"So what's it like?"

"Mountains, mountains, and more mountains."

"I heard your parents died in a crash. Sorry about that."

Rick interjected, "Yes, condolences."

"Thank you." Chris wondered if Abe could check his fake backstory with anyone he knew back in Wyoming.

"And you have no brothers or sisters?" Abe asked, resuming the conversation.

"None," Chris answered, with growing tension. So Abe had heard that, too.

"Unusual for out there. My parents adopted six kids. Three of us are black, and three are white. My dad said we were his retirement package and he was hedging his bets." Abe chuckled. "My dad knows everybody. I emailed him about you but he hasn't emailed back. He only checks his email when he remembers to."

"Uh, I forget." Chris didn't like the way this was going. He picked up his water bottle, and his gaze fell on his laptop, his attention drawn by a familiar name under the headline, LOCAL YOUTH ARRESTED:

Central Valley resident Ryan Sematov, 19, was arrested last night by Rocky Springs Police Department for attempted burglary of the Samsonite factory store at the ValleyCo Outlet 11. Police were called to the scene when the burglar alarm sounded and nearby residents dialed 911. Sematov was charged with attempted burglary, vandalism, and malicious mischief, and was released on his own recognizance pending a preliminary hearing.

"Oh no, look at this!" Chris said, seizing the excuse to change the subject. He realized that the arrest must've been one of the reasons that Raz was late this morning. "This is terrible news. I have his brother Raz in my class."

"What?" Abe came around the desk and read the screen. "Oh no, that *is* terrible. I had Ryan in my class last year. He was a terrific student. I have Raz now, he's nutty. I feel bad for the family. The father died over the summer."

Rick joined them, looking at the laptop. "That's too bad. I liked Ryan, and Raz is okay. He's a free spirit, that's all."

Courtney entered the classroom with her cell phone. "What's the matter?"

Abe answered, "Ryan Sematov was arrested for burglary."

"Are you serious?" Courtney grimaced. "I never had him, but that's so sad about that family. The father died over the summer."

"I know." Abe shook his head. "Ryan tried to break into a store at a ValleyCo mall. I seem to remember his mother is a higher-up at ValleyCo, in the corporate office."

Courtney came around the desk. "That can't be good for her. What a shame."

"That's tough." Chris sounded troubled, but not about Ryan or Raz.

About Abe.

Chapter Sixteen

Mindy couldn't get into her husband's Gmail, so she was upstairs in his home office going through their credit-card receipts, since they had a joint Amex and Visa. Last night, he'd come home at eleven o'clock, and when she'd asked why he was late, he'd said only that he'd gotten held up at the hospital. But he wouldn't meet her eye and bit his cuticle, which he never did. As a surgeon, he was meticulous about his hands and nails, even getting manicures to keep them neat.

A wife always knows, her mother had told her.

But that was completely untrue. Mindy had scrutinized Paul for clues about whether he was having another affair, but she had no idea what to look for. The last time, she'd had no idea that he was having an affair. She'd thought they were both happy, communicating well, and having sex as often as most married couples. She'd been fooled by an excellent liar, her own husband.

Mindy's cell phone rang, and she checked the screen. She only had until one thirty, when she had to leave for the game, bringing party trays, bottled water, and soda. Alcohol wasn't allowed at the games, but nobody would know her reusable water bottle held a G & T.

Her phone screen showed that one of the Boosters was calling, so Mindy answered the call. "Ellen, what's up? I'm in the middle of something."

"Did you hear about Ryan Sematov?"

"Is that Raz's older brother?" Mindy asked, regretting having taken the call. She had more important things to do than gossip. Like play Nancy Drew.

"Yes, he was arrested for burglary last night."

"Oh no." Mindy felt a pang. She had adored Neil Sematov, who was one of the saner parents. She tuned Ellen out and eyed the credit-card receipt.

". . . and he broke into a ValleyCo outlet. You know the mother works for ValleyCo . . ."

Mindy scanned the list of their credit-card charges, noting the name of the restaurants. They were all places she or Evan had been, so far. The only thing that had surprised her was that Evan was eating out so much at lunchtime. She didn't know why he couldn't buy in the cafeteria like everybody else. Or God forbid, bring a lunch from home. Maybe he really was becoming entitled, getting *affluenza*.

". . . I mean, I feel bad for her, truly I do, but let's be real . . ."

Mindy kept scanning, then froze. There was a charge from Central Valley Jewelers for $327.82, processed two weeks ago. She felt her gut twist. Paul had bought that nurse a bracelet from the same store, the last time around. And he had charged it on their joint credit card, which made no sense unless he were trying to get caught, a theory they'd discussed in approximately 172 therapy sessions.

". . . if your kids are having psychological problems, you can't pretend it's not happening, especially not these days . . ."

Mindy felt her heart start to pound. She wanted to know if he was having an affair—and she didn't, both at once. Was it really true? The charge was undeniable, its machine-printed numbers staring her right in the face. Did Paul buy this for another woman? Would he really do this to her again? At the same store? Did he really want her to divorce him? Or did he just want to hurt her?

". . . you can't stick your head in the sand these days, as a mother . . ."

Mindy flashed-forward to Ellen on the phone, calling everybody to gossip about her. *Did you hear? Paul is running around on Mindy again. You can't stick your head in the sand, as a wife today.*

". . . but you know what they say, everything happens for a reason. So maybe now she'll . . ."

Mindy felt stricken. The dark obverse of everything-happens-for-a-reason was that the reason should have been identified, and prevented. If Paul cheated on her again, there had to be a reason, and it was her fault. Her weight, for starters. Mindy had *let herself go.* She could almost hear her mother saying it, right now. *You blew up, dumplin.' What did you expect?*

Mindy had thought she was over it, but she wasn't, not if it was happening again. She had forgiven Paul, or at least she hadn't asked for a divorce, because she loved their family. And she loved Evan, who loved them both. But she couldn't go through it again. Everybody deserves a second chance, but nobody deserves a third.

Mindy felt her thoughts racing, rolling into a giant bolus of anxiety, anguish, and confusion. And still, part of her reflexively wondered if she was jumping to conclusions. Maybe Evan had bought a gift for one of the girls he was dating. He was supposed to ask first, but he had done that before. Or maybe the charge was fraud or a clerical error. That had happened before, too; once somebody charged $150 worth of athletic equipment at a Footlocker in Minneapolis, using their credit card.

"Mindy? Did I lose you? Mindy!"

"Oh sorry, I think it cut out." Mindy came out of her reverie. "The reception is bad upstairs."

"You have cold spots in your house? I have a wireless guy. I'll text you his contact info."

"Great," Mindy said, wondering about the cold spots in her house. Lately her entire house was a cold spot. She set the statement aside. "I should really go, okay?"

Chapter Seventeen

Heather heard her text alert coming from her uniform pocket, but it was probably nothing. The only texts she got were from creditors, written in a deceptively friendly way; *Oops, life happens! Reminder, your bill is ready.* Blue Cross texted her, too; *You have a private message waiting. Tap link to view.* It sounded tantalizing, but it was the same message. *You're late with your payment.*

Heather hustled to the kitchen. She was working yet another luncheon, this time for the Women's Service League of Central Valley. She entered the warm kitchen and grabbed three plated entrees, avoiding the new chef, a drama queen. She pushed through the swinging door for outgoing, expertly balancing the plates on her forearms. She crossed the hallway, entered the Lafayette Room, and beelined for the table. Coincidentally, it was the one in the corner, where she had served Mindy Kostis yesterday.

You look familiar to me.

Heather dismissed the thought, sidestepping fancy handbags and managing not to elbow anyone in the head, though she might have wanted to, since the Women's Service League had decided at the last minute to hold its speeches and raffles before the meal, backing up the entire schedule, so that Heather had no hope of getting out on time again. She reached the table with a professional smile, served as unobtrusively as possible, and headed back to the kitchen, hearing another text alert sound, which gave her pause. It could be Jordan. Something could've gone wrong at school.

Heather stopped by the wall near the restrooms, sliding her phone from her uniform pocket. The banner on the screen showed the text was from Jordan, and it had the first three words, **whoa mom u,** which she didn't understand, so she swiped to read the whole text.

whoa mom u wont believe it im starting

Heather read the text in astonishment, because something good had happened. Jordan had taken the top spot. Her heart filled with happiness and another emotion—hope. She felt unaccountably as if her son had lifted up their entire family in just one stroke. She texted back: **you're STARTING!?**

yes ☺

Heather felt wetness come to her eyes. It was the emoticon that got to her, a generic representation of a smile that was too damn long in coming. On impulse, she scrolled to her phone function and called him.

"Ma, hold on," Jordan answered, his voice low. Heather assumed he was going where he could talk to his mother without fear of embarrassment.

"Jordan, is this really true? You're starting pitcher for *varsity?*"

"Mom, do you believe it?" Jordan asked, his voice filled with happiness.

"No, no I don't!" Heather felt tears come to her eyes, but she blinked them away. "I'm so proud of you! You deserve it! You worked so hard, you practiced so hard!"

"Mom, it's unreal! Coach Hardwick just told me, like, in front of everyone. I felt bad for Raz, though."

"He'll be okay. What did Coach Hardwick say?" Heather wanted to know every detail.

"He said, 'starting roster for today' and read off the names, and when he got to the pitcher, he said my name. Awesome, right, Mom?"

"*So* awesome! So what did you say when he said that?"

"There was nothing to say. I got my glove." Jordan laughed, a carefree giggle that Heather remembered from when he was younger.

"Where are you now?"

"In the locker room, in a *stall*." Jordan laughed again, and Heather realized that he had no one to share his happiness with except her. Raz was his closest friend, so there was nobody else left. She wished she could be there to watch him pitch, and wetness returned to her eyes. She cleared her throat.

"Well, you have a wonderful game, sweetheart. Knock them dead!"

"I will. Love you, Mom."

"Love you, too, honey," Heather said, hoarsely. She had no idea why she was getting so choked up. The emoticon. That giggle. Her son, who had worked so hard for so long, had finally caught a break.

"Bye." Jordan ended the call.

Heather wiped her eyes with her fingers, then looked up to see her manager, Emily, striding toward her.

"Heather, what are you doing on the phone?" Emily asked, glaring.

"Sorry." Heather looked Emily directly in the eye. She wasn't about to deny it. She would take her lumps.

"Was it a personal call?"

"Yes. My son."

"Was it an emergency?"

"No."

"Doesn't your son know not to call you at work?"

"He didn't call me, I called him."

"For what reason?"

"None of your business." Heather felt anger flicker in her chest, underneath her name tag.

"Did you have an emergency?"

"No."

Emily's blue eyes hardened like ice. "You know you're not allowed to make personal calls at work. We're in the middle of a luncheon. We're trying to get everybody served."

"My station is completely served."

"How do you know they don't need anything? They could need something while you're outside in the hall, making personal calls."

"The call lasted three minutes, maximum. I was just in the dining room and I can go back in right now."

"Not the point. You broke the rules and you should know better. This is a warning, and if you do it again, you're fired. And you were on more than three minutes. You were on four."

"Are you *serious*?" Heather felt the anger burn brighter. "You timed my phone call?"

Emily didn't bat an eye. "Yes, that's my job."

"No, your job is to make sure the luncheon is going well and the club members are happy, which they are, at my station. You're just trying to catch me in a mistake because you have it out for me, from day one."

"And you made a mistake. Because you're not committed to this job."

"Of course I am! I've been doing it for seventeen years. If you look up 'committed' in the dictionary, you'll see a picture of me in this stupid dirndl."

Emily crossed her arms. "I don't like your attitude."

"I do. I *love* my attitude, and you know what, you don't need to fire me. I quit."

Emily's eyes flared. "You better think about what you're saying."

"I have," Heather said, though she hadn't. She was tired, finally of waiting. For nothing. For everything. For her life to start. She found herself untying the back of the white apron that went over the dirndl, which wasn't easy considering that she still had her cell phone in her hand.

"What are you doing?"

"What do you think I'm doing? I'm stripping in the freaking hallway." Heather balled up the apron and threw it on the rug. "And if I could, I'd take off this effing dress, too."

"Are you serious right now?" Emily asked, surprised.

"Abso-effing-lutely." Heather didn't know why she was using profanity. She never talked that way. Meanwhile, one of the new waitresses walked by, averting her eyes, and Heather thought that if this were a movie, people would clap, like at the end of *Bridget Jones*. But in the real world, people looked away. They didn't want to see somebody jump off a bridge. "Take this job and shove it" was a song, not a career move.

"Fine then." Emily snorted. "We'll send your last check to your house."

"Thank you." Heather turned away, heading for the locker room, her eyes suddenly dry and her thoughts newly clear. She would get her purse and change into her clothes. She was going to a baseball game to watch her son pitch for varsity.

One of the Larkins was in the Winner's Circle.

Chapter Eighteen

Susan slipped on her sunglasses and hurried through the parking lot to the baseball game. Thank God it was a sunny afternoon because she didn't want anyone to see her puffy eyes. Everyone would know about Ryan's arrest by now. She'd considered not going to the game, but she couldn't sacrifice Raz for Ryan.

Susan prayed Raz was pitching today. He derived so much self-worth from being the pitcher, believing that his athletic skill was the only thing he had over his more academic older brother. Susan saw so much in Raz that he didn't see in himself—his open heart, his carefree way of looking at life, his absolute joy in meeting people—all of it so much like Neil. But because those things came naturally to Raz, he didn't value them, and nothing she could do would convince him.

You're as smart as your brother, honey, Susan remembered saying to him when he brought home another borderline report card. *You can get better grades, if you try.*

Raz had laughed it off. *I'm fine being a dumb jock, Mom. And I'm so much hotter than Ryan.*

Susan squared her shoulders, putting the memories from her

mind. She felt exhausted after the endless night at the police station. She'd called a lawyer who had negotiated a plea agreement. Ryan would be charged with a misdemeanor and sentenced to probation, a fine, and restitution. The lawyer had said *this will go away,* but Susan felt absolute mortification. She'd called her boss to apologize, Community Relations to make a general statement, and her assistant to let her know that she was taking a personal day. By noon, Ryan's mug shot was on TV news. Her reliable son, who never gave her a moment's worry until his face was above the red banner, **ValleyCo Vandal.**

She passed the high school, a massive redbrick complex with two new wings, their construction supported by developers like ValleyCo. Susan herself had arranged for the top ValleyCo brass to be at the ground-breaking, posing with shiny shovels. She used to feel proud she worked for ValleyCo, but now she felt guilty. She had to scale back. Something had to give.

She approached the crowd of parents clustered to the left of the dugout, watching the game. It seemed like a big crowd, maybe fifty people standing, sitting in blue-cloth sling chairs, or eating the food that covered a long picnic table against the dugout wall. Susan reached the fringe of the crowd, still not able to see the pitcher's mound. She didn't know any of the other parents, so she didn't try to talk to them.

Joyful cheering came from the students hanging onto the cyclone fence, and Susan walked around the back of the crowd to home plate, behind the super-tall cyclone fence, angled down at the top. A player from the other team was at bat, and though Susan didn't remember who they were, they had on bright red uniforms, so she could tell the difference. That meant the Musketeers were pitching.

Susan kept walking and got a view of the pitcher's mound. Raz wasn't pitching, and Jordan was, in his place. She felt terrible for Raz. The change to the lineup would've been another blow, when he was least able to deal with it. This morning before he'd left for school, he'd looked as exhausted, raw, and ragged as she had been. He'd skipped breakfast and left with his long hair dripping wet from the shower, making a soggy collar of his Musketeers baseball T-shirt, which he practically lived in.

Susan looked over at the dugout, and at this angle, she could see Raz silently watching the game from a folding chair behind the Musketeers cheering at the fence.

"Susan?" said a voice beside her.

Susan turned, but didn't recognize the woman approaching her, a pretty, heavyset mom with a halo of blonde curls, bright blue eyes, and a sweet, if concerned, smile. She had on a Musketeers sweatshirt and jeans, which was obviously the right thing to wear at the game, because the other parents had on team logowear. Susan was wearing the black cable sweater and khakis she wore on casual Friday at work.

"I'm Mindy Kostis. Good to see you again."

"Oh, Mindy, right. Hi." Susan raced to remember what Neil had told her about Mindy. Nice lady, doctor husband, popular son. Evan was the catcher. Raz talked about Evan, too, though Susan got the impression that Evan was too popular a kid to be friendly with Raz.

"I just wanted to tell you, I'm so sorry." Mindy's face flushed with genuine emotion.

"Thanks." Susan swallowed hard, unsure what she meant. Ryan? Neil? *Pick a calamity, any calamity.*

"Neil was such a terrific guy. He used to help me so much at the games. We're all missing him today. I know you must be, most of all."

"Thank you." Susan's throat thickened. Meanwhile, if Mindy knew about Ryan, it didn't show. Maybe this was the best way to handle the situation, just pretend it hadn't happened.

"The Boosters would like to make an impromptu memorial to Neil at the end of the game, if that's okay with you. I didn't know you were coming today, so I took the liberty of asking Raz and he was fine with it."

"Of course, thanks." Susan felt gratitude, and dread, both at once.

"Would you like to say a few words at the ceremony?"

"No, no, thank you." Susan couldn't, not today, not ever. She had been a mess at the funeral. She realized she was still a mess.

"Then I will, don't worry about it. I know what to say." Mindy patted her arm, frowning in a sympathetic way. "How have you been?"

Susan didn't know how to answer. Mindy seemed to want an honest answer, but it wasn't the time or the place to open up. Susan didn't know if she needed to make a friend among the moms, or even how to start. It always seemed like a clique she wasn't a part of, though Neil had been, ironically. Besides, she doubted they had anything in common. Mindy was the Queen Bee of the Boosters with a perfect life, as compared with the Sematov Shit Show.

"Fine, thanks," Susan answered, turning away.

Chapter Nineteen

Chris thought the scene at the baseball game looked typically suburban. The sun shone high in a cloudless sky, and cheering spectators clustered around a perfect baseball diamond and a lush green outfield. He understood why baseball was America's pastime, but it just wasn't his. Sports bored him. He preferred higher stakes.

Chris coached third base, and Jordan had been striking out one batter after the next, until the third inning, when one of the Upper Grove batters connected and the ball hopped into the infield. Jordan had fielded it on the fly and thrown it to first base in the nick of time, and the crowd went crazy. The Musketeers players cheered for him almost constantly, yelling at the top of their lungs, shouting "Jordan, Jordan!" "Number 12" "Get it!" and "Bring it!"

"Strike three!" barked the umpire, ending the inning.

Jordan and the rest of the team jogged toward the dugout, and Chris jogged in after them. Raz, who'd subbed in the outfield, was up next in the batting order, and the team cheered for him, shaking the cyclone fence in front of the dugout. One of the Musketeers played Raz's walk-up music on the boombox, and the team went crazy, rapping at the top of their lungs.

The Upper Grove pitcher threw a fastball, and Raz swung quickly, missing.

"Strike one!" barked the umpire.

Jordan and the Musketeers cheered louder. "You can do it!" "Shake it off!" "You got this, you got this!"

The Upper Grove pitcher threw another fastball, and Raz swung again, missing.

"Strike two!" yelled the umpire.

The Musketeers hollered, "Cool down, Raz!" "Wait for your pitch!"

Chris noticed two moms cheering for Raz behind the fence and he recognized them from his research—Evan's mother Mindy and Raz's mother Susan. He'd been hoping to meet Jordan's mom Heather, but she wasn't here, and he assumed she was at work.

The next pitch flew across the plate, and Raz swung wildly, missing yet again.

"Strike three, you're out!" the umpire yelled.

Suddenly Raz whipped the bat into the air and threw it into the fence behind home plate. Raz's mother and Evan's mother jumped back, shocked.

"Son, you're out of here!" the umpire shouted, then Coach Hardwick scrambled out of the dugout, scurrying to home plate.

Chris patted Jordan on the back. "Don't let this get to you. You're doing awesome. Keep it up."

Jordan nodded, tense, and the team watched as Coach Hardwick marched Raz to the dugout, where everybody parted for him, stunned and nervous. Raz stalked inside and kicked the folding chair.

"Raz, enough!" Coach Hardwick bellowed, then pointed to Evan, who was next in the lineup.

The Musketeers burst into cheers for Evan, and as the game went on, they dominated inning after inning, scoring three more runs, and Jordan hit as well as he pitched. Chris spotted Jordan's mother Heather arriving late, an attractive woman with dark blonde hair in a white sweater and jeans, and he kept his eye on her throughout the game, waiting to make his move. He needed to get as close as possible to Jordan, and winning over his mom would help the cause.

The final score was five to nothing, the Musketeers' first win, and the team rushed Jordan on the mound, piling onto him and each other. They shook hands with Upper Grove, then streamed to the grassy area behind the visiting dugout, where snack food and drinks had been put out by the Boosters. Coach Hardwick said a few words, parents started talking to him and each other, and Chris made his way to Jordan's mom, standing at the periphery. He approached her with a grin, sticking out his hand.

"Hi, I'm Chris Brennan, the new assistant coach. Are you Jordan's mom? I saw you cheering for him."

"Oh, nice to meet you. Yes, I'm Heather Larkin." She extended her hand, and Chris clasped it warmly.

"Great to meet you. I also have him in AP Government and I'm so impressed with him. He's able, responsible, and hard-working. You guys raised a great son." Chris knew there were no "guys," only Heather, but he couldn't let on he knew.

"That's true, he really is." Heather beamed, and Chris noted she didn't correct him.

"I was thrilled to see that he started today, and you must be very proud of him."

"Oh, I am, I really am!" Heather's hazel eyes shone. "I'm so glad I came. It's my first game! I can't believe how great he played!"

"He really came into his own, and it's wonderful that you were there to share it with him."

"That's just how I feel!" Heather bubbled over with happiness. "I'm so happy I quit my job!"

"What?" Chris didn't know if he'd heard her correctly.

"I quit my job and I feel so great!" Heather burst into laughter. "I hated it, only I didn't *realize* I hated it! The new bosses are terrible! I'll find another job and I feel so happy to be free! And I got to be here!"

"There you go! Some things are meant to be, aren't they?" Chris grinned, though inside, he was shaking his head. She was a sweet person, but somebody should tell all the sweet people in the world, *Don't volunteer so much to complete strangers. Don't tell them the most personal things. Don't post every detail about your private life. You have no idea who is out there, preying on you, using that information to their advantage. Like me.*

"It really is meant to be! Thank you so much for coaching him!"

"I've only coached him for a day, but I'll take the credit." Chris laughed, and Heather joined him.

"Why not? That's the spirit!"

"Right!" Chris said, but just then, a stray sniffle came from one of the moms nearby, evidently about Raz's father.

Heather's pretty face fell. "What a shame. Neil was a great guy. He used to drive Raz and Jordan everywhere until they got their licenses." She leaned over, lowering her voice. "I think Jordan feels bad about starting instead of Raz."

"I can tell." Chris matched her subdued tone, liking the way this was going. The more compliments he paid Jordan, the happier she got, like any good mother. "He doesn't relish beating his friend. He's got a good heart."

"He wouldn't let it show though. He's not like that."

"I know he's not, he reminds me of someone—basically me." Chris was ad-libbing, but Heather smiled again, so he kept going. "I'll tell you what I told Jordan about the situation with Raz. I told him, 'You have every right to this position because you earned it. You are a combination of God-given talent and hard work, and that's what this is all about. Baseball, life, everything. You can't let anything hold you back. You're stepping into your destiny.'"

"You told him that?" Heather's eyes went wide, and Chris worried he was laying it on too thick, but she was lapping it up. She was eager to hear him, and he could tell she was lonely. She was cute in a natural way, with a great body, but he shooed his horniness away. His goal wasn't to take her to bed, but to manipulate her, so he kept talking.

"I love coaching baseball, but the thing you have to know, is that baseball is about these kids and their maturity, and helping them grow into who they were really meant to be. That's how I think of it. That's why I got into teaching in the first place."

"Really." Heather beamed.

"In fact, just FYI, I'm having a get-together tonight at my apartment for the team to introduce myself. Now it will be a victory celebration, thanks to Jordan."

"Oh." Heather blinked. "He didn't mention that to me, but he doesn't always tell me what he's doing."

"Of course, he wouldn't." Chris could see her falter, so he rushed to reassure her. "I didn't keep my mother posted on everything I did, either. No boy does."

"Right." Heather's smile returned.

"I just wanted you to know that I'm going to take very good care of him. And if you ever need to reach me, my number and email's on the website."

"Thank you so much." Heather nodded.

"I better go. Congratulations."

"You should say that to Jordan!" Heather shot back, with a final smile. "I'm just the mom."

"I meant congratulations for quitting your job."

"Oh, right!" Heather rolled her eyes, adorably. "God knows what happens next."

"We'll see!" Chris knew *exactly* what happened next, but that was for only him to know.

Chapter Twenty

C hris scanned the party under way at his apartment. Coach Hardwick had declined to come, but the players filled the living room, wolfing down pizza and talking among themselves. Everyone had arrived except Jordan, Evan, and Raz, and Chris was concerned. He hoped it didn't suggest a reconciliation between Jordan and Raz. He was looking for an opportunity to solidify his relationship to Jordan and finish Raz.

"I wonder where Jordan is." Chris stepped onto the balcony, which overlooked the pocket parking lot. A few of the players were freestyling, which gave Chris a headache, but Trevor and Dylan stood talking against the rail, so he went over to them. "Hey guys, great game! Way to go!"

"Hey Coach!" Trevor shook his fist in the air. "Awesome! Larkin's the man!"

"Trevor, I give credit to you guys, too. It's a team victory."

"Thanks, Coach." Trevor beamed.

"It's the truth. You hit two doubles today. And you, Dylan." Chris turned to the boy. "Dylan, that home run! I think that ball went four hundred feet."

"Not *that* far," Dylan corrected him, pushing up his glasses with a tight smile.

Suddenly their attention was drawn by noisy rap music coming from below, and they all turned to see Evan's BMW pulling into the parking lot with its convertible top down, blasting hip-hop. Evan was driving, Jordan was in the passenger seat, and Raz was wedged in the nonexistent backseat, his knees tucked under his chin. Evan parked and cut the engine, abruptly ending the music.

"Musketeers!" Trevor called to them, but Dylan looked over at Chris, worriedly.

"Are your neighbors going to be pissed at the noise?"

"Don't worry about it." Chris waved him off.

"Musketeers, pizza's hot!" Trevor hollered.

"Zaaaaaa!" Evan hollered back, looking up with a grin as he opened the car door and got out of the BMW.

Trevor pointed down at Raz, laughing. "Raz, you look like a dog! Did you put your head out the window? Did you get a treat?"

"Shut up, Trevor!" Raz called out, climbing out of the car, and just then, Chris thought he heard the telltale clink of a bottle from below. They must've been drinking, and he didn't approve. Alcohol was an X factor he didn't need right now.

Trevor called back, "Yeah, Raz, you're a good dog! What tricks can you do? Besides throwing your bat? That was smooth, dude!"

The boys on the balcony burst into laughter, and the players who were inside the apartment came out. "Yo!" they started calling out, "Raz! Evan!" Then they broke into a chant, "Jordan, Jordan, Jordan!"

Chris watched Jordan get out of the car and follow Evan and Raz to the back door, which he'd left open. "Excuse me, gentlemen," Chris said, making his way off the balcony and into the apartment, then opening the front door just as Evan and Jordan reached the top of the stairs with matching grins.

"Hey, Coach Brennan!" they both said in unison, then started shoving each other, Evan saying "Jinx," and Jordan saying, "What are you, in middle school?"

"Welcome, guys!" Chris clapped them both on the shoulder. "Come in and have something to eat. We're celebrating. Big home victory!"

"Totally, Coach!" Evan said, crossing into the apartment.

Chris shook Jordan's hand. "Jordan, you played incredible today. Congratulations."

"Thanks, Coach."

"Great to see your mom there, too."

"I know, right?" Jordan smiled, shyly. "She never came before."

"She brought you luck." Chris could see Raz coming up the stairs but didn't hurry to acknowledge him. "I introduced myself to her. We had a great talk about you. She was so proud of you."

Jordan shuddered. "She didn't say anything embarrassing, did she?"

"Of course she did. She told me what a good boy you were when you were a little baby."

"You're kidding, right?" Jordan's eyes flared in mock-alarm.

"I'm kidding. You did terrific today. You should be proud of yourself."

"Thanks, Coach." Jordan glanced over his shoulder at Raz, who lurched forward.

"Coach, your crib is sick!" Raz pushed past him.

"Hey, Raz." Chris caught a whiff of beer on Raz's breath, but not on the other boys. He closed the apartment door, watching as Jordan followed Evan toward the food table.

Raz stopped to look at the gun case. "Whoa, Coach! Are they loaded?"

"No," Chris answered, going over. "You like?"

"Awesome! Are you a good shot?"

"I'm not bad. How about you?"

"Never tried." Raz kept looking at the guns, and Chris couldn't tell if it was to avoid looking at him. Either way, it was time to twist the proverbial knife. There were many kinds of weapons in the world, and words could be the most lethal.

"Raz, I have to say, I was really disappointed when you threw the bat—"

"Sorry," Raz said, sullen. He raked back his hair, loose to his shoulders.

"I know you have a lot going on with your older brother, but—"

"I *don't* have a lot going on," Raz shot back, shifting his gaze back to the gun collection.

"Okay, then I stand corrected." Chris had brought it up because he wanted to see how Raz would react. "I'm talking to you, as your coach and as your friend. I'm looking out for you. You can't have a bad attitude. Between us, my buddy was there today. He saw what you did."

Raz's head snapped around, his dark eyes newly troubled. "You mean the guy you sent Jordan's video to?"

"Yes, but that's between you and me. I'm not even going to tell Jordan that. You've got to do better next time." Chris patted him on the shoulder, like *tough break.*

"What if there's not a next time, Coach?" Raz grimaced.

"I'm sure there will be," Chris answered, but his tone suggested exactly the opposite.

"But, there'll be other games. I'll get in as reliever, won't I?"

"That's up to Coach Hardwick, not me. You're going to have to dig yourself out of a hole."

"I got a single."

"True, but that's not the problem."

"What's the problem?"

"An attitude problem is the kiss of death for recruiters."

" 'The kiss of *death*?' " Raz's frown deepened.

"That's what my friend told me. No school will touch a kid with an attitude problem. They don't need the aggravation on the field or in the dugout."

Just then, Evan and Jordan came over holding plates of food, and behind them was Trevor and Dylan. Evan laughed. "Raz, we were just saying, that might've been your best pitch ever. Except that you pitched your *bat*."

Trevor burst into laughter. "Raz, what do you call that pitch? Was that a fastball? Or fast *bat*?"

Dylan smiled. "Dude, I think it was more like a curve. Don't you think it was a curve *bat*? I thought I saw it curve right before the plate. Or the *fence*."

"Or my *mom*!" Evan joined in, his eyes comically wide. "Raz, you almost cracked my mom's skull wide open!"

Trevor added, "And his *own* mom! He almost clocked his own mother! He pitched a curve bat!"

"Trevor, shut the hell up, you meathead!" Raz shouted, shoving Trevor.

"You shut up! Get your hands off me!"

Chris delayed acting for a half second, and just then, Raz shoved Trevor harder, and Trevor shoved Raz back.

"You're crazy, Raz!" Trevor shouted. "You're outta your mind!"

"Boys, Raz, stop it!" Chris reached for Raz, but just then, Raz threw a punch, missing Trevor, upending Evan's plate of food, and connecting with Jordan's face.

"Arhh!" Jordan jumped backwards, his hand flying to his cheek.

Raz whirled around on Jordan. "Oops, did I hurt you, rock star? You going to get a mark on your face now?"

Jordan recoiled, shaken. Raz's punch had broken the skin, making a cut that started to bleed, dripping down Jordan's cheek.

Trevor yelled, "You *suck*, Raz! You can't take it! You never coulda pitched the way Jordan did today!"

"I could so!" Raz lunged for Trevor in anger, knocking Evan and Jordan to the side.

"Stop, Raz!" Chris decided this had gone as far as he needed it to go. He grabbed Raz by the shoulders from behind, forced him backwards, and pressed him into a sitting position on the cabinet in front of the gun case, looking the boy in the eye. "Raz, you've been drinking, haven't you?"

"So what!" Raz yelled in Chris's face, and the boys fell stone silent. Jordan wiped blood from his cut, leaving a pinkish smear on his cheek.

Chris turned to Evan. "Evan, were you drinking, too?"

"No."

"Are you okay to drive?"

"Yes."

Chris believed him, only because Raz didn't call Evan a liar. "I want you to take Raz home."

"Okay, Coach."

"Thank you." Chris took Raz by the arm and lifted him off the cabinet. "Raz, get it together. You're your own worst enemy."

"Leave me alone, *buddy*!"

"Good-bye." Chris walked Raz toward the door, with Evan behind. When he opened it, Raz wrenched his arm away, stalked out of the apartment, and hurried down the stairs. Chris put a hand on Evan's shoulder. "Take him right home, please. No monkey business, no drinking."

"Okay, Coach." Evan motioned to Jordan. "Jordan, you coming?"

Chris interjected, "Evan, I want Jordan to stay. I need to check out his cut and see if he needs to go to the hospital."

Jordan shook his head, and blood dripped like a red tear down his cheek. "Coach, I don't need to go to a hospital. It's nothing."

"That may be, but I'll take you home. I'm responsible for you. I met your mom today. You can't go home and tell her you got injured at my house without her hearing from me. That can't happen, Jordan."

"Okay," Jordan said reluctantly. "Later, Evan."

"Later." Evan waved them off, leaving the apartment and going down the stairs.

"Jordan, let's take a look at that cut." Chris closed the door, satisfied that he'd accomplished his mission—or Raz had, for him.

And he wouldn't mind seeing Jordan's mother again.

Chapter Twenty-one

Chris stood next to Jordan as the boy opened the apartment door, and Heather looked up from her laptop. She was sitting on the couch in a sweatshirt and jeans, with her hair in a ponytail. She had one of those *Housewives* shows on mute, and her expression morphed from sleepy to shocked when she saw Chris entering with Jordan, who had a fresh wound on his cheek.

"Hey, Mom." Jordan closed the door behind them. "I'm okay, don't freak."

"Oh no, what's that on your face?" Heather moved the laptop aside, jumped up, and went over to Jordan, peering at his cheek. It had swollen pink, but the bleeding had stopped. "What happened, honey? Chris, what's going on?"

"It's nothing, Mom. I'm fine."

"He really is," Chris added.

"Tell me what happened. Did you fall?" Heather squinted at the cut, gripping Jordan's arm as if he would otherwise run away. "I hope you don't need stitches."

"I don't think he does," Chris interjected, speaking from experience, though it wasn't an experience he could share. "I looked at it carefully, cleaned it up, and left it uncovered so it could get air."

"I'm totally fine," Jordan said again. "It's really nothing,"

"So how did it happen?" Heather looked from Jordan to Chris. "Did it happen at your house? At the party?"

Jordan hesitated, and Chris realized they should've discussed this before now. The party had continued after Evan and Raz had gone, and Jordan had hung out, even helping Chris clean up afterwards. They'd talked about other things on the ride here, like the game and pitching mechanics, of course, always mechanics. Chris had been glad to get closer to Jordan at his most vulnerable, and Jordan's friendship with Raz had to be dead meat after tonight.

"Mom, it doesn't matter," Jordan answered, but Heather looked at him like he was crazy.

"It matters to me, Jordan." Heather wheeled her head back to Chris, her blue eyes so frank that it unsettled him. "What happened, Chris? You tell me, since my son won't."

"I'm sorry, but unfortunately, there was an altercation."

"An *altercation*?" Heather asked in disbelief. "With you?"

"No, with Raz," Chris rushed to explain. "I drove Jordan home to apologize to you, because it happened at my house."

"It wasn't really an *altercation,* Mom," Jordan said, edging away. "It's not a big deal."

Heather placed her hands on her hips, turning to Jordan as he backed toward the hallway. "Jordan, if it's not a big deal, don't make it one. What's the big mystery? Did somebody hit you? Tell me."

"Raz got in a bad mood, is all."

"Raz *hit* you? That's terrible!"

"He didn't mean to."

Chris didn't say anything. He knew that if he made Raz look bad, Jordan would only defend him.

Heather's eyes had gone wide. "Jordan, what do you mean?

How do you unintentionally hit somebody in the face? Are you saying it was an accident? Was it an accident?"

"Mom, no, but it's not a big thing. It's fine."

"Then it was on purpose? He hit you under your eye. He could've ruined your vision. Why did he do that? Were you guys fighting?"

"No, not really." Jordan backed up toward the hallway.

"So then why did he hit you?"

"He had a bad day. You saw, at the game."

"Hmph! Yes, I did see. I saw him throw a bat. That's bad sportsmanship, and it's dangerous."

Jordan looked at Chris as he left the room. "Coach Brennan, thanks for everything. Good night. Good night, Mom."

Chris gave him a wave. "No worries, Jordan. I'll see you at practice tomorrow morning."

Jordan turned away and headed down the hallway.

"Jordan, we'll talk later," Heather called after him, then turned to Chris with an exasperated sigh. "Sheesh! Is he really okay?"

"Yes, I'm sure of it."

"It was nice of you to take him home."

"Not a problem."

"Would you like a cup of coffee? Or is it too late for you?"

"A glass of water would be great." Chris realized that he could get something accomplished here, if he stayed awhile. Plus she really was cute.

"I have some cookies, if you're a cookie guy." Heather led him to a small dining area that was part of the kitchen, then gestured him into a seat at the table.

"Of course I'm a cookie guy. Who isn't?" Chris sat down, taking in the kitchen and the dining room. It was modest, and a weird reddish glow came from the curtains, from the Friendly's sign next door.

"It's Chips Ahoy. Not gourmet or anything." Heather reached into a cabinet above the counter, and Chris could tell from her residual frown that her mind was on what had happened to Jordan.

"There's no such thing as gourmet chocolate chips."

"Yes, there is." Heather opened the bag of cookies, shaking a few onto a plate she took from the dish rack. "They cost twelve bucks a pound at Whole Foods."

"Not worth it."

"I agree. You really want water? I have milk." Heather brought the plate of cookies over to the table and set it down. "Milk and cookies is better than water and cookies."

"Water and cookies is fine. I just won't dunk."

"Ha!" Heather brightened, heading back to the kitchen. "Everybody in my family dunked, we're big dunkers. Toast got dunked in coffee. Doughnuts, too."

"I like to dunk toast in coffee," Chris said, realizing it was the first completely true sentence he'd said since he'd come to Central Valley.

"Me too." Heather turned on the tap and poured water into a glass, then went to the freezer and popped a few cubes into the water. "We dunk Italian bread in gravy and—"

"Gravy?"

"Gravy is tomato sauce, that's what we always called it. My mother was Italian, from Brooklyn. It's my ex who was from here."

"Oh." Chris caught the reference to her ex, so now he could officially know what he already knew.

"My mother even dunked her bread in salad dressing. Vinegar and oil."

"That would be extreme dunking."

"They were dunking professionals." Heather smiled.

"I'm a dunking *champion*." Chris found himself smiling back.

Heather laughed as she brought the glass of water over and set it down, then took the seat opposite him. The table was small, and the only fixture was an overhead light, which was unusually cozy—at least it was unusual to Chris, because coziness wasn't a feeling he'd had often. In fact, he couldn't remember the last time he felt cozy.

Chris got back on track. "Obviously, I think Raz is having a hard time being replaced as starting pitcher. You might want to discourage the friendship for the time being."

"Tell me about it, I've been trying. I thought they'd sort it out, but maybe not. This is ridiculous."

"It's not fair to Jordan."

"No, it's not!" Heather raised her voice. "I feel bad for Raz and I don't mean to be mean. Please don't think I'm a gossip, but I don't know if you heard, his older brother Ryan was arrested last night."

"Yes, I did hear that." Chris noted she didn't say it in a gossipy way, but her tone was sympathetic.

"Okay, so they're having trouble in the family. I saw Susan at the game, but I didn't get to talk to her. I feel terrible that Raz's father died, too. But still, none of that is Jordan's fault. Jordan earned the position, all by himself. Nobody helped him. Everything he does, it's on his shoulders. He was never given any advantages."

Chris heard the emotion behind her words and sensed she wasn't talking about Jordan anymore. He broke off a piece of cookie and popped it in his mouth.

"I probably should have mentioned this, but his father and I broke up when he was born. He's grown up without a father and he's 'risen above his raisin' as Dr. Phil says."

"I don't think you need to worry. As you said, Raz and Jordan will sort themselves out, and this too shall pass."

"Right, I know." Heather pressed a stray strand of hair from her eyes, with a new sigh. "It's been a long day, I guess. A long, weird day."

"The day you quit your job."

"Right, the day I quit my job." Heather rolled her eyes, with a self-conscious giggle. "It's settling in."

"What is?"

"Reality. I don't have a backup plan."

"I always have a backup plan," Chris said, another thing that was true.

"Is that supposed to make me feel better?" Heather lifted an eyebrow, and Chris realized he'd said the wrong thing, thrown off-balance by her.

"No, what I was about to say is that you don't need a backup plan. Just go to the next step."

"What's that?"

"Find a new job."

"Ha!" Heather laughed, but it had a hollow sound. "That's not as easy as it sounds. I was just online at monster.com and Craig's List. I applied to fifteen jobs already, but there's not a lot of places looking."

"Nothing's as easy as it sounds. You can't let that stop you."

"Now you're talking like a coach."

"Well, I am a coach," Chris said, without thinking.

"Okay, then, coach me. I'm open-minded." Heather leaned back, crossing her arms, and Chris tried to think of something a real coach would say.

"Be positive."

"Good start."

"I'm sure a lot of businesses would love to have someone like you."

"What makes you say that? You don't even know me." Heather looked at him like he was crazy, the same way she had looked at Jordan, which was very cute. Totally cute.

"I do, in a way," Chris answered, and he wasn't even talking about his research on her. "Through Jordan."

"What about him? You don't know him that well, either."

"I know enough to draw some reasonable conclusions. He turned out great, and you just told me that you raised him by yourself, on your own."

"Yes, so?" Heather blinked. "What are you saying, that I should get a job as a nanny?"

"No, not unless you wanted to. What I mean is, you need to view your skill set more broadly."

"Skill set?" Heather threw back her head and laughed. "I have a *skill set*? That's news to me."

"No it isn't, it shouldn't be," Chris said, meaning it. His tone turned soft and he didn't even plan it that way. "It takes a lot of skills to be a single mother, raise a kid, and run a household by yourself. You have to pay the bills, repair what needs repairing, and make sure that Jordan gets to school and to the doctor and to practice, am I right?"

"Yes, when he was younger, I guess." Heather shrugged. "But I don't fix things, Jordan does. Or they don't get fixed."

"Then they didn't need fixing. And all the time you're working at a full-time job, so you have that to deal with. True or not?"

"True," Heather answered, with the trace of a smile.

"And I'm sure you were very good at your job, whatever you did, and you said you wanted to leave it, and you did that, too. So you have a broad skill set and you should move forward with absolute confidence."

Heather smiled, chuckling. "You're an excellent coach! You're getting me to think positive. Gung ho! Clear eyes, full heart, can't lose, all that."

"So it worked?" Chris chuckled.

"It kind of did!" Heather threw up her hands. "Go, team, go!"

"Ha!" Chris burst into laughter, realizing that the weirdest thing had just happened. He had been playing the role of a coach and saying whatever a coach would say, but somewhere between him and her, the words had become true. And above all, they had helped her, which made him feel good. He felt not only like a coach, he even felt more . . . human.

Suddenly a cell phone started ringing in the living room, and Heather looked over. "Oh, excuse me, I have to get that, but I'll be only a minute. It's my cousin in Denver and she just had a baby—"

"No, that's okay, I should go," Chris said, standing quickly. He had to stop what was happening between them. Whatever it was, it wasn't according to plan, backup plan, step one, or step two. It was basically something that couldn't happen at all, especially not with Heather. He needed to use Jordan, and her. They could only be the means to an end, in a dangerous and deadly game.

"You don't have to go. Give me a second." Heather hustled for the phone. "I just want to see if she's okay."

"No, it's late. Good night now." Chris crossed to the door, pulled it open, and let himself out.

It was no time to grow a conscience.

Chapter Twenty-two

An hour later, Chris was driving through thick, dark woods to a meet. The night sky was starless, and clouds swept across the moon, carried by unseen winds. He tried to put Heather out of his mind and focus on what lay ahead, but it wasn't easy. He'd been with his share of women, but she was different. He didn't want to figure out how, because any relationship with her could end only one way. So it had to end now, before it started.

Chris turned into a dirt driveway, and his Jeep's headlights raced over a peeling white sign with faded letters, COMING SOON, CENTRE MALL & FOOD COURT. He parked and cut the engine, scanning the scene in the scant light. It was a construction site for a mall, but the project had evidently been abandoned after the pad had been installed, paving a footprint for the strip of stores. The concrete glowed darkly in the moonlight, surrounded by trees that had been cut to black stubs.

Chris got out of the Jeep, dismayed to see that the silhouette standing next to the car wasn't the one he'd expected. Neither was the car. It was a gleaming black Audi coupe, not the nondescript black Ford SUV he knew so well. The man standing next to the car had on a Phillies cap, and there was only one man Chris knew who wore a ball cap thinking he was a Master of Disguise. The cap's brim put his face almost completely in shadow, which was fine with Chris because Aleksandr Ivanov was ugly as sin.

Chris walked over. "Hey, Alek. Where's the Rabbi? He said he'd be here."

"He couldn't make it."

"Why?"

"What's the difference? You miss Daddy? Deal with me. What's going on?"

Chris bit his tongue. He wasn't looking for trouble. "Okay, I have a guy. I'm in."

Alek snorted. "By 'guy,' you mean a kid. A high-school junior. This is some next-level shit, Curt."

Chris thought his real name sounded strange to him, but didn't say so. He realized he was mentally betwixt and between, after the cookies with Heather. He had to get his head back in the game. Alek had a bad temper, and the stakes were too high to get distracted.

"Who's the kid?"

"Jordan Larkin." Chris felt a twinge offering up the name, like a betrayal. But he shooed the thoughts away.

"So what's the problem? You called the Rabbi and told him you had a problem."

"I said I might have a problem." Chris didn't want to talk it over with Alek, who was half as smart as the Rabbi.

"Gimme a break, Curt. I don't have time to jerk around." Alek checked his watch, a neat swivel of his head under the cap.

"Turns out one of the teachers is from Wyoming. He knows Northwest College."

"You said that wouldn't happen." Alek snorted again.

"The odds were slim to none. It's a fluke." Chris's chest tightened. Alek always reminded him of one of his foster fathers, the worst one. A bully to everyone around him, like a prison guard to his wife, his other foster son, even the cat. Milly was the cat's name, a calico. The night Chris had finally left, he'd let Milly out and she ran off. She would never look back. Neither would he.

"What's his name, this teacher?"

"Abe Yomes."

"So what are you telling me for? Handle it."

"The question is how."

"You're a big boy. Don't ask me. Handle it. I gotta go. What a waste of time." Alek turned away, got in the car, and started the engine.

Chris watched him go, wishing the Rabbi had come. Together they would have assessed the risk and figured out what to do about Abe.

But if Chris had to handle it on his own, he would.

Chapter Twenty-three

Saturday morning dawned sunny, and Susan put on her sunglasses as she drove Raz to baseball practice. He kept his head turned to the window, cell phone in hand and listening to music through his earbuds. She'd hardly slept a wink, her thoughts on Raz and Ryan, torn between the two of them like when they were young and fought over the same toy. They'd tantrum, and she'd tended to get down in the weeds with them, but Neil would tell her:

Honey, when they fight, they spiral down. Don't go into the spiral. You're the parent, remember? If you go down the spiral, you'll all end up in the toilet.

Susan remembered his words as clearly as if it were yesterday, which was the problem. She remembered everything about Neil, how he had acted, what he had said, the jokes he'd made, the way they'd made love. She wished she remembered less. She wished he wasn't so present all the time, in her head and her heart.

Susan drove ahead, her thoughts churning. It had been almost a year since Neil died, and a year was the grief cutoff. He died in August and it was already April, so she had only four months left. Nobody said so explicitly, but she got the message. She saw an article in the paper that said, most widows return to their "pre-loss level of life satisfaction" after a year. So she knew she had four months to become a normal person. Still she didn't believe there could be a deadline to mourning the dead.

Susan stopped at a light. She knew what they were saying at work, behind her back. She was *milking it. She just wanted the sympathy.* She was *wallowing in grief* and not *moving on.* She was *dragging down* her sons, too. They're spiraling down to get *swallowed up* by the grief toilet.

The light turned green, and Susan glanced over at Raz. They were only a few blocks from school, and she wanted to make sure they understood each other.

You're the parent, remember?

"Raz?" Susan said, but there was no reply. "Raz."

"What?" Raz turned to her, his expression slack and his skin pale. His eyes looked bloodshot and puffy. His hair was wet from the shower, dripping onto his blue Musketeers T-shirt, darkening it around the neckline. He had on his gym shorts and sneakers, his feet resting on his backpack in the well of the passenger seat.

"I want to talk to you."

"So, talk." Raz blinked.

"Please take out your earphones."

"I can hear you."

"I'm not going to talk to you with your ears plugged up. This is important."

"Fine," Raz said tonelessly. He pulled out one of his earphones.

"Both, please."

Raz pulled out the other one.

Susan reminded herself to be patient. Neil had been, above all things, unbelievably patient. "Okay, so first thing this morning, what are you supposed to do?"

"Mom, I know."

"Yes, but tell me. I want to hear what you'll say."

"You mean like a rehearsal?" Raz's weary eyes flared in disbelief.

"Yes, exactly." Susan returned her attention to the road because his expression only made her angry. She drove ahead, passing the tall oaks, the clipped hedges, and the clapboard colonials with their shiny PVC fences.

"Okay, well, whatever, first I'm going to Coach Hardwick. I'm going to tell him I'm sorry I threw the bat."

"Right." Susan kept her eyes on the road. "Remember, the first words out of your mouth are 'I'm sorry.' Lead with 'I'm sorry.' "

"I know that. I *said that*."

"I want you to go to him before practice even starts."

Raz sighed heavily. "That's not going to be that easy, Mom. He's busy."

"Just go up to him and say 'excuse me.' "

"He doesn't like to be interrupted."

"He won't mind after he hears you say 'I'm sorry.' "

"Should I say I'm sorry for interrupting, too? How many things am I sorry for, Mom? Am I sorry for *breathing*?"

"Don't be fresh," Susan said, then an awful thought struck her. *I'm sorry for breathing.*

It was true. She was sorry that she was breathing, when Neil was not. She wished she were dead, and her husband was the one dealing with these angry, thankless children, who acted like they were the only ones who lost him, when exactly the opposite was true. Neil might have been their father, but he was her husband. She'd been there first. She'd loved him longer. He was more hers than theirs. She was his lover, his *wife*.

Susan's fingers tightened on the steering wheel, and she gritted her teeth not to turn around to Raz and *smack him in the face*. That's what she actually thought, a vicious notion that came out of nowhere, shocking her. *My son is driving me so crazy that I want to smack him.*

"Then I have to go to Coach Brennan and tell him I'm sorry that I ruined his party, even though I didn't ruin his party. They stayed after. They had a good time. It didn't end or anything. Jordan was fine, he didn't have to get stitches."

Susan roiled inside, enraged at his freshness, at his attitude, at his *selfishness*. He used to be a fun little boy, but he had turned into a total brat.

"Then I go to Jordan and tell him I'm sorry that I hit him. I'm not allowed to say that I didn't mean to hit him, because like you always say, 'When you do the act, the consequences always go with it.'"

Susan tried to press away her horrible thoughts. The high school was in sight. She breathed in and out, trying to calm down.

"Then, after I apologize to everybody at practice, I have to call Mrs. Larkin and apologize. I have to tell her I'm happy for Jordan if he's the starting pitcher because 'that's what friends are for.'" Raz made air quotes, and Susan turned left into the school grounds.

The road ran uphill, and she passed the student parking lot on her left. She glanced over at the entrance, where several Central Valley police cruisers sat in front of the school. She looked away, having seen quite enough police cars recently.

"Cops?" Raz frowned at the cruisers. "Wonder what's up."

Susan drove forward, having a schedule to keep. She had to drop Raz off, go home, and pull Ryan out of bed because she was taking him to a therapist at eleven o'clock. Susan would be meeting with her own therapist at the very same time, so two-thirds of The Sematovs' Shit Show would be on expensive couches.

"Mom, look, something's the matter," Raz said, alarmed, and Susan stopped the car. A group of uniformed police, teachers, and staff were leaving the school building, and some of the teachers were crying.

"Oh, my." Susan took one look and knew that someone had died. She had *lived* that scene. She *still* lived it, in her mind.

"That's Dr. McElroy, and Mr. Pannerman. And Madame Wheeler's freaking out."

"Who's Madame Wheeler?" Susan didn't know who Raz meant for a minute. Neil was the one who went to Parents' Night.

"The French teacher. Ryan had her, remember? She's the one in the front."

"Poor woman," Susan said, touched at the sight of the stricken teacher, holding a Kleenex to her nose. She left the building next to Dr. McElroy, whom Susan did recognize, with a bearded male teacher, also weepy. Three female students held each other as they cried, and a baseball player in a Musketeers T-shirt and gym shorts hurried from the entrance and started jogging toward the field.

"Hey, that's Dylan. Maybe he knows what's going on." Raz slid down the window, waving to get the attention of the tall, wiry kid. "Dylan!"

"Raz!" Dylan hustled toward the car, his backpack bouncing. "Hi Raz, hi Mrs. Sematov."

"Dude, what's up with Madame Wheeler? Why are the cops here?"

"Oh man, it's bad." Dylan bent over to peer inside the car, pushing up his glasses. Wrinkles creased his forehead. "Mr. Y died last night. Dr. McElroy's crying. They're all crying."

"What?" Raz gasped, shocked. "That can't be! I just saw him! How did he die?"

"Mr. Y is dead?" Susan recoiled. It was horrible news. Mr. Y was Raz's Language Arts teacher, and Ryan had him, too. They both loved him. That's how she knew the name, they talked about him so much.

"He committed *suicide*," Dylan answered, blinking behind his glasses.

Step Two

Chapter Twenty-four

Chris hurried up the sidewalk, his head down. The last thing he needed was another meet with Alek, especially one he had to drive to Philly for. Alek had set it for two o'clock, and Chris had barely had time to change after practice. It had been an awful morning, with the team distraught over Abe's death.

Chris hustled toward the massive sandstone-and-brick tower, rising seventeen stories and occupying the entire block of Second and Chestnut Streets, in the colonial section of the city. The building was on the National Register of Historic Places, though its history was undoubtedly irrelevant to the people outside, enjoying the last few puffs of their cigarettes.

He reached the building and hustled up the steps, through the stainless-steel doors, and inside to the metal detector, while his eyes adjusted to the darkness. There were no windows in the entrance area, and the brass fixtures were vintage, shedding little light. He slid his wallet from his back pocket—not his Chris Brennan wallet with his fake driver's license, but his real wallet with his true Curt Abbott ID, his true address in South Philly, and his heavy chrome badge, with a laminated card identifying him as a Special Agent in the Philadelphia Field

Division of the Bureau of Alcohol, Tobacco, Firearms, & Explosives, or ATF.

Chris handed his open wallet to the guard, who scrutinized his ID and handed it back. He worked undercover, and he had to show his ID because he wasn't at the office enough to be recognized by the security guards, especially on the weekends. He put his ID on the conveyor belt with his keys, walked through the metal detector, and collected his belongings; then entered the lobby. He experienced a sense of awe every time he crossed the dark marble floor, starting from twelve years ago, when he was first hired by ATF.

The massive space was flanked by two carved staircases and topped by an ornate plasterwork rotunda that soared three stories high. At its apex shone a circle of daylight rimmed by an upper deck with a stainless-steel railing. To Chris, the history of the building mirrored the history of ATF, and he was proud to be an ATF agent, even though he had to report to Alek Ivanov, who acted like a gangster even though he was a Washington bureaucrat transferred to the Philadelphia office.

Chris pressed the elevator button, uncomfortable to be in public as himself, as if he were wearing the wrong skin. He hated coming in while he was undercover. It wasn't procedure, and he knew it wouldn't have happened during any other operation, further evidence of the lack of support he was getting from Alek.

The elevator arrived, and he stepped inside and pressed the button, his thoughts churning. As a child, he hadn't known what he wanted to be when he grew up, but he wanted to help the underdog—maybe because he *was* the underdog, raised in so many different foster homes. He'd been drawn to law enforcement and after college, had chosen ATF, an underdog of an agency that lived in the shadow of the FBI. Chris's favorite movie was *The Untouchables* about the legendary ATF agent Eliot Ness, and after a string of successful operations, he'd felt honored when everyone started calling him The Untouchable. But lately, the nickname bothered him, reminding him that he was literally untouchable, disconnected from people.

He got off the elevator, took a right, and walked down a hallway that ended in a locked door, intentionally unmarked so that no member of the public would know it was ATF. For the same reason, ATF wasn't listed on the directory downstairs and none of the security guards would confirm that ATF was even in this building, having been instructed not to do so. ATF's Philadelphia Field Division employed two hundred people— Supervisors, Special Agents, Task Force Officers, Detectives, Certified Explosives Specialists, Fire Marshals, Intelligence Research Analysts, and many others, but none of their names was on the directory, either. Unsung didn't begin to describe their status. Unknown was closer to the truth.

Chris unlocked the door and let himself into the office, which was as quiet as expected on a Saturday afternoon. He went down a gray-carpeted hallway past walls of institutional yellow, un- adorned with any artwork. The hallway led to a large room of gray cubicles that looked like an insurance office except for the Glock G22 or subcompact Glock G27, agency-issued weapons, hanging in a shoulder holster on the cubicle's corner, evidence that an agent was in.

Chris reached the conference room and opened the door to see Alek sitting at the head of the round table. The Rabbi was nowhere in evidence, though he was supposed to be here, too. "Hey, Alek."

"Curt, thanks for coming in." Alek half-rose and extended a hand, which Chris shook, though he could barely bring himself to meet Alek's small, dark eyes, set deep in a long face. His dark hair thinned in front, and a thin scar on his cheek looked like it was from a knife fight, but it was from a car accident at the mall.

"Where's the Rabbi?"

"He'll be right back." Alek sat down. "You know, that's all you ever ask me. 'Where's the Rabbi?' 'Where's the Rabbi?' "

Suddenly the door opened and the Rabbi came in, holding his laptop. "Curt, so good to see you!" he said with a broad grin, showing teeth stained from excessive coffee. His real name was David Levitz, but everyone called him the Rabbi because he was the smartest agent in the Division.

"Hey!" Chris gave the Rabbi a bear hug, almost lifting him off his feet, since the Rabbi was only five-foot-five and maybe 160 pounds. He was fiftysomething with frizzy gray hair, sharp, dark brown eyes behind thick, wire-rimmed bifocals, and his thin lips were bracketed by deep laugh lines, earned over the years.

"Sorry I missed you last night," the Rabbi said, which was code for *Sorry I didn't rescue you from Alek.*

"No worries," Chris said, which meant, *Can we shoot our boss and get away with it?*

"Let's get started, lovebirds." Alek gestured Chris into the seat opposite the Rabbi, rather than next to him, and it struck Chris that Alek was the Coach Hardwick of ATF. Technically, Aleksandr Ivanov was the Group Supervisor, or GS, of the Violent Crimes Task Force, and the Rabbi was Chris's contact agent, to whom he reported when he worked undercover.

"Okay, so Alek, why did you call me in?"

"I'm pulling the plug."

"On my operation?" Chris wasn't completely surprised. "There's no reason to do that, Alek. I disagree—"

"I went out there to meet you. Sleepy little town in the middle of nowhere. It's nothing but a total waste of time, and now that some teacher offed himself last night, there's a possibility of you being blown."

"I won't be, and anyway, I'm not so sure it's a suicide. The jury's out for me, and it could be connected to the case." Chris still couldn't believe that Abe Yomes was really gone. He had liked Abe, and it had shocked him to the marrow to hear that he was dead, much less by his own hand. It was awful, and it sent up red flags in terms of the operation, which had been dubbed Operation Varsity Letter.

"What facts do you base that on?"

"His personality. It doesn't make sense that he would commit suicide."

"You didn't know him that well. You've been there two days."

"I get the guy. He's a fun, upbeat guy. Connected to friends and students. They all loved him, they called him Mr. Y." Chris flashed on the scene at practice this morning. The players had been so distraught when they heard the news. Raz had been dropped off by his mother, after he had obviously been crying. Coach Hardwick had made them practice anyway, but they played horribly and left crestfallen.

"I don't see the point."

"That's because you never heard the justification for the operation. You were in D.C. when I got the authorization—"

"I read the file. I'm completely up-to-date on your reports."

"It's not the same thing, and besides, there's no downside. It costs nothing. My rent is $450, and I buy my own clothes."

"Don't forget we had to pay to place you in the school. The superintendent wanted four grand to send the teacher and her old man on a vacation." Alek rolled his eyes. "Your tax dollars at work."

"But still, it's cheaper than a house or a boat, and the upside is great."

"You know what your problem is, Curt? Your premise is wrong."

"How? It's cost–benefit. The typical budgetary analysis—"

"No, your premise is that you're the one who makes that analysis. But you're not. I am. I'm shutting you down."

"You haven't given it a chance. Let me break it down." Chris commandeered the Rabbi's laptop, logged into the network using his password to get beyond the ATF firewall, then found his private files. "Did you see the video? Did you even look at it?"

"I read—"

"It'll take fifteen seconds. Watch." Chris hit PLAY, and the video showed a shadowy image of a tall figure forcing open a door in a dark shed, then hurrying toward bags of ammonium nitrate fertilizer. The figure reached for one of the bags, and as he did so, he came closer to the camera. The man's features were obscured by a ball cap, but it captured the lettering of his blue T-shirt, which read Musketeers Baseball.

"So?" Alek sighed theatrically.

Chris hit STOP. "We know that ammonium nitrate fertilizer is the go-to ingredient for IEDs made by domestic terrorists and that its purchase, transport, and storage is strictly monitored by Homeland Security and it's restricted to those with a permit, mostly farmers. The only other way to get it is theft." Chris pointed to the screen. "This video was taken by Herb Vrasaya, one of the farmers in Central Valley, whose farm is located five miles from the high school. Mr. Vrasaya grows corn and he has a permit to buy and store the fertilizer. He installed the camera two weeks ago, because he thought rats were getting into the shed and he wanted to see how."

"I read that part."

"Mr. Vrasaya sent the video to our office, like a good citizen. 'If you see something, say something,' and he didn't want his permitting jeopardized. I think this video is evidence of a bomb plot that has a connection to the baseball team at CVHS. The blue Musketeers T-shirt is issued to only the varsity players, the boys I coach. It's a badge of honor. I'm infiltrating the team to identify this kid and learn why he's stealing fertilizer. And it would be no problem at all for an underage kid to rent a box truck in Central Valley. All the locals know where to go, to a guy named Zeke. I went there myself to see how hard it would be to rent a truck and what the pitfalls would be. I met the guy. He always has them available, and there's no paperwork."

The Rabbi interjected, "Remember that it's April, Alek.

April 19 is the anniversary of the Oklahoma City bombing. Anybody trying to blow something up would be stockpiling fertilizer now. It takes a ton of fertilizer for a major explosion. That's fifty bags. Bottom line, I agree with Curt. I'm backing him."

Alek threw up his hands. "Why? Because some kid has a T-shirt? He could've gotten it at Target. Curt, you said so in your own report, didn't you?"

"What I wrote in my report was that I talked to the manager at Target, and he told me that only the Booster moms buy T-shirts at Target. The store never sells any large or the extralarge, only the extrasmall and small." Chris thought ahead to preempt Alek's next objection. "And don't think that the kid in the video wore the T-shirt to frame a member of the baseball team, because there's no way they could've known about the security camera."

Alek scoffed. "But what kind of an idiot would wear a team uniform to steal something?"

"Not an idiot, a kid. I've been a teacher for two days and I can tell you they do dumb stuff. Especially the boys. They don't think anything through."

"Not that dumb. All it takes is one kid to buy the T-shirt or one mom to buy a larger size."

"Then assign another agent to follow up with Target. I can't do it myself with my cover, and the video alone isn't enough for probable cause. We can get the name, address, and credit card of everybody who bought a Musketeers T-shirt in the past five years. I think it was a newish one because the color stayed true." Chris had washed four T-shirts thirty times to see when the color faded. The answer was, the twenty-third time.

"We don't have the agent to spare."

"I'm making progress. Like I told you, I'm in: I picked my guy, Jordan Larkin."

"Is that the name of your unwitting?" the Rabbi asked. An unwitting was the ATF term for an informant who was being pumped for information without knowing that he was part of an undercover operation.

"Yes, and he's perfect. It took me only two days to befriend him, that's step one, and step two, I'll cast my net wider to find who stole the fertilizer." Chris hit REWIND, stopping the video when the shadowy image first entered the room. "The height of the doorway in the shed is eighty inches, and this figure is over six feet tall, between six-one and six-five. There are five boys on my varsity team who are over six feet tall. Three of them are the ones in my AP Government class, including my unwitting— Jordan Larkin, Raz Sematov, and Evan Kostis." Chris kept talking, though Alek glanced at his watch. "Step two is to get to know the other two players who are over six feet tall, Trevor Kiefermann and Dylan McPhee. I'm investigating them and I know I'm going to get a break."

"When?" Alek snapped.

"I have three days left until the nineteenth, if what they're planning is an anniversary bombing. Give me three days." Chris pointed again at the video. "In addition to which, the timing makes absolute sense for it to be a baseball player. A player leaving practice when it was over would arrive at Mr. Vrasaya's farm, park his car, and run to the shed exactly when this happens, which is 6:20. I drove the distance myself. Then he still gets home in time, and nobody is the wiser, except for the fact that his trunk is filled with ammonium nitrate."

"What does he do with it then? Does he hand it off? Does he store it at his house?"

"I don't know but I'm gonna find out."

"One question, Curt," the Rabbi interjected. "What about your unwitting, Larkin? Do you suspect him?"

"No," Chris answered. "Again, I'm going with my gut. Jordan Larkin doesn't fit the profile for a domestic terrorist. He's quiet, a rules follower, and a good kid."

Alek ignored them both. "I still don't understand what the

teacher had to do with it. Yomes, the one who committed suicide."

"Maybe Abe knew something. Maybe he saw something. Maybe he overheard something. He was a connected, inquisitive guy. It's too coincidental otherwise." Chris hadn't yet found the connection, but he'd asked around at practice and determined that all five boys had Abe Yomes for Language Arts. "He was the one who asked me about Wyoming."

"So it was a lucky break he died."

"No, it wasn't," Chris shot back, cringing inwardly. He couldn't think of Abe's death that way, and before Abe had died, Chris had decided to immerse himself in Wyoming trivia, in order to answer Abe's many questions.

"It's a suicide, no question, according to the locals. Yomes hung himself. His boyfriend told them he had a history of depression."

The Rabbi interjected, "Curt, I understand that Yomes was African-American and gay. Did you see any facts that would suggest the possibily of a hate crime? Any evidence of a neo-Nazi group? Are you seeing anything like that at the high school, or on the team?"

"Not yet," Chris answered, then turned back to Alek. "Let the locals think whatever they think. Yomes told me about his depression himself, but it sounded like it was in the past. I'm going to follow up."

"But Yomes has no connection to the baseball team, does he?"

"Other than he taught my five guys? No, not that I know of, yet." Chris had been wondering if there was some secret connection there, maybe one of the players was in the closet, but he didn't have enough information on which to float a theory.

"Curt, I'm unconvinced." Alek shook his head. "We have bigger cases."

"The Oklahoma City bombing was the most deadly act of

domestic terrorism in the country. It doesn't get much bigger than that. In this political climate, with feelings against the government, it's only a matter of time until it happens again."

"We're not hearing anything. Nothing unusual, no chatter, no leads."

"That could mean they're good at it. Or a small group. Or a loner. I've got my eye on a few kids on the team, who spoke against the goverment in one of my classes. I did an exercise to see who felt that way. I'm asking for three days. Three more days, until the anniversary on the nineteenth."

Alek frowned. "Curt, you're killing me. You've made a name for yourself in the most dangerous operations. I can't believe you want this one, with a bunch of high-school kids. It's like Jump Street, for God's sake!"

"The hell it is," Chris said, simmering.

The Rabbi turned to Alek. "Let him see it through. We owe him that, don't we? After Eleventh Street?"

Alek kept frowning, but said nothing.

Chris thought back to the Eleventh Street Operation, in which he'd gone undercover as a Kyle Rogan, a low-level cocaine dealer, infiltrating a gang of violent dealers near Wilmington, Delaware, believed to have connections to the Sinaloa cartel. Chris had been about to make a "buy-bust" in a run-down house on Eleventh Street, but the moment of truth had come when the drug dealers had insisted that Chris sample the product, which was one of the few things that the movies actually got correct— undercover ATF and FBI agents were typically asked to sample the product to prove they weren't cops. In theory, it was otherwise illegal activity, or OIA, since the government had an acronym for everything. But refusing could endanger their lives. Chris had thought of another way out.

No can do, Chris/Kyle had said to the three thugs sitting opposite him, behind the black duffel bag of bricks wrapped in plastic, which the bearded drug dealer had split open with a key.

You won't try some? Why?

I can't. No liquor, no drugs. I'm a Muslim.

Who are you kidding? You're white as a sheet. A Ku Klux Klan sheet. The bearded dude had burst into coarse laughter, and so had his cohorts.

So? Chris/Kyle had-shrugged. *I'm a Muslim. Muslims can be white.*

I don't believe for one minute you're a Muslim, said a skinny black man on the end, the only African-American in the room.

So Chris/Kyle had launched into a recital of the most important passages of the Koran, which he had memorized in anticipation of being quizzed. It had convinced the thugs of his bona fides, and they made the buy. Afterwards, they'd left the house, where ATF agents had arrested them all, including Chris, to preserve his cover.

The Rabbi was saying, "Alek, look at it this way. If Curt is right, you come out looking like a rose because you gave him the approval. If he's wrong, everybody will understand why you gave him a freebie. It's win-win, for you."

Alek sighed heavily, then turned to Chris. "Three days. That's it."

Chapter Twenty-five

Chris walked next to the Rabbi past the well-maintained stone row houses, reflexively keeping his head down through Fairmount, an artsy city neighborhood with indie coffeehouses, historic pubs, and used bookstores, as well as the Philadelphia Museum of Art, Barnes Foundation, and Free Library. The Rabbi and his Portuguese wife, Flavia, were always nagging him to go to author lectures at the Free Library or folk dancing at the Art Museum, which would never, ever happen.

Chris was going to the Rabbi's for dinner only because he wouldn't take no for an answer, but Chris felt out of sorts. He was angry at Alek's attempt to shut down the operation, and Abe's death was beginning to haunt him. Heather was at the back of his mind, too, but he pressed her away as they reached the Rabbi's house, which was different from the others, since Flavia was an artist and had wanted their window trim to be purple, pink, and green.

"Flavia is so excited you're here," the Rabbi said, unlocking the front door.

"Me, too." They went inside, and Chris found himself surrounded by chatter, music, and delicious aromas of broiled fish.

Soft bossa nova music played on an old-fashioned stereo system, and the sound of laughter and women talking floated from the kitchen.

"And the girls are home," the Rabbi said, meaning his twin daughters, Leah and Lina, who shared an apartment in Center City.

"Terrific." Chris looked up as their chubby brown mutt, Fred, ran barking toward them, his long ears and pink tongue flying.

"We're home, honey!" the Rabbi called, bending down as the dog jumped up on his shins and got a scratch behind the ear.

"In the kitchen!" Flavia called back, and the Rabbi headed toward the back of the house with Chris and Fred on his heels. They walked through the large, funky living room, with its green tufted couch and hot pink chairs grouped around a glass coffee table covered with books, drawing pads, and colored pencils. The walls were a soft turquoise, and vivid oil paintings covered every square inch with abstract scenes of flowers, fruits, and pottery.

"Curt!" Flavia appeared at the threshold of her aromatic kitchen, threw open her arms, and hugged Chris, barely coming up to his chest because she was as short as the Rabbi.

"Hello, Flavia," Chris said, hugging her back. She felt warm and soft, and he breathed her spicy perfume and garlic smells from cooking. Inwardly, he struggled to cross the Chris/Curt divide to her, the family, and the house. It was an occupational hazard of an undercover cop to always be inside himself, but Flavia and the Rabbi reached into his heart and yanked until he gave it to them, so Chris surrendered as best as he could. At least he knew he wanted to, even though he was The Untouchable.

"How have you been, Curt? Long time, no see!"

"Wonderful, you?"

"Terrific. I'm so glad you could come. You know we love when you hang with us."

"I love to hang with you."

"Yet you won't come dancing with us? David told me he asks you."

"I can't right now—"

"You always say that!" Flavia pouted, pretending to be offended, her dark eyes flashing. Her features were beautiful in an exotic way, with a large curved nose, full lips, and striking cheekbones. Her figure was part of the same package, voluptuous in a flowing peasant dress. Black curls trailed freely to her shoulders, framing her lovely face.

"Curt!" the twins said in unison, looking up as they set the table. They were a matching mixture of Flavia and the Rabbi, with their mother's round brown eyes, the same dark curls, and a ready smile from their dad.

"Ladies!" Chris couldn't tell them apart for a minute, though he had known them a long time. He felt a pride in them as if they were his own daughters, which he knew was a ridiculous thought, even as he had it.

They laughed, coming over and giving him a quick hug. "I'm Leah, she's Lina," Leah said, smiling up at him.

"Wow! When did you two grow up?"

"When you got old!" Leah shot back, laughing.

"Curt, meet our friend Melissa Babcek." Lina gestured behind her, and a slim blonde came out of the pantry with some cans.

"Hi, I've heard a lot about you," Melissa said, and Chris realized that Flavia and the Rabbi were trying to set him up, yet again.

"Nice to meet you too. I'm—" Chris was about to say Chris Brennan, but he stopped himself. "Curt Abbott."

"I hear you're, like, the best ATF agent ever."

"Not exactly," Chris said, eyeing the Rabbi. "So much for confidentiality."

The Rabbi waved him off. "Don't give me that, Curt. She doesn't need clearance to know you're a star."

Chris laughed it off, and they all sat down to a delicious dinner of vegetarian risotto and roasted branzino, covered with tomatoes, onions, and red peppers. He wolfed down a second helping as the conversation circulated easily, lubricated by chilled Sancerre. Melissa was a nice woman, telling funny stories about her life as an associate at a big law firm, and although Chris gave the right responses and said the right words, he felt apart from everyone. It was as if he could go only so far but no further, and by the end of dinner, Chris could feel the Rabbi's eyes on him.

"Chris, let's go outside. I need a cigar."

"Sure, okay." Chris followed him from the kitchen, through a set of French doors, and out to their back patio, a flagstone rectangle framed by a privacy fence covered by ivy and climbing rosebushes. At the center of the patio was a table and wire chairs painted red, and on the table sat a blown-glass ashtray with a half-smoked cigar and a Bic lighter.

"Sit down, please." The Rabbi sat down, picked up his cigar, lit it, and took a long drag to bring it back to life. "So what did you think of Melissa?"

"I think she's a lovely young woman who will make some guy a great wife." Chris sat down.

"But not you?" The Rabbi's cigar flared orange-red, and he leaned back in his chair.

"Not me." Chris could see inside the kitchen through the glass doors, and Flavia and the three girls were talking, laughing, and feeding Fred bits of fish, which he kept dropping on the tile floor. A warm golden glow emanated from the kitchen, and soft jazzy music floated through the screen door.

"What's going on, Curt?"

Curt. Chris. He tried to reposition himself in space and time. "Nothing."

"I'm not buying that." The Rabbi tilted his head back and exhaled a wispy funnel of cigar smoke, which was swept away by the city air.

"Alek ticks me off. I appreciate your going to bat for me."

"Happy to do it, you know that. I think you're right."

"Thank you." Chris glanced inside the kitchen, through the window, and he could see Fred walking on his hind legs for more fish. The women burst into laughter.

"Why do you want to stay with the operation so much?"

"Like I said. Something's not right, and we've gotten away with too many peaceful Oklahoma anniversaries. We're pressing our luck and—"

"And that would be the party line."

"What do you mean?" Chris looked over, surprised at a new skepticism in the Rabbi's tone.

"Don't get me wrong, I believe you. But you've been undercover for years. There's no operation you turn down, no matter how big or how small. And this one, you reached for, as soon as that video came in. You wouldn't be denied."

"Is something the matter with that?" Chris felt stung. "I'm doing my job."

"Curt." The Rabbi took another drag on his cigar, and its thick ash flared at the fat tip. "As your boss, I appreciate your dedication and your commitment. But as your friend, I don't like it."

"Why?" Chris scoffed. "Don't treat me like I'm some cliché, the undercover burnout. I'm not that at all. I'm fine. I'm stable. I'm not showing any signs of PTSD."

"That's *exactly* what bothers me." The Rabbi's dark gaze narrowed behind his glasses. "You like undercover work too much. You don't want to leave it."

"Because I like what I do. I'm a workaholic, like you."

"No, wrong, I hated undercover work. You know why? I like who I am and I love my life. I love Flavia and the girls, and I even love that fat dog." The Rabbi gestured to the kitchen, but his gaze remained on Chris. "You like being under too much because it gives you an identity. Someone to be. A role to play."

Chris's mouth went dry, and the Rabbi's words resonated in

his chest. But he didn't know if he could admit it, not even to himself, much less to the Rabbi.

"I think that's why you want to continue this operation, and why you leapt on the opportunity. The operation was your idea, and you rammed the authorization down Alek's throat. That's why he's coughing it back up. You want to be under forever, that's what I worry about."

Chris didn't know what to say, so he didn't say anything. He wished he had a cigar so he had something to do with his hands, something that would distract him from the sweetly domestic scene on the other side of the window. It struck him that he'd lived his entire life on the wrong side of the window, with everyone else on the other side, the normal side, easy to see and within reach, but only through glass, separated from him. The Rabbi was right. Still Chris couldn't say anything.

"And the question is, if that's true, what do you do about it? The answer is simple—come in, for good. You can't start figuring out who you are until you get rid of Chris Brennan, Kyle Rogan, Calvin Avery, and the other aliases. They're not you. They're just roles you played. I want you to stop before you lose yourself."

Chris swallowed hard. "I'm not sure if that's possible," he said, quietly.

"Stopping or losing yourself?"

"Stopping." Chris knew the other one was possible. That, he knew.

"Of course it is." The Rabbi gestured at the kitchen window again. "You can have everything that I have. A wonderful wife, two great kids to drive you crazy, a dog on a diet—"

"What if I need to play a role to be the best agent possible?" Chris heard himself say. It must've been the wine, loosening him up.

"You don't. You're already the best agent possible. The rest is just dressing. Like clothes or a scarf. Overlay. The distinction is form over substance." The Rabbi eyed him. "And Curt, you're all substance. Always have been."

Chris warmed inside, almost believing him. "So I won't lose my superpowers?"

"No." The Rabbi chuckled.

"I met someone," Chris said, after a moment

"Really?" the Rabbi asked, intrigued. "Who?"

"One of the moms. Larkin's mother. Heather." Chris liked her name. It was so feminine. He hadn't said it aloud until this very minute.

"You like her?"

"Yes." Chris had to admit it. He liked Heather. He flushed. It felt like high school, which, in a way, it was.

"You're sure the son's not a suspect?"

"Pretty sure."

"You're not letting your feelings for the mom cloud your judgment about the kid, are you? I'd hate to see you get hurt."

"I'm sure."

"So then. You know the rules." The Rabbi emitted a puff of cigar smoke. "A man's got to do what a man's got to do."

Chris burst into laughter, like a relief of a pressure valve. He'd never gotten involved with any woman on an operation before, but he knew it happened. "I wouldn't do anything, and it's not going anywhere. Nothing can jeopardize this operation now that Alek's on my ass."

"But even wanting it, that's a step in the right direction." The Rabbi's expression softened. "It's good to want a relationship. You're getting older. You're entitled to a family."

Chris didn't know if he was entitled to a family. He had gotten this far without one.

"I want you to think about what I'm saying. Curt Abbott is one helluva guy, and I really like him. So does Flavia, and she's smarter than I am, and the girls, and Fred. Don't stay out because you're afraid to come in."

"I'm not," Chris shot back, but he wasn't sure which was in and which was out. To him, he was in, and they were out.

"Then why? Why this operation, really? This is just us, now. You're going toe-to-toe with Alek, for what?"

"I know why," Chris said, thinking aloud. "I want to protect my kids. These kids. One of them is mixed up in something, maybe more than one of them. But they're good kids and they can't know what they're getting into."

"You don't know that."

"True, but it's a hunch. They're young. Naïve. They're *all* unwitting." Chris felt a new conviction and heard the truth in his own words. Maybe the kids were standing in for him, for all of his boyhood. No one had protected him, and he knew how that had felt. Now he could protect them. He hadn't realized it until this minute, clarifying his mission anew.

"Then stay. And however it ends, I hope that woman is still there for you."

"We'll see." Chris checked his watch. "Gotta go."

Chapter Twenty-six

The neon sign glowed **REGAL CINEMA MULTIPLEX CENTRAL VALLEY**, and Chris joined the back of the crowd swelling into the theater, mostly teenage boys. He had learned from his audiotapes that Evan and Jordan were going to the movies tonight, and after he'd left the Rabbi's house, he'd had just enough time to wire himself. He'd taped the microphone to his chest under his polo shirt, and the controller was in his pocket so he could turn it off and on remotely, saving him hours of listening to irrelevant details of a target's everyday conversation.

Jordan and Evan shuffled ahead in the middle of the throng, visible because they were so tall, and Jordan had on his Musketeers baseball cap, worn twisted backwards. The crowd shifted forward, and Chris kept his eye on them as they went through the door. He watched them join the line at the concession stand, where every teenage boy was buying oversized tubs of popcorn and sodas.

Chris lingered at the back of the lobby, pretending he was reading the menu, which was endless, including nachos, hummus, and pizza. He couldn't remember what they sold in the movies when he was little; he'd been to the movies only once, as a child. He didn't even remember which movie he'd seen. All he remembered was that when he'd looked over, his foster mother's eyes had been teary. He hadn't had to ask why.

Evan and Jordan got their popcorn and sodas, headed to the ticket taker, and had their phones scanned, and Chris followed. Jordan and Evan went down the hall to the theater and went inside, and Chris let a few people pass before he entered and took the first seat on the left. He passed the next few hours watching the movie, a decibel-blasting superhero sequel, but in the back of his mind was his conversation with the Rabbi.

It's okay to want a relationship. You're getting older. You're entitled to a family.

After the movie was over, Chris got a bead on Jordan and Evan, heading toward the side exit. It was time to make his move, and he left his seat just as they were reaching the line. "Jordan, Evan!" Chris called to them, managing a look of surprise.

"Hi, Coach!" Jordan smiled, but he looked unusually drawn, and Chris flashed on the scene at practice this morning, remembering how upset they'd been over Abe's death.

"Yo, Coach," Evan said, already looking down at his phone, and the three of them left the theater together, squeezing into the hallway.

"How's your face feel, Jordan?" Chris gestured to the injury on his cheek, which had scabbed over.

"A lot better."

"Good. What did you think of the movie?"

"Awesome," Jordan answered.

"Totally," Evan answered, still looking at his phone. They trundled out to the main lobby, to the exit doors, and out of the building. People passed them, lighting cigarettes, checking phones, and pulling out car keys as they left for the parking lot.

Chris stayed close to Jordan. "Hey guys, you want to go out and grab a coffee or something? It's not that late, and I know you've had a tough day, after what happened to Mr. Y. We could go next door. We don't have to move the cars."

"Okay." Jordan smiled with a shrug.

"Why not?" Evan said, texting.

The night was dark and cool, and they walked the length of the multiplex with Evan texting on his phone. Jordan fell into step with Chris, who put his hand in his pocket, found the remote control for the wire, and pressed ON. "It's so sad about Mr. Y," Chris said after a moment.

"Yeah." Jordan walked with his head down, the flat lid of his backwards-baseball cap pointing up at a moonlit sky.

"How are you feeling about it?"

"It's sad, like you say."

"Obviously I didn't know him that well, but he took the time to welcome me. Suicide is a terrible thing, an awful thing."

"I know. How can you *hang* yourself? That's, like, hard to do."

"It must be." Chris didn't explain that, in fact, the opposite was true. It wasn't that difficult to hang yourself, and if the ligature were positioned correctly, it wouldn't be suffocation that would be fatal, but the breaking of the hyoid bone at the base of the throat, crushing the windpipe.

"God, it sucks," Jordan said, as they approached the restaurant. "It's so hard to believe that Mr. Y is dead. It's, like, final. You can't change it or take it back."

"Right, I know." Chris had actually had the same thought about death. That it was final, and forever. "It's difficult to wrap your mind around."

"Is this place any good?" Evan asked, still texting as Chris opened the door to the restaurant, which was packed.

"My mom likes it," Jordan said, and Chris felt a twinge at the mention of Heather. He pointed at an empty table, and a harried waitress gave him a nod. They went over and sat down at a tiled circle, fitting with the island scheme of the restaurant.

Chris eyed both boys, but only Jordan was paying attention.

"Sorry you had to practice this morning, guys. I was surprised that Coach Hardwick held it after the news about Mr. Y."

Jordan nodded sadly, but didn't reply. Chris could see Heather's features in her son's face, the warmth of her eyes and the shyness of her smile. He wondered what it would be like to have Jordan as a son. Or to have a son at all.

Evan glanced up. "Coach Hardwick holds practice, no matter what. I think his wife could die and we'd still have practice."

"Jordan, Evan, you know, the school's worried that any time you have a suicide, you guys are going to start getting strange ideas. They're going to have grief counselors there on Monday." Chris wasn't lying. He'd already gotten a flurry of emails from Dr. McElroy informing the CVHS community of Abe's death and setting up preventative counseling for CVHS students. "Do I have to worry about you guys? You wanna talk about it?"

"You don't have to worry about me, Coach." Jordan managed a smile.

"Me, either," Evan said, still texting away, his thumbs flying.

"I'm glad to hear that. But just let me know, don't be ashamed. Everybody gets down sometimes, when you just don't feel like yourself." Chris sensed he was talking about himself, but stayed on track. He needed information about his four suspects—Evan, Raz, Trevor, and Dylan. "You know, being new, I don't know the team very well, but what about some of the other guys? Raz, for example. And Trevor and Dylan?"

Jordan sighed. "Raz was upset, but I don't think he would ever do anything like that. I hope not, but since his dad died, you know, he's been down."

"No way, he wouldn't." Evan shook his head as he texted.

"I'll keep an eye on Raz. I know he's got some trouble at home he's dealing with, so this is a hard time. But I've got his back."

"Good, Coach." Jordan smiled, and Chris wanted him reassured so that the two boys didn't become close again. Raz was on Chris's list of suspects and had chosen the Bill-of-Rights side in Chris's classroom exercise. The profile of his suspect would be a kid with a grudge against the government, which had been Timothy McVeigh's motivation in blowing up the Alfred P. Murrah Federal Building in Oklahoma City.

"Jordan, tell me about Trevor. He's a helluva third baseman, and I got to talk to him a little at the game. What's he like?"

"Beef, he's a nice guy," Jordan answered, as the waitress came over with a tray of water glasses, setting them in front of them with a hurried "be right back," which made Chris think about Heather.

I quit my job!

Suddenly Evan looked up from his phone with an excited grin. "Dude! Looks like Brittany freed up. She wants me to come over."

Jordan's gaze shifted sideways. "You mean Miss Booty Call?"

"Ha! Coach, you mind if I bounce? She goes to a different school, and I never get to see her. Check her out." Evan scrolled through his phone, swiping through photos, then held one up of a pretty blonde making a duck-face kiss. "I mean, you feel me? This girl is haaawwwt!"

"Go ahead, Evan. As between me or her, I'd choose her too." Chris turned to Jordan. "I'm assuming you guys took Evan's new car. If you did, I can take you home, so Evan can go."

"Uh, okay." Jordan smiled. "We did take his car. He loves that car. He'd sleep in it if he could."

"Dude, you love my ride, too." Evan jumped up. "Coach, sorry. Later, Jordan." Evan took off, leaving Jordan alone with Chris, who paused before he resumed the conversation.

"How about Evan? You ever worry about him becoming depressed?"

"No, are you kidding?" Jordan looked at Chris like he was crazy. "He has too much to live for. He's dating, like, four girls in rotation."

"He's got a varsity and a JV?"

"Hell, he's got a farm team."

"Ha!" Chris wanted to know more about Evan, who was on his suspect list. "He seems like a pretty happy guy to me. Is he?"

"Yes, totally. He's, like, so popular."

"But Mr. Y was popular, so that doesn't tell you anything."

"Right." Jordan's face fell.

"What's Evan like?"

"Like what you see. Easy, cool. I'm not that friendly with him, but he's got nothing to be bummed about. His family is rich, and his dad is a big deal. They belong to the country club my mom works at, er, quit from."

"She told me. Good for her."

"Right." Jordan brightened. "She hated that job."

Chris felt fleetingly the warmth of the bond he shared with Jordan, especially in Heather, but he put her out of his mind. "So does Evan have a lot of friends outside of school?"

"Not friends, just girls. If it's a girl, he's there. They come to him."

Chris moved on, so it wouldn't seem like an interrogation. "Tell me about Trevor. What's he like? He seems so outgoing."

"He is. He gets along with everybody. He's a farm boy."

"You mean he lives on a farm?" Chris didn't understand. He had researched Trevor online and learned that the boy lived with his family in a development in Central Valley. Trevor's social media was sparse except for the weight lifting videos.

"Oh, whoops, I guess I shouldn't have said anything." Jordan grimaced. "It's, like, secret."

"What's secret about it? I won't tell anybody."

"Trevor doesn't live at the address they have for him at school." Jordan leaned over. "Like, it's the wrong address in the Booster directory. His family has a farm but it's outside the school district, near Rocky Springs. They told the school he lives at his uncle's address in town so he could go to CVHS."

"Is it a dairy farm or what?" Chris's ears pricked up. If Trevor lived on a farm, he could have access to fertilizer and a place to store it. But he'd need fifty bags or so to make an IED powerful enough to blow up a building, which would explain why he'd be stealing more from Herb Vrasaya's farm.

"I don't know, I've never been to the farm. But that's how he got so big. He can bench press, like, 250. He's a monster."

"What's his personality like? You don't think he would be the kind of guy to get depressed, do you know?"

"Nah. The only thing is he's got a temper."

"I saw, at the party. How about Dylan?" Chris was ticking off the names on his suspect list. He'd pump Jordan until he struck oil.

"Dylan's a nice guy."

"He seems it." Chris was starting to see the shortcomings of his unwitting. Jordan liked everything and everybody, and Chris would have to pull teeth to get better information. "But he's the quiet type, isn't he?"

"Totally. He works so hard. He gets really good grades. Evan thinks he's a total geek."

"Do you know Dylan?"

"Yes, him, I know. He played JV with me, too. He's not superhard-core into baseball. Don't get me wrong, he's a great player and I don't want to dis him to you—"

"No, I get that."

"He plays because his parents make him, and he's so tall, like the tallest on the team, and it helps him in the outfield. And he can hit. His mechanics are good."

"Right. Where are they tonight, Dylan and Trevor? Do you know?"

"I don't know."

"Who do they hang with?"

Jordan shook his head. "Nobody I know. They're both, like, loners. Trevor especially. He never goes anywhere because he has so many farm chores."

"Where's the farm?"

"On Skinny Lane Road. It's called Skinny Lane Farm. I remember the name because Raz said it should be called Meathead Lane Farm, for him." Jordan sipped his water, chuckling.

"How about Dylan? Who's he friendly with?" Chris's research on Dylan's social media had shown that the boy had only six friends who were people and the other fifteen were scientific organizations like CERN, NASA's Hubble Space Telescope, and Curiosity Rover. Chris thought it didn't get lonelier than having an inanimate object for a friend.

"Nobody, he studies all the time. Like on the bus to away games, he puts his headphones on and keeps studying. Once I asked him what he was listening to, and he said 'nothing, I just want to block you guys out.' "

Chris had another thought. "I wonder why he's not in our AP Government class. He must be on the AP track, right?"

"Yes, but he took Government last year. He takes everything ahead of everybody else. He's on an independent study now. He took Physics last year, too."

"How about Chemistry?" Chris asked, since Dylan's interest in the sciences was a red flag.

"I don't know." Jordan shrugged. "Come to think of it, Dylan is kind of weird. Maybe you should be worried about him, with depression and all. He seemed weird this morning when we heard about Mr. Y. Everybody was upset, but he wasn't. He told all of us about it like it was a news story."

"Yeah, I noticed that," Chris said, meaning it. Dylan showed a marked lack of empathy when he told everyone about the scene at the high school, with the crying teachers. In contrast, Raz had been holding back tears, his face mottled with emotion, not to cry in front of the team.

Jordan wheeled his head around. "Wonder what happened to the waitress? Maybe we should just go?"

"Okay, it's getting late. Your mom's probably wondering where you are." Chris didn't want to arouse Jordan's suspicions and he was looking forward to seeing Heather again. Maybe they'd have another talk over water and cookies.

"No, not tonight." Jordan stood up. "She's out on a date."

"Oh, good," Chris forced himself to say, rising.

Chapter Twenty-seven

For Heather, the check couldn't come fast enough. She hadn't ordered dessert, but her date had, oblivious to the fact that she was having a horrible time. She sat across from him, muting him in her mind, like a commercial she couldn't fast-forward. He was decent-looking and had a great job, but she didn't want looks or even money. What she wanted was a man who was interested in *her,* and she knew that her date wasn't interested in her by the appetizer, a mixed green salad.

It only went downhill from there, when, in response to her *so what do you do for a living,* he started mansplaining title insurance. They'd ordered entrees, and she'd listened to him drone on through her poached salmon with yogurt dill dressing. She could've put up with it if he had just asked one question about her. That was her test for first dates—whether he learned as much about her as she did about him.

But by the time the check came, he still had no idea whether she had children, a job, a dog, or preexisting illness. That didn't stop him from pawing her in the parking lot on the way to her car and forcing his tongue into her mouth. She pushed him away, got in the car, and drove home, looking forward to taking off her bra, getting into her pajamas, and watching her DVRed shows, which were backing up like a Things To Do List for the unemployed.

Suddenly her cell phone rang, and she glanced at the screen, surprised to see it was Raz, so she answered. "Raz? How are you?"

"Sorry to call you so late, Ms. Larkin."

"That's okay." Heather didn't know what was going on, but Raz sounded upset, his voice shaky.

"I've been calling Jordan. Do you know where he is?"

Heather hesitated. She didn't relish being the one to tell Raz that Jordan was with Evan. She wondered if he and Jordan had talked since practice. Jordan had been upset about Mr. Y's suicide and had spent the day in his room, on his computer and doing homework. She told Raz, "I think he's at the movies. Maybe he has his phone on silent."

"Who did he go with?"

"Evan, I think," Heather answered, because it couldn't be avoided. She didn't know what Raz could have expected after he'd punched Jordan. She heard a woman's voice in the background, probably Susan, but the words were indistinct, like it said on closed captioning. WORDS INDISTINCT.

Raz cleared his throat. "See, uh, I wanted to say I'm sorry to you, too. I lost my temper and I didn't mean to hit Jordan, I'm sorry about that."

"Well, that's nice of you to say. But I think Jordan is the one you owe the apology to."

"That's why I'm trying to reach him."

"Well, good. It's between the two of you. You have to make it right."

"I know, I went too far."

"Yes, you did." Heather felt a pang of sympathy for him, he sounded so upset. But still, she'd been happier knowing that Jordan was out with Evan and she sensed Jordan had been looking forward to it, too. Not that he'd told her as much, but he'd put on a clean T-shirt and jeans. And Heather couldn't believe it when she saw Jordan and Evan driving off in a BMW that cost more than she made all last year.

"Mrs. Larkin, my mother wants to talk to you."

"Okay, no problem, good night."

"Good night," Raz said miserably, then Susan came on. "Heather? I'm so sorry about what Raz did. I hope you accept his apology."

"Of course I do," Heather said, softening up. She felt guilty that she hadn't gone up to Susan at the game. "I'm so sorry about Neil, and you have my sympathies. I know that couldn't have been easy for you yesterday."

"Right, thanks." Susan sounded shaky, too. "It's been so hard, and I'm not saying this is an excuse, but Raz has been very upset about losing his father."

"I can't imagine," Heather said, though she could. Jordan never knew his father, but he still never punched his friend in the face.

"He's been so angry lately and withdrawn, and he spends a lot of time in his room on the laptop. I'm beginning to worry what he's up to." Susan's tone turned vulnerable, which surprised Heather. They didn't know each other at all.

"Jordan spends a lot of time in his room too. They all do. They're growing up."

"I know, but this is different. I think he's withdrawing and I don't know who he's online with, all the time."

"Tell me about it." Heather steered onto Central Valley Road, almost home.

"I hope that what happened won't affect his friendship to Jordan. I always liked that they were friends. Jordan is such a good influence on Raz."

"Thank you." Heather didn't think Jordan should have to raise Raz, but whatever. The traffic on Central Valley was light since most of the businesses were closed, the storefronts darkened and their signs turned off. Only the Friendly's sign was still on, blasting into her apartment. She always thought, *Not so Friendly, are you?*

"Heather, I need to ask you a favor. I'm hoping there's something you could do to facilitate things between the boys. You could broker a peace."

"How?" Heather asked, unprepared for the request. Susan had a big job at ValleyCo, so maybe she was used to asking for things. Heather had always wished she could be more like that. She never asked anybody for anything. She relied on herself. She *waited.* As Dr. Phil would say, *How's that working for you?*

"Please talk to Jordan and tell him that Raz is having a hard time. I don't know if you heard, but his brother Ryan was arrested last night for vandalism, and that's upsetting everybody."

"Oh, my," Heather said, as if she hadn't heard, though she had.

"I hope you'll try to just get us through this time. It's a rough patch and I think Jordan would really be key to helping Raz. Jordan hasn't answered his calls."

"He was at the movie, so maybe he didn't get it."

"Raz has been calling him all afternoon, too. And texting. Jordan's not responding. He would've apologized to him at practice but for the news about Mr. Y. It's so terrible. I feel like we're all in a bad patch lately, don't you?"

"In a way, yes. I just left my job." Heather reached her apartment building and turned left into the driveway, then had a thought. "Susan, you work for ValleyCo, don't you?"

"Yes, I'm Marketing Manager."

Heather hesitated, then thought of Dr. Phil. "Do you know of any openings, for me?"

Chapter Twenty-eight

Mindy scrolled through Facebook on her phone in bed, not bothering to comment on the funny animal videos, baby pictures, or inspirational sayings. Usually she was a Facebook slut, liking all her friends' posts and counting the likes on her posts. But not tonight. She was completely preoccupied, waiting for Paul to come home. He was late, the second night in a row. And again, he'd only texted, **got held up at the hosp, sry.**

She kept scrolling, watching the posts flip by like a slot machine. She remembered when she used to read in bed, but Facebook had replaced books. She'd been happier back then, but that could have been a coincidence. Finally she heard Paul's car pull into the driveway and glanced at the bedside clock: 12:15.

The house was quiet, and Mindy waited for him to get inside, so that when he finally did, she could almost hear the mechanical *ca-chunk* of his key turning in the lock downstairs, then the slight squeak of the front door opening, and the comforting sealing sound as it was shut and the deadbolt thrown. She knew Paul's routines so well, the way a wife does a husband's, so that she knew he would drop his keys jingling on the console table, which he did, then his messenger bag on the chair beside the console table, *thud,* then he'd turn off the light she'd left on for him, and last would come a sigh, which she used to think of as a sigh of contentment. But after he'd had his affair, she wondered if his sigh was one of resignation, like, *I'm home, having no other choice.*

Mindy focused her attention on Paul's heavy tread on the steps. One footfall then the other, each beat like the tick of a clock, signaling that she was running out of time on a decision. She hadn't decided what to do about the mysterious jewelry charge. She could let it go or she could confront him—but she couldn't be accusatory, she had to use I-words, and not point her finger, literally. Their ground rules had been laid down by their marriage counselor, though Mindy couldn't believe that her husband was threatened by her manicured fingernail.

Mindy knew that when she forgave Paul, she was letting him off the hook, but she didn't want him thinking that he was off the hook forever. She had consulted a divorce lawyer, unbeknownst to him even to this day, and the lawyer had told her about the "one free bite" rule, which was the law in Pennsylvania with respect to dog bites—every dog gets one free bite before the owner is liable. Well, her dog had had his free bite, and after the next one, he was getting neutered.

Mindy tried to make a decision. To confront or not to confront? The footfalls disappeared, which meant that Paul was crossing the carpeted hallway, then he materialized in the doorway, looking tired, though she didn't know if that was an act.

"Hey honey, sorry I'm late," Paul said, flashing her a tired smile, though he barely met her eye.

"It's okay." Mindy's instant impression was *he's hiding something.* He was tall, a trim six-footer with dark hair going prematurely gray, and it looked slightly greasy, since he had a nervous habit of raking his hair. His dark brown eyes were small, set far apart, and slightly hooded for a forty-five-year-old, with deep crows'-feet. Mindy always thought he had the weight of the world on his shoulders, being an oncology surgeon, but now she was wondering where he had been. She asked him, lightly, "What kept you?"

"The last case took forever. My feet are killing me."

"You poor thing. What was it?"

"The case?" Paul slid out of his suit jacket, which he tossed on the cushioned bench at the foot of the bed. "Lawson. I think I told you about him. He'll make it, Thank God."

"Great. I don't remember you mentioning a Lawson. What was the problem?"

"Honey, you know I don't like to talk about my cases. Let me leave it at the hospital, please." Paul came around the bed and gave her a quick peck on the cheek.

"Mm, okay." Mindy received his kiss like a happy wife, though she sniffed him like a hound dog. Or maybe a cadaver dog. Was their marriage dead or alive? Was it buried under some rocks, waiting to be rescued?

"How was your day?" Paul kicked off his shoes.

"We had some bad news."

"What?" Paul slid out of his tie and threw it on top of his suit, then began to unbutton his shirt around his growing paunch, which pleased Mindy more than it should have. She hated that Paul did nothing to stay thin, which was metabolically unfair. Plus he would've been dieting if he were having another affair. Last time, he'd started going to a gym and dyeing his hair, a Hubby Renaissance that would've tipped off any wife but her.

"You know Mr. Y, Evan's Language Arts teacher? He committed suicide."

"Whoa." Paul frowned. "That's terrible. How?"

"I know, isn't it? He hung himself." Mindy felt terrible about Mr. Y's death, but she was happy to have some actual news to tell Paul. Ever since the affair, she'd worried that she was boring.

She tried to think of stories that happened to her during the day, just to have something to tell him. Sometimes she even made them up. *See, I'm not just a housewife. I'm fascinating!*

"Wait. Language Arts is English, right?"

"Right."

"Why don't they call it that?"

"Progress?" Mindy answered, as Paul slid out of his pants, hopping around in his socks to stay on balance. She bit her tongue not to tell him to sit down when he took his pants off, because he always said she sounded like his mother. She wondered if every man married his mother, then hated his wife for being his mother, or if he didn't marry his mother, then he would eventually act like such a child that he would turn his wife into his mother.

"Be right back." Paul stripped to his undershirt and boxers, then went into the bathroom and closed the door behind him, which he never did. Hmmm.

Mindy eyed her phone without seeing a word. She realized she was tallying the clues about whether Paul was having another affair, like an Infidelity Ledger. In the No Affair column he was *gaining weight,* and in the Divorce column was *home late, lame explanation, oddly tired, shut the bathroom door, and mysterious jewelry charge.* Mindy heard him washing his face, buzzing his teeth clean, flushing the toilet, then he left the bathroom and was back in the bedroom.

"God, I'm beat," Paul said, which Mindy knew was marital code for *I don't want to have sex.* He walked around the bed, climbed in, and pulled up the covers with a grunt. Of satisfaction? Of pain? Why hadn't she noticed before that he made so many noises?

"Me, too," Mindy said, which communicated, *I don't want to have sex either, so don't sweat it, I won't hold this one against you—unless you don't want to have sex because you just had sex with someone else. In which case, I've got a divorce lawyer who's dying to take half of your money, and I'm keeping Evan and the house. And I'm melting your Porsche for scrap metal.*

"How was your day?"

"Fine, but it's so sad about Mr. Y. The school is having grief counselors on Monday, and Evan was upset about it, too. He really liked Mr. Y. He spent most of the day in his room."

"Bastard!"

"Who? Evan?"

"No, the teacher." Paul inched down in bed. "What kind of teacher does that? He's not thinking about the kids."

"Well, I think people who commit suicide are in despair. They don't see a way out."

"Yes, there is one. Work through your problems like an adult."

"It's not that easy—"

"Of course it is. Mindy, you're too soft."

Mindy cringed. She heard everything he said as a criticism of her weight, ever since he told the therapist he wanted her to lose thirty pounds. She had to stop the drinking, that's what did it, the sugar. Then the thought struck her. She was too soft, and Paul was too hard.

"I see my cases, like Lawson tonight, fighting for his life. If these people spent one day in my OR, they'd see what life is worth. Everything."

Mindy didn't reply, because he didn't need any encouragement to talk anyway. She *was* too soft. Her hand went to her tummy, and she squeezed the roll under her T-shirt. She held it like a security blanket, trying to decide whether to confront him. He seemed irritable tonight. Maybe he really had been at the hospital.

"People don't have a governor anymore. They do whatever they please. They don't control themselves. They don't think of the consequences. They lack discipline. Willpower."

Mindy cringed again. Once Paul had told her that she was fat because she didn't have willpower.

"So what's the school going to do for a *Language Arts* teacher now? What about the class? These are high-school juniors. Can't screw with their grades right now." Paul turned over, his back to her.

"I suppose they'll figure out something." Mindy switched off the bedside lamp, plunging the bedroom into darkness, the way Paul liked it. He would've been perfectly content to sleep in a cave, and she used to call him Batman. The consolation prize was that she had custom curtains made with a lovely Schumacher fabric that she'd used for the headboard, bench, and two side chairs.

"Good night, honey."

"Paul, there's something I wanted to mention," Mindy said, making her decision to confront him.

"I know, I forgot to bring up the recycling bin when I came in. Does it really matter?"

"No, it's not that." Mindy lightened her tone, as if she were a violinist playing a Stradivarius instead of a wife asking her husband a legitimate question.

"What is it?" Paul said, staccato, and Mindy wished she could see his face, but she couldn't. He was turned away, and it was dark, the only bright spot in the room was his undershirt.

"I was going through the Visa bill and I noticed a charge I didn't understand."

"Like what?"

"A three-hundred-twenty-seven-dollar charge at the jewelers, you know, the one in that strip mall? Do you know if that was Evan or you? Because if it was Evan, I told him to ask me before he bought any more jewelry."

Paul fell silent a beat. "That was my charge."

"For what?" Mindy felt relieved and nervous, both at once, and it was a struggle to maintain her falsely light tone. He wasn't denying it, which was a good sign. It went into the No Affair column on the Infidelity Ledger.

"Carole's birthday, remember? The new secretary? I got her a fancy picture frame. I picked it up on the way to the hospital. I thought I paid cash for that, but I was short that day. I charged it."

"Oh, well, thanks." Mindy's chest eased. That was a reasonable explanation, and more importantly, a verifiable one. She could double-check Carole's birthday. She used to note all of the staff's birthdays to buy them their gifts, but after therapy, they decided that Paul should buy his own gifts, since he never liked what she picked out anyway.

"It really bothers me that you do that," Paul said coldly, after a minute.

"Do what?" Mindy said, but she knew. *Here it comes.*

"You question me."

"I wasn't questioning you." Mindy hated Paul's habit of construing every question as an accusation. Except this time it was.

"You *were* questioning me. You're questioning me all the time. I mean, I do a nice thing, handle my own people myself, even though I have *no time.* I got the present myself, and here you are, fly-specking the credit cards."

"I'm entitled to that—"

"No, you're not, you're not at all." Paul huffed. "What the hell, Min? I'm walking on eggshells around here!"

"*I'm* the one walking on eggshells, not you." Mindy would never understand how he always accused her of things he did, but he got it out first, so he won.

"I don't deserve this, not in the least. I get called in on a Saturday, no less, and I work my ass off. I'm in the OR all day, then this pain-in-the-ass daughter of one of my cases is asking me four hundred questions. I barely get dinner and when I finally get to bed, you question my integrity."

Mindy rolled her eyes, since he was turned away. Sometimes she gave him the finger behind his back or when they were on the phone. "Look, I'm sorry, but you can understand it—"

"No I can't."

"A jewelry store charge? From the *same store*?"

"Okay, listen, Min." Paul flopped over in the darkness, facing her. "You have to let it go. We've been through the mill. We've worked through it and we did everything we're supposed to do. We're past it now."

"Are we?" Mindy heard herself say, her genuine voice poking through her self-editing, like a blade of grass peeking through a crack in a pavement.

"Yes, we absolutely are. I love you." Paul's tone softened, and Mindy felt her heart ease.

"I love you, too. I really do."

"Okay, so remember that, Min. You love me, I love you."

"But I worry—"

"So, don't. Don't worry so much. You have absolutely nothing to worry about." Paul reached out, pulling her to him for a hug.

"Well, good." Mindy hugged him back, burying her face in his undershirt, which was when she realized something. He didn't smell like he'd been in the OR. Those odors always clung to his undershirt, an acrid antibacterial tang and even the metallic scent of blood. And he always took his undershirt off when he'd been in the OR, a habit he probably didn't even know he had. Then she thought back to when he'd first come in the bedroom. His hair had been greasy, but he hadn't had helmet head from his surgical cap, like he always did. She would've bet money that he hadn't been in any OR tonight.

"Good night, honey." Paul kissed her again on the cheek, then flopped back over.

"Good night." Mindy lay in the darkness, looking up at the ceiling, her heart sinking as she added another two items to the Divorce side of the Infidelity Ledger.

Which only made her think about what she would do next.

Chapter Twenty-nine

Chris hunched over his computer and watched the videotape of Trevor Kiefermann at the team party, his suspicions beginning to focus on the boy because of what Jordan had told him. Chris had called the office to see if the Kiefermanns or Skinny Lane Farm was registered with Homeland Security to purchase and store ammonium nitrate fertilizer, but he hadn't gotten a call back yet. It always frustrated him that it took so long to get answers, not like in the movies with split-second replies, magical indexes, and seamlessly shared intel. In truth, federal law enforcement too often functioned like any other government bureaucracy. Except that lives were at stake.

Chris watched the video, and the scene changed to Trevor standing in front of the gun case, telling his teammates about the weapons. The boy seemed to have a working knowledge of firearms, which was consistent with the profile of a domestic terrorist, though not dispositive. And Trevor and his family had lied to school authorities about his true address. That wasn't proof either, but it sent up red flags. It was likely that any bomber would be part of a conspiracy, even a family conspiracy like the Tsarnaevs in Boston and Bundys in Montana.

Chris eyed the screen, concerned. He didn't know Trevor's political leanings because the boy wasn't in his Government class, but there was an array of antigovernment groups on ATF's radar: neo-Nazis, Ku Klux Klan, skinheads, Nationalists, Christian Identity, Originalists, Constitutionalists, and militia groups. Plenty of them were in rural Pennsylvania, and Trevor and his family could belong to any one of them. Or be lone wolves.

Chris checked the clock, which read 2:03 A.M. He wasn't tired, but jazzed. He closed out the computer file and grabbed his phones, keys, and windbreaker on the way out. He hurried from the apartment, left the townhouse, and hustled to the Jeep as he thumbed his phone to Google maps and plugged in Skinny Lane Farm Rocky Springs PA.

Fifteen minutes later, he was driving the deserted streets of Central Valley, then leaving town behind as he headed north. The outlet malls and chain restaurants gradually gave way to open farmland, and he rolled down the car window. He passed barns and farmhouses set far from the road, their windows black. There was no traffic and no ambient light. The moon hid behind a dense cloud cover, and only Chris's high beams illuminated the road. Bugs dive-bombed in the jittery cones of light, and dark fields of new corn rustled in the chilly breeze.

He drove on and on, following the twists and turns, and the only sound was the coarse thrum of the Jeep's engine, the mechanical voice of the GPS app, and outside the window, the constant chorus of crickets. Chris's nostrils filled with the earthy scent of cow manure and the medicinal odor of chemical fertilizer, and he breathed deeply, letting his thoughts run free.

Scraps of memories floated into his consciousness, and they were times he didn't want to remember, especially not on the job. He wasn't a little boy anymore, a ten-year-old on a ramshackle farm in the middle of nowhere, the only foster son of the Walshes, chosen by the local DHS for their allegedly wholesome life.

You don't listen, boy.

Chris kept going as he approached the sign, SKINNY LANE FARM, HORSES BOARDED, SELF-CARE, at the end of a dirt road. Up ahead, the road bottomed in a compound that included a small gray farmhouse, nestled among two white outbuildings, a chicken coop, and a large red barn. He turned off his headlights and steered onto a narrow dirt road between vast cornfields. Corn was the primary crop fertilized with ammonium nitrate, but ammonium nitrate wasn't generally used by farmers on the East Coast, where humidity turned it to rock quickly, rendering it less spreadable. It wasn't impossible that Trevor's family could legitimately have ammonium nitrate fertilizer, and there was only one way to find out.

Chris traveled up the dirt road slowly, and when he was about a quarter of the way toward the house, he cut the engine. He got out of the car, closed the door, and stayed still for a moment, waiting for the bark of a dog. There was no sound. He ran down the road toward the house, turned into the cornfield so he wouldn't be seen, and kept going. It was pitch-black, and he ran with his hands in front of him, got the pattern of the rows, then angled to the right toward the main house. Bugs flew into his face, and dust filled his nostrils. He reached the end of the corn rows and peeked out. The farmhouse was to the right, and the barn and the outbuildings were to the left. There was still no barking dog, so he hurried from the cornfield, and ran to the barn, where the smell was unmistakable. Horses.

You don't listen, boy.

Chris used to love horses, one horse in particular, an old mare. The Walshes had been horse brokers, of the worse sort, and the mare didn't even have a name. She was a brown quarter-horse from some third-rate racetrack, on her way to a kill pen, for horsemeat to Canada or other countries. He had named her Mary, for which the Walshes had teased him.

Chris put the thoughts out of his mind as he walked down

the center aisle of the barn, four stalls on each side, and he could see the shadows of the horses, the graceful curve of their necks and their peaked ears wheeling in his direction. He hustled to the end of the barn, knowing that there would be a feed room and hayloft. He opened the door, slid out his phone, scrolled to the flashlight function, and cast it around. There was nothing untoward, only galvanized cans of feed, labeled with duct tape, Purina Senior, Flax Seed, Alfalfa Cubes.

The Walshes never had treats like alfalfa cubes, but he used to pull grass to feed to Mary, and she had loved it, following him everywhere. He would find excuses to stop his chores and groom her, pick her feet, or pull her mane, imagining she enjoyed the attention. It was when she developed a cut that started to fester that was the beginning of the end. But Chris refused to think about that now.

His flashlight found a stairwell in the corner, and he hurried up the stairs. He shined the flashlight around the neatly stacked bales of hay on both sides of the loft, next to a pile of extra feed. He went over to make sure nothing was hidden behind them, then hurried back downstairs and out the feed-room door. He glanced around, but there was no sound, except for the horses' occasional shuffling in their stalls. There was another door across the way, presumably the tack room. He opened the door, closed it behind him, and shined his flashlight on saddles, grooming boxes, and blankets, then shelves of the typical supplies—Ventrolin, Corona hoof dressing, and a white jar of Swat, a salve for wounds.

On impulse, Chris walked over, picked up the Swat, and unscrewed the lid, releasing the pungent smell, and for a second felt lost in a reverie of emotion. It all came rushing back to him then, and he couldn't stop it if he tried. His mare had cut herself on a nail on the fence, a cut that would've healed if he'd been able to treat her. It had been the height of summer, hot as hell, and the horseflies were biting the mare alive, laying eggs in the wound. All it would've taken to heal her was Swat, which he'd seen an ad for in one of the farm newspapers. The salve only cost nine dollars then, and it would've fixed everything.

Walsh wouldn't spend the money, and so one day, Chris had bought Swat himself with money he'd saved and covered Mary's wound, before he turned her out at night. But the telltale pink stain on her neck showed Walsh that Chris had been treating the wound, and Walsh had smacked him so hard that he went flying down the aisle of the barn. Then Walsh found the Swat, dug his dirty fingers inside, and smeared two pink globs on Chris's cheeks, like rouge.

You don't listen, boy.

Chris hustled out of the barn and went past the chicken coop, also well maintained. Ahead lay the two outbuildings, the first a white woodshed with a peaked roof. He went to the door, which had a galvanized turn handle, but stopped before he opened it. Going inside the shed was an unlawful search, and he never would have been able to get a subpoena. The fact that Trevor was on the baseball team, lived on a farm, and was the requisite height wasn't sufficient for probable cause.

Chris couldn't break and enter, under the law. Undercover ATF agents weren't allowed to engage in otherwise illegal activity, OIA. If they needed to engage in OIA, they were supposed to get prior approval, which was laughably impractical. Chris remembered the time he'd infiltrated a human-trafficking ring smuggling young women from the Philippines, and he'd been offered one of the girls. It not only revolted him, but it would've constituted OIA. He'd declined, coming up with what became a classic line around the office—*I never paid for it in my life.* He took a special pride when those traffickers were convicted and sent to jail for twenty years.

But with the outbuilding, Chris was willing to bend the rules. It wasn't locked, so he wasn't breaking in, and it could prevent an impending bombing. He opened the door, stepped inside, and flicked on his flashlight. He looked around for fertilizer or anything suspicious, but it looked normal, even first-rate. Just an old tractor and a Kubota front-end loader with keys in the ignition. Hanging neatly were pitchforks, brooms, shovels, a hedge clipper, blowers, and the like.

He left the shed and hustled ahead to the other outbuilding, with a similar type of door, but it was padlocked. The shed could be used to store fertilizer, it was a cool location and it would be prudent to be kept under lock and key. He didn't smell anything but ammonium nitrate fertilizer was odorless. Chris thought about breaking the padlock, but didn't. It would be discovered, and even so, he made a distinction between going through an open door and breaking into a locked one. It drove him crazy that law didn't always lead to justice, and often thwarted justice, like now.

Chris needed a work-around. The situation came up on undercover operations, and the way that ATF dealt with it was through a "walled-off" operation. Most common was when he knew there were suspects driving around with contraband or explosives, but they couldn't be stopped without blowing an agent's cover, so the higher-ups at ATF would call the local constabulary. The locals would then make a traffic stop on the vehicle, finding a broken taillight, cracked windshield, or expired inspection sticker. It happened every day, but Chris couldn't do it without a call to the Rabbi, and he couldn't get it done tonight. He turned from the door, which would stay locked another day.

And he ran back toward the Jeep.

Chapter Thirty

Mindy reached for her phone and touched the screen, which came to life—3:23 A.M. She had been awake since Paul had told her that the mysterious charge at the jewelry store was for Carole's birthday. Mindy hadn't been sure whether she wanted to know the truth, but she had reached a decision.

She thumbed to the calendar function, scrolled to March, and scanned the entries on her calendar, color-coded: red for family, blue for Boosters, pink for Hospital Auxiliary, and green for Miscellaneous. An entry for Carole's birthday would have been, Miscellaneous, but she scanned the entries with a sinking heart. There was no entry for Carole's birthday.

She scrolled to April, and there was no entry for Carole's birthday there either. She searched the calendar under "Carole," because she remembered entering the secretary's birthday, and the entry came up, October 23. Mindy got a sick feeling in the pit of her stomach. Carole's birthday wasn't last month. It hadn't even come yet. No amount of staring at the phone would change that fact. Paul had lied to her.

Tears came to her eyes, but she was more angry than sad. What did Paul think, that she wouldn't check the bill? How stupid did he think she was? Even brain-dead housewives can read Visa bills. Why did she let him handle all the money in the first place? In fact, she had offered to handle their household finances more than once, but Paul felt strongly that it was *his* money.

Mindy wondered how many other charges had gone unnoticed. Questions flooded her brain, and she had the sickening realization that it was happening all over again. Did he take her out to eat? Who was she? Was she married? The reason he'd gotten caught last time was that the nurse had started calling him. Maybe this time he'd wised up. Practice made perfect.

Mindy's phone blinked into darkness, and she glanced over at Paul, snoring soundly away. Then she remembered something he had said.

I thought I paid cash for that, but now I remember. I was short that day. I guess I charged it.

Mindy thought it was an odd thing to say. It got her thinking. Maybe *that* was his improvement, that he started paying cash. Maybe *that* was why she hadn't seen any other charges. He wasn't charging anymore. Her heartbeat quickened. It made perfect sense. If he was paying cash, he would have been using his ATM card to withdraw cash. She never checked those before because she'd been so focused on the charges.

Mindy got out of bed, padded out of the bedroom, and went back downstairs to the kitchen. She flipped on the light and went directly to the drawers in a pocket office off the kitchen, where they kept bank statements, which she had rifled through only this afternoon. She'd been looking for the wrong thing, for canceled checks and charges. She should have been looking at cash.

She went to the first stack of envelopes, which she kept in chronological order with the most recent on top. March was the first statement, and she grabbed the thick envelope, slid out the three pages, and scanned for cash withdrawals that looked unusual. Paul generally withdrew cash in two-hundred-dollar amounts, and she saw one on March 7, March 14, then March 21, and then another on March 28, also two hundred dollars. In other words, nothing unusual or suspicious.

She felt stumped. She replaced the March statements, refilled the envelope, and reached back for February. She withdrew the February statements, another three pages, and scanned them as well. There was a two-hundred-dollar cash withdrawal on February 1, 8, 15, 22, and 28. She noticed they were all around lunchtime at the same ATM, Blakemore Plaza, at the hospital. Again, not suspicious.

Mindy put the February statement back and reached into the drawer for the January statement. But when she pulled it out, she noticed that it wasn't from their joint account—it was a February statement from Evan's account. They had opened the account for him, and the balance was about $32,000. Evan deposited money he got from them and from Paul's wealthy parents, who had been generous with gifts for their only grandson. The statement was still sealed, since she never bothered to open them when they came in. Evan didn't bother either, evidently taking it for granted, defeating her purpose in opening the account in the first place. She could almost hear her father's voice, saying, *you have to teach him the value of money,* and that had been her intent, but somehow she ended up with a son who had affluenza.

Mindy tore open the envelope, which read at the top, **Dr. Paul & Mrs. Mindy Kostis in custodianship for Evan R. Kostis,** and she scanned down to the bottom for the balance, which was $22,918. That was a lower balance than she remembered, but she could have been mistaken. There had been no deposits that month, but oddly, there had been a withdrawal, in the amount of $5,000.

Mindy gasped. Why had there been such a large withdrawal, or any withdrawal at all? Who had withdrawn it? She, Paul, and

Evan were all authorized to make withdrawals, and no permissions were required. Mindy hadn't withdrawn the money, so that left Paul or Evan. She didn't know if Paul had withdrawn the money to buy his new girlfriend a present, or if Evan had withdrawn the money to buy whatever girlfriend he had a present.

Mindy felt flabbergasted. In the past, Evan had bought presents for his girlfriends at Central Valley and other high schools, probably five gifts in total, but he had never used his money to do it and the most he'd ever charged was three hundred dollars, which was when she'd laid down the law that he had to ask first. So what could Evan have possibly done with $5,000? Or Paul, for that matter?

She set the statement aside, went back in the drawer, and started looking for the previous statement, which she found, also unopened. She was kicking herself now. She'd simply assumed Evan's account was dormant.

She examined the envelope, postmarked February 12, then extracted the statement, scanning it. She spotted a withdrawal of $3,000 on January 16. She couldn't believe what she was seeing. Why would Evan take so much money out of his account? Why would Paul? How many gifts where they buying? What was going on? Where was all of Evan's money going?

Mindy's heart began to hammer. What was going on in her own house? Her own family? She set the statement aside, went back in the drawer, and rummaged until she found the December statement for Evan's account. She tore it open, pulling out the single-page statement with hands that had begun to shake. Again, on December 13, about a month previous, there was another withdrawal, for $2,000.

Mindy's mind raced with possibilities. Drugs? Gambling? She went back to the drawer, collected all of the statements from Evan's account, and opened every envelope, checking to see if there were any cash withdrawals. Half an hour later, she'd found none earlier than December.

Mindy sat cross-legged on the floor, the statements around her in a circle. So there had been three withdrawals, totaling $10,000 in cash, but she didn't know if they were by Evan or Paul. Her heart told her that they had to have been made by Paul, but she knew a way to answer her own question.

She returned the statements to their envelopes, put them back in the kitchen drawer, then hurried from the kitchen and headed for Evan's room.

She was going to get to the bottom of this, right now.

Chapter Thirty-one

Chris sped toward town, his head pounding. It drove him crazy that there could be ammonium nitrate fertilizer in the Kiefermanns' shed and he was leaving it behind. He'd already called and texted the Rabbi to set up a work-around, but the Rabbi hadn't called or texted back yet, and Chris suspected it couldn't happen until tomorrow or the next day. Which could be too late.

Chris accelerated down the country road, racing past dark farms and fields. He gripped the wheel tight, grinding his teeth and clenching his jaw. He *knew* he was right about a bomb plot at CVHS and he wasn't going to stop digging until he stopped *them*. He felt a rush of adrenaline that focused his thoughts and clarified his mission, a drive that dedicated him to a higher purpose—protecting people, saving lives, serving *justice*.

He glanced at the speedometer and saw he was nearing a hundred miles an hour. He let off the gas. Central Valley lay ahead, and he followed the route to Dylan McPhee's house. Chris had been making nocturnal rounds of the four suspects since he moved to town, regularly cruising their homes. Now he knew that with Trevor, he'd been staking out the wrong house, a split-level in Central Valley proper. No wonder he hadn't seen Trevor there. Trevor didn't live there. Chris was kicking himself, but it showed why an undercover needed an unwitting.

He took a right turn off the main road, then wended his way through the upscale Golfing Park neighborhood, where the homes were large, with a stone or brick façade. Most were built fifteen years ago, when the developers came in to support the outlet boom. He turned onto Dylan's street, Markham Road, and parked at the corner, giving him a diagonal view of the house, number 283, three doors down.

He cut the engine, not wanting to wake anyone up. The street was quiet and still. Houses lined up behind the hedges, and perennials sprouted through fresh mulch. Newer cars sat in the driveways, though some houses had garages. Several of the garage doors were left open, indicating that the residents felt safe and secure, but Chris knew otherwise. People thought no harm could ever come to them, but the harm was already here.

He sat eyeing Dylan's house, a standard four-bedroom on two acres, bordered by a high stone wall that enclosed a kidney-shaped pool and a small putting green—Chris knew from Google Earth, which had given him every detail of the homes he staked out. Dylan's bedroom was around the back, and the boy's was the only window that stayed lighted after the family had gone to bed. Chris had binoculars and he used them to see Dylan through the open curtains, the boy's head bent over the lighted screen of his laptop, sitting at his desk until almost one in the morning, every night.

Chris glanced at Dylan's window, but it was dark, which made sense since it was 4:15 A.M. The kid had to sleep sometime. Chris picked up his phone, thumbed to the camera function, enlarged the view, and took a picture, reviewing what he knew about Dylan's family. The father, David McPhee, was a workmen's comp lawyer in town who had no website and little social media. His mother was a dental hygienist, also in town, but she had no activity on social media, and the other kids were younger, Michael, age ten, Allison, age nine, who had been in the local newspaper for winning a spelling bee. There were two cars in the driveway; a green Subaru Outback and a new Honda Fit, a shiny eggplant color.

Chris had a bad feeling about the McPhee family, not because of anything he saw, but because of what he didn't. It was strange that even the mother wasn't on social media, especially with kids who had academic and sports success. It struck him as secretive, and he'd also noticed that the family only rarely went out, except to church on Sundays, attending United Methodist in Central Valley. Chris had been making the rounds to different churches, temporarily becoming the religion his suspects were, but so far, it had been impossible to keep track of everybody on Sunday morning, which was why he needed more manpower.

Suddenly, he spotted something in motion behind the hedges at the house next to the McPhees'. It was moving fast, maybe a deer. He reached inside the glove box, retrieved his binoculars, and aimed where the shadow had been. It took him only a second to focus the lens, and he saw something race across the McPhees' driveway behind the cars.

Chris watched through the binoculars, astonished. It was a person, and in the next minute, a figure climbed on top of the stucco wall and walked along the edge to the house, climbed a trellis affixed to the wall, and used it like a ladder toward the window. It had to be Dylan, because in the next minute, the boy reached his window and scrambled inside.

"Holy shit," Chris said under his breath. He kept his binoculars trained on the window as Dylan closed the sash. A moment later, the bluish light of the laptop screen went on, and the boy appeared in view, his profile silhouetted as he sat down at his desk.

Chris tried to make sense of what he had seen. He'd been here many nights and seen Dylan at the computer, but there had never been any suspicious activity. Dylan had obviously sneaked out somewhere, which didn't fit his nerdy profile. It wasn't inherently suspicious that Dylan was sneaking out, but the questions were obvious.

Chris kept an eye on the window, and Dylan stayed on his laptop. Chris wished that he could legally get inside the kids' computers, but again, the law thwarted him. He didn't have probable cause for a subpoena and even the Rabbi wouldn't let him go phishing, that is, sending the boys a false link to hack into their computers. Again Chris understood the reason for the law, but it kept thwarting him when he was trying to save lives. He would just have to keep investigating the old-fashioned way, around the clock.

Chris waited, watching, and in the next few minutes, Dylan got up from his desk and disappeared from view. The laptop screen blinked to darkness, and the window went black. Chris stayed waiting and watching, just in case anything else happened. After twenty minutes, he turned on the ignition, pulled out of the space, and left the street, heading home with another set of questions to answer.

The anniversary of the Oklahoma bombing was less than three days away.

Chapter Thirty-two

Mindy reached the door to Evan's room, listening. No sound came from inside, so she twisted the knob as quietly as she could and entered. Moonlight shone through the open window, and she could see the familiar form of her son, his breathing soft and regular. Evan's iPhone was recharging on his night table, and she tiptoed over, unplugged it, then backed toward the door, and slipped outside, closing it again.

She hurried across the hall into Paul's home office, then ducked into its bathroom, and closed the door behind her. She didn't know Paul's phone password, but she knew Evan's—and Evan didn't even know she knew. She had been curious who he was texting all the time, so one day, when he didn't realize she was looking, she'd watched him plug his password into his phone. A not-so-dumb housewife, after all.

She sat on the toilet lid and touched the phone screen, then plugged in the passcode 0701, the birthday of their old Lab, Sam. The passcode worked, revealing the home screen, a photo of Miley Cyrus in a wacky outfit, with her tongue out and showing a dream-catcher tattoo on her side. Mindy thumbed to the text function and scanned the list. The boys' names jumped out at her because there were so few of them and they were his teammates—Jordan, Trevor, Raz. Mindy didn't bother to look at those texts because Evan wasn't buying presents for his teammates. Then she had a second, scary thought. What if Evan was doing drugs and buying them from one of the boys? She didn't know Jordan or Trevor very well, but Raz was a wacko and his brother had just been arrested.

Mindy was just about to take a screenshot of the people Evan texted with, but she realized that if she did that and sent it to herself, Evan could tell from his Sent email box, so she got her phone and took a picture of the screen, then scrolled down and took another picture, then another, and finally a fourth, until the names finally started to repeat. She couldn't believe how many people Evan texted with. It was a miracle that he got anything else done.

Mindy started with the girls, opening the text from the first girl, Brittany, and reading the text bubbles:

> **Brittany: where r u? i thot u were coming over**
>
> **Evan: cant**
>
> **Brittany: why not? what r u doing?**
>
> **Evan: movies**
>
> **Brittany: w who? r u w maddie rn**
>
> **Evan: larkin**
>
> **Brittany: wht about after? wanna come over?**
>
> **Evan: cant**

Mindy paused. Brittany seemed needy, and Evan never had liked that kind of girl. Mindy used to worry if he'd find a long-term girlfriend, but high school wasn't the time for that, anyway. In any event, Mindy didn't get the impression that Evan was buying Brittany any presents. To double-check, she scrolled backwards, trying to get closer in time to the cash withdrawal in March, but there were so many damn texts it was taking forever to load and she didn't want to get caught.

She thumbed to the other girls Evan texted, and touched the screen on the next girl's name, which was Maddie:

> **Maddie: i thought we were going to rita's**
>
> **Evan: cant make it**
>
> **Maddie: why where r u? mall? we can meet you**
>
> **Evan: w the guys**
>
> **Maddie: where?**
>
> **Evan: movies**
>
> **Maddie: want us to come?**
>
> **Evan: no gotta go**

Mindy shook her head, feeling sorry for the girl. She wished Evan didn't lead them on. She scrolled backwards to see if the earlier texts showed a relationship that would justify gift-giving, but she wasn't finding anything. It looked as if Maddie was always asking for Evan's time, but he wasn't coming around. Mindy knew the feeling.

She thumbed back to the list of girls Evan texted and touched the third name, which was Amanda, a name she didn't recognize. It must've been one of the girls who didn't go to CVHS or a girl in a different class. The text opened, and the screen filled with a nude photo of a girl—showing her full breasts, tiny little tummy, and a completely shaved pubic area. Her legs were partly opened, a crudely pornographic pose.

Mindy recoiled, shocked. This was a *sext,* for God's sake! What were these girls thinking? What the hell was going on? The photo didn't show the girl's face, but it was a selfie of her body, and she had a tattoo of a dream catcher on her side, too, like Miley Cyrus.

She scrolled backwards through Evan's texts with Amanda:

Amanda: ur at movies? don't u kno what ur missing?

Evan: oh man

Amanda: did u forget?

Evan: no way

Amanda: get here. im so wet.

Evan: cant

Amanda: i need u. get over here. i need it hard

Evan: gimme ten

Amanda: dying 4 u luv u

Evan: luv u 2

Mindy felt aghast. She scrolled backwards, and the texts were a blur of dirty talk and nude selfies—Amanda's perfect butt, fleshy breasts, tan tummy, and a belly button as taut as a frown. It was positively pornographic, but Mindy couldn't help but look at the girl's waistline with envy. Her own waist had never looked like that, and her belly button was a thing of the past.

Mindy went into contacts, looking for more information about Amanda. She searched under A, but there was no other contact information but a phone number. Mindy took a picture of the contact information, then went back to the screen of people Evan texted, touching the next girl's name. She wanted to make sure there weren't any other girls he was buying presents for, or whatever was going on.

She went through one girl, then another, and then finally the third, but it was getting late. Plenty of those girls had sent him naked pictures, but something told Mindy that Amanda was the one Evan was buying gifts for, or maybe he was even giving money to. Mindy had to figure out what to do, but she couldn't do it now.

She turned off the phone, left the bathroom, and headed back toward Evan's bedroom. She crept inside, replaced the phone, plugged it in, and slipped out, closing the door behind her. She headed down the hallway, turned into her bedroom, and crawled under the covers beside her snoring husband.

She stared at the ceiling and realized she still didn't know for sure who was withdrawing the money, since both Paul and Evan could withdraw from the account. It seemed more likely that it was Evan, but she didn't know why, and that left the question why Paul had lied to her about Carole's birthday.

You have to let it go. We've been through the mill. We've worked through it, and we did everything we were supposed to do. We're past it now.

Mindy didn't know if she'd ever get to sleep.

Chapter Thirty-three

S unday morning dawned sunny and cool, and Chris joined the back of the crowd filing into the modern church. Dr. McElroy had sent the CVHS faculty an email saying that Abe's passing would be mentioned at the church service this morning, the first Sunday after his death on Friday night, since he and his partner Jamie Renette had been such active members of the congregation. Chris had decided to come and follow up on Abe's suicide because he couldn't put his doubts to rest until he had investigated from this angle.

Meanwhile, he'd worked all night reviewing his tapes and research files, but learned nothing more about Dylan or Trevor. The Rabbi was setting up the work-around on the Kiefermanns', but that wouldn't happen until tomorrow, if then. Chris was running out of time.

He spotted a man he assumed was Jamie at the front, talking with the female pastor and a group of teary men and women, presumably close friends of the couple. There were also faculty from CVHS, among them Dr. McElroy, Courtney and her husband, Rick Pannerman and his wife, and Coach Natale and his wife. Behind them was a weepy clutch of students but so far, Chris didn't see anybody from the baseball team.

They filed into the church, a modern building made of sandstone-faced bricks with stained-glass windows depicting flowers, trees, sunny skies, and a cross. A tan spire soared at its center, and the glass entrance was flanked by banners that read, *Everyone Is Welcome at Our House of Worship.* Chris had been raised without a religion, and as an adult, his career infiltrating neo-Nazis, drug cartels, and human traffickers had provided him ample evidence that God needed to do a better job.

Chris reached the church and entered a hall with an American flag, a Pennsylvania flag, and a rainbow flag. The congregation filed into sleek oak pews, greeting each other with hugs, then settling into seats. He sat on the end of a pew in the back, and the church was shallow and wide, so he could keep an eye on Jamie, his friends, and the CVHS faculty. The pastor appeared on the elegant altar, flanked by banners with an embroidered cross and a white dove. Live music began, a string quartet in the balcony.

The pastor crossed to the pulpit. "Ladies and gentlemen, friends of our church. We welcome those who are here today to support Jamie in the heartbreaking loss of his partner, our beloved Abe. We thank you all for being here at this difficult time."

Chris heard sniffling, and Dr. McElroy patted Jamie on the back.

"Before we begin the service, allow me to remind you that God does work in mysterious ways, and at times like these, we are at a loss to understand the mystery of those ways." The pastor's voice softened. "I say this because there is no one in this congregation who does not have an Abe Yomes story. Mine is the time he told me I shouldn't wear green vestments because 'nobody looks good in green except leprechauns.'"

Chris heard teary chuckles and wished he had gotten to know Abe better.

"Abe was a fixture at all of our volunteer efforts—he happily doled out the carbohydrates at our Thanksgiving Day meal, he worked on our voter-registration drive, and he delivered Christmas gifts to the children of those less fortunate." The pastor smiled sadly. "He was the least credible Santa Claus, because he was way too thin and refused to wear the beard."

The congregation laughed, and there was more sniffling and hugs. Chris realized that Abe had earned this tribute by his relationships with everyone—a partner, a set of friends, students, and a larger community, grieving together. Only the Rabbi, Flavia, and the twins would show up for Chris's funeral.

"Abe's death is especially difficult to understand because it came by his own hand." The pastor paused. "I don't want to avoid that topic because this church is about honesty. No one of us knows the struggles that others undergo. Abe experienced hardships, but they made him a better servant of God and a better friend to us. They gave him the empathy and the sensitivity that carried him through every day, through his volunteer work, his teaching, and his home life."

A group of female students burst into tears, and Dr. McElroy, Courtney, Rick, and Coach Natale tried to comfort them. Chris realized that no one from the baseball team had come. He couldn't seem to puzzle out the connection between the team, the plot, and Abe's death, but that only told him that he needed to keep digging.

"Our church has always been about love, and today we celebrate our service to God and rededicate ourselves to His community, as we know that Abe would want us to. And now, let us begin."

Chris watched as the pastor led the congregation in prayer, hymns, and a homily about universal understanding. The service ended in signs of peace, and he hugged the people near him, relieved that he wasn't wearing a shoulder holster. He filed out of the church, and the congregation went outside. Dr. McElroy,

Courtney and her husband, Rick and his wife, Coach Natale and his wife, and a weepy group of friends and students clustered around Jamie, and Chris approached the group, who turned and smiled at him.

"Chris, how wonderful of you to come," Dr. McElroy said, reaching over for a hug. She didn't have her knee scooter anymore, but her big black orthopedic boot was on, matching a black dress.

"Deepest condolences, Dr. McElroy."

"Thank you." Dr. McElroy gestured to Coach Natale. "I assume you've met?"

"Yes. Hi, Victor." Chris shook his hand. "Sorry about this loss. This is very sad."

"It sure is." Victor gestured to his wife. "Please, meet Felicia. I think I mentioned her to you. She knew Abe, too."

"Yes, of course, the reading support specialist." Chris shook Felicia's hand, and she smiled back.

"Hi, Chris." Courtney gave him a hug, her eyes puffy, without her usual sparkle. She had on a black pantsuit and sagged against her husband, a blocky linebacker type with blond hair. Chris remembered that Abe had called him Doug The Lug.

"Courtney, I'm very sorry about your loss."

"I can't believe he's really gone. I *don't* believe it." Courtney rallied to motion to her husband. "Please, meet Doug."

Doug extended his hand. "Chris, nice to meet you. So I heard you're from Wyoming."

"I went to school there. Are you from Wyoming?" *Please don't be from Wyoming.*

"No, I'm from here. Abe was a great guy, and it's nice that you came today. It's been hard on Courtney."

"I'm sure." Chris noticed a crestfallen Rick standing next to an attractive Japanese woman with long dark hair, presumably his wife, Sachi, dressed in an artsy black smock. Chris turned to greet them, extending a hand. "Rick, I'm so sorry about Abe."

"Thanks. You, too." Rick squeezed Chris's hand. "It's not possible. It doesn't seem real. We were just together. Remember, we were joking? 'Mr. Y?'"

"I know." Chris turned to Rick's wife. "And you must be Sachi."

"Yes, nice to meet you." Sachi smiled sadly. "Have you met Jamie, Abe's partner?"

"No, I haven't." Chris extended a hand, and Jamie shook it, managing a shaky smile. His brown eyes were bloodshot, and grief etched lines into his smooth face. He was trim and compact in a sharply tailored dark suit with a crisp white shirt and blue-patterned tie, a stylish standout in the crowd of outlet gear.

"Oh, you're Chris Brennan. It's so kind of you to come today. Abe told me about you."

"I'm so sorry about your loss," Chris said, meaning it. "Abe was a wonderful man, and you have my deepest condolences on his loss."

"Thank you." Jamie's eyes glistened. "He was *so* excited about you. No one from Wyoming ever comes out here. He hadn't lived there in so long, but he was nostalgic about the place. He had even pulled some pictures for you."

"How nice." Chris felt touched.

"You know, a few of the other teachers and our closest friends have set up a little brunch back at the house. I'm not ready to be alone, and my friends know that. Why don't you come back to the house? It would mean so much to me if I knew that you saw the pictures. He wanted you to see them."

"I'd love to, thank you."

"Terrific. You can follow us."

Chapter Thirty-four

Heather cracked an egg into the Pyrex bowl, humming happily to herself. Susan Sematov had known of three job openings, one as an assistant in ValleyCo's corporate office and two from the outlet stores for Wranglers and Maidenform. She had already applied online for all three jobs and was planning a shopping trip to get a nice interview outfit.

Heather scrambled the eggs, making a yellow funnel so perfect it could've been in a surf movie. She wasn't Ina Garten yet, but she was on her way. She was going to surprise Jordan with French toast because he needed cheering up. He had been sad about Mr. Y's suicide, returning home from practice subdued and staying in his room all day. She'd tried to buck him up at dinner, telling him the good news about her job prospects, but that hadn't worked.

Heather added a dash of vanilla, feeling good about herself for the first time in a long time. If she got an office job, with nine-to-five hours, she could be home and make dinner every night. From recipes. With fresh herbs. And pretentious butter from Whole Foods. She'd spent last night fantasizing about that ValleyCo job, which could become a stepping-stone to a real career. ValleyCo had a scholarship program for employees, and Heather vowed she'd never be in a dirndl again.

She lifted a piece of bread into the egg mixture, then sprinkled on cinnamon, and let it soak, her thoughts straying to a fantasy that had nothing to do with gainful employment. She'd found herself thinking about Chris, more and more. He was a total hunk, and sensitive, but in a manly way. He listened to her, learned about her, and he'd coached her, to boot. And he was so good to Jordan. She knew that it was an inappropriate fantasy, but no fantasy worth having was appropriate. The man was Marriage Material on Wheels.

"Hey, Mom." Jordan shuffled into the kitchen in his Musketeers T-shirt and jersey shorts that hung around his knees.

"I'm making French toast!" Heather looked over, expecting applause, but Jordan was reaching for the pot of brewed coffee in the machine.

"Good, thanks."

"I even have powdered sugar for the top." Heather's mood was too good to be brought down that easily, like a balloon that refused to pop.

"Great." Jordan set his phone on the counter, reached into the cabinet for a mug, and then filled it with coffee. Just then, a text alert sounded on his phone, and Heather glanced over, reflexively. The text was from Evan, and it read **sharing is caring**—underneath a photo of a woman who was completely nude from shoulder to thigh. Her face wasn't showing, but her breasts and private parts were crudely exposed.

"Jordan! What is *that*?" Heather almost dropped the fork. "Evan is sending you naked pictures?"

"Mom, wait." Jordan reached for the phone, but Heather grabbed it first and went to the table, where the light was better. The photo was like something out of *Playboy*, but a real girl. She had a small dream-catcher tattoo on her side.

"Jordan, what is going on here? Is this a girl Evan knows? Do you know this girl?"

"I don't know, I never got one of these from him."

"One of *these*? What does that mean?"

Jordan flushed. "I heard that sometimes he sends pictures to the guys on the team."

"Are you kidding me?" Heather felt shocked. She'd seen this on *Dr. Phil.* "Do you swear he never sent a naked picture before?"

"I swear. It's a group text to the team. I was never on it before. Mom, you don't need to freak."

"Yes I do! This is terrible! This is *wrong*!" Heather felt disgusted. She had been happy that Jordan had become friends with Evan, but no longer.

"The girl sent it to him—"

"I don't care! Two wrongs don't make a right. She shouldn't be doing that, but she doesn't expect him to send it around!" Heather tried to calm down. "I mean, how does this even happen, like, how does it work? How did you get this picture?"

"Mom, guys do it. It happens—"

"How. Does. It. Happen?"

"Well, she probably sent it to him by Snapchat or she texted it to him."

"What is Snapchat again?" Heather couldn't keep up.

"Snapchat is when you send a picture to somebody, and it disappears."

"A picture, like a sext? This is a sext, isn't it? I heard about that."

Jordan half-smiled. "Okay, yes it is."

"And if you send it by Snapchat, it disappears?"

"Yes."

"Do you have Snapchat?"

"Yes, but I never use it." Jordan rolled his eyes.

"Good." Heather felt a little better. "Okay, so why does Evan still have it if it was on Snapchat? Why didn't it disappear?"

"Either he took a screenshot of it or she didn't send it on Snapchat. She could have texted it to him. Mom, chill." Jordan put up his hands like he was being robbed. "I didn't do anything wrong. I'll delete it, okay? Now can I please have my phone?"

"You wait one minute." Heather went back in the kitchen, grabbed her phone, and before Jordan could stop her, she took a picture of the sext.

"Why are you doing that?"

"I want proof. This is outrageous." Heather wasn't exactly sure of the answer. It seemed like something a good mother would do, and she wasn't falling short anymore.

"Mom, it's not, everybody does it."

"*You* don't, do you?" Heather was pretty sure he was still a virgin.

"No, of course not."

"Jordan, I *never* want you to do this. Even if a girl sends you a picture like this, I don't want you to send it to anybody else. It's wrong. It's embarrassing. It's probably even illegal."

"Okay, Mom, whatever, can I have my phone?" Jordan held out his hand.

"Do you think Evan's parents know that he's sending pictures like that? Because if you were doing that, I'd want the mother to tell me. I should call her, right now."

"Mom, please, no, don't." Jordan's eyes flared.

"I think I should, I think I have to." Heather dreaded calling Mindy and telling her that her son was a dirtbag, which wasn't going to ingratiate her with the Winners' Circle. She didn't know if Mindy would believe her or if she would be furious with her. The messenger always got shot, didn't they?

"Mom, don't call his mother. Please, that would be so embarrassing."

"For who? For you? *You* shouldn't be embarrassed. *He* should be embarrassed."

"But Mom, Evan will be so pissed at me."

"And Evan will be in trouble if I don't. Which is worse?"

"Oh man." Jordan sighed, walking around to his seat at the table.

"I can't do nothing about this, Jordan. I'm not going to pretend I didn't see it."

Jordan sighed again. "Can we eat?"

"Damn!" Heather turned to the stove, but the French toast was already burned.

Chapter Thirty-five

Chris pulled up in front of the modern A-frame that looked like a European ski lodge, set off by itself on one of the wooded hilltops outside of Central Valley. He parked, cut the ignition, and got out of his car at the same moment as Dr. McElroy emerged from her Subaru, struggling because of her orthopedic boot.

"Oh my, I'm not doing very well," she said, leaning on the car.

"Let me help you." Chris went to her side.

"Thanks. I forgot that they have this damn hill."

"Not to worry." Chris took Dr. McElroy's arm and guided her up a gravel walking path that wended up in a gentle curve. Massive evergreens flanked the path and surrounded the house. "This is a major house, isn't it?"

"Yes, Jamie owns a real estate company. He does very well for himself, and he and Abe designed the house together and had it built. It's quite something."

"It sure is." Chris wanted to pump her for information because the newspapers had no details about Abe's suicide. "I'm sure it's going to be hard for Jamie to live in a place they designed together."

"Yes, though it wasn't a *complete* surprise to him. Abe did have a history of depression."

"Really. But depression is one thing, and suicide is another."

"Well, confidentially, Abe tried to end his life once before." Dr. McElroy lowered her voice as she labored to walk uphill with the cumbersome boot. "We kept it hush-hush at school and we thought he had recovered. Abe wasn't even in therapy anymore. It's just awful that this time, he succeeded."

Chris mulled it over. The previous attempt did make it more likely that it was suicide, but still. "I heard that he hung himself. Where did he do that? And was it Jamie who found him? I'd like to get the story before we go in, so I don't say the wrong thing."

"Of course. Jamie called me after it happened so we could figure out how to deal with it at school. Jamie is very responsible that way, and very caring."

"Good for him," Chris said, keeping her talking.

"Anyway Jamie told me that he came home late Friday night. He was showing some homes then met with the PR man from the Chamber of Commerce, out past Sawyertown. He didn't get home until one o'clock in the morning and the house was empty, so he assumed that Abe was out late. They have a great circle of friends and they love to socialize." Dr. McElroy sighed. "Anyway, when it got to be about three in the morning, Jamie started to worry. He knew Abe wouldn't be out that late, and also Abe wasn't answering any of his texts or calls. By the way, Abe's car was in the driveway but Jamie didn't think that was unusual because when Abe thought he might be drinking, he never drove. Jamie assumed he had a designated driver."

"Of course." Chris nodded, guiding her along.

"So Jamie called their friends, and Abe wasn't out with any of them. Then Jamie checked the cottage and that's when he found Abe, hanging from the rafter." Dr. McElroy shook her head. "He had hung himself with the power cord from his computer. Isn't that so horrible?"

"Yes, awful." Chris paused. "But what cottage are you talking about? I thought you said Jamie found him at home."

"They have a cottage out back, behind the house." Dr. McElroy motioned to the A-frame, as they drew closer. "Abe called it his writing cottage. You know he loved literature and he wrote short stories and poems. I think he might have entertained the notion of writing a novel."

"Really," Chris said, as they were approaching the front door. "So where is the writing cottage?"

"It's in the backyard. I'm terrible at measuring distances. That was where Abe did his writing, he used it as his own private retreat. Other writers do that, he told me once even Philip Roth did that."

Chris tried to visualize it. "If the writing cottage is in the backyard, I'm surprised that Jamie didn't see the lights on and know that Abe was there."

"The lights weren't on. Jamie told me he thinks Abe left the lights off on purpose, so he wouldn't see him and stop him."

"Oh, I understand." Chris still had his suspicions. "So I assume there wasn't a suicide note?"

"No, there wasn't a note." Dr. McElroy shuddered. "It's so sad to think of the pain that Abe must've been in. I'm glad he didn't leave a note, and the police told me that it's not uncommon for there not to be a note."

"Oh, you spoke with the police?"

"Yes, they came to the school yesterday and talked to me about Abe. I told him about the previous attempt, but Jamie had told them already, too." Dr. McElroy sighed heavily. "So tomorrow morning we'll have an assembly, and grief counselors will be there, and Jamie told me that there will be a proper memorial service later this month."

"When is the funeral?" Chris had read the online obituary, but it hadn't given any details about scheduling.

"There's no burial. Abe wanted to be cremated, so Jamie honored that request."

"Of course." Chris masked his dismay. If Abe's body had since been cremated, it couldn't yield any further evidence about whether he had been murdered. Under state law, there had to be an autopsy, but it must have been routine, since suicide was suspected. A toxicology screen wasn't done routinely, but it would've showed if there was alcohol, tranquilizers, or another drug in his system, which could have incapacitated Abe and facilitated someone's hanging him. Now that evidence would be gone. It wasn't a mistake that a big-city medical examiner would've made, but Central Valley was a small town.

"I'm sorry this happened, so early in your time with us. We're usually a quieter town than this."

"After you." Chris opened the front door for Dr. McElroy, who stepped inside, and he followed her into a house brimming with guests.

Dr. McElroy got swept up with some students, and Chris got the lay of the land. The living room was of dramatic design, with glass on the front and back walls, and a ceiling that extended to the floor in an immense triangle. To the right was a living area furnished with tan sectional furniture around a rustic coffee table, and on the left was a glistening stainless-steel kitchen. A few casseroles, a sandwich tray, and soft drinks sat on a table, and a handful of guests talked in small, subdued groups. Jamie was in the kitchen, surrounded by an inner circle of friends that included Courtney and her husband and Rick and his wife.

Chris headed for the back of the house, so he could get a better look at the writing cottage. The backyard was lush grass, with a pool covered by a green tarp, and behind that was a smaller version of the A-frame main house, the writing cottage. He sized up the distance, and if the lights had been off inside the cottage at night, there would have been no way to see Abe inside. Ambient light would have been nonexistent, and there had been a cloud cover Friday night.

He eyed the cottage with more questions than answers, the obvious one being who was the last person or persons to talk to Abe before he died? What had been his state of mind? Why now? Had he given any indication that he was about to commit suicide? Where was his phone? His computer?

Chris turned from the window, scanning the crowd. He didn't know any of the couple's friends, but he knew Courtney and Rick, and they seemed the best place to start, so he went over. "Hey, everyone, how are you all?" he asked, when he reached them.

"Horrible, I still can't believe it. He seemed fine to me." Courtney shook her head sadly, and her husband Doug put his arm around her, drawing her close.

"I know." Chris sighed. "You know, it's shocking because we all got together for lunch on Friday? Abe seemed fine."

"That's what *I* keep saying." Courtney looked at Rick, stricken. "Right, Rick? We can't believe it. His parents are so upset, too. They'll be here tonight. They're the nicest people."

Rick sighed. "They are. We met them when we went out there. It's just awful. But I get it, I understand. We went through it with him, last time he tried. He took pills. We all thought he was over it, but I guess he wasn't."

Chris remained skeptical, but hid it. "Had you noticed him becoming depressed again?"

"Honestly, I didn't," Courtney interjected, her bloodshot eyes bewildered. "I think he was having a hard time with the rejection though, I know that. He told me that."

Next to her, Rick nodded. "I think that's what did it. It put him over the top."

"What rejection?" Chris asked, keeping his tone less urgent than he felt.

"His poems," Rick answered. "He was trying to get his poems published. You should read them. But he kept getting rejection after rejection."

Courtney scowled. "These agents, they're really the worst. He wrote to one in New York, and the agent emailed him, 'We don't have time to take any more clients, and if we did, we wouldn't take you.' Isn't that so *mean*?"

"That's terrible." Chris supposed it answered why Abe would commit suicide now, but still. "Rick, did you talk to Abe Friday night? Did he call you or anything?"

"Well, yes." Rick's expression darkened, and a deep frown creased his forehead. "He did call me, but I couldn't take the call. I keep thinking, what if I had? What if I just taken the five minutes to talk to him? Maybe he wouldn't have—"

"Rick, no, don't say that." His wife, Sachi, rubbed his back, her expression strained. "We were at my mother's that night, and she's been in chemo, so she wasn't feeling well. Rick was helping me with her—well, you don't need to know the details. I asked Rick not to take the call right then, I thought it was a social thing. I never realized that . . ."

Courtney nodded, her eyes glistening. "Rick, it wouldn't have made a difference if you'd taken the call. Nobody knows that better than me. He called me that night, too, and I talked to him. He was upset about the rejection, but I never would've thought he would *kill* himself."

Doug chimed in, "Honey, like the pastor said, everyone has their own struggles. You did your best. You were on the phone with him a long time."

"Was I? I didn't think I was." Courtney reached into her purse, thumbed to her phone screen, and showed it to her husband. "Look, he called me at 9:35 P.M., and I was only on for fifteen minutes. I wish it had been longer."

Rick glanced at Courtney's phone, nodding sadly. "It must've been right after he called me."

Courtney nodded. "Probably, and like I say, he was disappointed but not *suicidal*. He even asked if we could get together Saturday night, last night. He wanted us to go out to dinner, but we couldn't."

Doug frowned, glancing at Chris. "I had a work thing last night. My boss's birthday. I couldn't miss that. We had to say no."

Courtney's eyes glistened with new tears. "But I feel like Rick does, what if I had said yes? What if we made the plans? He needed friends this weekend, and I wasn't there for him."

Chris still had no answers. "Courtney, you can't blame yourself for this. You were a wonderful friend to him, and so were you, Rick."

"Thanks," Rick said, miserably.

Courtney wiped a tear from her eyes. "I just really loved him. We all did."

"He knew that." Chris noticed over Courtney's shoulder that there was a lull in the guests greeting Jamie. "Folks, excuse me, I'd like to pay my respects to Jamie, okay?"

Chapter Thirty-six

Susan picked up the dirty laundry in Raz's bedroom while he showered in his bathroom, getting ready for their therapy session. Ryan was already at his therapist's office, and her therapist had wanted to see her and Raz together. She had agreed, though she couldn't deny the unease in the pit of her stomach. She knew the family needed professional help, but all three of them in simultaneous therapy put their crisis in relief—Neil's survivors were barely surviving.

Susan picked up sweat socks, which reeked, then his favorite jeans. It had been a long and difficult day yesterday, with Raz coming home after practice, emotionally drained about Mr. Y's suicide. Raz had even stayed inside last night, alone in his room. It was the first Saturday night he hadn't gone out in a long time.

You're the parent, remember?

Susan picked up a stained T-shirt and tried not to think about what Neil would've said about the mess in this room. He was the one who used to nag the boys about their room, their shower schedule, and whether their homework was done. He always had a running timeline of their quiz, exam, and midterm schedules. He checked their grades on the CVHS portal and he shepherded

them through the PSAT, SAT, AP testing, and college application process.

She kept picking up clothes, going through the things that
Neil used to do, and she hadn't even realized how many tasks
there were until he had passed. She picked up a wet towel, then
straightened up, suddenly assessing the scene. Raz's bedroom
had always been a pigsty, but she found herself seeing it with
new eyes, and for the first time, she realized that it bordered on
hoarding.

Raz's bed was flush under the window, but the sheets looked
grimy. Piles of dirty laundry lay around the bed on the floor and
some had been stuffed under the bed, mixed in with sports
pages, *Sports Illustrated,* empty cans of Red Bull, and Snickers
and gum wrappers. Dirty underwear and sweatshirts were
mounded on top of the television, and video games were strewn
about. The controllers were buried under old CDs, which Raz
never even bought anymore.

Susan blinked, appalled. She didn't know when it had gotten
this way. She had to be the worst mother ever born. Her own
son had been burying himself in filth and she hadn't even
realized it until this very moment. She felt shocked at the realization, horrified at her own neglect. How had she been so selfish? So blind?

She resumed picking up the clothes, distraught. She collected
a dirty T-shirt, a soiled blue Musketeers Baseball shirt, and
another one identical to the first. She had no idea how Raz had
accumulated so many Musketeers Baseball T-shirts, maybe he
was buying them instead of washing them, or he was getting
them from the team. Either way, she stepped from one pile of
dirty clothes to the next, cleaning up his room, and when her
arms were totally full, she went over to the hamper, which he
kept in the closet.

The hamper overflowed, and she set the clothes she'd been
holding onto the rug, looked inside, and saw that it was taken

up by sheets and a blanket. She pulled the sheets and blanket out, but at the bottom, she felt something hard. Instinctively she withdrew her hand. It could be something crusty with mold, pizza crust, or God-knows-whatever. She had seen enough stiff socks to last a lifetime, mostly because Neil would find them and show them to her to make her laugh. Today, she wasn't laughing.

She reached her hand into the hamper again, but whatever she felt was hard and solid. She grabbed the object and pulled it out, shocked to see what sat in her palm.

A gun.

Susan felt thunderstruck. Where had he gotten it? Why was it here? Why was he hiding it? How had she lost control of her own home? They didn't have guns in the house. They didn't know anything about guns. Neil hadn't known a damn thing about guns. She didn't know much about guns, either, but she knew enough to know that this one was a revolver, with a silvery muzzle and a brown handle.

She walked the gun over to the bed and set it down carefully, with the muzzle facing away from her. She didn't know if it was loaded and she didn't know if the gun had a safety, or if revolvers even *had* safeties. She didn't understand why Raz had it or where he had gotten it. But she was going to find out. She went to the bathroom and heard the shower water still running. She knocked on the door and tried to open it, but it was locked. She didn't know why Raz had locked the door. Did he always do that? Did he ever do that? And why didn't she know?

"Raz!" Susan shouted, banging on the door. "Raz, come out!"

"I'll be out in a minute!"

"Now!" Susan shouted, louder, then got her temper in check. Being angry wouldn't help, and she wasn't angry, she was terrified. "Raz, please, right now!"

"All right!" Raz called back, irritably, and the next minute, the shower water went off.

"Hurry, please, I want to talk to you." Susan tried the knob again. She wanted him out of that bathroom. She wanted to see his face. Panic rose in her chest, for some reason.

"Mom, what's your problem?"

"Come out!" Susan turned the doorknob and pushed at the same moment that Raz opened the door, and she almost fell inside the bathroom. "Why is there a gun in your hamper?"

"A gun?" Raz's dark eyes went wide. A towel was wrapped around his waist, and he had barely dried off his chest, slick with water. She hadn't seen him naked to the waist in a long time, and she realized he wasn't a kid anymore, but a full-grown adult man, who had secrets.

"Raz, are you telling me you didn't know there was a gun in your hamper? Where did you get it? What's it doing there?"

"Oh, jeez." Raz stepped out of the bathroom, tucking the towel tighter around his waist.

"Is it loaded?" Susan pointed at the bed, but Raz made no move toward the gun.

"Yes, I think."

"Raz, you had a *loaded gun* in your room? Where did you get it?"

"From Ryan."

"Ryan!" Susan couldn't begin to process the information. Just when she thought it was bad, it went worse. Now both boys were involved. "Where did he get it from? And why do you have it?"

"Are you mad at me? Don't be mad."

"I'm not mad, honey," Susan said, realizing that the words were absolutely true. "I'm just trying to understand what's going on. You and Ryan have a gun? Why? How?"

"He got it from a guy that he knows."

"*What* guy?"

"He didn't say, I don't remember."

"You don't remember or he didn't say?" Susan thought he was lying.

"I don't know, it was, like, awhile ago, and he gave it to me and he asked me to put it in my room, so I did."

"Did he tell you what he got it for?"

"No."

"Do you have any idea?"

"No."

"Oh God." Susan found herself rubbing her face. She had put on makeup for the therapy session, but her foundation was coming off on her finger pads.

"Don't be mad," Raz said again.

"How do you know it's loaded?"

"He told me."

"Did it come that way or did he buy bullets?"

Raz smiled his goofy smile. "Bullets are like batteries. They're not included."

Susan didn't laugh. "This isn't funny."

Raz looked at her directly, seeming to focus. Then after a moment, he said, "I'm sorry."

"I am too," Susan heard herself say, her voice softening.

"What are *you* sorry for? You're just the mom."

Susan felt the words cut through her chest, though Raz hadn't meant it in a bad way. "I haven't been acting like a mom, not for a long time, and I'm sorry about that."

Raz frowned. "It's all right, I get it. It's because Dad died."

"No, it's because he *lived*. I stopped being the mom when he was still alive because he was such a good father. But you still needed me. You still needed a mom."

"It's not your fault." Raz swallowed hard.

"Yes, it is. I'm sorry I let you down. I'm sorry I didn't notice your room was getting this bad. I'm sorry I didn't know how sad you were."

Raz blinked, and for a moment he didn't say anything fresh or come back with a wisecrack. "I am sad."

"I know, honey. I know that now." Susan reached out, hugged

him, and held him again, the same way she had the other day in the car, and she stopped herself from saying *I'm sad too.* Because it couldn't be about her anymore, not for another minute. She held him close, her youngest son, as wet and slick as the day he was born and she had held him in her arms for the first time, and she realized that she had hugged him more in the past two days than she had probably in the past two months, and when she let him go, they both wiped tears from their eyes.

"I just had the gun for safekeeping, Mom. I wasn't going to do anything with it."

"I'm afraid you were," Susan said, her heart speaking out of turn.

"No, I would never hurt anybody."

"I know that." Susan kept her tone quiet, even grave, which wasn't hard to do because it was exactly how she felt. Deep inside, she knew the answer to the question she was about to ask him, as if her very soul housed the two of them, mother and child, the way her body once had, long ago, back at their very beginning. "I know you'd never hurt anyone else. I'm worried you would've hurt yourself. Did you ever think about that, honey? Did you ever pick up that gun and think about that? About hurting yourself?"

Raz nodded, then his lips began to tremble, and tears came to his eyes. Susan reached for him again, hugging him closer while he began to cry, and they sank to the floor together, surrounded by the debris of their lives. She cradled him against her chest while she told him that she loved him more than she had ever loved anybody in her life, that he was her special and spirited son, and that she would always be there for him and that they were going to sort this out together, the three of them.

As a family.

Chapter Thirty-seven

C hris made his way to the kitchen and shook Jamie's hand. "Jamie, thanks for having me today. I really am so sorry about Abe. He really was such a nice guy."

"Thanks." Jamie met Chris's eye, his gaze sad, but strong. "I'm glad you could come. It was so kind of everyone to bring the food, and they won't leave me alone, which is fine with me. And Abe would have loved that you came and got the pictures. I know you two would've been great friends. The Wyoming thing and all."

"I think you're right." Chris felt guilty. He realized that, unlike his typical operation, he was undercover among a wonderful group of people, a true community. It affected him in a way he'd never experienced, conflicting him. But he reminded himself to stay on track.

"It's just so hard to imagine that we're here, but he's not. I mean, I know he was depressed and I guess you heard he tried once before, everybody knows, he was open about that. He even volunteered at a suicide hotline.

"He didn't give any sign or anything, this time?"

"No, I knew the rejections were starting to mount up. He

counted them and there were twenty-one." Jamie shook his head. "I think the number just got too high. He felt hopeless, like it would never happen for him."

"Did you talk to him Friday night?"

"Yes. He called me around eight o'clock, asking me how long I'd be, and we spoke for about five minutes. I couldn't talk longer, I had people. He sounded bummed about the latest rejection, he told me about how there were twenty-one. He said he wanted to talk to me when I got home."

"Did he say what about?"

"I assumed it was about the rejections."

"That's what Courtney and Rick said, too. I wonder if he talked to anybody else."

"No, he didn't. I asked everybody. So when I came home, that's why I figured he wasn't here, that he went out to forget about it and have a drink. But otherwise he was looking forward to summer." Jamie paused. "And those pictures he pulled for you, he couldn't wait for you to see them. I'd love to show them to you but," Jamie hesitated. "They're in the cottage. I guess you heard that's where he . . ."

"Yes, I did. That must be so difficult for you."

"It was, it is, finding him was the most horrific thing that's ever happened to me in my life." Tears came to Jamie's eyes, but he tilted his chin up. "We designed this house together, and the cottage is where he loved to go. It was his man cave, only with books instead of a TV. I just ran out when I saw him and called 911. I left everything in there."

"What do you mean by everything? His phone?"

"No, his laptop. He probably had his phone on him when they took him away, and I assume the police or the funeral home have it. I know the Wyoming pictures are in the cottage because I saw them Thursday night, on his desk. He printed them out for you."

"If you want, I can go in there and get that stuff for you. I can see if his phone is there, too." Chris kept his tone low-key, but he was asking for legal reasons. A consent search was lawful, and if any evidence of foul play turned up, it would be admissible.

"Would you do that?" Jamie asked, hopeful. "I mean, I just don't want to do it myself. Our friends are already talking about me moving, but I would never do that. This was our house."

"Of course, you have memories here. I'll go look for his phone and get the pictures."

"Thank you, I'd love that. Don't forget about his laptop. He had a passcode that I don't even know, but I'd feel better if the laptop was in the house." Jamie gestured to a glass door at the end of the kitchen. "You can take the back door and go across the lawn to the cottage."

"Is there a key or is it open?"

"It's open. We never lock anything."

Chris didn't bother to correct him. Once again, the illusion of safety rendered people unsafe. "Be right back."

"Thanks again."

Chris headed for the back door, left the house, and walked across the lawn, then reached the cottage and opened the door, stepping inside and throwing the deadbolt behind him so he wouldn't be interrupted.

Chris looked around, sizing it up. It was an A-frame with one large great room, which was undisturbed, with no signs of a struggle or a forced entry. A cherrywood table dominated the room, cluttered with papers and a MacBook Pro. Books lined both sides of the room on matching bookshelves, and the tall triangle of the ceiling was constructed of the same rustic wood as the house, with three thick oak rafters.

Chris crossed the room and stood underneath the middle rafter. Sadly, it was easy to see that it was the one Abe had hung himself from—or had been hung from. A stain soiled the beige rug, and Chris surmised that it was from bodily fluids, postmortem.

Chris gazed at the stain, and it struck him as obscene that such a kind soul had died on this very spot, now flooded with sunlight. The back wall was also entirely of glass, offering a view of a flagstone backyard, two green Adirondack chairs, and the woods beyond. There was a back door, and Chris opened it and went outside, trying to understand how Abe could have been murdered.

He passed the patio and kept going to the edge of the woods and looked down. There were trees all the way down a steep hill, and at the bottom was a single-lane country road. He could see that the trees weren't that dense, so a killer could have parked along the road, climbed the hill to the back door of the cottage, and let himself inside. Escape would've been accomplished the same way, with the car left on the road below, which looked hardly traveled, like the roads he had taken on the way here.

Chris returned to the cottage, entered, and went directly to the spot, deep in thought. There was a random cherrywood chair sitting near the middle rafter. He looked over at the desk, seeing that the chair's mate was sitting in front of the desk and that it also matched the desk chair itself, which was on rollers.

Chris mentally reconstructed the murder. The killer wouldn't have chosen the desk chair because it had rollers, so the side chair was a rational choice. The killer could've entered the back door, surprised Abe at his desk, and either chloroformed or injected him to incapacitate him, then used the side chair to hang him. Abe would have kicked the chair over in his struggle or death throes. It was likely that the police, when they came to cut him down and take the body away, would have righted the chair.

Chris reasoned there had been more than one killer, because Abe would have been too heavy for one person to lift and hang from a rafter, deadweight even if he wasn't struggling. Chris walked over to the desk but didn't touch anything, looking around. His first impulse was to go to the computer, but Jamie had said it was under passcode that even he didn't know.

The bright sun illuminated the cluttered desk, covered with correspondence, pages of poetry in draft, and notes written on lined paper. He read the notes to try to see if they contained any clues, but no luck. He slid his phone from his pocket and took pictures of the papers, the desk, the rafter, the stain, and everything else, to be reviewed later, in case he had missed anything.

Chris stood next to the spot, looking around in a 360-degree turn. The circular motion stirred up dust motes, the tiny specs visible in the solid shaft of sunlight, sending them swirling. It brought him to a realization. If killers had come in and hung Abe, there would have been signs of a struggle, even if they only had to hoist the body up. But the room was undisturbed, which meant that everything had been put back in order—and if that had happened, the proof could be in the dust.

Chris bent over and looked at the desk more closely. There was a clean square, book-sized, on the left side of the desk, and it was the only place not dusty. His gaze went to a paperback dictionary, which sat on top of another note-filled legal pad. It was the same size as the dictionary. So somebody had moved the book, and that wasn't something the police would do. They might have righted the chair, but they wouldn't have straightened up a desk.

Chris felt his heart beat faster. He continued scrutinizing the desk, finding more blank spaces where an object had been but was placed somewhere else. He didn't get the impression that the desk was searched, but merely put back in order so it would look as if Abe had simply been reading his rejection letters, rose from them, moved the side chair, and hung himself with the power cord.

Chris felt a bitter taste in his mouth, knowing it would be difficult to prove murder now that Abe had been cremated. But even so, he had to know who killed Abe and why. His gut was telling him that it was linked to the baseball team, but he couldn't connect the dots.

Chris moved papers on the desk to find the phone, but didn't see one, also consistent with his theory. The killers could have taken the phone, worried that it contained information or phone calls that implicated them. The police wouldn't have taken a personal effect, and the funeral home would have let Jamie know by now. Chris's best guess was that Abe's phone was in the hands of whoever had killed him, so cruelly.

Chris became aware that he was taking too long, so he picked up the laptop and gathered the Wyoming photos, taking pictures of them for later. They showed a scenic array of mountains, a lovely home in the woods, then Abe's parents and siblings, Jamie, Courtney, Rick, and their respective spouses.

Chris knew they would be grieving for years to come. He made a silent vow to the murdered teacher.

I'll get your murderers, Abe.

And I'm sorry I didn't get them before they got you.

Chapter Thirty-eight

Mindy glanced at the kitchen clock, on edge. It was 11:15, and she couldn't wait for Evan and Paul to get home. When she'd awakened this morning, having overslept through yoga, there'd been a note from Paul saying he and Evan had gone to play golf. She'd texted back, **come home ASAP, family meeting,** and he had texted back, **will be home after nine holes.**

She paced, getting angrier. She thought that Evan had withdrawn the money and spent it on Amanda, but it was still possible that Paul had, on his new mistress. She was going to confront them both at the same time. She wanted the truth to come out, unvarnished and unprepared for, once and for all.

She checked her phone, which showed one of the naked pictures she'd found in Evan's phone. There were more than one girl because they had pierced nipples, weird body jewelry, and tattoos, which she thought was disgusting. Plus you had to be eighteen to get a tattoo, so Mindy had no idea what was going on in the world anymore.

She heard the sound of Paul's car in the driveway and reminded herself to stay in control. She didn't want to fall into the Hysterical Mom category, in which Paul and Evan were so willing to place her. They acted like she was the numbskull in the house, and she was finally over it. She hadn't had anything to drink, no G&T yet or wine. Deep inside, she was angriest at herself, for medicating herself with alcohol. For telling herself she had a happy marriage and perfect son, when she had neither. For not knowing what was happening under her own roof. That had to end, right now.

Mindy stormed out of the kitchen just as Paul and Evan entered the house, flush, happy, and sweaty in their golf clothes. "Boys, in the family room!"

Evan's smile faded. "Mom?"

"Honey?" Paul did a double-take.

"We're having a meeting in the family room." Mindy stalked into the family room, seeing it with new eyes—a cheery red couch with matching side chairs, a beautiful glass coffee table, three walls of eggshell white, and a red accent wall. She had decorated it herself, but right now, she wanted to set it on fire. Mindy pointed to the couch. "Sit down, both of you."

"Honey?" Paul said, in wonderment as he took a seat.

"Mom, you okay?" Evan asked, mystified, sitting next to him.

"No, I'm not okay, and I'll tell you why." Mindy scrolled to the saved photos on her phone, held up her phone to face them, and started an XXX-rated slideshow for her son and her husband. "Evan. What in God's holy name are these photographs doing on your phone? Who is Amanda? Why are there so many different ones? And are you texting the photos to anybody else, because if you are, Heaven help you, I am going to rearrange your very handsome face."

"Oh no!" Evan's eyes flew open.

"Oh no," Paul said, aghast.

"Oh, yes," Mindy corrected. "And Evan, before you answer, I also want to know who you're buying presents for, and what you're doing with the money, because you've withdrawn ten thousand dollars from your account over the past three months. So either you're buying drugs, buying women, or buying tattoos—"

"I can explain, Mom—" Evan interrupted, panicky, but Mindy wasn't finished venting yet.

"Evan, why are these girls sending you these photos?" Mindy stood above Paul and Evan, folding her arms, and she had never felt more powerful in her life. "Do you ask or do they offer? If you sent them to anybody, you're transmitting child pornography, do you realize that? You can go to jail! Everybody you sent them to can go to jail, if they send it on. If you have an explanation, you better start explaining right now!"

"I can explain," Paul interjected, his tone quiet, and Mindy wheeled around to him.

"Paul! Don't tell me you *knew* what this is about! If you knew and didn't tell me then you're going to have more to answer for than Carole's real birthday, because the one you told me was a lie!"

Paul grimaced. "Honey, I didn't know about the pictures—"

Evan interjected, "Mom, Dad didn't know about the pictures, he didn't know about any of it—"

Paul shook his head. "I knew about the money, Evan. I can explain about the money—"

"Dad, you don't have to." Evan put a hand on Paul's arm, and Mindy could see they were trying to protect each other. Boys will be boys, covering each other's asses against Mean Mommy, The Disciplinarian, the Mother of Us All, the *Boss Bitch*.

"No more games, either of you!" Mindy barked. "I want the truth and I want it now."

Paul sighed, then said, "Honey, as I started to say, I can explain about the money, it went to pay for—"

"I got a girl pregnant," Evan said, finishing the sentence.

Mindy almost fell over. She wasn't sure she had even heard him right. "You *what*?"

Evan reddened, flustered. "Mom, I'm sorry, I'm really sorry.

It was an accident. I always use protection, I do. I know you told me, I know all about it. But this one time I didn't, she was drinking, and I was drinking, and it was legit consent, but we didn't use protection, and then she told me she was pregnant and she wanted to, well end the pregnancy—"

"An abortion?" Mindy groaned, stricken. She had a million thoughts at once. An abortion, a baby. Evan got a girl pregnant. A baby had been aborted. Her son's baby. Her *grandchild.* It was too much, and she sank into the couch opposite them, suddenly powerless, helpless, useless.

"Mom, don't be upset, really, it's all fine now, we took care of it, that's what the money was for." Evan leaned forward urgently. "When it happened, when she told me, I went to Dad and I told him that the girl didn't want the baby. Believe me, I didn't have a choice even if I wanted a baby, she wasn't about to have it and neither were her parents—"

Mindy listened, appalled. Paul knew. Her parents knew. Everyone knew but Mindy. She didn't know what to say. She didn't interrupt her son, who was talking a mile a minute anyway.

"—I went to Dad because I didn't want to upset you, and he said I had to pay for it out of my own money because that's my fault and I have to learn to accept the consequences and all that. So we took it out of my own account and we knew you never look at my statements, so we thought it would be fine."

Mindy's mouth had gone completely dry, and she turned to Paul. "You thought this would be *fine*? You paid for a girl to abort your son's first child and you didn't even tell me? And you thought *that was fine*?"

"Yes, I'm sorry, honey." Paul kept his surgeon's demeanor, experienced at delivering bad news. "I thought it would be the best way to handle it, just Evan and me. I didn't want you to get upset, and we knew that you would. So we took care of the problem ourselves."

"The problem?" Mindy shouted. "It wasn't a problem, it was a *baby,* our *grandchild,* and I had a right to know that baby existed. You didn't tell me because you thought I would say no, because I could stop you, so you just ignored the fact that I exist. How could you? How could you keep it from me?"

"I thought it was best, considering, that last year was so difficult—"

"Ha! Oh, I get it! So, because you kept your affair a secret, which almost ended our marriage, you also decided to keep this a secret, too. Which therapy session did we cover that in? Because I must've missed that one!"

Paul frowned, glancing at Evan. "Honey—"

"What?" Mindy knew Paul didn't like that she'd just let Evan know about his affair, but she was beyond caring. "Yes, Paul, you had an affair, and now Evan knows it, too. Our son is not a child anymore, since he *made a child of his own.* The jig is up, wouldn't you say, *Gramps?*"

Evan said nothing, without looking over at his father.

Paul sighed, contrite. "I'm so sorry, honey. I should've told you. I just wanted to make it easier on you, and that may have been a mistake, but I own that."

"Oh you *own* that?" Mindy hated that Paul used therapy-speak but had learned zero in therapy. "Don't you think that's wrong, that that's *terrible,* that your son got a girl pregnant? When did you buy him the BMW, before or after?"

Evan made a little hiccup, his eyes suddenly brimming with tears. "Mom, I'm really sorry, I really am. I would never do it again, and if I could take it back, I would—"

"Evan." Mindy felt unmoved, turning to him, shaken to her very foundations. She felt as if she were seeing him with new eyes, as if she had been sleepwalking through her own life. "Evan, I don't know what to say to you. I don't know what to do about this."

"Mom, you don't have to do anything, it's over now."

Paul nodded. "Honey, it is over. I swear to you. It's over. We dodged a bullet, and we came out fine."

"You don't even know how bad it got," Evan added.

"No, I don't, why don't you tell me?" Mindy realized that she had never disliked her son before, and now she hated him. Hated her own child. Hated the man he was growing into, or had already grown into. Hated her son and her husband. *Hey Facebook, how do you like the Kostis Klan now?*

"Mom, she started to ask for more money because she wanted to get the abortion in New York so nobody would know, and we said yes, because we were worried that everybody at school would find out—"

Paul interrupted, "And at the club and the hospital, too. We didn't want it to get around."

"Oh God." Mindy moaned. Her phone rang in her hand, and she glanced down to see who was calling, but it was a number she didn't recognize, so she pressed the screen to send it to voicemail.

Evan was saying, "Dad took care of it. We gave her as much money as we could, and she took, like, two weeks off from school. She stayed at a hotel in New York, it cost a lot."

Paul nodded. "I cut her off at ten grand in cash, and she accepted it, and so did her parents, and it's over. They don't want it to get around, either. It's a terrible chapter in our lives, but it's over."

"It's not over for me. It's just begun for me."

"What do you mean, Mom?" Evan asked, his voice cracking. He wiped the tear from his cheek.

"What's this girl's name, Evan? Is it Amanda, the girl sending you the naked pictures? Excuse me, *one* of the girls sending you—"

"Mom, no, it's not Amanda."

"So it's a *different* girl? You got one girl pregnant, and another one's sending you naked pictures? You told Amanda you love her, and she said she loves you!" Mindy couldn't even follow. "What's the name of the girl you got pregnant?"

"Mom, what's the difference? She's not from here. She goes to a different school."

"How dare you! You answer this question! What is her name? Which one is she?" Mindy reached for her phone. "Is she one of the girls in this phone?"

"No, I said, I don't see her anymore."

"Evan, what's the matter with you?" Mindy exploded. "What are you, a sex addict?"

Paul interjected, "Mindy, you don't need to know her name."

"Why, Paul? Because you don't want me to look her up, to call her? You better tell me her name or I'm going to divorce you on the spot. You can go up and pack right now." Mindy pointed upstairs again. "Right now."

Evan answered, "Okay, her name is Cynthia Caselli. She goes to Rocky Springs. But, please don't call her. You're just gonna make everything worse."

Paul chimed in, "Honey, he's right. I dealt with these people. The Caselli's are lowlifes. Let it go."

"The hell I will!"

"Mom!" Evan jumped up, as tears spilled from his eyes. "You shouldn't've been in my phone in the first place! You invaded my privacy! How do you even know the passcode? Why do you have to stick your nose into everything? Why can't you just let it go?"

"How dare you!" Mindy rose, squaring off against Evan. "I can't let it go because you're my son. Don't throw a tantrum about me not trusting you—if you're not worthy of trust!"

"Mom, you didn't know that when you went in the phone. You were just snooping around in things that aren't your business." Evan started to move toward the door, and Mindy went after him.

"You're my business, and everything you do is my business!"

"I've had it with you! I've had it with you *both*." Evan stormed out the door, letting it slam behind him.

"Don't walk out when I'm talking to you!" Mindy started to go after him, but Paul appeared at her side, holding her arm.

"Let him go, honey. He needs to cool down. Let him think it over."

"Oh, what do *you* know?" Mindy wrested her arm out of his hand as if he were a complete stranger, which was exactly how she felt. "He can't walk out on me when I'm talking to him. That's rude and disrespectful, and he needs limits. When are you going to figure that out? When he gets another girl pregnant? How many BMWs can you buy him, *Dr. Kostis*?"

"Min—"

"He's sick of the two of us? I'm sick of the two of *you*!" Mindy turned and ran upstairs to her bedroom to figure out whether the Kostis Klan could be saved.

Or should be.

Chapter Thirty-nine

Susan went downstairs as soon as she heard Ryan come home from therapy and head into the kitchen. She'd called and postponed her and Raz's session until later this afternoon because the situation needed to be dealt with immediately, not by a therapist, but by her. She had the gun wrapped in a pink towel from her bathroom, without really knowing why. She didn't feel angry anymore, only sad, and underneath that, she had a renewed sense of purpose. To put the Sematovs back together, however reconstituted, after Neil's death.

Susan entered the kitchen, and Ryan was standing in front of the refrigerator with the door open, staring at it like it was a television. He'd been doing that since he was little, and she used to yell at him for wasting electricity. Not today. He looked predictably drained, his skin pale and his blue eyes washed-out. He looked so much like her, with her dark brown hair, which he wore short, and he had a longish nose with thin lips, which right now were pursed.

"Ryan, hi."

"Hi," Ryan answered, without looking over. He was very tall, six-foot-four, but he hunched rather than stood, his head slightly forward. He'd lost weight since Neil's death, which emphasized his bad posture, or maybe he'd just been downcast since then.

Susan set the wrapped gun on the kitchen table. "You hungry?"

"Just thirsty. I did a drive-through on the way home."

"Oh, good," Susan said, not sure she believed him. She'd have to stop herself from second-guessing his every move. It wouldn't be productive right now. "Why don't you grab a soda and come sit with me? I want to talk about something."

"Really, Mom?" Ryan sighed. "I'm kind of talked out."

"I'm thinking there's no such thing. Grab something to drink and come on over."

"Fine." Ryan closed the refrigerator door without getting anything to drink, making a point, but Susan didn't remark on it. He was so much like her it wasn't even funny.

"What is it?" Ryan flopped into the chair and pressed it away from the table with an annoying scraping sound. Behind him, a small strip of sunlight came into the kitchen through the narrow window over the sink, and Susan felt bothered by that, for the first time. The kitchen was large, but it was dark, with walnut cabinets that made it seem darker. It needed more light. More windows. Maybe she could renovate and blow out a wall, later.

"How you feeling?" Susan asked, testing the waters.

"Okay."

"How was your session?" Susan liked the way he met her eye directly. She was pretty sure that he hadn't been drinking today. She realized how much she had missed the steadiness of his gaze, and the intelligence there. He was the rational one, and she'd always been able to talk to him. Even though he was closer to Neil, he was *of* her.

"It was okay. I liked it better than yesterday."

"Good." Susan peeled aside the corner of the pink towel

revealing the silvery metallic barrel of the gun. "I just found this in your brother's room."

Ryan's face went white, and he sighed again, audibly.

"I'm not mad, I just want to understand. Did you give it to him?"

"Yes, I did."

"When?"

"After Dad died, like a month or two."

"Where did you get it?"

"I don't know, Mom." Ryan shook his head, newly impatient.

"Ryan, you have to know where you got it." Susan softened her tone, nonaccusatory.

"Honestly, I don't."

"Did you buy it in a gun shop?'

"No, from a guy."

"What guy?"

"I don't know." Ryan averted his eyes. "I don't remember."

"Ryan, you bought a gun and you don't remember who from?" Susan maintained her calm tone, for which she deserved an award. She didn't have to be a detective to know that he was lying. "Okay, when did you buy it?'

"Like, a month after Dad died."

"How is it that you remember that, but you don't remember who sold it to you?"

"Because." Ryan hesitated, returning his focus to her, with a frown. "I was at a party, Mom. I drank too much. I blacked out, and I bought the gun."

"How much was it?" Susan asked, incredulous.

"Like I say, I don't know."

"Who was at the party?"

"A lot of guys I don't know, mostly guys, some women, I just didn't know the crowd."

"Whose party was it? Where was it?"

"Just some people I met at this bikers' bar, in Rocky Springs.

They said you want to come over and party, and I went to some house, I don't remember where it was. All I know is that I got drunk and I bought the gun."

Susan tried to understand. "But a gun has to cost a couple hundred dollars. You never have more than twenty dollars on you. You weren't working then, either. Who's going to sell you a gun for twenty bucks?"

Ryan blinked. "I don't know, I don't remember."

Susan bore down. "Honey, I love you. I just don't feel like you're telling me the truth. It doesn't make sense."

Ryan fell silent, and she could see him going inward, which was his way. Her way, too. She got that from her father. Her side of the family kept it all inside, until they exploded.

"Ryan, just tell me. I won't be mad. I've been thinking about a lot of things and we are going to make a lot of changes here for the better." Susan hesitated, then tried to explain, the way she had with Raz. "We're all hurting since your dad died, and we've lost our way, as a family. Me most of all. I think I delegated so much to him, he was the true head of our household, and without him, well, there's been kind of an emptiness, a power vacuum."

Ryan seemed to be listening, and Susan realized that he was probably unused to her taking the time to sit down with him this way, not to mention being so vulnerable, so she continued.

"You know, there's an expression, 'nature abhors a vacuum.' That means when there's a power vacuum, things go wrong. The world gets out of whack. Well, I think our world has been out of whack. I haven't stepped into that power vacuum yet, but I'm going to now. I have to be the head of this household. I made a lot of mistakes, but I'm going to try to get it right from now on. So please, tell me where you got the gun and why?"

"I stole it," Ryan answered, after a moment.

"You *stole* it?" Susan asked, unable to keep the incredulity from her tone. Ryan was her mild child, the rules follower, the one who never did anything wrong—until his father had died.

She arranged her face into a mask of calm, but inwardly, her emotions were all over the map. "How did you steal it? From where? From a store?"

"No, from a guy. I mean, everything I just told you about the party was true, and we all drank too much and I didn't know those people, but there was this guy and he fell asleep and I saw the gun sticking out of his jacket pocket, and I just took it and I left."

Susan knew it was the truth, as shocking as it was, because his gaze stayed level and his voice had a ring of authenticity. "Okay, why did you steal it, then?"

"For protection."

"Why did you think you needed protection?"

"Not for me, for you," Ryan answered softly.

"For me?" Susan said, touched.

"I mean, after Dad died, I felt that way . . ." Ryan's forehead buckled with pain, and his voice trailed off. "Okay, maybe it's like you said, I felt like I needed to be, like, the man of the house. I had to protect you and take care of you, and Raz, too. Then when I thought I was going back to school, I gave it to Raz, so he could protect you, and himself, and the house."

Susan felt speechless, then realized it wasn't the time for words anyway. She got out of her chair, went around the side of the table, and put her arms around her beloved firstborn, holding him close to her. He turned and wrapped his long arms around her waist, and neither of them said anything, clinging to each other. She didn't have to say anything to him, unlike Raz, because he knew her so well, and deep inside, she knew that he was coming back, returning to her again.

And more important, coming back to himself.

Chapter Forty

Chris drove away from Abe and Jamie's house, feeling a pang. He hadn't known Abe that long, but the teacher had made an impact on him, maybe in the way of all teachers. Chris had always loved school because it was his only constant; it was always him and a teacher, even as the schools changed, because he never had many friends. He'd earned good grades, eager to please those who had provided him even a temporary sanctuary, and he realized now that Abe had become for him every teacher who'd helped him, sheltered him from the hell of his home life, and encouraged him to go to college and find a career that actually helped people, in return.

Chris knew in his bones that Abe had been murdered, but he didn't know who had done it or why. He sensed it was connected to the baseball team, but he couldn't tie the two together. There was a piece of the puzzle missing, and he had faith that he would find it—just not in time. The Rabbi still hadn't gotten back to him about the work-around on the Kiefermanns' farm, and he still didn't know where Dylan had been last night, when he sneaked out of his house.

Gravel popped under his tires as he accelerated onto the

country road. He had been in this situation before, but he'd been part of a larger operation and had access to the full array of ATF resources—other special agents would be deployed, police records and other official records subpoenaed, CIs, or confidential informants, questioned, and there would have been electronic surveillance for months, plus visual and cyber surveillance. The general public had no idea how much personnel, resources, techniques, and electronic fact-gathering was demanded by a major ATF operation. But that wasn't Operation Varsity Letter, manned by one undercover agent.

Yet as Chris drove, he felt more motivated and determined than ever. In other operations, he had been instrumental, but he'd also been a cog in the wheel, working with the Rabbi and other agents. This time, he was completely on his own, with only his wits and experience to guide him, and it struck him that he felt like a cowboy, from Wyoming of all places.

Chris whizzed by farmhouses, cornfields, and horses grazing in pastures, seeing all around him that which he wanted to protect—innocent people, this beautiful countryside, his homeland. The buildings of Central Valley rose in the distance and he couldn't wait to get home to study his audios, lay out the information he knew, review the photographs he had taken and all the mental notes he had made, to try to make sense of things, to find the missing piece, solve the puzzle, and connect the dots.

Suddenly the text alert sounded on his phone, and he looked over. The text was from the Rabbi, and it read:

Something is going down. Meet us in 15 mins. Same place.

Chris felt a surge of new energy. Information must be coming in, and the "us" referred to Alek, so it must be big. If Alek and the Rabbi had the missing piece, they could bust the conspirators. Nobody else had to die, nobody else had to get hurt.

Central Valley could go on living its quiet life. Jordan would be safe, and so would Heather.

Chris turned the car around and raced toward the abandoned development.

Step Three

Chapter Forty-one

Y ou can't shut me down!" Chris said, furious.

The Rabbi and Alek stood opposite him, with the Rabbi looking pained and Alek in his stupid ballcap and aviator sunglasses, like the Unabomber on a federal payroll.

The Rabbi said, "Curt, we have to, this is big—"

"No!" Chris interrupted. "You were supposed to get back to me with the work-around. I'm *this* close, I'm one inch from the finish line. I'm telling you, the teacher was murdered. It wasn't a suicide. And I caught one of my suspects sneaking out last night. All I have to do is put it together."

The Rabbi shook his head. "I hear you, but this is bigger, and we need you up north. I'm going up myself. You fly with me."

"Are you serious?" Chris guessed that Alek had made the Rabbi do the talking, because this wasn't a conversation, it was a sales pitch.

"There's no time to waste. We believe it's about the Oklahoma anniversary. We have one day to figure it out, and it's all hands on deck."

"Where up north? Why?"

"I can fill you in on the way."

"Fill me in now. Because I don't want to get pulled off this."

Alek interjected, "Curt, we don't need to justify this to you."

"Yes you do," Chris shot back. "I've taken it this far, I know I'm close. I'm not gonna drop everything just because you say so."

Alek pursed his lips. "I'm your boss. You work for me."

"I work for ATF, not for you. There was a you before you and there'll be a you after you. You're all the same guy. I'm doing the right thing."

"Keep it up and I'll fire you."

The Rabbi stepped between the two men as if he were separating two boxers. "Curt, hear *me*. Here's what we got. About two hours away from here, the northern part of the state, that's part of Marcellus Shale, you ever heard of that?"

"Not really," Chris said, though he had. He just didn't feel like cooperating, even with the Rabbi. If they wanted him to drop everything, they were going to have to lay it out. He'd been on too many wild goose chases sent by bureaucrats like Alek who had no idea what they were doing.

"The Marcellus Shale is one of the largest deposits of natural gas in the country, and it's one of the major fracking sites. In fact, the most fracking sites in the entire country are in Pennsylvania, on the Marcellus in Susquehanna County and a bunch of others. Towns like Dimock, Montrose, Springville, Headley. As you know, the gas companies use explosives to drill and they have the FELs."

"Okay, I got it, what's the point?" Chris knew that FELs stood for Federal Explosives License, which allowed companies to buy and sell explosives necessary in the course of their business.

"So you know that under the regs, the gas companies have to monitor their inventory of explosive devices and detonators, like blasting caps. If over a certain number get lost or stolen, they have to report that and they're subject to fines."

"Yes, so?" Chris knew all this and it bored him. It was part of ATF routine monitoring under the new Homeland Security regulations, but it was administrative and handled by a separate team in the office.

"So you know how this works, we send agents out there, they inspect the gas companies' operations. We fine any company that has an excessive theft report, which, business being what it is, sometimes they cheat. They underestimate the number of blasting caps that were lost or stolen to avoid the fines."

"Okay, so what? Somebody is lying about the blasting caps? Take away their FEL. Recommend they be prosecuted."

"If that's all it was, we wouldn't be shutting you down."

Alek interjected, "Yes, we would."

The Rabbi ignored him, continuing, "So we got a report from a resident of Headley, a town up there, that while he was hunting, he found a burn site. He figured it was a burn pile or maybe kids playing with fire, but when he started digging, he found blasting caps. He called the locals, who called us."

Chris felt his gut tense, knowing that it was a valid cause for concern. Domestic terrorists who made IEDs typically field-tested their explosives, leaving burn sites and testing grounds, sometimes killing even small animals or neighborhood pets. Still he wasn't going.

The Rabbi continued, "We sent some agents up there to talk to the gas companies and double-check their inventory of blasting caps. Long story short, we found out that somebody's been stealing blasting caps, just under the amount that would trigger the reporting requirement, from different drilling sites in the area around Headley. And one of the companies reported theft of Tovex."

"Again, so?" Chris knew Tovex was a water-gel explosive used instead of TNT. "Are they finding reports of stolen fertilizer? They still need an oxidizing agent."

"No, but there's not much farming up there anymore." The Rabbi pursed his lips. "Curt, I know you're committed to your operation. I know you believe in it, and you think you're onto something. But it's time for triage. We need you up north. You have to admit, this alters the cost–benefit analysis."

"But you have no plan to deploy me. I can't get undercover in a day. And with whom? Do you have any suspects?"

"Not yet, and granted, we don't have a specific role for you as yet. We have to get up there, see which end is up, and figure out the best way to deploy you. It may not be undercover at all. We need all hands on deck."

Chris had a random thought. "What if the blasting caps are related to my operation? To my fertilizer?"

Alek interjected, "It's up north. It's two different places, two different *types* of places. One had nothing to do with the other."

"It's only two hours away," Chris said, thinking out loud. "Look, I *know* that one of my kids stole fertilizer, it's on that video. What if someone down here in farm country is getting the fertilizer, and someone up there is getting the blasting caps? Together they go boom. Let me work it from my angle, and you guys work it from yours. I need to get into that locked shed. Did you set up the work-around?"

Alek interjected again, "There's no work-around, I wouldn't authorize it. There's no point and there's no time."

The Rabbi's face fell. "Curt, we need you to come with us."

"I can't go, I'm not going," Chris shot back.

Alek threw up his hands. "You've lost your mind! We have *confirmed* intel that there's a testing ground upstate, but you're going to play with high-school kids?"

Chris stood his ground. "Alek, you said I had three days. I have one day left. Do without me for one day."

The Rabbi frowned, interjecting, "Curt, one day is all we have."

"It's all I have, too, and I've come this far. I swear to you, I'm close."

"We're closer. You're our best agent. We need you."

Chris had never gone against the Rabbi's advice, though he'd gone against orders from even more annoying bureaucrats than Alek. But Chris's gut was telling him to stay, and so was his heart. Maybe it was time for him to grow up. "Rabbi, I'd do anything for you. I'm sorry, I can't turn my back on these kids. If they're involved, if they're being used, then I'm gonna protect them. Because they're my boys."

"Curt, I'm your boss, too. Don't make me order you."

"Don't make me call in my chit. You owe me one. I'm asking now."

"You're gonna do that to me?" The Rabbi looked like he'd been punched in the gut.

"Yes, really." Chris didn't have to remind the Rabbi of the story. The only man Chris had ever killed was in his very first operation, when he and the Rabbi were undercover in a ring of dangerously violent gunrunners. One of the thugs had pulled a gun on the Rabbi, and Chris had revealed his identity as an ATF agent per procedure. The thug had taken deadly aim anyway, but Chris had tackled him, grabbed his knife from his ankle holster, and stabbed him in the throat, killing him. Chris had pulled out the blade too soon, a rookie mistake, but he had saved the Rabbi's life.

The bust had followed, the gunrunners had been arrested, and an investigation by ATF's Incident Review Team followed. Chris had been exonerated when they'd found deadly force had been justified, since he'd had a reasonable belief that there was imminent danger of death or serious physical injury. And the Rabbi had never forgotten that Chris had saved his life. It gave Chris a chit that he'd never intended to call in, until this very moment.

Alek exploded. "Curt, you're an arrogant prick!"

"Keep me posted, Rabbi." Chris turned away and strode back to his Jeep while Alek ranted and raved, calling after him.

"Curt? Curt!"

Chris climbed into the Jeep, started the ignition, and hit the gas.

Chapter Forty-two

Heather sat at her kitchen table, trying to decide what to do. She had called Mindy, but Mindy hadn't answered, so she'd left a voicemail introducing herself and asking for a call back, but not giving any details. Heather had followed up with a text, but Mindy hadn't responded to that either. Then Heather had called Susan, but Susan hadn't picked up. Heather had left the same voicemail message and follow-up text.

Now she was fresh out of ideas. Jordan was sulking in his room, angry that she had confiscated his phone, which rested on the table in front of her. She'd taken his laptop too, so he couldn't text or G-chat. She didn't want any more online shenanigans until this mess was sorted out. She was beginning to hate the Internet altogether.

Heather sipped her coffee, which had turned cold, and her troubled gaze fell on the Friendly's sign outside the window. TRY OUR FRIBBLE MILKSHAKE FRESH AND FROTHY! She'd never eaten in Friendly's, though she could've recited every item on its menu, including made-up words like FRIBBLE and FISH-A-MAJIG, which appeared regularly on the sign. Maybe when this was over, she and Jordan could go over and have a Hunka Chunka PB Superfudge. Or maybe she could go over there with Coach Hunka Himself. Chris, her Inappropriate Crush.

Suddenly Heather got an idea. She could call Chris about the pictures. She wasn't even using it as an excuse. If Evan had really sent these photos to everybody on the baseball team, then somebody on the coaching staff should be made aware of it. Heather had never met Coach Hardwick and she felt intimidated by the horrible stories about him. But she knew Chris. It would make sense to contact him, though it wouldn't be the romantic beginning she'd been hoping for—*Hey Chris, did you see the dirty pictures the team is looking at?*

Suddenly Jordan's phone rang, and she reflexively looked over at the screen. It read, **Evan Kostis calling,** and impulsively, she picked it up. "Evan, this is Jordan's mom."

"Oh, Ms. Larkin, is Jordan there? Can I speak to him?"

"Actually, no you can't, not yet." Heather thought Evan sounded upset. "Before I tell Jordan that you're calling, I need to deal with something. I've called your mother but I haven't heard back from her yet. May I speak with her?"

"Uh, I'm not home."

"Okay, well then." Heather hesitated. "I happened to see an inappropriate picture you sent to Jordan, and I'm very concerned. I think—"

"Mrs. Larkin, I'm really sorry, I already talked to my mom and dad about it, and they're angry, too. I know I never should've done that, and I'm very sorry. I apologize to you and Jordan."

Heather felt a pang of sympathy, but she wasn't about to let him off the hook. "Evan, I'm glad you feel remorseful, but this is a very bad thing. I don't even know the implications myself. There might even be legal issues—"

"I know, I know, my mom said the same thing, and I'm really sorry. Can I talk to Jordan?"

"No, you may not." Heather thought Evan was trying to rush

her off the phone. "I would like to understand the situation better. Who else did you send the picture to?"

"Just the team."

Heather rued the day that Jordan finally made varsity. *Winner's Circle, my ass.* "Who's this girl in the photo? Is it your girlfriend? Does she know that you sent this picture around? Evan, this is a terrible thing to do—"

"Mrs. Larkin, my parents are all over it, so you really don't have to worry about it. Now can I please talk to Jordan?"

"No." Heather didn't like his attitude. "You can talk to Jordan when you've answered my question. You sent my son a photograph that can get him in trouble with the law. I want to know what you did—"

Suddenly the call went silent, and Jordan came rushing into the kitchen. "Mom, was that my phone? Was that for me?"

"Yes, it was Evan, and you'll be happy to know he sent that photo to the varsity players only, so only the best players will be going to prison."

Jordan's eyes flared. "Mom, did you just talk to him right now? Did you yell at him?"

"I didn't yell, but I told him 'no,' and if you ask me, it's about damn time."

"Mom, what are you doing? You're not his mom!" Jordan's mouth dropped open.

"His mom didn't call me back and neither did Raz's."

"You called *her*, too?" Jordan threw up his hands. "Mom, you can't do this! You're telling on everybody! Why did you do that? Evan's going to be so pissed at me!"

"First off, that shouldn't be your main concern, and second, Evan's parents already knew."

"How do you know?"

"He just told me."

"Mom, give me my phone, please." Jordan held out his hand for the phone, but Heather tucked it into her back pocket.

"You're not getting your phone or laptop 'til we figure this out."

"Mom, it's my phone."

"Not anymore."

"I paid for it. I bought it with my own money."

"It's under my roof, and so are you."

"Give it to me!" Jordan took a step forward, but Heather stood her ground, realizing for the first time that she wasn't big enough to stop him if he needed stopping. She realized that she and her son were crossing a parenting point-of-no-return. She looked him in the eye as fiercely as she could, for a woman who was accustomed to waiting for a living.

"And don't even think about trying to take it from me."

"You're ridiculous!" Jordan yelled, then walked out of the room.

Heather exhaled, wondering if other mothers had their sons walk out on them on a regular basis. She picked up her own phone and redialed Mindy. It was the right thing to do since she had just yelled at Evan. The call rang and rang, then went to voicemail, so she left a message: "Mindy, this is Heather, Jordan Larkin's mom, calling again. Could you please call me when you get a moment? It's very important."

Heather hung up, followed it up with a text, then phoned Susan.

Chapter Forty-three

Mindy sat on her bed with her laptop, scrolling through Facebook, but this time she wasn't posting or reading feeds. She typed Cynthia Caselli into the SEARCH window, and a long list of thumbnails of young girls, older women, and even a Maltese puppy came up. She scanned for local entries and found Cynthia Caselli, who went to Rocky Springs High.

Mindy clicked the thumbnail. Cynthia's face popped onto the screen, a gorgeous, blue-eyed blonde with a dazzling smile. Mindy thought of the baby and how pretty he or she would have been. Her grandchild. Mindy had looked forward to the day when she'd be a grandmother, since all of her older friends at the club talked about their grandchildren all the time. They said it was an experience like no other.

Mindy felt tears well up, but blinked them away. She looked at the Facebook page and, unfortunately, couldn't learn more about Cynthia Caselli, since the girl kept her page private except for the profile picture and the basic information.

Mindy opened a new window, went into White Pages, and typed in Cynthia Caselli, which called up a list of names and addresses. At the top was Paul and Gloria Caselli, 383 Hilltop Drive, Rocky Springs, PA, with a telephone number.

Mindy picked up her phone, then hesitated. She didn't know why she had the urge to call. On the one hand, it was a dumb idea, and she didn't know what she would say. On the other hand, she didn't like being left out of the equation, and at the very least, she owed them an apology. Paul could call the Casellis lowlifes, but Mindy and her spoiled son were no better than this girl or anybody else.

Mindy called the number, and the phone was answered after two rings by a woman. "Hello, is this Gloria Caselli?"

"Yes, who's calling?"

Mindy felt her heart start to pound. She couldn't believe that she was actually talking to the other grandparent of her grandchild, and it was strange to be connected through blood to a woman she had never met. But now that connection was gone, making it even stranger. "This is Mindy Kostis, Evan's mom."

"Oh, yes, how are you, Mrs. Kostis?"

"Please, call me Mindy. In the circumstances, I think it's appropriate." Mindy's mouth went dry. Now she had to think of what to say, and it was awkward. She wished she had a drink, but those days were over, so she had to tough it out.

"Okay, call me Gloria. Now, can I help you with something?"

"I don't know where to begin." Mindy felt so ashamed of Evan, Paul, and herself. "I guess I'm just calling to say that I didn't know what was going on with Evan and Cynthia, and I'm sorry about all of it. I am truly sorry."

"Well, there's nothing to be sorry for. They're young. It happens."

"It does?" Mindy asked, surprised. She would have expected Gloria to be furious with her and Evan.

"Yes, sure. They dated awhile, and Cyn was very hurt when Evan broke up with her. But she has a new boyfriend, so all's well that ends well. I don't like when teenagers get serious too soon, do you?"

"Well." Mindy felt flabbergasted. She'd been trying to be delicate, but it wasn't working. "I meant about the baby. I'm sorry that that happened. They didn't tell me about it. They kept it from—"

"What baby?"

"The baby, you know, their baby. Cynthia and Evan's."

Gloria gasped. "Wait. What baby? I don't know what you're talking about."

Mindy froze. Paul and Evan had told her that Cynthia's parents knew about the baby. But what if they had lied to her? What if the Casellis hadn't known? What if they were hearing it for the first time from Mindy? And now the baby was gone. Mindy didn't know what to say. Anything she said would break Gloria's heart.

"Mindy? What baby?"

"They got pregnant," Mindy blurted out, stricken. "Cynthia got pregnant and she had an abortion out-of-state, in New York. Evan and my husband gave her the money and put her up in a hotel. I thought you and your husband knew about it—"

"Are you *serious*?" Gloria sounded shocked. "That's not true at all! Cyn didn't become pregnant or have an abortion! Nothing like that happened."

"Yes, it did."

"No it didn't," Gloria shot back, firmly.

"I'm sorry if you're hearing this for the first time from me, but they told me you knew."

"There's nothing to know. It didn't happen. Trust me. You're wrong."

Mindy didn't understand. "I'm not, we just discussed it. They just told me. Maybe she just didn't tell you, or maybe she told your husband and not you. That's what Evan did, he told his father and not me."

"No, wrong. It's just false."

Mindy felt completely bewildered. Maybe Gloria was in denial. "Believe me, I don't mean to offend you, but sometimes we don't know what's going on in our own houses—"

"Mindy, if you really must know, my daughter had a torsed ovary at fourteen, and it was removed in emergency surgery. She's been on birth control ever since, to make sure she doesn't lose both of them. So the odds of Cyn's getting pregnant are slim to none. Now, I'm done with this conversation."

"Oh, my I'm sorry. Good-bye." Mindy hung up, shaken. She had no idea what was going on, but she didn't cry, and she didn't hesitate.

She got up, left the bedroom, and went downstairs to find Paul.

Chapter Forty-four

Mindy reached the bottom of the stairwell and didn't have to go any farther, because oddly, Paul was in the family room, where he never spent any time. He was sitting on the couch and staring at the ceiling, his head resting backwards in the cushion. A crystal tumbler with two fingers of Scotch rested near his hand.

Mindy entered the room, and Paul shifted his gaze to look at her. His gaze looked weary, exhausted, and bleary from the alcohol, but she still didn't feel sorry for him. In fact, she felt nothing for him.

"Paul, I just got off the phone with the Casellis." Mindy stood over him. "Would you like to explain to me what the hell is going on?"

Paul blinked, dully. "You called the Casellis," he said quietly. "Of course you did."

"What does that mean? What's going on?" Mindy didn't understand the way he was acting. He seemed to be decompensating, which was completely unlike him. "Did Cynthia Caselli have an abortion or not?"

"No, she didn't."

"*What?*"

"Evan didn't get her pregnant. It was a total lie."

Mindy had no idea how to react. She felt dumbstruck, astonished, and shocked. "Is this a joke? Are you kidding? Evan *didn't* get that girl pregnant?"

"No, he didn't."

"Did *you?* Did *you* get somebody pregnant?"

"Of course not, nobody got anybody pregnant." Paul sounded almost bored, reaching for his Scotch.

"Don't say 'of course not' to me," Mindy said calmly. She didn't feel the need to shout, with him acting so strange. "Are you telling me that you and Evan lied to me?"

"Yes. Well, to be precise, Evan made it up and I went along with it."

"What do you *mean?* Why? What's going on? Did you plan this?"

"No, we didn't plan anything. I didn't think you'd find the withdrawals and neither did he."

"Paul, why would you make up such a horrible story? I was so upset that he got a girl pregnant, that he aborted the child, our grandchild."

"I just told you, I didn't make up the story. He did, on the spot." Paul sighed. "He's a teenager. He was making it up as he went along. The good news is he's not that good a liar."

"Not as good as his father."

"No, not at all."

Mindy didn't like the way he was acting, almost comatose. She began to feel a tingle of fear. Something was terribly wrong with him. "Paul, tell me what's going on."

"You need to sit down."

"Don't tell me what to do, just tell me what you did."

"Mindy, this is bad. This is as bad as it gets. I suggest you sit down." Paul's unfocused gaze met hers, and something told

Mindy to follow his advice. It wasn't a power struggle anymore, because Paul was acting absolutely powerless.

"What is it?" Mindy asked, sitting opposite him on the chair.

"I was trying not to tell you because I thought I had it handled. I thought it would blow over, but that's not happening. You're going to find out sooner or later because I'm going to be indicted next week. So there you have it."

"Indicted?" Mindy gasped.

"Yes, I've been the target of a federal investigation for the past six months, from the IRS and the FBI. Not one, but two federal agencies. Two." Paul held up two fingers like a victory sign.

"What are you talking about?" Mindy felt like she was in a bad dream. This didn't make any sense. It couldn't be possible. He could still be lying. She didn't know who he was anymore. Her husband, the stranger.

"I'm about to be indicted for Medicaid fraud, money laundering, and income-tax evasion."

Mindy felt the blood rush to her head, as if she would faint. She leaned on the soft arm of the chair.

"Would you like a drink? I know you drink." Paul held out his tumbler of Scotch, smiling crookedly.

"No." Mindy found her voice, choked. "Is this really true?"

"Yes. Next week, I'm going to be indicted." Paul didn't bat an eye. He stayed preternaturally calm, almost mechanical. "I took the money out of Evan's account. He didn't even know about it. I needed a criminal lawyer who specialized in white-collar crime. They wanted a retainer. I couldn't write them a check because I knew you would see it, and our assets are about to be frozen when the indictment is filed."

"Paul, no." Mindy reeled. It was too much to take in all at once. Part of her still wasn't sure it was true. She felt gaslighted. "Are you lying again? Is this real?"

"Mindy, my dear, this is as real as it gets. They've been making my life a living hell every day since they sent me the target letter, you don't even know. That's where I've been, all these times I've told you I'm working late. I've been meeting with my lawyers and the IRS and FBI, trying to hammer out a deal."

"What did you do? Did you do these things?" Mindy struggled to process the information, all at once. If he was telling the truth now, he wasn't having an affair. He was doing something much worse, but all he felt was self-pity.

"Yes, I did these things."

"What, exactly? How?" Mindy couldn't wrap her mind around what she was hearing. Paul was a selfish jerk, but he never did anything illegal, that she knew of. And they had plenty of money to pay taxes with.

"I'll simplify it, because my lawyers aren't here to cite chapter and verse. I don't have to worry about your testifying against me at trial, even if you divorce me, because we're not going to trial. And you're in the clear, though you did sign our returns."

Mindy felt stunned. The words made no sense. *In the clear. Trial. Testify.* Her life was coming apart at the seams. She was too stricken to speak so she let him continue.

"Long story short, we've been charging for tests we don't perform and surgeries we don't perform, and we put the claims in and we keep the money. Of course we have to hide the money, which at this point is almost $7.2 million, and we've been dividing it equally among the three of us."

"*Seven million* dollars?" Mindy began to get her bearings, hearing the number. The money made it real. It was real. "Where's it all going?"

"Our share is over 2 million, and we've been spending it on this very couch, our club membership, Evan's BMW, and the Caymans' vacation, which really was fun, I have to tell you."

Mindy had no idea why he would do such a thing. Money had never been a problem, so she didn't know why he would take such a risk.

"Mike, my beloved pal, told his lovely wife, Linda, and Linda made him tell the feds, who offered him a very sweet deal. In return for that, he became what's known as a CI, or a confidential informant. He's been wearing a wire under his lab coat for the past six months."

"Mike, your *partner*?" Mindy had always liked him and Linda. They'd been friends since Mike joined the group.

"Yes. They've also been tapping my cell phone and my office phone, and by the way, Carole was in on it too. We needed her cooperation to fake the billing. That's why we hired her and that's why I bought her the jewelry. To keep her happy and quiet. I know it's not her birthday." Paul sipped his Scotch, then made a clicking sound with his teeth, knocking it back. "Mike gave them the whole case. We would've gotten away with it—we *were* getting away with it—but he handed it to the feds on the proverbial silver platter. Which also happened to hold my head."

"Paul, did you really do these things?" Mindy asked in disbelief.

"Yes, I did."

"Why?"

"Money, primarily. The money is just too good. And frankly, I'm angry."

"You're angry about *what*?" Mindy shook her head, dumbfounded. "You have everything. We have everything."

"I'm angry at managed care, or rather, mismanaged care. I'm sick of being told what tests I can run, what procedures I can bill for, what drugs I can order, and which drug companies I can use." Paul glowered. "So I found a way to get them back. I'm making up the money I would have been earning if they hadn't been interfering with my cases."

Mindy heard the self-pity eke into his voice and she began to grasp the implications of what he was telling her. "So what are you saying? You're going to prison?"

"Yes. I'm going to make a deal, Min. I'm going to plead guilty. I'll get twenty-two months."

"You're really *going to jail?*" Mindy felt incredulous.

"Yes, and the government is taking everything. Everything we own, everything in this room." Paul gestured around at the furniture. "It's going to be sold to pay the fines and make restitution. It's being seized, the whole house, the cars, everything we own."

Mindy felt her lips part in shock. Her hand went to her chest. Her heart thundered. She understood everything now, but she didn't care about the house, the car, or the couch. The only thing that concerned her was Evan. "What does Evan have to do with this? You didn't mix him up in this, did you?"

"No, he's in the clear."

"What do you mean 'in the clear'? Why did he make up the story? What happened?"

"After I got the target letter, he heard me talking on the phone, trying to hire a lawyer. He overheard the whole conversation and he asked me about it. I didn't mean for him to know. I thought it would never get this far, I didn't think they could prove their case. I didn't figure that Mike had turned into *their* partner, instead of mine." Paul shook his head, clucking his tongue again. "And I was so good to that jerk. I took him into the group when nobody else would have him. He's not that good a surgeon. He's practically a butcher, I'm telling you—"

"So then what happened with Evan?"

"Well, I suppose I confided in Evan from time to time, and he wanted to know. He saw what I was going through, and believe me, he's as angry about this as I am. He saw what they were doing to me." Paul sipped his Scotch, draining the tumbler. "It's been a nightmare, honey. You have no idea how much power the government has, and when it turns on you, you don't stand a chance. Not a chance."

"So you've been confiding in Evan all this time?"

"I needed the support, frankly."

"Your son isn't supposed to support you, you're supposed

to support him." Mindy felt anger burn, like hot steel. "You shouldn't have told him, you should have told me."

"I didn't want to worry you—"

"Stop lying to yourself. You didn't want to *face* me." Mindy controlled her temper. Paul didn't matter anymore. Only Evan did. "So you let your son pay for your lawyer? You let your son take the rap for you? You let him lie to me? You let him hide what you did from me?"

Paul sighed heavily, shifting his gaze back to her, unfocused. There was no love in his eyes, nor was there any remorse. "I was about to tell you the truth, and if you think back, you'll remember that. I started to tell you, but he cut me off and he came up with this crazy story about an abortion, and I thought, why not go along with it? But I'm going to have to plead guilty. So you're going to find out sooner or later and you're finding out. Sooner."

"Where did Evan go?"

"I don't know. I have no idea."

"Is that really true?"

"Absolutely. Probably with his friends or one of his girlfriends. Our golden boy. He leads a charmed life."

"Does he?" Mindy said, rising. She began to panic. It was dark and they hadn't heard from Evan. She couldn't imagine him driving around for so long, and he had to be shaken to the core. He had lied to protect his father, who didn't deserve him. Or her.

"I'm sure he'll be fine."

Mindy's brain began to function. This was too heavy a burden for Evan, or any kid. His life was about to come tumbling down, and his father was going to jail. He would lose his home. Everybody at school would know, his teammates, his friends, his teachers. "Did you call him? Or text him?"

"No."

"Nice. Perfect. Great." Mindy reached for her phone and read the home screen. She'd gotten some texts from some moms but the text that jumped out at her was from Evan. She hadn't even heard it come in, maybe it came in when she was on the phone with Gloria Caselli. She swiped to read the text, which said:

mom, don't worry im fine. call u asap. love u

"Min, did he text you?"

"Yes, he texted me, but he doesn't say where he is or when he's coming home." Mindy took no comfort from the text. In fact, it worried her more. She called Evan again, but the call rang and rang then went to voicemail. She texted him.

call me asap please im worried about u

"If he texted, he's fine. He'll be home when he cools down."

"I wonder if he's with that girl, Amanda." Mindy went into her phone, scrolled to the photo she'd taken of Amanda's phone number, and called. The call rang and rang, then went to voicemail, a recorded message with a mechanical voice. She waited for it to end, then said: "Amanda, this is Evan's mother. Is Evan with you? Please have him call me right away. If he isn't with you, I want *you* to call me back right away. Right away!"

Paul called from the couch. "Min, who's Amanda?"

Mindy didn't bother answering, reflexively going to the window. Evan's BMW was gone, of course. He could be with Amanda or sitting alone in a car somewhere, distraught. She scanned the street, but there was no BMW. The moon shone on McMansions, manicured hedges, and mulched beds of daffodils. Everybody had a new car and a basketball hoop, and they all recycled. Mindy mentally kissed it good-bye. She only wanted her son back.

Her mind raced. She prayed that Evan wasn't running away. She looked down at the other texts and started opening them. Somebody had to know where he was.

Evan, where are you?

Chapter Forty-five

Chris worked in his home office, multitasking in high gear. He'd isolated the videotapes of the four suspects—Raz, Evan, Trevor, and Dylan—and was playing them. Their recorded voices echoed through the room while he reviewed the photos he'd taken of Dylan's house. It was the way he always worked a case, immersing himself in the investigation, reviewing all the facts and studying each detail. Every time, something popped out at him that he hadn't noticed before. He'd never been under such time pressure, but he performed better under the gun.

He shifted to the photos that he'd gotten from Abe's cottage and scanned each one. They showed scenes of white-capped mountains, a wildlife museum, Abe's older parents sitting in a porch swing, and Jamie, Abe, and the other teachers and their spouses at a pool in their bathing suits, smiling with their arms around each other. Abe stood happily at the center, and Chris felt a pang at Abe's loss, a sign of how deeply this operation had sunk into his bones. He couldn't let Abe's killers get away with murder and he had to stop them from killing anybody else. There *had* to be a connection.

Chris heard voices and a knocking at the door downstairs, but he ignored it. He wasn't expecting anyone. They must have the wrong building. It happened because the townhouses in the development looked alike.

A woman called out, "Chris, are you home?"

Chris recognized the voice. It was Heather's. As much as he liked her, he didn't have time to deal. He waited, hoping she would go away.

"Chris, it's Heather and Jordan! Are you home? Your car is here!"

Chris would see what they wanted and get rid of them fast. He closed the file, hurried from his office, and hustled to the front door, buzzing them in. He stepped outside his apartment door to greet them on the landing, as they came upstairs. Heather looked stressed, her hair loose and her hands shoved into her jacket pockets, and Jordan lumbered behind her as if they weren't even together.

"Oh hello, guys," Chris said quickly. "Sorry, you caught me at a bad moment."

"Chris, hi." Heather flashed a tight smile, reaching the landing. "We're really sorry to bother you."

Jordan interjected, "Hey Coach. My mom wanted to come, not me."

"Thanks. Jordan." Heather shot him a tense look, then turned back to Chris. "Chris, I wouldn't be here if it weren't important. Something came up that you need to know about, as coach. I didn't want to go to Coach Hardwick because, well, I don't know him, and I didn't want to call the principal if we could keep it to the team. In-house, as it were."

"Okay, how I can help you?" Chris resigned himself to dealing with it, then getting them out of here.

"Well, can we come in?" Heather blinked. "I don't want to talk about it out here."

"Oh, sure, right. Excuse my bad manners." Chris ushered them inside, but left the door open.

"Well, this is awkward to talk about, but here goes." Heather frowned, barely glancing around the apartment. "Jordan got an inappropriate picture in a text from Evan today. It's of a girl that Evan's dating, a sext. Jordan thinks they call her Miss Booty Call, but whatever. Evan sent it to the entire varsity team and apparently he has done this before. I don't know what to do, but we have to do *something*."

"I understand." Chris had no time for a high-school sexting drama. "I'll deal with this first thing tomorrow morning when—"

"I just want to say, it's the first time that Jordan ever got one of these pictures from Evan. Jordan wasn't on varsity before. I don't want my son to get in trouble for something that Evan is doing. Jordan needs a baseball scholarship and if this goes on his record—"

Jordan interjected, "But I don't want to get Evan in trouble. I called him but he didn't call me back."

"Jordan, really?" Heather shot Jordan another look, then returned her attention to Chris. "I called Mindy, Evan's mother, but this is the least of her worries right now. She's beside herself. She just found out that her husband's going to jail for tax evasion."

"Really," Chris said, surprised.

"Yes, and they had a big family fight. She doesn't even know where Evan is."

"Evan is missing?" Chris's ears pricked up.

"Well, not missing, just not home." Heather pursed her lips. "But Evan isn't my problem. That family can afford to write a check for college, but we can't, and I'm not going to let Evan hurt Jordan's chances to be recruited."

"I agree, Jordan shouldn't get in trouble. But it's Sunday night, so I can't contact Coach Hardwick, Dr. McElroy, or anybody in the office." Chris walked to the door. He sensed that something was going on with Evan and he had to get back to his desk. "Guys, I really appreciate your bringing this to my attention, but

I'm in the middle of something. I will discuss this with them first thing in the morning—"

"Chris, I must not be making myself clear, this is so awkward." Heather took a phone from her pocket and scrolled through it as she talked. "Maybe you need to see what I'm talking about to understand. It's a *very* inappropriate picture. Look!"

"I assumed it was—" Chris started to say, but stopped when Heather held up her phone. Its screen showed the naked body of a woman whose face wasn't shown but whose legs were parted, leaving nothing to the imagination. She had a tattoo on her side, a dream catcher.

"Heather, let me see that." Chris felt something nagging at him.

"The sext?" Heather handed him the phone. "Kinda weird of you, but okay."

"Excuse me for one minute." Chris eyed the photo, handed her back the phone, and edged backwards toward his office. "Just wait here."

Chapter Forty-six

Chris hustled into his office, closed the door behind him, and hurried to his desk for the pictures from Wyoming. He found the one he was looking for, the photo of Jamie, Abe, and the other teachers and their spouses in bathing suits. His gaze went straight to Courtney, who was wearing a black two-piece suit. She had a tattoo on her side, and he looked at it closely but couldn't tell what it was. If it had been a digital photo, he would simply enlarge it, but he didn't have a scanner.

Chris tore open his desk drawer, found an old-school magnifying glass, and held it up to the photo. He moved it over Courtney's waist, and the ink came into focus. Courtney's tattoo was a dream catcher, and it was on her right side, in the same position on her body as in the nude selfie. He compared it with the phone, and it was a match.

Chris blinked. So Courtney was the woman in the sext, and she and Evan must've been having an affair. But something else was far more concerning. Heather had said that Evan's father was about to go to jail for tax evasion, a federal crime. Evan was so upset that he'd left the house. That could give Evan a motivation for a grudge against the government. But where was Evan? Could he be with Courtney?

Chris felt adrenaline surge into his system. He turned to his computer and plugged in Courtney's name and Central Valley PA, and the first address was hers:

Courtney Wheeler, 297 Mole Drive, Central Valley, PA

Then Chris's gaze fell on the third address, under **previous addresses of Courtney Wheeler,** and the entry read:

Courtney Shank Wheeler, 938 Evergreen Circle, Headley, PA

Chris's thoughts raced. Headley, PA. Where had he heard that name before? The Rabbi had said it. It was up north in Marcellus Shale. Courtney and her family were from the Marcellus Shale area. *She* could have been the connection to the baseball team—and if so, that meant Evan was the boy in the Musketeers Varsity T-shirt, stealing the bags of ammonium nitrate fertilizer from Herb Vrasaya's farm.

Chris felt the revelation electrify his system. If Evan was missing, it could be going down tonight. Or Evan could be in mortal jeopardy.

Chris reached for his phone and was pressing in the Rabbi's number when he heard the door opening.

"Chris?" Heather stood in the threshold with Jordan, her bewilderment plain.

Chapter Forty-seven

"Chris, what are you doing?" Heather asked, aghast.

"Excuse me." Chris hustled out of the office and closed the door behind him. "I'm sorry, but you both have to go, and so do I."

"What do you mean?" Heather recoiled, frowning. "What's going on?"

"I can't explain more. You both have to go. Please."

"But aren't you going to deal with this situation?" Heather folded her arms. "I'm not just going to let my son—"

"Heather, please. Evan could be in grave trouble." Chris grabbed his windbreaker from the hook and his keys from the side table.

"But what about Jordan? Jordan matters, too. I'm surprised you would treat him like he doesn't. I thought you cared about him. About us."

"Heather." Chris felt pained. He wanted to touch her but he didn't. Instead, he said, "Of course I care about you both. But please, for now, go."

"Why?" Heather asked, wounded.

"Coach, what's up? Why are you acting so random?" Jordan's

lips parted, and Chris could see how hurt they were, which made him feel terrible. He had deceived her and Jordan, who had trusted him. They had been his unwitting, and he'd never felt bad about it before. He owed them an explanation.

"Heather, Jordan, there's something I have to tell you. I'm a Special Agent with the Bureau of Alcohol, Tobacco, Firearms, and Explosives, and I'm working undercover."

"Chris? You're a *what*?" Heather asked, astonished. "You mean, you're not really a coach?"

"Correct, I'm not a coach. That was a cover story. I have to go now. We all do." Chris had no more time to lose. He crossed the room and removed the false front from a shelf in the entertainment center, which concealed a small safe that he'd built into the wall himself.

"Whoa, Coach, I mean, for real?" Jordan gasped. "Are you kidding right now?"

"Jordan, I'm sorry I lied to you, but I had to." Chris dialed the safe's combination, opened the door, and took out his wallet and shoulder holster with his Glock. He closed the safe, walked back to Heather and Jordan, and showed them his ID and badge. "Here's my ID, so you know."

"It says Curt Abbott," Heather said, shocked. "Chris isn't your real name?"

"No, now that's all I can tell you and I shouldn't even be telling you that. I'm asking you to keep this completely confidential. Tell no one outside of this room. This is a federal matter, and we are handling it." Chris felt a wrench in his chest to see Heather edge backwards, her eyes showing the sting of betrayal.

"Chris, is this really true?" she asked, her tone newly hushed. "You lied to us to help Evan?"

"No but I can't explain more," Chris rushed to say, slipping on his shoulder holster and checking the snap on the thumb break, which held his Glock securely in place. "You'll be contacted by an ATF agent within the hour. They'll confirm what I'm saying. Now let's go, hurry."

Chris hustled them downstairs, then ran for his car, pulling out ahead of them.

It was go-time.

Chapter Forty-eight

Chris tore out of his development, heading toward Court-ney's. Mole Street was in the Murray Hills development, and he knew the way. He reached for his phone and called the Rabbi, who answered immediately.

"Curt, hi. I'm at the burn site, and we got nothing. Tell me something good. Improve my mood."

"Can do. I think the kid who stole the fertilizer is Evan Kostis, from my baseball team." Chris steered right, then left through the deserted streets. "He was having an affair with a female teacher at the high school, Courtney Wheeler, and she's origi-nally from Headley. Her maiden name is Shank, and she used to live on Evergreen Circle. I'm going to her house in Central Valley right now."

"So they *were* connected. Nice work! You need backup? I'll get the locals over there."

"Yes, but I don't want them to tip her off if she's there."

"Think she will be?"

"No. She could be up there with Evan. You need to send people over to her family home in Headley." Chris told him the address.

"So you think the kid's in the conspiracy with the teacher?"

"Yes." Chris whizzed past the outlet malls, their stores darkened and closed. "His father is about to be indicted for tax evasion, a doctor at Blakemore Medical Center in Central Valley. Ask your AUSA and IRS pals what the deal is. That might be the source of Evan's gripe against the government."

"Okay. How are they traveling? You got a vehicle or a tag?"

"Not for Courtney, but Evan is driving a new black BMW. I'll text you photos of the tag, the car, and him." Chris had a photo of the BMW in his phone from that day in the parking lot, at school.

"What does this have to do with the dead teacher, Abe Yomes?"

"Not sure yet, but Abe was close friends with Courtney. You got anybody to call my unwitting, Jordan and Heather Larkin? I had to blow my cover, it couldn't be avoided. They need handholding."

"Text me the information, and I'll get somebody over there."

"Thanks. We have to assume any bomb plot is now in progress. If it was an anniversary bombing, they're not waiting anymore." Chris would fill him in about the sexting later, which would have accelerated the plot.

"Agree, they have to know we're onto them by now. Meantime we'll liaise with Homeland Security, the Joint Terrorism Task Force, and the FBI. They're all here. You need to get up here after you assess the situation at the Wheeler house."

"Okay. You going to send a helo for me?" Chris knew that getting a helo wasn't always easy for ATF, which no longer had an aviation fleet. It received air support from DEA and U.S. Customs & Border Protection, through a Memorandum of Understanding, or MOU.

"Yes, we got all the toys up here."

"Good. Let me let you go. Call the locals and I'll meet them there."

"Stay safe."

"That's no fun," Chris said, hearing the bravado in his own voice. He used to say things like that all the time, but the words didn't fit so easily in his mouth anymore. He'd liked risk before, when he had nothing to lose. Now, it was different. Or it could have been.

Chris turned right, then left. At the first red light, he texted the Rabbi the photos from his phone. When the light turned green, he headed through the quiet suburbs late on a Sunday night, when everybody thought their biggest worry was work or school the next morning.

He had to make sure they were right.

Chapter Forty-nine

Chris turned into Murray Hills, and the development was quiet, the houses still and darkened. He turned onto Mole Road, found the house, parked in front, and hustled out of the Jeep. He had beat the local police.

The Wheeler's house was quiet, still, and dark, but a black BMW sat parked in the driveway behind a white Acura. It had to be Evan's. Chris hustled to the BMW, pulling out his phone and switching to the flashlight function. He reached the car, scanning inside, but saw nothing.

"Evan?" he called out, but there was no response, and Chris prayed the boy wasn't in the trunk, alive or dead. He would've popped it but he had to get inside the house. He jogged across the patch of front lawn, and when he reached the concrete steps in front of the door, he noticed that the front door stood partway open behind the screen door. The house was darkened inside.

Chris slipped his phone in his back pocket and pulled his gun from his shoulder holster, entering as quietly as possible. He found himself in a small living room and though the lights were off, he could see a dark figure lying motionless on the floor.

"Evan!" Chris rushed to the figure's side, kneeling and holstering his weapon. But the figure wasn't Evan. It was Courtney's husband, Doug, lying on his back. Blood soaked his T-shirt and the rug around his body, filling the air with its characteristic metallic odor.

"Doug!" Chris palpated under Doug's chin to feel for a pulse, but there wasn't any. The man's flesh felt cool, and his body remained still.

Chris began CPR, pressing down on Doug's chest, but there was no hope. The vast darkening stain on the rug showed that Doug had sustained a catastrophic loss of blood.

Chris kept compressing Doug's chest, but it practically caved in from the pressure. He could feel that Doug's sternum had been shattered and his ribs splintered, so there must have been two or three gunshots. Blood squeezed between Chris's fingers as he pressed down, and he glanced around to assess whether someone else was in the house, either dead or alive. He was taking a chance that he could be ambushed but he sensed he was alone and he had to give Doug every chance to survive.

"Come on, Doug," Chris said, trying to massage the man's heart back to life, but it wasn't happening. He finally stopped the compressions, feeling as if he were abusing a corpse.

Chris rose, wiped his hands quickly on his jacket, reached for his weapon, and began his walk-through. Courtney could be lying dead somewhere in the house, and so could Evan. He crossed the living room to the kitchen and scanned the room, but it was empty, its red pinpoint lights from the dishwasher, coffeemaker, and microwave clock glowing like a suburban constellation.

Chris hustled back into the living room and spotted a stairwell at the far left, so he went to it and climbed upstairs, looking around. There was a bathroom at the head of the stair, but it was empty, then he advanced down the hallway, ducking into the first room on his left, a master bedroom. Moonlight spilled through its two windows, and he could see there was no one else in the bedroom, which looked in order, not showing signs of struggle or ransacking, as if from a burglary.

Chris ducked out of the first bedroom and went to the second, evidently a spare bedroom with a single bed in the corner, and there was no activity or disturbance in there either.

So far, so good, Chris thought, relieved to see that Evan wasn't dead and neither was Courtney, at least not at this location. He left the bedroom, hurried back down the hall, and descended the stairwell. He spotted a side door, so he hurried inside, and down a set of stairs. He found himself in a finished basement with a bar, big-screen TV, and framed football jerseys on the wall. It was undisturbed, and there was no exit.

Chris ran upstairs and returned to the living room, where he saw Doug's body, and he looked down at the fallen man with a stab of anguish. Now two men had been murdered, and there would be more lives lost if he didn't succeed. He couldn't bring himself to even think the word, *fail.* Suddenly he heard the sound of sirens a few blocks away. The local police were en route.

Chris walked to the front door and switched on the light switch with his elbow, illuminating the room to signal that he was inside. The locals must have reached the block because the sirens became earsplitting, and he spotted another light switch next to the door, for the exterior fixture. He flicked it on with his elbow too, casting a yellowish cone around the front door.

Flashing red-and-white lights chased each other around the walls of the living room, accompanied by the blare of sirens, and Chris realized his hands were covered with Doug's blood. He raised his hands palms up, standard procedure in case the locals hadn't gotten the message that he was on the scene, an occupational hazard for undercover agents. He knew of a case where two undercover agents almost killed each other, each believing the other was the criminal.

Chris positioned himself in full view as three police cruisers, with their distinctive brown-and-yellow Central Valley emblems, pulled up in front of the house and braked, their car doors opening immediately. Uniformed police officers jogged toward the house.

"I'm Special Agent Curt Abbott, ATF," Chris shouted, as loudly as possible to be heard over the sirens.

"Copy that! Everybody, stand down!" shouted the police officer who took the lead, and none of the locals drew their weapons, so Chris opened the front door and stepped outside, meeting the lead cop at the front step. He seemed stocky in his brown uniform, in his fifties.

"Hello. Special Agent Curt Abbott, ATF," Chris said, in case they hadn't heard him. "I'd shake your hand, but mine are bloody."

"Officer Mike Dunleavy," said the lead cop, his expression grim under the patent bill of his cap.

"We have a gunshot victim dead in the living room, name Doug Wheeler. I believe this is his residence. I performed CPR but it's too late and—"

"A *murder*?" Officer Dunleavy interrupted, shocked. "I don't think we have two murders in Central Valley in a year."

"I also did a cursory walk-through and found no other bodies, dead or alive. Your guys may want to double-check. I didn't have time to check the backyard."

"We'll follow up. But a *murder*. What's this about, do you know?"

"Sorry, Officer Dunleavy, I can't share that with you."

"You got any suspects?"

"I can't share that with you, either."

"Jeez, was it a bomb, guns, or something like that? I figure, since you're ATF—"

"Sorry, I can't explain further."

"I get it, if you tell me you have to kill me." Office Dunleavy chuckled, without mirth. Behind him, cops were shutting off the sirens, setting up a perimeter with yellow caution tape, and putting on gloves and booties. Lights went on in the other houses on the street, and heads appeared at windows.

"Officer Dunleavy, have your boss call my boss and they'll fill you in. They'll complete whatever reports you need." Chris motioned to Evan's car. "Before I go, I need to check inside the BMW's trunk."

"Let me go back to my cruiser, I got a crowbar." Officer Dunleavy jogged off, while neighbors began to file out of their houses to watch, their coats draped over their bathrobes and pajamas on the chilly night.

Chris kept his face down and walked over to Evan's car. He prayed Evan wasn't dead in the trunk and he bent over and checked underneath to see if anything was dripping, just in case the trunk's seal wasn't perfect. The driveway underneath the BMW remained dry.

Chris straightened up, coming eye level with the license plate, then he did a double-take. The license plate read RET-7819, but that wasn't Evan's license plate, unless Chris remembered it wrong. He slid out his phone, thumbed to the text function, and scanned through the photos. He found the one of Evan's BMW that he'd just sent to the Rabbi. The license plate was PZR-4720.

Chris pressed redial to call the Rabbi, who picked up after one ring. "Rabbi, I got good news and bad news."

"What's the bad news?"

"Don't you want the good news first? Everybody wants the good news first."

"Not Jews. We're tough. Give it to me straight."

"I found Courtney Wheeler's husband, Doug Wheeler, murdered in the house, three gunshot wounds to the chest. I tried to revive him but I couldn't."

The Rabbi groaned. "Okay, that's bad news. What's the good news?"

"I'm looking at Evan's black BMW, but it doesn't have the

right tag. Evan's tag is PZR-4720, as in the picture, but now it's RET-7819."

"So they switched the plates."

"Exactly. You need to find the vehicle with Evan's old tag. My bet is it's on a van, and you know what I'm thinking." Chris didn't elaborate because a local cop was within earshot, unrolling crime-scene tape.

"The van is a bomb on wheels," the Rabbi answered, finishing the thought.

"Bingo. If you run the plate I'm looking at, it'll tell you the make and model of the van."

"And it'll turn out to be a stolen vehicle."

"Agree. I think I'm done here. Where's my ride?"

"In the air, ten minutes away. Where do you want him?"

"The baseball field at the high school, southeast of the main building. That will jerk Alek's chain."

"You're enjoying this, aren't you?"

"Only a little bit. And tell the pilot not to mess up the clay on the baselines. My boys just raked it."

The Rabbi chuckled. "Don't push it."

"Did you learn anything new? Or do I have to do all the work around here?"

"We're on our way to the farmstead now. Evidently the Shank family is well-known to the locals. Everybody knows everybody up here."

"Tell me what you got."

"The mother died a long time ago, and father about six months ago, heart attack. Two older sons, David and Jim, both barroom brawlers. The Shank brothers, everybody calls them. No neo-Nazi, biker, Christian Identity, or alt-right affiliations. No college degree, no criminal record. Anti-frackers. Write letters to the editor of the local paper. Go to the rallies. Courtney is the only one who graduated college, the youngest of three. She's the one who got away."

"Good to know." Chris noticed Officer Dunleavy returning with a crowbar. "I'm about to break into the BMW to make sure there's nothing in the trunk."

"Attaboy. Stay in touch."

"Will do. Good-bye." Chris hung up, and Officer Dunleavy reached him, extending the crowbar.

"Special Agent, you want to do the honors?"

"No, have at it. The anti-theft system is going to give you a headache."

"All in a day's work." Officer Dunleavy wedged the crowbar under the lid of the trunk, pressed down, and popped the lid. The car alarm went off instantly, beeping in a night already abuzz with activity. Neighbors lined the sidewalk, watching, talking, and smoking cigarettes.

Officer Dunleavy pulled a flashlight from his utility belt and shined it inside the trunk, and Chris looked. There was nothing inside but a baseball glove and a blue Musketeers ball cap.

Chris swallowed hard at the sight. "Thanks, I gotta go," he said, jogging toward his Jeep.

Chapter Fifty

Chris flew northward in the helo, an older Black Hawk UH-60 on loan from DEA, which was being piloted by a Tony Arroyo, an African-American subcontractor who'd served two tours in Iraq. A dizzying array of dials, levers, and controls filled the dashboard in the all-glass cockpit, glowing an array of colors in the darkness, and though the big rotors whirred noisily over head, the helo barely shuddered in Tony's experienced hands.

Chris kept his head to the window, his thoughts racing. The bomb plot was being rushed and that was when criminals started taking bigger risks—which made them even more dangerous. If the Shanks had killed Doug, they hadn't bothered to disguise the murder as a suicide or a home invasion. They could be setting Evan up as the fall guy. They had left Evan's car in the driveway, and the switching of the license plates would point to Evan's guilt. Maybe the scenario they were trying to sell was that Evan had killed Courtney's husband in a jealous rage.

Chris tried the theory on for size, and it worked. Reasoning backwards, that meant that the stolen vehicle, presumably a van, had probably come from the Central Valley area, because it would be a location to which Evan had access, not the Shanks.

Chris mulled it over as he looked at the land below. They were flying roughly along Route 81 to 476. The sky was dark, and they passed Allentown and were coming up on Hazleton, due north. The terrain below turned wooded, then rural, signified by vast dark spaces with only intermittent houses, towns, or signs of civilization. The moon shone brightly on the left side of the sky, and Chris found himself checking it as they flew farther north, knowing that its incremental sinking meant it was getting later. Soon the sun would rise, and it would be Monday morning.

Chris shuddered to imagine people going to work with their cups of coffee, phones, and newspapers, boarding trains and buses to get themselves to a city, to a building, and finally to a desk to start the workday. They wouldn't know that their lives and the lives of everyone around them were about to end in a violent death.

Chris thought back to the Oklahoma City bombing, the WTC bombing on 9/11, and a string of other deadly bombings that made him want justice for the victims and their families. It was his job to never let it happen again.

He clenched his jaw as the helo zoomed north, heading toward the Shank farmstead in Susquehanna County, and ten minutes later, he could see the change in the terrain. Bright white lights twinkled below in a regular grid pattern, like a box of connect-the-dots in the dark night.

"What's that, over there?" Chris asked Tony, speaking into the microphone in his headset.

"Drilling wells for natural gas. We're coming up on the Marcellus Shale."

"Tell me about it, would you?" Chris should know, but didn't.

"The Marcellus Shale runs under the Appalachian basin and

includes seven states, like Pennsylvania, New York, New Jersey."
Tony pointed left. "Over there, that's the fairway, where the
shale's deep enough to extract."

"What's shale exactly?"

"Sedimentary rock that traps oil and gas in the layers. In the
old days, they tried to locate where the gas was and drill for it,
but now they frack for it." Tony pointed again. "I fly over this
all the time, doing VIP pickups. It changes every year. More well
pads and more drills."

Chris absorbed the information without judgment. He knew
fracking was a political hot button, but he'd always been apo-
litical. His job was to save lives, and he couldn't be distracted or
people died.

"Ten minutes to landing," Tony said, and Chris checked his
watch. It was 4:32 A.M.

Dawn would be here before he knew it, and the first order of
business was to find the target. ATF and the other federal agencies couldn't shut down every highway, bridge, and tunnel in the
Northeast. They couldn't issue a warning to all federal buildings
and state buildings. They had to learn where the disaster was
going to strike, so they could avert it.

The helo began to descend in the night sky, tipping forward.

Chris felt like a guard dog straining against a leash. He
couldn't wait until they touched down, setting him loose.

Chapter Fifty-one

Chris hustled from the helo toward the staging area, a white tent that had been erected on the front lawn of the Shanks' farmstead. Bright klieglights flooded the area, illuminating folding tables, chairs, and laptops that had been set up. Federal agents hustled back and forth in blue windbreakers labeled JTTF, FBI, and ATF. The local uniformed police stood at the perimeter around their squad cars.

Chris looked beyond the staging area to the farm, a compound that struck him as a poor man's version of Skinny Lane Farm. Its layout was almost identical, with a stone farmhouse behind a pasture, an old barn, and several outbuildings, albeit in disrepair. Faded blue shutters hung askew on the windows, and its clapboard was peeling in patches. The roofs sagged, and the barn had faded to a dried-blood color. The pastures had been overrun by tangled overgrowth of scrubby weeds, and the fences missed boards everywhere. Farm equipment, a truck, and an old car sat rusting on cinder blocks.

Chris spotted the Rabbi running from the farmhouse to meet him. "Hey, you got anything new?"

The Rabbi reached him out of breath. "The joint is jumping,

and the gang's all here. Let me brief you before we get inside. We're on top of each other in there."

"Okay." Chris hated that, too. Neither of them played well with others.

"Let me show you my phone. I got two videos. Check this out." The Rabbi held up his phone and pressed PLAY. "We ran the tag you gave us, and it belongs to a pickup, 2014 black Dodge dually, reported stolen from a used car lot outside of Central Valley. The locals sent us a traffic cam video."

"Good." Chris watched the video, in which a dark Ford Ranger pickup pulled up in front of a used-car lot and someone got out of the passenger seat wearing a black ski mask, black sweatshirt, and black pants. Unfortunately, the license plate wasn't in the frame.

"Now here's the video from the used-car lot." The Rabbi began thumbing through his videos, stopping at another one. He pressed PLAY, and the video showed the ski-masked figure breaking into the dually, with its characteristic double tires in the rear for bigger payloads. An old black cap covered its bed. The figure climbed inside and presumably hot-wired the dually, because he drove it out of the used-car lot.

"So far, so good."

"Stay tuned," the Rabbi said, and on the video, the dually drove away, but one moment later, was followed by the Ford Ranger pickup. The last frame showed the license plate of the Ranger before it slipped out of the frame.

"So you ran a plate on the Ranger."

"Yes, and it's Jimmy Shank's. So we got Jimmy on auto theft, and it got us into the farmhouse."

"You got anything on the target? And where's Evan and Courtney?"

"Nothing on Courtney or Evan, but come in and I'll brief you. We've narrowed possibilities for the target, and we put out a BOLO for auto theft. JTTF doesn't want to notify the public that we're talking about a domestic terrorist." The Rabbi headed for the farmhouse, and Chris fell into step beside him, checking his watch.

"But it's almost five o'clock in the morning. People are going to work soon."

"Tell me about it."

"Can't we issue some kind of general warning?"

"We're not calling the shots. JTTF is."

"But it's our operation."

"We know that but nobody else does." The Rabbi lowered his voice. "Humor them, Curt. It's the best way to get along. We divided the labor, and so far, we're living in harmony."

"So what's the division of labor?" Chris hid his frustration. He hated bureaucratic crap.

"Their guys searched the farm, and everybody's gone— the Shank brothers, Courtney, and Evan. We all went through the house, and the FBI found some of the files, and we found some others."

"What files?"

"I'll show you inside."

"Where's the burn site, the testing ground?"

"At a farm five miles away. Owner is Jason Zucker, and he's been in the hospital for a long time. Lives alone. Zucker is friends with the Shanks, so it makes sense that the Shanks would have used his backyard for testing while he was away."

"And nobody goes there?"

"It's in the middle of the woods. The FBI's command post is there. They think that's where the Shanks built the IED but they haven't found any bomb-making equipment yet." The Rabbi picked up the pace as they approached the farmhouse. "The Shanks took their laptops. We know they had them because there are boosters in two of the rooms. They left nothing behind. They're not coming back."

"But they're not suicide bombers."

"No, I don't think so. They must have a getaway plan."

"They're going to make Evan do it, aren't they?" Chris felt his chest tighten. "They're going to make Evan drive that dually. They're going to kill that kid."

"You're assuming he's not in on it."

"He's not in on it."

"Even with the IRS indictment?"

"Even so, I just don't see it going that far. I just don't see him or Courtney going that far."

"Evidently they are."

"You don't know if Courtney or Evan's with them."

"I got a good guess." The Rabbi hurried along. "Another possibility is that Courtney and Evan went off together. Killed her husband and took off. Let the brothers bomb their hearts out, but the kid runs off with the teacher."

"The brothers wouldn't let them get away. They couldn't take that risk."

"You think they'd turn on their sister?"

"You tell me. I never had a sister."

"Instead of life in prison? Yes. And the youngest always gets picked on, especially a girl. I drove my sister nuts."

They reached the front door, and Chris followed the Rabbi into the crumbling farmhouse, which had thick stone walls, low ceilings, and small rooms that were typical of homes built during the colonial era, but the décor was hardly historic. The walls had been paneled and decorated with deer heads in baseball caps, and worn mismatched furniture and a fake leather recliner sat around an old television on a metal cart. Beanbag ashtrays overflowed with cigarettes, and the air smelled like stale smoke.

"Love what you've done with the place," Chris said, then his gaze fell on a grouping of family photos that hung at crooked angles. He spotted Courtney's pretty face, a bright-eyed young girl with missing teeth in her school picture, then a First

Communion picture, and group pictures with her two older brothers, who had none of her good looks, though they shared her dark hair and dark brown eyes. Both brothers had broad smiles, which became flatter over the years.

The Rabbi pointed. "That's David, age thirty-eight, on the left and Jimmy, forty-five, on the right. We circulated a better one, but that gives you an idea."

"Got it." Chris took out his phone and snapped a photo, just in case.

"Come this way." The Rabbi led him from the living room and down the hall, past two crummy bedrooms to a back room, which appeared to be a spare bedroom. On the bed were piles of paper, correspondence in accordion files, and scattered court pleadings with blue backers.

"What's this?"

"More bad news." The Rabbi gestured to the papers. "The Shank family has had a dispute for the past five years with the Commonwealth of Pennsylvania, the Pennsylvania Department of Environmental Protection, the EPA, and Frazer Gas, which has leases to frack the neighboring farms. The problem is that three of the neighboring farms leased their land to Frazer Gas for fracking. Under Pennsylvania law, if three contiguous farms lease to frackers, the gas company can drill underneath your parcel, whether you leased or not. They drill horizontally."

"Really." Chris walked over to the papers, picked up the first packet, and started thumbing through the letter on top, to Frazer Gas, which read:

. . . You have ruined our home and our business. We used to sell top-quality horse and alfalfa hay, but then it was only good for mushroom hay and now even the mushroom farmers won't buy it. We can't sell it to anyone. You ruined our family business. We built a reputation as the best hay dealer on the quality of our

hay and now that has gone down the tubes. We could not even give it away, not once they found out where it came from and we are not willing to lie to people to take their money like you will . . .

"Pennsylvania's law allows it, and the fact is, you can own the surface rights of your property, but not the mineral rights. Lobbyists and politicians strike again."

Chris picked up the second packet, looking at the date, 2010. It was scientific testing of some type, attached to a letter.

Dear Sir,

We demand that Frazer Gas, the PADEP, and the EPA cease and desist their drilling! They have destroyed our property and made us sick, especially my elderly father! We demand justice and we have proof! You can see by this report that the air is contaminated and killing us and our horses and dogs!!!!

Chris flipped to the report, skimming down the list of chemicals:

BTEX (benzene, toluene, ethylbenzene', m-xylene, p-xylene, o-xylene); carbon tetrachloride, chloromethane, methylene chloride, tetrachloroethylene; trichlorofluoromethane . . .

The Rabbi continued, "The Shanks claim that as soon as the fracking started, their farm went to hell. The air turned bad, the water turned bad, and Frazer Gas and the state government ignored them. The state eventually conceded on the water quality when it caught fire."

"The water *burns*? Is it methane?" Chris turned to the next letter, also to Frazer Gas:

**. . . You give us water buffaloes but that's barely enough
for us to drink but we don't have drinkable water for the
horses and they all got so sick after you started drilling
they were bleeding out their noses, losing weight, and
refusing their grain until they died of starvation!!! My
hunting dog died the same way . . .**

"Evidently. The same thing happened in Dimock, if you heard
about that. So the Shanks and their neighbors complained and
complained, and the state finally sent in some water buffaloes."

"Water buffaloes?"

"It's not an animal, it's a big tank of potable water. The water
buffalo was for the family, not for the animals, and the Shanks
had horses. They had no choice but to give the horses the water
from the well, and over time, the horses got sick and died, except for one."

Chris felt for the Shank family and understood their griev-
ance. Whatever the cause, it would've been disastrous to lose
their farm and animals. He kept reading the letter.

**. . . You sold my neighbors a bill of goods. You made our
lives a living hell and now our houses are worth nothing.
Nobody will buy them and we can't even move away.
Your landsmen told them they would be getting royal-
ties from the drill leases and that was a TOTAL LIE.
They have yet to see a dime. You would say anything to
get what you want, and that is a TOTAL CRIMINAL
FRAUD that you perpetrated on . . .**

"They have forty-five acres, you'll see it out back. It's all open
until you get to the well pads drilling the neighboring farms. It's
not a pretty sight."

Chris looked out the window of the bedroom, but all he could see was darkness, and above it, the moon beginning to thin to transparency. Monday morning was on its way. He returned his attention to the letter:

> **... You were aided and abetted by the government! You know who to pay off and you have your lobbyists lining the pockets and kissing the asses of the politicians in Harrisburg and Washington. That is not LEGAL AND IT IS NOT JUSTICE. You don't care if you ruin family farms like ours. The Shanks have been in Pennsylvania since day one! Do you even know that William Penn named our beautiful Commonwealth Pennsylvania because that means Penn's Wood? He wanted it to be full of trees, not drilling pads ...**

"Then about two years ago, the father, Morris Shank, develops nosebleeds, nausea, headaches, heart trouble. The Shanks start a letter-writing campaign, file suits, make all the noise they can. They get stonewalled by the state and federal government, Frazer Gas countersues them, and six months ago, Morris Shank dies of a heart attack."

"Oh boy." Chris eyed the papers, dismayed. "And they blame the gas company, the state, and the feds."

"Exactly." The Rabbi gestured at the papers again. "So what you're looking at is antigovernment animus. Motivation. The Shank boys get angry. David starts drinking too much, and believe it or not, they blame that on fracking too. And they don't have a bad argument. The locals tell me that alcoholism and crime increases in fracking areas. Also traffic accidents, because of the heavy machinery using roads not meant to carry the loads and noise."

"Really."

"I'm not making a judgment, I'm telling you what they're telling me. The locals say people who leased their land aren't happy and haven't seen a dime in royalties, but it's too late. And it's not our focus. The target is."

"Right, the question is, what's the target? The Shanks want justice, and I don't think they got it. The federal courthouse in Philly is the logical target."

"That's the consensus. JTTF sent everybody that way after you called me. It's only 160 miles away. Three hours by car. Remember, it's the Byrne Courthouse on the south side, twenty-six floors, and on the north, the Green Federal Building, ten floors—1.7 million square feet, all told."

"How many people work there?" Chris shuddered to think of the loss of life.

"In the courthouse about a thousand, including appellate and district judges, magistrates, clerks, and staff, but it's higher with jurors and visitors." The Rabbi looked grim, his lined forehead buckling and his mouth a flat line. Grayish stubble marked his chin. "The Green Federal Building holds regional offices of the FBI, IRS, DEA, Secret Service, U.S. Marshal Service, Federal Probation Services, and other federal offices. It has about the same number of employees but more members of the public. We think we're talking, all told with foot traffic, thirty-five hundred people. And that doesn't count the businesses nearby."

"Oh man. The FBI and the IRS are relevant to Evan." Chris regretted his words as soon as they left his lips. "But I think they're setting him up, framing him."

"Maybe," the Rabbi said, averting his eyes, and Chris knew he wasn't on board.

"Does the target change, given the fact that we're onto them?"

"Unsure. In terms of targets, if they change their plans, we're close to the New York state border, and Harrisburg, the state capital, is three hours away. There's an endless number of soft targets—train stations, bus stations, bridges, and tunnels. It could be anything, if they change tacks."

"You get no bang for your buck in Harrisburg." Chris set the file back down. "If you want to get attention for a cause and kill a lot of people, you go to Philly or New York."

"Luckily, there's no major bridge between here and Philly. There's a few tunnels through the mountains, but they aren't much. I'm guessing they're going into Philly, and most of the federal buildings are around our office in Old City and—" The Rabbi fell abruptly silent as a cadre of FBI agents lumbered down the hallway and into one of the other bedrooms. "Let's go back outside and talk."

"When can I go?" Chris wanted to get back in the air, heading to the courthouse.

"We have to wait for authorization from JTTF. They'll call Alek and he'll call me."

"Are you serious?" Chris couldn't control his impatience. "I have to ask permission to work my own case?"

"Go along to get along, Curt."

"Man!" Chris sighed inwardly. He followed the Rabbi down the hall, nodding to the FBI agents, a group of JTTF types, and two men in suits. The Rabbi opened the front door, but they both saw at the same moment that their staging area was full of uniformed locals helping themselves to coffee and doughnuts.

"Follow me." The Rabbi gestured to the right, and Chris fell into step with him. They walked toward the rusted cars in front of the abandoned pasture, with the red barn behind. Chris took a deep lungful of air, but it didn't smell like country air, but vaguely acrid and foggy. The Rabbi leaned against an ancient blue Taurus, fishing in his breast pocket and pulling out his cigar and lighter. "You're not asking where Alek is."

"Don't tell me, let me guess. He's with the cool kids."

"Yes. Taking credit for your investigation. All the *machers* are up here, and he's angling for a promotion to JTTF. He only used us as a stepping-stone."

"I feel so cheap."

The Rabbi chuckled. "The party line is that he was behind you every step of the way."

"Fine with me. Let's get him promoted out. The next Alek can't be worse than this Alek."

"Ever hear of the Billy Goat's Gruff?"

Chris shrugged it off. "Were you able to get an agent to the Larkins?"

"Yes, is that your crush? Heather Larkin?"

"Yes." Chris had forgotten that he'd told the Rabbi about her.

"I sent Marie over. She's a great agent, nicer than you."

"Thanks," Chris said, grateful. He flashed on Heather's pained expression when she'd learned his true identity. "I'm not sure Heather's going to be speaking to me after this."

"Och." The Rabbi waved him off. "You save the day, you get the girl. That's how it works."

Chris smiled, for the first time in a long time. "I didn't save the day yet."

"Added incentive." The Rabbi blew out a cone of smoke. "Was there ever any other? Every rock star in history says he did it to get girls."

"But they don't get shot at."

"There's that."

Chris looked around the pasture, noticing the bright lights in the distance and hearing the mechanical thrumming of drilling machinery, an unnatural sound. "Do they drill at night, too?"

"I assume so."

"The Shanks were hay farmers." Chris eyed the abandoned equipment behind one of the old cars on cinder blocks. "That's nice equipment over there. A haybine, hay tedder, and that rusty thing with the round tines is a hayrake. That fluffs the hay into windrows."

The Rabbi turned, looking. "I always forget you're a country boy."

"I'm a country boy, I'm a city boy, I'm a whatever-you-want boy. I wonder why they didn't sell the equipment." Chris heard the distinctive sound of a horse nickering. "Somebody's unhappy."

"The horse? The FBI guys said he's crazy. They said he was going in circles. I told them, maybe he's hungry."

"When horses are hungry, they kick the stall door." Chris heard the horse nicker again. "That's strange. He's bothered. Something is bothering him."

"Probably the activity."

"No, he'd have gotten used to it by now." Chris found himself edging backwards to listen harder. "Let's go look into that."

"The FBI already did."

"Like I said," Chris said, heading for the barn.

Chapter Fifty-two

Chris heard the nickering of the horse as they approached the barn door, which stood open. "What's in the other out-buildings?"

"Equipment and junk. The FBI searched it pretty thoroughly."

They walked down the aisle between the empty stalls. The barn had eight stalls, four on either side, and cobwebs festooned the rafters like a Halloween ghost barn. The stalls were empty except for the one at the end, on the right. The manure odor was strong, so the stall hadn't been picked recently.

"That's funny," Chris said, thinking aloud.

"What?" the Rabbi asked, puffing on his cigar.

"If you have one horse, the normal thing to do would be to put him in the first stall. That way you don't have to walk to the end to turn him out." Chris gestured to the feed room, directly across in the first stall, the conventional layout. "And that's where you get the grain from. Why would you put the horse so far from the grain?"

"I don't know. Darryl and Darryl aren't Einstein?"

Chris approached the stall, and the horse stood tall, his ears facing stiffly forward at the intruders. "Ho, boy," he said, sing-song.

"You speak the language."

"You could too. Horses are easy to understand. They're flight animals, not fight animals. They're worried by new things, especially if they don't have a herd or buddy. You can get them a goat or a pony to keep them company."

"Horses have pets?"

"They don't like to be alone." Chris heard himself talking, realizing that maybe he was a fight animal. Maybe he didn't need a herd or a buddy. Maybe he truly was untouchable.

"There he goes." The Rabbi gestured with his cigar, as the horse circled the stall.

Chris looked at the straw, which had been so churned up that it had scattered to the edges of the stall, breaking up the manure. The hayrack was empty, and so was the feed bucket affixed to the side of the stall. The water bucket was empty, as well. "He needs hay and water. But something's up. He's bothered. Frightened."

"Is it the cigar?"

"I don't think so. The Shanks smoke, I smelled it inside." Chris turned on the barn lights, flickering fluorescents that needed to be replaced. The horse was an old brown draft, sweaty with nervousness. "He seems afraid in his own stall, which makes no sense. Their stall is the one place that horses are never afraid."

"Who knew?"

"Stand aside a sec, okay?" Chris lifted the nylon halter from its hook and opened the stall door, stepped inside, slipped the halter over the horse's head, and fastened the buckle. He led the horse out, and he quieted almost as soon as he stood in the aisle.

"That worked."

"Hold this." Chris handed the Rabbi the lead rope.

"Really?"

"There's no crossties." Chris returned his attention to the stall, walked back inside, and toed the hay that had been disturbed, revealing a layer of screenings, standard subfloor. He had bedded more stalls than he could count, and he recognized new shavings by their light gray color. They hadn't been here more than a day.

"Chris, what do I do with this thing?"

"Ride him or put him in another stall."

"He's looking at me."

"Maybe he thinks you're cute."

"He's scary."

"Put him away."

The Rabbi hustled the horse into the neighboring stall, and Chris dug the toe of his loafer into the shavings until he got to the floor, which was plywood. No stall that he knew of had plywood in the bottom. It should have been a rubber mat or dirt.

"You need to see this," Chris said, starting to dig. He cleared the hay, screenings, and manure to expose a plywood door locked with a padlock.

"Oh, whoa," the Rabbi said, over his shoulder.

"Can I get a pair of bolt cutters?"

"It could be booby-trapped."

"I doubt it. They were not expecting anybody to be here." Chris yanked at the padlock, then stood up and kicked it, but it wouldn't come off. It was new and shiny, unlike everything else on this farm. He ran his finger along the edges of the door. "They didn't just make this. It's been here awhile. Only the padlock is new."

"Be right back." The Rabbi took off, returning quickly with bolt cutters and some ATF, FBI, JTTF, and uniformed locals, who gathered in the aisle outside the stall.

Chris felt his heart pound as he cut the padlock, removed it, and pulled the latch to open the door. It looked like the entrance to an underground bunker of some sort, but it was too dark to see anything.

"Here's a flashlight," the Rabbi said, handing him a small one from a uniformed cop.

He shined it inside the hole.

Chapter Fifty-three

Courtney!" Chris shouted, when the jittery cone of light found her bound and gagged on the floor, her body facing him. Blood clotted her hairline, and dirt streaked her lovely face. Her eyes closed above a red bandanna covering her mouth. They opened, squinting in the sudden light, and she began to make whimpering noises.

"It's the sister?" the Rabbi asked, urgent. "Is she alive?"

"Yes, Courtney Wheeler, alive." Chris stuck his head in the hole and shined the flashlight around. Evan wasn't there. The bunker contained a plastic table cluttered with bomb-making equipment—a leftover pile of white ammonium nitrate fertilizer in crystalline form, a soldering iron, wiring, wire cutters, pliers, and other tools—plus ashtrays, an old CD player, and empty soda cans. There were two folding chairs, one knocked over. The bottom floor was earth, about six feet or so away.

"Courtney, it's Chris, I'll be right there!"

Courtney responded with frantic sounds, writhing, and Chris jumped down through the hole, landed hard, and rushed to her side. Tears came to Courtney's eyes, and she tried to get up, making whimpering noises as he elevated her upper body, undid the bandanna over her mouth, and dug out a sock that had been cruelly stuffed inside it. Instantly she began to cough, a hoarse hacking that wracked her chest.

"Chris . . . Chris . . ." Courtney tried to talk between coughs. "Thank God . . . somebody came . . . they put me here . . . to die . . . my *own* brothers . . ."

"Where's Evan?" Chris helped her sit up, then scrambled to untie her hands from behind her back, putting the flashlight between his teeth.

"They took him . . . they made him go . . . oh, Chris . . . Chris . . . it's all my fault . . . I'm so sorry . . ."

"Your brothers took Evan? Where? When?" Chris untied the rope around her shins, bound on top of her jeans. She only had one shoe.

"To . . . Philly . . . the courthouse . . . don't know when . . . they're going . . . to blow it up . . ."

"Rabbi, did you hear that?" Chris shouted out the open lid, taking the flashlight out of his mouth.

"Got it!" the Rabbi called back. "Get her underneath the door. We'll hoist her up."

"Courtney, can you stand? Hold on to me." Chris took her arm, looped it around his neck, and supported her as she struggled to her feet.

"Chris, you don't know what . . . they've done . . . they killed Doug." Courtney started to cry, but Chris couldn't let her lose it now.

"Courtney, keep it together. We have to get you out of here. Let me lift you, then reach up, okay?" Chris positioned them under the door, hoisted her up, and lifted her upward.

"I can't, I can't . . ."

"Climb on my shoulders, you can do it."

"Help me!" Courtney struggled to get her legs onto Chris's shoulders, and in the next moment, she was pulled up through the trapdoor into the stall. He grabbed a chair, stood on it, and boosted himself out of the hole. The Rabbi helped a weepy Courtney to a sitting position against the wall, as he identified himself and Mirandized her. Behind him, ATF, FBI, and JTTF agents started videotaping her with their phones. Somebody handed Courtney a bottle of water, which she drank thirstily while Chris went to her side, kneeling.

"Courtney." Chris knelt at her side. "You're okay, you're gonna be fine. We need you to help us now."

"Chris, I don't . . . understand." Courtney's eyes brimmed with tears as she took in the crowd. "Who are . . . all these people? What are you doing here?"

"I'm an ATF Special Agent and I was working undercover at the school. My real name is Curt Abbott. I have to stop your brothers and find Evan. You're sure they're going to blow up the federal courthouse in Philly?"

"Yes, but . . . Chris? Curt?" Courtney's bloodshot eyes flared with disbelief. "Really, is this you? You're not . . . a teacher?"

"It's true but we don't have time to talk about it. When did they leave? How long have you been down there?"

"I don't know . . . what time is it now? What day is it?"

"It's almost six in the morning, Monday morning. You've been there since when?"

"Since midnight last night." Courtney began to cry, her chest heaving with hoarse sobs. "I didn't know they were going to do it, I swear . . . I thought they were going to blow up the well pads, but not when anybody was around . . . that was what we all said . . . that Frazer was going to pay for what they did to my father"—Courtney's words ran together in one anguished stream—"we were never going to kill anybody . . . that's what I told Evan . . . he went along with it because of me, because of his dad . . . I asked him to do it, he did it . . . he helped steal the fertilizer to blow up the pads, but not a courthouse . . . not with *people* in it . . ."

"I understand," Chris said, glancing at the Rabbi, who looked grim.

"They *killed* Doug . . . right in front of me, they *shot him* . . . they had a gun and I didn't even know they had . . . a silencer on it." Courtney sobbed, her skin mottled. Tears streamed down her face.

"Where is the bomb? Is it in the dually, the black dually?"

"Yes . . . Evan came to my house and Doug wasn't supposed to be there . . . he was supposed to be away for the weekend . . . but he came home early."

"Then what happened?"

"Jimmy *shot him* . . . and I got hysterical . . . but they said they would kill me and Evan if I screamed . . . I never saw them like that . . . they've gone crazy, they've lost their minds."

"So then they put you in the dually?"

"Yes, we were in the dually . . . and they had a gun to Evan's head, and in the back of the dually was the fertilizer . . . the bomb we were going to use to blow up the well pads, but I was crying . . . and they said 'change of plans, that's not what's going on.'" Courtney dissolved into tears, breaking down completely, her head drooping. "Nobody was supposed to die . . . nobody was supposed to get killed, ever . . . I think they killed Abe, too . . . They said they didn't, but I think they did."

"Why did they kill Abe, Courtney?"

"It's my fault, it's all my fault . . . he found out about me and Evan, he saw me texting Evan and he was so . . . upset with me, so disappointed . . . and I was so stupid, I told my brothers that Abe knew . . . but I think they *killed him*."

"How are they going to bomb the courthouse? They can't all be in the same van."

"Jimmy has a pickup . . . it's black . . . and he's going to follow the dually to Philly. Evan's going to drive the dually to the courthouse . . . and they're going to blow it up . . ."

"Does Evan know that?"

"No, they told him that they would kill his parents . . ." Courtney hiccupped sob after sob, ". . . if he didn't go with them . . . they told him that they'd get him out . . . before they blew the dually up . . . but that's not what's going to happen . . . they have a remote control . . . they're going to blow him up in the dually."

"Courtney, hang in." Chris touched her shoulder, and she looked up at him.

"Chris, don't let them hurt Evan . . . He did it for me . . . I got him into this . . . I know it was wrong to have the affair but . . . he gave me so much attention . . . and I felt young and pretty again . . . Doug was never home . . . and now, he's dead . . . all because of me . . ."

"Okay, hang in." Chris rose, having all the information he needed and not a moment to spare. "Rabbi, I gotta go, authorization or no."

"Agree. Your helo's waiting." The Rabbi left the stall with Chris, and they hurried down the aisle, clogged with law-enforcement personnel, including ATF. The Rabbi directed them on the fly. "Mark, get Ms. Wheeler some medical attention and take her into custody. Don't move her from the farmhouse until you hear from me. Don't let anybody talk to her unless they're authorized by me or Alek. Jenny, call Alek and brief him. We're supposed to run everything through JTTF."

Chris fell into step beside him. "And somebody, please feed and water the horse."

"I did already." The Rabbi winked. "He's my buddy now."

"Nice." Chris glanced at the sky as they left the barn, which was warming to a soft rosy blue, an unwelcome sight. Time was running out.

Meanwhile, the Shank compound had become a scene of controlled pandemonium, since word had spread the target had been confirmed. JTTF and FBI personnel met in groups, raced back and forth, clustered around laptops, and talked on phones or walkie-talkies. Police cruisers and black SUVs appeared out of nowhere, parking on the overgrown pasture, and three other helos sat waiting on the field with his.

Chris asked, on the run, "So what happens now? Do they cut off I-95? I-76? Inform the public, now that we have confirmation?"

"I don't know. Not our call." The Rabbi shook his head. "JTTF makes all the decisions. They liaise with Homeland Security, the FBI, the Philly police, the Pentagon, and the White House." They hustled toward his helo, and Chris felt the gravity of the situation. "I'm thinking of those tourist attractions across from the courthouse, like the Liberty Bell Pavilion. School field trips go there from all over. Plus the Federal Reserve Bank, the Bourse, the African-American History Museum, WHYY—"

"They *have* to tell the public." Chris spotted his pilot, Tony, running toward the helo.

"They don't want to induce panic. It's a major American city, 1.5 million people. If you go public, the residents, businesses, employees, and tourists freak out. It would be mayhem, dangerous for them and us." The Rabbi shook his head. "And the Shanks might switch targets. The courthouse is on the other side of the Ben Franklin Bridge to Jersey. They could decide to blow up the bridge or hop on it to New York. They could stop at any exit, hide out, wait, steal cars—"

"They'd terrorize the entire Eastern Seaboard. Paralyze business." Chris watched Tony climb into the helo, and in the next moment, the rotors whirred into life. "Looks like I'm good to go."

"Okay." The Rabbi hugged Chris impulsively. "Good luck, son."

"Thanks," Chris said, touched. He raced for the helo.

Chapter Fifty-four

The helo flew toward Philadelphia, and Chris kept an eye on the horizon like a stopwatch. The sky was cruelly clear, and the rising sun streaked it in rosy swaths. It promised a beautiful day that could end in a horrific loss of life. Chris would never forget 9/11, which was one of the loveliest mornings of September until it became the most tragic.

Chris scanned the terrain below as the helo flew south down Route 81. The Shanks had an overwhelming head start, and he assumed they were already in the city. Nevertheless, he kept his head down and his eye on the traffic, looking for the black pickup or the dually. As they flew southward, Route 81 widened and grew more congested with cars, trucks, tractor trailers, school buses, and vans. Chris ran possibilities in his mind for the next step, trying to formulate a Plan A and Plan B.

"Curt?" Tony's voice was transmitted through the headset into his ear. "I have a phone call for you from Supervisor Alek Ivanov. I'm going to patch him in. You'll hear his voice next in your headset."

Terrific. "Thanks." Chris heard a crackling sound, then a click.

"Curt? Are you in the air?"

"Yes, headed toward Philly. What's going on? Are they going to close the courthouse? Are they going to inform the public?"

"No decision yet. There are a lot of moving parts. JTTF will liaise with the other agencies and the city, and those decisions will be in their very capable hands."

"Okay." Chris thought Alek sounded unusually official and assumed that his boss was speaking for the benefit of others overhearing the conversation.

"Curt, you may not have been told that ATF is no longer primary in Operation Varsity Letter. JTTF is. JTTF didn't authorize your deployment to the target zone. You've done a great job, Curt. I couldn't have asked for more. But JTTF has its own people in the air, handpicked. Turn around and return to the Shank farmstead."

"No." Chris hadn't come this far to quit. "JTTF doesn't know how this may go down. Anything can happen. I may be needed. I'm the only one who knows Evan. I have his trust and his confidence—"

"Curt, Evan Kostis is a domestic terrorist, armed and dangerous, engaged in a conspiracy to blow up a courthouse and murder thousands of innocent people—"

"No, you're wrong, he's not a willing participant. They're using him as a human shield. Courtney confirmed it to us, just now. Call the Rabbi, he'll tell you. Evan is a *hostage.*" Chris felt fear tighten his chest. He could read between the lines. They were going to shoot to kill Evan. The boy was about to become collateral damage. If Evan didn't get killed by the Shanks, he'd get killed by the feds.

"Curt, we're talking about one person as against thousands."

"No, it's not that way. I would never sacrifice thousands of people for Evan, but I don't think we have to sacrifice anyone. I want to stop the Shanks and get Evan out of there." Chris had to sound reasonable or he would never convince Alek. "You already put the word out about the dually and the pickup. We're going to start getting sightings. We'll be able to locate them. They've got to be in the city or close by. When you start to get those sightings, we can coordinate our extraction of Evan—"

"There's no *extraction* of Evan. That's not JTTF's plan. Their order is for you to come back."

"But JTTF needs me. What if they have to defuse the bomb? I can do that. I'm a certified explosives specialist. You know that—"

"Again, not JTTF's plan. Bomb squads are already headed to the target. Turn around and come back to the farmstead." Alek's tone turned angry, but controlled for the sake of the others listening.

"No, I can't. I'm asking for one shot. I'm not gonna let you kill this kid. There's no reason to. He's a victim, not a perp."

"Pilot, return to the farmstead."

"No, don't," Chris told Tony, then said to the headset, "Alek, please, I promised Evan's mother I'd bring him home and I want to try—"

"Pilot, turn around and return to farmstead." Alek's tone hardened like steel. "That's an order."

"Roger that," Tony answered.

"Over and out," Alek said, then there was a click on the headset.

Chris turned to Tony in appeal. "Please, don't go back. They're going to kill a kid for no reason, a seventeen-year-old boy. I can get him out of there. I've got to try. Let me try."

Tony looked over, grim-faced. "I'm not going back. I heard you. We're going to give it a shot."

"Wait, what?" Chris didn't get it.

"I don't take orders from your boss, I'm a subcontractor. I'm a father, too. I'll follow your lead."

"Thanks." Chris's hopes soared. Evan had been given a stay of execution.

"I can switch channels and listen to the chatter from the

other pilots. We'll hear about the sightings as soon as they do. Nobody will know we're in the sky until they see us." Tony shot him a warning glance. "But if it goes south, I'm turning back. I'm not going to let you get us killed."

"Fair enough," Chris said, turning to the city.

Chapter Fifty-five

Chris spotted the cluster of Center City buildings he knew so well—City Hall topped by William Penn, the spiky ziggurat of Liberty Place, Commerce Center, and the Cira Center to the west, and to the east, Carpenter Hall, the U.S. Mint, and the Federal Detention Center. Straight ahead was the redbrick and smoked-glass tower that was the target, the James A. Byrne U.S. Courthouse and the William J. Green Federal Building.

Chris shuddered to think about the horrific loss of life if the Shanks succeeded, and the deaths would extend to people in the nearby office buildings, retail shops, restaurants, and tourist attractions clustered in the historic district of Philadelphia. It made him sick to his stomach. He wished the helo could move faster, but they were flying as fast as safely possible.

Chris listened to the constant crackling chatter through the headset. There had been no sightings of the dually or the pickup, according to the bulletins from the Philadelphia police and the other federal agencies, all with their own lingo and codes, telling the story of a major American city under terrorist threat, unfolding in real time. The public had been just been notified of a credible bomb threat on the federal courthouse, and Homeland

Security had issued a severe threat level for the City of Philadelphia, shutting down the airport, and train, subway, and bus lines.

The Ben Franklin, Walt Whitman, Betsy Ross, and Tacony-Palmyra Bridges had been closed, and cars stuck on the bridge at the time of the closure were being escorted off by Philly and Port Authority police. The federal courthouse and all municipal offices and courts had been closed, and all employees, judges, staff, personnel, and jurors evacuated. People flooded the streets and sidewalks in panic, waiting their turn to be bused to shelters uptown. But none of this could be accomplished quickly, and tens of thousands of people were terrified, frantic, and in mortal jeopardy.

Tony looked over, eyes narrowed. "You seeing anything below?"

"No." Chris watched the traffic as they flew over I-95 south, six lanes of wall-to-wall traffic, the drivers honking in fear and driving erratically as they fled the city. A fleet of Black Hawks and bigger helos from JTTF, FBI, and the Philly police filled the sky, searching the highway traffic, main streets, side streets, and parking lots for the dually and the pickup.

"This is JTTF. Pilot, identify yourself," crackled an authoritative voice in the headset.

Tony looked over. "Tony Arroyo. I'm a subcontractor for DEA."

"Who are you with, Arroyo?"

"Special Agent Curt Abbott, ATF."

"Special Agent Abbott, do you copy? We were told you returned to base."

"Negative," Chris said, and just then, the voice was overridden by an urgent voice through the headset:

"Subject vehicles sighted at Ninth and Race Streets, heading east." Suddenly the headset exploded with orders, reactions, and sightings, a frenzied cacophony of official business as every helo in the air and vehicle on the ground started barking orders, notifications, and alerts.

"They found them!" Chris said, his heart pumping.

"Copy that. We're on." Tony steered the helo eastward. The other helos turned and headed east as if on cue.

Chris and Tony's helo was among the closest and they beelined for Race Street, flying over the concrete complex of buildings that was Hahnemann Hospital, then the Roundhouse, Philadelphia police headquarters. They zoomed east on Race Street and fell into formation with the other helos in hot pursuit.

Chris scanned the city streets. He didn't see the dually or pickup. Traffic was being stopped in a ten-block radius around Race Street. Race Street was in the process of being cleared by police cruisers blaring their sirens, herding motorists off the street or to the curb.

Chris scanned the city streets as they descended, flying over Chinatown, which was bisected by Race Street. They flew directly over the ornate red-and-green gate that was the entrance to Chinatown, then zipped over Ninth, Eighth, Seventh, and Sixth Streets, where Chris spotted the police chase and felt his heart leap into his throat.

"There!" Chris pointed to the black dually and pickup, careening down Race Street at high speed. Blue-and-white Philadelphia police cruisers, boxy black SUVs from JTTF, FBI, and ATF, and emergency vehicles raced after them at top speed. Adrenaline surged through Chris's system.

"Uh-oh." Tony shook his head. "They're not turning for the courthouse. They're heading for the Ben Franklin Bridge."

"The bridge is full of traffic." Chris felt his heart sink, looking at the Ben Franklin, the massive blue suspension bridge arching over the Delaware River. Cars, trucks, and BOLT buses sat stopped across its span like a parking lot.

Meantime, the Shanks kept trading positions on the street, sometimes driving side by side, sometimes one leading the other.

"This does not look good." Tony clenched his jaw.

"Stay with the dually." Chris saw with horror that one of the unmarked helos was aiming a long gun out of the window, a sniper getting ready to take a shot.

"No!" Chris cried out, too late. The rapid popping of gunfire filled the air. He looked below on the street, stricken. Bullets ripped through the pickup. It zigzagged down Race Street and crashed into a line of parked cars.

Tony said grimly, "They're shooting to kill."

Chris said into the headset. "This is ATF, Special Agent Abbott. Do not fire on the dually. Repeat, do not fire on the dually. The dually contains a fertilizer bomb. Firing on the dually will result in its detonation and drastic loss of life and property."

"Special Agent Abbott?" several voices replied, crackling with static. "To whom do you report?"

"Supervisor Alek Ivanov at the Philly Field Division, ATF. In the dually is domestic terrorist David or Jimmy Shank and also a hostage, minor Evan Kostis. I need to get the hostage out of there. If the bomb goes off on the bridge, you're going to kill thousands of people and destroy the Ben Franklin Bridge. Do you copy?"

"Stand by," "Negative," "Affirmative," came a torrent of replies, crackling with static.

Chris turned to Tony. "You got binoculars? I need to see inside the dually."

"In the compartment at your feet."

"Can you get me to the passenger side of the dually? I want to see if the boy is driving or in the passenger seat." Chris opened the compartment, found the binoculars, and trained them on the dually as they bounced along.

"Going south, hang on." Tony swung the helo around, provoking excited chatter in the headset, which Chris ignored.

"This is Special Agent Abbott, going in for a visual to determine location of the hostage and detonator." Chris ignored the responding chatter and looked through the binoculars, trying to focus in the bumpy ride.

Suddenly he spotted Evan in the passenger seat, hair blowing back from his terrified expression. A large pink bruise distorted the right side of the boy's face, swelling his right eye. Evan's hands were handcuffed in front of him. He wasn't holding the detonator. Chris tried to see if Shank had the detonator, but had no luck. There was no time to lose. A protective fury gripped Chris's chest, the closest he'd experienced to a paternal feeling.

"This is Special Agent Abbott. Preparing to extract the hostage. The hostage does not have a detonator. Do not fire on the hostage or the dually. Repeat, do not fire on the hostage or the dually." More excited chatter crackled through the headset, and Chris heard a few "copy thats" from the other helos. He turned to Tony. "You got a ladder?"

"Sure, behind your seat."

"If I hang a ladder outside, can you get me down to that dually?" Chris climbed out of the seat and into the belly of the helo, opening the trunk and rummaging to find a rope ladder of yellow nylon.

"You'll see the clips on the wall there."

Chris located the clips, secured the ladder to the helo wall, and opened the door. Wind buffeted him crazily, but he grabbed the handle and righted himself, saying into the headset, "This is Special Agent Abbott. Deplaning to extract the hostage."

Frenzied chatter came nonstop.

Chris looked over at Tony. "I'm going. Thanks."

Tony nodded, tense. "I'll keep talking to them. Go with God."

"Thanks." Chris slid off the headset, grabbed the ladder, and climbed out of the helo.

Chapter Fifty-six

Chris got hit full force by a powerful wind current. It almost blew him off the rung but he kept his grip. The ladder swayed sideways as their helo swept toward the Benjamin Franklin Bridge, a major span of seven lanes with a center divider heading to and from Camden, New Jersey. Two massive anchorages stood at either end of the bridge, and along the span were arches with lighted signs to shift lanes in off-peak hours.

Chris climbed down the ladder, flying over the sign that read WELCOME TO THE BENJAMIN FRANKLIN BRIDGE, DELAWARE RIVER PORT AUTHORITY. Below him, the black dually barreled around the curve at Fifth Street onto the bridge. Tony steered their helo farther south, overshooting the dually, then circling back toward the city for the one pass that Chris would get to grab Evan.

Chris kept climbing down the ladder, buffeted by the wind and the wash from the other helos, circling like hornets. Again he spotted a long gun poking through the passenger-side seat of one of the helos.

He couldn't stop them now. He could only hope that the gun was aimed at Shank and not Evan or the bomb. His feet reached the final rung, and he flew through the air at the end of the ladder.

Tony turned the helo west, then south to complete the circle, at the same time lining up with the dually.

Pandemonium broke out on the bridge. Drivers sprang from the parked cars and abandoned them, running for their lives toward the nearer side of the bridge.

Suddenly Chris realized that their helo was zooming toward one of the arches over the bridge, which would crush him. Tony jerked the helo upward just in time, sailing Chris over the top of the arch, but they'd missed their first pass.

The other helos circled or hovered, creating major turbulence, setting Chris swinging crazily on the ladder. He could barely manage to hang on.

Below, the dually barreled up the incline of the bridge. Shank started firing at the helos. The helos returned fire or jerked out of the way, evading the bullets. Chris was still armed, his Glock in his shoulder holster, held securely by the thumb break.

He kept his eyes on the dually as Tony began another pass, circling again to the north, then toward the west, and then south again, ultimately beginning his descent to the dually. It would be Chris's last chance to save Evan.

He spotted another long gun poking through the back door of one of the larger Black Hawks. He intuited that they were waiting for him to get in position to take their shot. Meanwhile, Shank kept firing on them.

The dually sped to the summit of the bridge, and Chris kept an eye on Evan as Tony flew their helo closer, within fifty feet, then forty, then thirty.

Evan looked out the passenger-side window, spotting Chris, his eyes wild with fright. He shouted, "Help, Coach!"

The helo was twenty feet from the passenger side, then ten feet, and Chris could see Shank pull Evan away from the window.

The second arch of the bridge zoomed toward Chris at warp speed, and he made his move. It was do or die.

Chris linked his legs through the bottom rung of the ladder, flipped down and backwards, and reached both hands down. The ladder swung toward the dually with him facing away and upside down. Momentum carried him to the passenger side window. He arched his back and stretched out his hands toward Evan.

"Evan, catch!" Chris shouted, on the downswing.

Evan thrust his handcuffed arms out the passenger side of the dually and grabbed Chris's arms.

Chris grabbed him back, gripping Evan's arms as tightly as he could, and in the next moment Tony flew their helo up and away, lifting Evan from the speeding dually and clearing the second arch.

The air filled with a lethal barrage of automatic weapons fire. The snipers must have hit Shank. The dually veered to the left.

Chris secured his hold on Evan, straining with all his might to hold on to the boy as they flew through the air. Evan looked up with terror in his eyes, his hair blowing wildly, locking his fingers around Chris's forearms.

"I got you!" Chris shouted to Evan.

Below, the dually barreled toward the cars that had been abandoned, parked every which way, along the north side of the bridge. Motorists scrambled safely out of its path.

Chris watched the scene unfold with his heart in his throat.

The dually headed straight for a Corvette and drove squarely onto its low front end, kept going onto its hood like a ramp, and took off over the side of the bridge. The dually soared away from the bridge into thin air, its wheels still spinning, then plummeted into the Delaware River.

Chris held his breath. There was a muffled *boom*. The fertilizer bomb exploded underwater, producing a massive bubble of white water and ripples in all directions. The bridge shuddered at the percussive wave, but the explosion was far enough from its anchorage not to damage them.

People fled toward both ends of the bridge, but none of them was harmed or injured.

"Yes!" Chris cheered inwardly, keeping a tight grip on Evan as Tony completed his final circle.

Flying them toward safety.

Chapter Fifty-seven

Their helo flew back toward the Philadelphia side of the bridge and descended slowly. The ladder dug into the back of Chris's knees, cutting off his circulation and weakening his leg hold. The ache in his shoulders and arms intensified, supporting Evan's weight.

Chris felt Evan grow heavier, as if the boy could no longer hold himself up, the handcuffs hobbling his grip. Chris formed his fingers in a vise, praying that they landed soon. He feared that Evan had been beaten, suffering internal injuries.

The street below was being hastily cleared and a makeshift helipad was being formed at the base of the bridge, in front of a small grassy park that contained a monument to Benjamin Franklin, a silvery lightning bolt piercing the sky. Their helo descended slowly, and Chris worried whether they'd clear the lightning bolt, but he had confidence in Tony, who'd more than proved his mettle.

Both Chris and Evan hung their heads, looking down at the chaos below. JTTF, FBI, and ATF vehicles, Philly and Port Authority police, firefighters in heavy coats, and EMTs and other emergency personnel clustered around a slew of fire trucks, ambulances, and a bloodmobile. There were SWAT team members in boxy paramilitary vehicles, white Bomb Squad trucks, and bystanders, gawkers, and other civilians, who must have left or been evacuated from their offices, businesses, and homes.

The helo dropped lower and lower, and each person watched the sky or held up a smartphone, iPad, or tablet to videotape the dramatic descent. A throng of reporters and media stood filming from white vans bearing network and cable-TV logos.

Chris realized that it was the biggest news story that had ever happened in the Philadelphia area and it was being recorded, filmed, and photographed by professional outlets as well as guys with flip phones. He looked back at the smartphones, lenses, and cameras with the sickening knowledge that he was blown. His undercover career was over. His face, his image, and his true identity would be posted online, shared, and broadcast everywhere around the country, maybe even the world, starting right now.

Chris Brennan/Curt Abbott was about to go viral, and there would be no more hiding in plain sight. No disguise would be good enough, not after today. Chris had saved Evan but he'd lost his job, and the only life he knew.

And it struck him that if he didn't know who he really was, he was going to find out.

Chapter Fifty-eight

Chris didn't release Evan from his grip until the boy's feet touched the street, then all hell broke loose. Philadelphia police, JTTF, FBI and ATF agents, federal marshals, and EMTs rushed Evan from all directions, crouching to avoid the rotors and wash of the helo as it hovered above the street.

"Coach, Coach!" Evan shouted, as they hustled him away, his voice lost in the din of the rotors and blaring sirens.

"Get him to a hospital!" Chris shouted, as Evan was whisked into the nearest ambulance, its back doors hanging open at the ready.

Chris kept his grip on one side of the ladder, unhooked his legs from the rung, and swung his feet down to the street, righting himself as a noisy slew of official personnel engulfed him. He scanned the crowd for an ATF windbreaker, but there was too much of a commotion. The rotor wash subsided as Tony pulled the helo up and began his ascent, still trailing the yellow ladder.

Chris looked up, and Tony flashed him an okay sign, then climbed higher and steered northward.

"Special Agent Abbott, come with us, this way!" shouted one of the Philly police, barely audible over the din. "Special Agent Abbott, this way! There's a command post at the United States Attorney's office. We've been instructed to take you there unless you require medical attention."

"I'm fine, let's go!" Chris shouted back, jostled in the crowd, and the cadre of police whisked him to a waiting cruiser surrounded by more cruisers, emergency vehicles, and paramilitary vehicles. The media and the civilians beyond the perimeter surged forward, trying to get a look at him and cheering, applauding, or shouting to him.

Chris hustled to the backseat of the cruiser, closing the door behind him. The sirens kept blaring, preventing conversation with the uniformed officers in the front seat. He didn't feel like talking anyway. He worried about Evan and how the boy would be dealt with by the law. It wasn't a fate that Chris could save him from, but maybe the time for saving Evan was over.

The cruiser began to make its way through the crowd as official personnel cleared a path for it to pass. Chris couldn't hear anything because of the sirens and the people cheering, clapping, or calling to him, though he couldn't make out any of the words. They waved at him or flashed him thumbs-up. One woman blew him a kiss, and another one held up a hand-scrawled sign that read, MARRY ME!

Chris looked away, thinking of Heather. He didn't know what she'd think of him now or if she still felt betrayed. Same with Jordan, which hurt, too. Chris didn't want to be untouchable anymore, but he might have blown his chance.

The cruiser inched along, and he looked out the window at the cheering mob. His thoughts were in a quieter place, Central Valley. It struck him then that everything he'd said to Dr. McElroy in his job interview was absolutely true. He'd thought he'd been lying to her, but he'd been lying to himself. Central Valley *did* feel like home to him, and it was the kind of place where he'd want to settle down and raise a family.

He just didn't know how, or even if, he could ever get back there.

Chapter Fifty-nine

The next few hours were a blur, during which Chris was escorted to the United States Attorney's office, a concrete monolith on Chestnut Street in Philadelphia. The Rabbi gave him a relieved hug and Alek shook his hand, acting as if Chris had followed his orders to the letter, a charade in which Chris played his part. After that, Chris, the Rabbi, and Alek met with the heads of JTTF, Homeland Security, FBI, and ATF, in addition to the United States Attorney for the Eastern District of Pennsylvania, the Middle District of Pennsylvania, the mayor of Philadelphia, and the police commissioner. Chris met so many members of the top brass that he lost track of the names, the uniforms, the suits, and the badges.

Everybody needed to be briefed, and he answered all the questions they had, though they answered none of his. The most he could get out of them was that they were getting ready to give an official press conference at six o'clock today, at which he was expected to speak. Chris couldn't ask the Rabbi and Alek about it because they weren't alone until the end of the day, when he hustled them down the hall to the first private room he could find, which was a large supply closet.

"Why do I have to speak?" Chris asked Alek and the Rabbi, closing the door behind them. "That's not how we roll. We don't parade the details of our undercover operations in front of the public."

Alek looked at him like he was nuts. "Operation Varsity Letter is a major victory for federal law enforcement. You're the hero. You're a celebrity. You're truly the new Eliot Ness. You *are* The Untouchable!"

"Curt, listen to me." The Rabbi placed a hand on Chris's shoulder, his lined face weary. "I know you hate the limelight. But you got it done, and this was a major operation. We thwarted a domestic terror attack. We need to explain that to the media and the public."

"We never did anything like this before, had an undercover agent speak."

"Correct, and you know why?" the Rabbi asked, patiently. "Because this scenario is unprecedented. We didn't stop the Oklahoma City bombing. But we stopped the Philadelphia bombing, and you're blown anyway."

"Rabbi, I know that, but what about the next undercover agent? How many questions are we going to answer? How much of the story are we going to tell? Rather, am *I* going to tell?"

Alek dismissed him with a wave. "Just the basics, Curt. Nothing granular. This is ATF's time to shine. If you don't do it for yourself, do it for them."

"You mean *us*. You're still ATF for another hour or two, aren't you?"

Alek's smile faded. "I'm still your boss, Curt. You're still reporting to me. You'll go to that press conference and you'll say what ATF needs you to say."

"On one condition." Chris had gotten an idea during those endless debriefings with the nameless suits. In fact, it was his own personal Plan B. "If I can't work undercover anymore, I still won't work a desk. After the dust settles, I want a different job."

"What do you want?" Alek asked, his smile back, though he was still ugly.

"I want to start a field-training program for undercover agents, over and above what we had at Glencoe, based on my experience. It could start as a pilot program in Philadelphia and extend to the other divisions around the country."

Alek hesitated. "A field-experience program? That job doesn't exist."

"I know, I want to create it. I want to teach everything I know to undercover agents coming up."

Alek frowned. "Curt. This is the government. We don't create jobs willy-nilly, and you won't get any more money."

"I don't want more money. I'll stay at my pay grade." Chris was a GS-13, making a little over a hundred grand a year.

The Rabbi interjected, "I think that's a great idea, Curt. You know so many tricks of the trade, and I think it would be great if you could impart that knowledge to our newer agents."

"Thanks." Chris returned his attention to Alek. "If I can look forward to a new job, I'll be happy to speak at the press conference."

"Oh, I get it. We're negotiating." Alek folded his arms. "You never give up, do you?"

"Lucky for you, no."

Alek thought a minute, then his grin returned. "Curt, a field-experience program is an *excellent* idea. I was just thinking the same thing myself!"

Chapter Sixty

Police guarded the doors, and Mindy sat in the waiting room of the emergency department waiting for Evan to come back. He had taken ten stitches through his eyebrow and had bruises on his right cheek, though his orbital bone hadn't been fractured or his eyesight impaired. He was being X-rayed because they suspected two cracked ribs, but otherwise, he would be physically okay.

Mindy had cried all the tears she could cry. She could never live with herself if more people had been killed. She felt exhausted, sitting next to her new lawyer, Maxwell Todd, Esq., of Logan & Dichter. Todd specialized in the legal problems of the children of their corporate client CEOs. Mindy would never have guessed there were enough spoiled brats to support a law practice, but maybe affluenza was contagious.

Evan was in police custody, and he was going from here to the Federal Detention Center until his arraignment. The charges against him had yet to be decided upon, but Mindy would be there for him, not to excuse him, but to help him deal with whatever sentence they gave him. A mother was a lighthouse in a storm, and she would stand with him always. And even though, if she'd said yes to him before, when she should've said no, they both still had time to turn it around. She could change, and so could he.

She glanced at Paul, sitting several rows away from her with his criminal lawyer. They were the only people in the waiting room, which had been cleared by the police. Her phone rested in her lap, but she didn't look at it. She'd stopped checking Facebook when the posts about Evan started appearing in her feed, mostly horrible and vile. She was ditching Facebook and going back to real books.

Mindy's gaze found the TV mounted in the corner, playing on mute. There was a car commercial, and the screen returned to the the courthouse and the rescue, above the banner BOMB PLOT FOILED. Then came a shot of Evan's latest school photo, then photos from his Facebook and Instagram accounts, a continuous slideshow of media coverage.

Mindy watched the coverage, having an out-of-body experience. She couldn't believe that Evan was on TV, that hers was the family they were talking about, that she was *inside* the news, even though they were real people. They weren't a story. It was her, Evan, and Paul.

The screen switched to a photo of Coach Brennan above the title UNDERCOVER HERO CURT ABBOTT. Mindy watched as the video in which Coach Brennan—she still called him that in her mind— flew upside down like a trapeze artist, holding on to Evan as they soared over the Benjamin Franklin Bridge.

Mindy felt tears come to her eyes. Coach Brennan had saved Evan's life, as well as the lives of thousands of innocent people, and risked his own. Her first impulse had been to call him and she'd gotten his cell phone from the Booster directory, but her lawyer had advised her not to call him.

Mindy picked up her phone, scrolled to the text function, and typed a message, straight from the heart.

Coach Brennan, this is Mindy Kostis. I'm not supposed to be communicating with you, but what's right is right. Thank you very much for saving Evan's life. God bless you.

Mindy swallowed hard. Her attention returned to the television, and she found herself watching her own Facebook album, the Kostis Klan in the Kaymans.

"Mrs. Kostis?" said a female voice, and Mindy looked up to see the doctor entering the waiting room, with a professional smile.

"You can see Evan now. He's asking for you."

Chapter Sixty-one

Heather tossed the salad, alone with her thoughts while Jordan sat in the living room with the television blaring CNN.

". . . this is Wolf Blitzer, welcoming our viewers in the United States and around the world. We're only five minutes away from our coverage of the press conference, which we will be bringing you live from Philadelphia, regarding the terrorist bomb plot that was thwarted today by federal law enforcement, working in connection with state and municipal law enforcement . . ."

Heather screened out the TV, trying to process her emotions. She couldn't wrap her mind around the fact that Chris wasn't who he said he was. She had a crush on a guy that didn't exist. Worse, Chris, or Curt, had used Jordan to get information. She still didn't know the details and she didn't care if she ever found out. The bottom line was that she had been lied to, and so had Jordan.

She kept tossing the salad, bringing up the tart scent of the apple-cider vinegar, which she'd never used before. She'd finally had the time to make an Ina Garten recipe, a corn salad made from real corn, not canned, with red pepper, red onion, and fresh basil. She'd never used kosher salt either, so she'd gone to Whole Foods to buy some, celebrating the fact that she had a job interview on Wednesday, as an administrative assistant in the corporate headquarters at ValleyCo.

Heather smiled to herself. She felt confident about her prospects, considering that her boss would be Susan, who had all but told her that she'd get the job. Almost overnight her life had changed, and she had the possibility of a new job with a desk, a nameplate, and a tuition-matching program. Not only that, she could wear whatever she wanted as long as it came from a ValleyCo outlet, which was where she shopped anyway. She was even baking a poached salmon filet, filling the small apartment with an expensive, culinary aroma known only to home cooks, like her.

". . . stand by for a briefing from the Director of Homeland Security, who will be outlining the details of today's breaking news, the thwarting of the bombing of the James A. Byrne U.S. Courthouse and the William J. Green Federal Building in Philadelphia, which would've caused thousands upon thousands of deaths in and around the building. The loss of life and property would've been catastrophic, but for Operation Varsity Letter. You will hear from Special Agent Curt Abbott of the Bureau of . . ."

Heather screened out the name, which was much less appealing than Chris Brennan. She wondered how he had chosen his alias, and if he had actually looked up online for friendly-sounding names that would fool single mothers who were desperate enough to believe anything.

She tossed the corn salad and tried not to think about it. Jordan had come home from school early and had spoken with her only briefly before he went to his room and closed the door. He'd been shaken by the fact that Evan had almost been killed, as well as being involved in a lethal terrorist plot. In fact, he had come out of his room only ten minutes ago, to watch the press conference on TV.

"Mom, it's about to start," Jordan called from the living room.

"I'm making dinner. I can hear it from here."

"Mom, are you serious?"

Heather didn't answer, and in the next moment, Jordan appeared at the entrance to the kitchen in his baseball sweats.

"Mom, you're not going to watch?"

"I've heard it all day, the coverage has been nonstop. You've been at school, you don't know."

"We had it on there, too. That's all anybody's talking about. It's major, Mom. You have to watch."

"They're not going to say anything new. It's all the same thing. We know it all. We lived it all. It's about *us*."

"Don't you care about Evan? They *arrested* him. He wasn't in school today. I think he might be going to jail."

"Of course I care about Evan." Heather felt terrible for Mindy, for what she must have been going through. Heather never would've thought it could happen to a family like the Kostises.

"Everybody says he was in with those guys, but I don't think he was."

"I'm sure he wasn't," Heather said, though she wasn't sure. She didn't know Evan, but her father always said, *If you go through life with your path greased, you could end up on your ass.*

"I mean, it's so random that it was Madame Wheeler in the picture, but Evan is not a *terrorist*. He wouldn't *kill* anybody, he wouldn't blow up a courthouse." Jordan glanced at the TV, where CNN was teasing the press conference. "Mom, come on. I want to see what happens."

"Jordan, I'm cooking—"

"Why are you being so weird?"

"I'm not being weird." Heather kept tossing the salad like a madwoman. Maybe she *was* being weird. A weird version of Ina Garten.

"You're acting like you're mad."

"Well, I *am* mad." Heather turned to him. "Aren't you? How

do you feel? You went in your room and vanished after school. Do you want to talk about it?"

"Okay," Jordan answered, less certainly. "It's a big deal, and I think you should watch the press conference. Don't you want to hear what the coach has to say?"

"He's not *the coach*."

"Okay, I know that. Whatever."

"Curt. It sounds like Chris, but it's not Chris."

Jordan cocked his head. "Are you mad at him?"

"Aren't you?" Heather told herself to calm down. She let go of the serving fork and spoon. "How do you feel about it, Jordan? You believed he was a coach, didn't you?"

"Yes."

"And you believed he liked you, that he was showing interest in you as a friend. As a coach. Isn't that right?"

"Okay, yes." Jordan shrugged uncomfortably. "Why are you acting like a lawyer? You sound like a lawyer."

"I'm trying to understand how you feel. Don't you feel angry that you were lied to? That he lied to us both? Did he ever ask you questions about Evan or the other boys on the team?"

"Yeah, I guess. Once."

"So he was using you for information. He was pumping you for information. He was only pretending to be your friend, and mine. Doesn't that make you angry?"

"Um, it's not great, I admit."

"It's more than *not great,* Jordan. It's a lie. I teach you not to lie. I don't like people who lie. But he lied to us, and I'm mad at him, so you'll understand if I don't want to watch the stupid press—"

"That's not what I think," Jordan interrupted her, which he rarely did, especially to offer his thoughts.

"What do you think?"

"I know he lied and all, and that's not right, but I still think he liked us." Jordan blinked sadly, and Heather felt a wave of guilt for her son, let down not only by his father, but by his father figure.

"Maybe he did, I'm sure he did. But I don't like being lied to."

"Mom, he *had* to lie, don't you see?" Jordan gestured at the TV, where Wolf Blitzer was counting down. "He saved Evan's life and he saved the lives of all those people. Like they just said, thousands of people would have been killed."

"But he deceived us. He pretended to be somebody he wasn't."

"He had to, for the greater good. He did what he had to do to save people's lives. It's like he really was a coach, and we're all the team. Mom, he did the right thing for *the team*."

"But he's not a coach," Heather said, softening, thinking back to that night in this very kitchen, when Chris had coached her to think about her skill set.

"It doesn't matter if he really was. He did what a coach would do, a really great coach. He went to the standard, Mom. The standard did not go to him. It's seventeen inches, Mom."

"What?" Heather had no idea what he meant.

Jordan shook it off. "It doesn't matter. All I'm saying is, he flew upside down through the air holding on to Evan. He *rescued* him. He achieved *excellence*."

Heather felt a glimmer of new pride in Jordan. "You know, you should express yourself more often. You make sense."

"So you agree?"

"No."

"Mom, come on." Jordan took her hand and tugged her into the living room, where they sat down in front of the TV, side by side, something they hadn't done for some time.

Wolf Blitzer continued, "We take you directly to Philadelphia, where the press conference is beginning." The screen morphed to a man in a suit standing behind a lectern with a cluster of men in suits. To the man's right was a tall ugly guy, a shorter older man, and on the end, Chris.

"There's Coach!" Jordan leaned forward, resting on his knees.

"Not a coach," Heather said reflexively, though her gaze went immediately to Chris and stayed there. It was so strange to see him in such a different role, on TV to boot. She couldn't deal with the fact that it was the same man. She couldn't help but think, *If nothing he said was true, is it the same man?* Then she answered her own question, *Of course not, you idiot. But he's still hot.*

"My name is Ralph Brubaker, Chief of the Joint Terrorism Task Force. I'm here to brief you on the thwarting today of an act of domestic terrorism whose goal was to destroy the James A. Byrne U.S. Courthouse and the William J. Green Federal Building in Philadelphia, murdering the persons inside and causing considerable property damage. The plot was foiled by JTTF and many other law-enforcement agencies, but first mention goes to the Philadelphia Field Division of ATF, headed by Group Supervisor Alek Ivanov, Special Agent David Levitz, and the hero of Operation Varsity Letter, Special Agent Curt Abbott."

Jordan hooted. "Woohoo!"

Heather grumbled. "Hmph."

". . . Law enforcement scored a major victory today in our ongoing battle against domestic terrorism. We have no reason to believe that there are other conspirators or participants in this plot, so the City of Philadelphia and the region remain safe. Structural engineers are inspecting the Ben Franklin Bridge, and it will remain closed until further notice. We will retain the severe threat level, out of an abundance of caution. Most important, no confirmed lives were lost today in connection with this plot, except the perpetrators, brothers James and David Shank of Headley, Pennsylvania."

Jordan looked over. "Mom, can you believe Madame Wheeler sent Evan that selfie? I *knew* I should've taken French."

Heather rolled her eyes. "Spanish is more useful."

"Ha!"

"I'm just wondering why Evan was dumb enough to send you all her picture. Why didn't he just keep it to himself?"

Jordan snorted. "Mom, are you kidding? Did you *see* her? If I got a girl who looked like that, I'd send it around, no doubt."

"Don't tell me. I don't want to know."

Chief Brubaker continued, "We have taken into custody Ms. Courtney Shank Wheeler, the younger sister of the Shank brothers and a teacher at Central Valley High School in Central Valley, Pennsylvania. We also have in custody a seventeen-year-old junior at Central Valley High School. Neither Wheeler nor the minor have been charged, as yet. We are investigating their participation in the plot and it is unclear at this time."

Jordan looked over with a worried frown. "What does that mean? Why don't they say his name?"

"Privacy, I guess? Because he's a minor? Anyway, it means they haven't figured out what Evan did yet."

Jordan grimaced. "Do they really think he's one of the bad guys? He doesn't know Madame Wheeler's brothers. They beat him up. You could see his face in the videos."

"Shh, let's listen."

Chief Brubaker continued, "There are many details of this Operation Varsity Letter that we do not have or cannot make public for security reasons. We are holding this conference before we have the totality of the facts because we want to inform the press and public, giving correct information rather than the rumors circulating online or in social media."

Jordan turned to Heather. "He has to say that. Twitter is blowing up."

Heather kept looking at Chris/Curt. She wondered if he was even single. Maybe that had been a lie, too. Her gaze went to his left hand, but she couldn't see if he had a wedding ring. Maybe he kept it at home, with his wife. And seven children. Also a dog and a cat.

Jordan listened as the spokesman continued, but Heather kept her eye on Chris/Curt, trying to read his mind. He was probably thinking that he was a hero, that he did his job even if it meant telling a whopper. He may have served the greater good, but still, she didn't like being lied to. The *lesser* good still mattered, and she and Jordan were the lesser good. She wondered if she'd ever hear from Chris/Curt again, then if she *wanted* to hear from him again.

Suddenly she realized that the odor of salmon was permeating the apartment, and the fish was burning.

"Dammit!" Heather said, jumping up and running into the kitchen.

Chapter Sixty-two

It wasn't until midnight that Curt got home to his spare, one-bedroom apartment on the second floor of a row home in the Italian Market, a city neighborhood of open-air stalls selling fruit, produce, and fish, packed cheek-by-jowl with old-school Italian restaurants. The air always smelled like fresh basil and rotting food, but the neighborhood suited him. He could pick up prepared foods anywhere, and it was easy for him to blend in, since the Market bustled with employees, shoppers, and tourists.

He'd come home tonight completely unnoticed, the shops closed, tarps drawn over the stalls, and the few tourists inside the restaurants. He'd kept his ball cap on just in case, after having spent the day feeling like a celebrity poseur, being clapped on the back, congratulated, and even hugged by a pretty lawyer in the U.S. Attorney's office, who reminded him of Heather.

Curt flopped on his bed, which was made by the cleaning lady who came in every other week, whether he was home or not. There was nothing on the white walls of his bedroom because he'd never had time to decorate, nor had he truly cared to, but tonight it looked lame, beyond bachelorhood into psycho hermit.

Oddly, he missed his apartment in Central Valley, and by now, other ATF agents would be routinely fingerprinting, taking photographs, collecting his laptop and going through his videotapes and audiotapes for the government's case against Evan. None of the possessions in that apartment belonged to him, except the clothes, but he would leave them behind, shedding the Chris Brennan identity like a snake does its skin. It had never been a problem before, but now, he felt vaguely like a real snake.

He picked up the remote, turned on a news channel, and watched the coverage of the operation on mute. There was one talking head after another, then the screen played the video of him flying upside down, with Evan hanging on.

Curt felt odd. He had never seen himself on television before. The camera focused on the sheer terror in Evan's battered face, and Curt's heart went out to the boy. He thought of the text that Evan's mother Mindy had sent him earlier today, thanking him. It made him feel good inside, but still he worried about Evan, and of course, Jordan and Heather.

The TV screen changed to a replay of the press conference, and Curt watched himself on the dais, knowing that he had been thinking about Heather the whole time. He wondered if she had been watching and what she must be thinking of him. He thought about calling her, then glanced at his watch. It was 2:15 A.M. He'd lost track of time with so much going on.

A wave of exhaustion swept over him, and Curt let his eyes close, thinking about her. He wanted to apologize to her, and to Jordan, and to all of them—for the first time ever, he felt guilty after an operation was over, even though by any objective measure, it had been successful. But he didn't feel successful, he felt like a jerk. He had gotten justice for the murders of Abe and Courtney's husband, Doug, but justice never was an eye for an eye, not for him. All that was left was death and destruction, leaving him feeling more alone than ever.

Curt drifted to sleep, knowing that it would never be any other way—unless he changed something. And so three nights later, after the hoopla was subsiding and he was returning to a normal schedule, with his new position as yet unspecified, Curt found himself lying on his bed again, looking up Heather's phone number online in the Boosters' directory, pressing in the numbers, and waiting while the call rang.

"Hello?" Heather answered, her tone vague, probably because she didn't recognize the number of his new phone, since he'd turned in his old one as evidence. Still, hearing her voice brought him back to Central Valley, and knowing she was on the other end of the line made him feel different, too. Better, the way he had felt back then.

"Heather, it's Chris, I mean, Curt." Curt thought he had gotten used to using his true name again, but evidently not.

"Oh, hi." Heather's voice sounded cold, which he had expected.

"I waited a few days but I wanted to call you to say, well, I'm sorry. I'm sorry that I lied to you about who I was. I hope you understand—"

"I get it."

"It's my job. It *was* my job anyway."

"I said, I get it." Heather paused. "Jordan gets it, too. Team player, greater good, seventeen inches. Got it."

Curt didn't, but let it go. She sounded unhappy talking to him. "I wanted to apologize to Jordan too, but I didn't want to contact him without asking your permission first."

"Fine with me, if you call him."

"Good, thanks."

"You should. You lied to him, too."

Curt felt a pang, hearing the sting in her words. "I'm sorry. I know it must've been really strange for you, both of you, to find out I was undercover."

"It was."

"Is there anything you want to ask me? I mean, you're enti-tled to know the truth."

Heather didn't answer except to chuckle, not in a good way.

"I mean I never contacted anybody after an operation before, but this is different."

Heather didn't say anything.

Curt felt he should explain further, especially because she was saying so little. "I usually work undercover with drug dealers and thugs, but this time, I was infiltrating good people, like you and Jordan."

"So?"

"So—" Curt hesitated, unsure what to say next. "So it's un-usual for me, and I know it must be for you too, finding out that I'm not a coach or a teacher."

"Yes, it was. It was for Jordan too, although mostly he's con-cerned about Evan."

"Sure, right." Curt had been relieved that both Evan and Courtney were negotiating plea deals to a whole list of charges, since circumstances had shown that they had voluntarily and completely renounced their participation in the conspiracy.

"School is just now getting back to normal."

"Did you ever get a new job?"

"Actually, yes. I start at ValleyCo as an administrative assistant next week."

"That's wonderful!" Curt thought he heard a softening in her voice, or maybe he imagined it. "Well, I was wondering if you ever wanted to have dinner with me."

"Why would I do *that*?" Heather asked coldly, which gave him his answer. It had been a terrible idea, calling her. He had lost her, as he feared. But he couldn't ignore his feelings for her. He'd been thinking about her all the time and he wanted to give it his best shot.

"Heather, I really liked meeting you and getting to know you, and I have more of a normal life now."

"I have to think about it," Heather interrupted. "I'm not sure that's something I want to do."

"I understand," Curt said, disappointed, and the sad part was, he really did understand, completely.

"Now, excuse me, I have to go. I have something on the stove."

"Sure, but can I give you a call again in a few days?"

"Try a month," Heather said, hanging up.

Curt hung up, defeated.

Luckily, he had a Plan B.

Chapter Sixty-three

Curt waited a month to put Plan B into action, wanting to show Heather that he respected her wishes. He put the time to good use, hammering out his job description with a ridiculous number of bureaucrats and filling out a ton of paperwork, and serving as the *de facto* assistant to the new head of Philadelphia Field Division, the Rabbi himself, David Levitz. Curt couldn't have been happier that the Rabbi had finally received the promotion he deserved, and they were both delighted that Alek had gotten kicked upstairs to JTTF, never to be heard from again. At least until the next terrorist attack, which gave them an ulterior motive to keep the country safe.

Curt couldn't look out the window since the shades were down. Central Valley was finally returning to normal, and the story had just begun to fade from the headlines. He turned down the requests for interviews, as well as offers of movie and book deals. Evan and Courtney had begun serving their sentences—Courtney for twelve years, and Evan for five.

Curt had spoken with Raz, who was doing better than ever, taking over Evan's position as catcher for Jordan, who was pitching a winning season for the Musketeers. Curt had even gone to a game, and Coach Hardwick had greeted him with a completely unexpected bear hug, thanking Curt for his service and inviting him to come to practice anytime he wanted—even if he had to come late. Curt and Jordan texted each other all the time, and Jordan had helped arrange this date tonight. Or at least, what Curt had hoped would be a date.

"Mr. Abbott, can I get you anything besides the water?" the waitress asked, hovering over him with a smile.

"No, thank you." Curt smiled back, having gotten used to being sociable, as a matter of necessity. He'd met more people in the past month than he'd met in his entire life. He couldn't remember the last drink he'd bought himself and he wasn't complaining. Everywhere he went, people shook his hand, thanked him, and wanted a selfie with him. It was forcing him to come out of his shell, and Curt was learning that he actually liked the people he had sworn to protect.

In fact, his fame was one of the reasons that he'd been granted this favor tonight. He'd asked the restaurant to close to everyone except him and Heather, because he knew that if the regular crowd were here, they wouldn't get a private moment. He'd offered to pay for shutting down the place, but they'd done it as a personal favor, living up to their name.

Friendly's.

Curt checked his watch. It was 6:30, and according to Jordan, this was the exact time that Heather would be coming home from her new job and heading into the kitchen to start dinner. He couldn't look out the window so he didn't know if she was coming. They'd closed the shades so no one would see that he was inside, and he kept them closed. He had asked Friendly's to take down the usual promotion on their sign in favor of something special, and he wondered if Heather had read it yet:

H, PLEASE MEET ME HERE FOR DINNER TONIGHT? CURT

Curt checked the table to make sure everything was in place. He'd brought a bag of Chips Ahoy, two bottles of water, and two nice glasses. He'd also bought a bouquet of a dozen long-stemmed red roses in a clear glass vase, but when he'd gotten here, he realized that the color of the flowers inadvertently matched Friendly's logo. He'd messed that up, but okay. He was new at romance, and it wasn't easy. On the contrary, it was easier to hang upside down from a helo.

Curt sipped his water, trying not to be nervous, a new sensation for him. He'd met a lot of nice, smart, and attractive women in the past month, and he'd gotten plenty of fan mail, emails, and photos from them. He was red-blooded enough to look at the photos, but none of the women appealed to him like Heather. She was nice, smart, and attractive in a way that felt *real* to him, and he couldn't explain it any better than that. If she felt the same way, she would be walking through the door in the next few minutes.

So far, no luck.

Curt felt his heart beat faster, giving him a tingle that he'd never experienced before. He never thought he could get a tingle from anything but his job, but that was about adrenaline. This time, it was about emotion. About feelings that went to the core of who he was, flowing to and from his heart, like the very blood that gave him life. He was only just now finding out who he really was, meeting new people and trying a new job, but he wanted to go deeper than that. He wanted to be the man he was meant to be, for himself, and for Heather and Jordan. Maybe he could be a husband and father. Maybe he could have a family, with an overweight dog of his own.

Curt looked up, and his mouth went dry when he saw the door opening and Heather walking in with a surprised smile. She looked adorable with her hair down, wearing a blue dress,

Nordling, Elizabeth Wildman, Caitlin Dareff, Talia Sherer, Kim Ludlum, and all the wonderful sales reps. Big thanks to Michael Storrings, for outstanding cover design. Also hugs and kisses to Mary Beth Roche, Laura Wilson, Samantha Edelson, and the great people in audiobooks. I love and appreciate all of you!

Thanks and love to my agent, Robert Gottlieb of Trident Media Group, whose dedication guided this novel into publication, and to Nicole Robson and Trident's digital media team, who help me get the word out on social media.

Many thanks and much love to the amazing Laura Leonard. She's invaluable in every way, every day, and has been for more than twenty years. Thanks, too, to Nan Daley for all of her research assistance on this novel, and thanks to George Davidson for doing everything else on the farm, so that I can be free to write.

Finally, thank you to my amazing daughter (and even coauthor), Francesca, for all of her support, laughter, and love.